Praise for
The Expanse

"The science fictional equivalent of A Song of Ice and Fire."
—*NPR Books*

"The Expanse series is the best space opera series running at full tilt right now." —*io9*

"This is the future the way it's supposed to be."
—*Wall Street Journal*

"Superb...a thrill to follow."

—*Washington Post*

"Combining an exploration of real human frailties with big SF ideas and exciting thriller action, Corey cements the series as must-read space opera." —*Library Journal* (starred review)

LEVIATHAN WAKES

BOOK ONE OF THE EXPANSE

JAMES S. A. COREY

orbit

www.orbitbooks.net

Copyright © 2011 by Daniel Abraham and Ty Franck
Excerpt from *Caliban's War* copyright © 2011 Daniel Abraham and Ty Franck

Orbit
Hachette Book Group
1290 Avenue of the Americas
New York, NY 10104
www.orbitbooks.net

Printed in the United States of America

RRD-C

First edition: June 2011
TV tie-in edition: November 2015

10 9 8 7 6 5 4 3 2 1

Orbit is an imprint of Hachette Book Group.
The Orbit name and logo are trademarks of Little, Brown Book Group Limited.

The Hachette Speakers Bureau provides a wide range of authors for speaking events. To find out more, go to www.hachettespeakersbureau.com or call (866) 376-6591.

The publisher is not responsible for websites (or their content) that are not owned by the publisher.

The Library of Congress has cataloged a previous edition as follows:

Library of Congress Cataloging-in-Publication Data
Corey, James S. A.
Leviathan wakes / James S. A. Corey.—1st ed.
    p. cm.
ISBN 978-0-316-12908-4
1. Interplanetary voyages—Fiction. 2. Space warfare—Fiction. I. Title.
PS3601.B677L48 2011
813'.6—dc22

2010046442

ISBN: 978-0-316-39068-2 (TV tie-in)

For Jayné and Kat, who encourage me
to daydream about spaceships

Prologue: Julie

The *Scopuli* had been taken eight days ago, and Julie Mao was finally ready to be shot.

It had taken all eight days trapped in a storage locker for her to get to that point. For the first two she'd remained motionless, sure that the armored men who'd put her there had been serious. For the first hours, the ship she'd been taken aboard wasn't under thrust, so she floated in the locker, using gentle touches to keep herself from bumping into the walls or the atmosphere suit she shared the space with. When the ship began to move, thrust giving her weight, she'd stood silently until her legs cramped, then sat down slowly into a fetal position. She'd peed in her jumpsuit, not caring about the warm itchy wetness, or the smell, worrying only that she might slip and fall in the wet spot it left on the floor. She couldn't make noise. They'd shoot her.

On the third day, thirst had forced her into action. The noise of the ship was all around her. The faint subsonic rumble of the reactor and drive. The constant hiss and thud of hydraulics and steel bolts as the pressure doors between decks opened and closed. The clump of heavy boots walking on metal decking. She waited until all the noise she could hear sounded distant, then pulled the environment suit off its hooks and onto the locker floor. Listening for any approaching sound, she slowly disassembled the suit and took out the water supply. It was old and stale; the suit obviously hadn't been used or serviced in ages. But she hadn't had a sip in days, and the warm loamy water in the suit's reservoir bag was the best thing she had ever tasted. She had to work hard not to gulp it down and make herself vomit.

When the urge to urinate returned, she pulled the catheter bag out of the suit and relieved herself into it. She sat on the floor, now cushioned by the padded suit and almost comfortable, and wondered who her captors were — Coalition Navy, pirates, something worse. Sometimes she slept.

On day four, isolation, hunger, boredom, and the diminishing number of places to store her piss finally pushed her to make contact with them. She'd heard muffled cries of pain. Somewhere nearby, her shipmates were being beaten or tortured. If she got the attention of the kidnappers, maybe they would just take her to the others. That was okay. Beatings, she could handle. It seemed like a small price to pay if it meant seeing people again.

The locker sat beside the inner airlock door. During flight, that usually wasn't a high-traffic area, though she didn't know anything about the layout of this particular ship. She thought about what to say, how to present herself. When she finally heard someone moving toward her, she just tried to yell that she wanted out. The dry rasp that came out of her throat surprised her. She swallowed, working her tongue to try to create some saliva, and tried again. Another faint rattle in the throat.

The people were right outside her locker door. A voice was

talking quietly. Julie had pulled back a fist to bang on the door when she heard what it was saying.

No. Please no. Please don't.

Dave. Her ship's mechanic. Dave, who collected clips from old cartoons and knew a million jokes, begging in a small broken voice.

No, please no, please don't, he said.

Hydraulics and locking bolts clicked as the inner airlock door opened. A meaty thud as something was thrown inside. Another click as the airlock closed. A hiss of evacuating air.

When the airlock cycle had finished, the people outside her door walked away. She didn't bang to get their attention.

They'd scrubbed the ship. Detainment by the inner planet navies was a bad scenario, but they'd all trained on how to deal with it. Sensitive OPA data was scrubbed and overwritten with innocuous-looking logs with false time stamps. Anything too sensitive to trust to a computer, the captain destroyed. When the attackers came aboard, they could play innocent.

It hadn't mattered.

There weren't the questions about cargo or permits. The invaders had come in like they owned the place, and Captain Darren had rolled over like a dog. Everyone else—Mike, Dave, Wan Li—they'd all just thrown up their hands and gone along quietly. The pirates or slavers or whatever they were had dragged them off the little transport ship that had been her home, and down a docking tube without even minimal environment suits. The tube's thin layer of Mylar was the only thing between them and hard nothing: hope it didn't rip; goodbye lungs if it did.

Julie had gone along too, but then the bastards had tried to lay their hands on her, strip her clothes off.

Five years of low-gravity jiu jitsu training and them in a confined space with no gravity. She'd done a lot of damage. She'd almost started to think she might win when from nowhere a gauntleted fist smashed into her face. Things got fuzzy after that. Then the locker, and *Shoot her if she makes a noise.* Four days of not making noise while they beat her friends down below and then threw one of them out an airlock.

After six days, everything went quiet.

Shifting between bouts of consciousness and fragmented dreams, she was only vaguely aware as the sounds of walking, talking, and pressure doors and the subsonic rumble of the reactor and the drive faded away a little at a time. When the drive stopped, so did gravity, and Julie woke from a dream of racing her old pinnace to find herself floating while her muscles screamed in protest and then slowly relaxed.

She pulled herself to the door and pressed her ear to the cold metal. Panic shot through her until she caught the quiet sound of the air recyclers. The ship still had power and air, but the drive wasn't on and no one was opening a door or walking or talking. Maybe it was a crew meeting. Or a party on another deck. Or everyone was in engineering, fixing a serious problem.

She spent a day listening and waiting.

By day seven, her last sip of water was gone. No one on the ship had moved within range of her hearing for twenty-four hours. She sucked on a plastic tab she'd ripped off the environment suit until she worked up some saliva; then she started yelling. She yelled herself hoarse.

No one came.

By day eight, she was ready to be shot. She'd been out of water for two days, and her waste bag had been full for four. She put her shoulders against the back wall of the locker and planted her hands against the side walls. Then she kicked out with both legs as hard as she could. The cramps that followed the first kick almost made her pass out. She screamed instead.

Stupid girl, she told herself. She was dehydrated. Eight days without activity was more than enough to start atrophy. At least she should have stretched out.

She massaged her stiff muscles until the knots were gone, then stretched, focusing her mind like she was back in dojo. When she was in control of her body, she kicked again. And again. And again, until light started to show through the edges of the locker. And again, until the door was so bent that the three hinges and the locking bolt were the only points of contact between it and the frame.

And one last time, so that it bent far enough that the bolt was no longer seated in the hasp and the door swung free.

Julie shot from the locker, hands half raised and ready to look either threatening or terrified, depending on which seemed more useful.

There was no one on the whole deck: the airlock, the suit storage room where she'd spent the last eight days, a half dozen other storage rooms. All empty. She plucked a magnetized pipe wrench of suitable size for skull cracking out of an EVA kit, then went down the crew ladder to the deck below.

And then the one below that, and then the one below that. Personnel cabins in crisp, almost military order. Commissary, where there were signs of a struggle. Medical bay, empty. Torpedo bay. No one. The comm station was unmanned, powered down, and locked. The few sensor logs that still streamed showed no sign of the *Scopuli*. A new dread knotted her gut. Deck after deck and room after room empty of life. Something had happened. A radiation leak. Poison in the air. Something that had forced an evacuation. She wondered if she'd be able to fly the ship by herself.

But if they'd evacuated, she'd have heard them going out the airlock, wouldn't she?

She reached the final deck hatch, the one that led into engineering, and stopped when the hatch didn't open automatically. A red light on the lock panel showed that the room had been sealed from the inside. She thought again about radiation and major failures. But if either of those was the case, why lock the door from the inside? And she had passed wall panel after wall panel. None of them had been flashing warnings of any kind. No, not radiation, something else.

There was more disruption here. Blood. Tools and containers in disarray. Whatever had happened, it had happened here. No, it had started here. And it had ended behind that locked door.

It took two hours with a torch and prying tools from the machine shop to cut through the hatch to engineering. With the hydraulics compromised, she had to crank it open by hand. A gust of warm wet air blew out, carrying a hospital scent without the antiseptic. A coppery, nauseating smell. The torture chamber, then. Her friends would be inside, beaten or cut to pieces. Julie hefted her wrench and prepared to bust open at least one head before they killed her. She floated down.

The engineering deck was huge, vaulted like a cathedral. The fusion reactor dominated the central space. Something was wrong with it. Where she expected to see readouts, shielding, and monitors, a layer of something like mud seemed to flow over the reactor core. Slowly, Julie floated toward it, one hand still on the ladder. The strange smell became overpowering.

The mud caked around the reactor had structure to it like nothing she'd seen before. Tubes ran through it like veins or airways. Parts of it pulsed. Not mud, then.

Flesh.

An outcropping of the thing shifted toward her. Compared to the whole, it seemed no larger than a toe, a little finger. It was Captain Darren's head.

"Help me," it said.

Chapter One: Holden

A hundred and fifty years before, when the parochial disagreements between Earth and Mars had been on the verge of war, the Belt had been a far horizon of tremendous mineral wealth beyond viable economic reach, and the outer planets had been beyond even the most unrealistic corporate dream. Then Solomon Epstein had built his little modified fusion drive, popped it on the back of his three-man yacht, and turned it on. With a good scope, you could still see his ship going at a marginal percentage of the speed of light, heading out into the big empty. The best, longest funeral in the history of mankind. Fortunately, he'd left the plans on his home computer. The Epstein Drive hadn't given humanity the stars, but it had delivered the planets.

Three-quarters of a kilometer long, a quarter of a kilometer wide—roughly shaped like a fire hydrant—and mostly empty space inside, the *Canterbury* was a retooled colony transport.

Once, it had been packed with people, supplies, schematics, machines, environment bubbles, and hope. Just under twenty million people lived on the moons of Saturn now. The *Canterbury* had hauled nearly a million of their ancestors there. Forty-five million on the moons of Jupiter. One moon of Uranus sported five thousand, the farthest outpost of human civilization, at least until the Mormons finished their generation ship and headed for the stars and freedom from procreation restrictions.

And then there was the Belt.

If you asked OPA recruiters when they were drunk and feeling expansive, they might say there were a hundred million in the Belt. Ask an inner planet census taker, it was nearer to fifty million. Any way you looked, the population was huge and needed a lot of water.

So now the *Canterbury* and her dozens of sister ships in the Pur'n'Kleen Water Company made the loop from Saturn's generous rings to the Belt and back hauling glaciers, and would until the ships aged into salvage wrecks.

Jim Holden saw some poetry in that.

"Holden?"

He turned back to the hangar deck. Chief Engineer Naomi Nagata towered over him. She stood almost two full meters tall, her mop of curly hair tied back into a black tail, her expression halfway between amusement and annoyance. She had the Belter habit of shrugging with her hands instead of her shoulders.

"Holden, are you listening, or just staring out the window?"

"There was a problem," Holden said. "And because you're really, really good, you can fix it even though you don't have enough money or supplies."

Naomi laughed.

"So you weren't listening," she said.

"Not really, no."

"Well, you got the basics right anyhow. *Knight*'s landing gear isn't going to be good in atmosphere until I can get the seals replaced. That going to be a problem?"

"I'll ask the old man," Holden said. "But when's the last time we used the shuttle in atmosphere?"

"Never, but regs say we need at least one atmo-capable shuttle."

"Hey, Boss!" Amos Burton, Naomi's earthborn assistant, yelled from across the bay. He waved one meaty arm in their general direction. He meant Naomi. Amos might be on Captain McDowell's ship; Holden might be executive officer; but in Amos Burton's world, only Naomi was boss.

"What's the matter?" Naomi shouted back.

"Bad cable. Can you hold this little fucker in place while I get the spare?"

Naomi looked at Holden, *Are we done here?* in her eyes. He snapped a sarcastic salute and she snorted, shaking her head as she walked away, her frame long and thin in her greasy coveralls.

Seven years in Earth's navy, five years working in space with civilians, and he'd never gotten used to the long, thin, improbable bones of Belters. A childhood spent in gravity shaped the way he saw things forever.

At the central lift, Holden held his finger briefly over the button for the navigation deck, tempted by the prospect of Ade Tukunbo — her smile, her voice, the patchouli-and-vanilla scent she used in her hair — but pressed the button for the infirmary instead. Duty before pleasure.

Shed Garvey, the medical tech, was hunched over his lab table, debriding the stump of Cameron Paj's left arm, when Holden walked in. A month earlier, Paj had gotten his elbow pinned by a thirty-ton block of ice moving at five millimeters a second. It wasn't an uncommon injury among people with the dangerous job of cutting and moving zero-g icebergs, and Paj was taking the whole thing with the fatalism of a professional. Holden leaned over Shed's shoulder to watch as the tech plucked one of the medical maggots out of dead tissue.

"What's the word?" Holden asked.

"It's looking pretty good, sir," Paj said. "I've still got a few nerves. Shed's been tellin' me about how the prosthetic is gonna hook up to it."

"Assuming we can keep the necrosis under control," the medic said, "and make sure Paj doesn't heal up too much before we get to Ceres. I checked the policy, and Paj here's been signed on long enough to get one with force feedback, pressure and temperature sensors, fine-motor software. The whole package. It'll be almost as good as the real thing. The inner planets have a new biogel that regrows the limb, but that isn't covered in our medical plan."

"Fuck the Inners, and fuck their magic Jell-O. I'd rather have a good Belter-built fake than anything those bastards grow in a lab. Just wearing their fancy arm probably turns you into an asshole," Paj said. Then he added, "Oh, uh, no offense, XO."

"None taken. Just glad we're going to get you fixed up," Holden said.

"Tell him the other bit," Paj said with a wicked grin. Shed blushed.

"I've, ah, heard from other guys who've gotten them," Shed said, not meeting Holden's eyes. "Apparently there's a period while you're still building identification with the prosthetic when whacking off feels just like getting a hand job."

Holden let the comment hang in the air for a second while Shed's ears turned crimson.

"Good to know," Holden said. "And the necrosis?"

"There's some infection," Shed said. "The maggots are keeping it under control, and the inflammation's actually a good thing in this context, so we're not fighting too hard unless it starts to spread."

"Is he going to be ready for the next run?" Holden asked.

For the first time, Paj frowned.

"Shit yes, I'll be ready. I'm always ready. This is what I *do*, sir."

"Probably," Shed said. "Depending on how the bond takes. If not this one, the one after."

"Fuck that," Paj said. "I can buck ice one-handed better than half the skags you've got on this bitch."

"Again," Holden said, suppressing a grin, "good to know. Carry on."

Paj snorted. Shed plucked another maggot free. Holden went back to the lift, and this time he didn't hesitate.

The navigation station of the *Canterbury* didn't dress to impress. The great wall-sized displays Holden had imagined when he'd first volunteered for the navy did exist on capital ships but, even there, more as an artifact of design than need. Ade sat at a pair of screens only slightly larger than a hand terminal, graphs of the efficiency and output of the *Canterbury*'s reactor and engine updating in the corners, raw logs spooling on the right as the systems reported in. She wore thick headphones that covered her ears, the faint thump of the bass line barely escaping. If the *Canterbury* sensed an anomaly, it would alert her. If a system errored, it would alert her. If Captain McDowell left the command and control deck, it would alert her so she could turn the music off and look busy when he arrived. Her petty hedonism was only one of a thousand things that made Ade attractive to Holden. He walked up behind her, pulled the headphones gently away from her ears, and said, "Hey."

Ade smiled, tapped her screen, and dropped the headphones to rest around her long slim neck like technical jewelry.

"Executive Officer James Holden," she said with an exaggerated formality made even more acute by her thick Nigerian accent. "And what can I do for you?"

"You know, it's funny you should ask that," he said. "I was just thinking how pleasant it would be to have someone come back to my cabin when third shift takes over. Have a little romantic dinner of the same crap they're serving in the galley. Listen to some music."

"Drink a little wine," she said. "Break a little protocol. Pretty to think about, but I'm not up for sex tonight."

"I wasn't talking about sex. A little food. Conversation."

"I was talking about sex," she said.

Holden knelt beside her chair. In the one-third g of their current thrust, it was perfectly comfortable. Ade's smile softened. The log spool chimed; she glanced at it, tapped a release, and turned back to him.

"Ade, I like you. I mean, I really enjoy your company," he said. "I don't understand why we can't spend some time together with our clothes on."

"Holden. Sweetie. Stop it, okay?"

"Stop what?"

"Stop trying to turn me into your girlfriend. You're a nice guy. You've got a cute butt, and you're fun in the sack. Doesn't mean we're engaged."

Holden rocked back on his heels, feeling himself frown.

"Ade. For this to work for me, it needs to be more than that."

"But it isn't," she said, taking his hand. "It's okay that it isn't. You're the XO here, and I'm a short-timer. Another run, maybe two, and I'm gone."

"I'm not chained to this ship either."

Her laughter was equal parts warmth and disbelief.

"How long have you been on the *Cant*?"

"Five years."

"You're not going anyplace," she said. "You're comfortable here."

"Comfortable?" he said. "The *Cant*'s a century-old ice hauler. You can find a shittier flying job, but you have to try really hard. Everyone here is either wildly under-qualified or seriously screwed things up at their last gig."

"And you're comfortable here." Her eyes were less kind now. She bit her lip, looked down at the screen, looked up.

"I didn't deserve that," he said.

"You didn't," she agreed. "Look, I told you I wasn't in the mood tonight. I'm feeling cranky. I need a good night's sleep. I'll be nicer tomorrow."

"Promise?"

"I'll even make you dinner. Apology accepted?"

He slipped forward, pressed his lips to hers. She kissed back, politely at first and then with more warmth. Her fingers cupped his neck for a moment, then pulled him away.

"You're entirely too good at that. You should go now," she said. "On duty and all."

"Okay," he said, and didn't turn to go.

"Jim," she said, and the shipwide comm system clicked on.

"Holden to the bridge," Captain McDowell said, his voice compressed and echoing. Holden replied with something obscene. Ade laughed. He swooped in, kissed her cheek, and headed back for the central lift, quietly hoping that Captain McDowell suffered boils and public humiliation for his lousy timing.

The bridge was hardly larger than Holden's quarters and smaller by half than the galley. Except for the slightly oversized captain's display, required by Captain McDowell's failing eyesight and general distrust of corrective surgery, it could have been an accounting firm's back room. The air smelled of cleaning astringent and someone's overly strong yerba maté tea. McDowell shifted in his seat as Holden approached. Then the captain leaned back, pointing over his shoulder at the communications station.

"Becca!" McDowell snapped. "Tell him."

Rebecca Byers, the comm officer on duty, could have been bred from a shark and a hatchet. Black eyes, sharp features, lips so thin they might as well not have existed. The story on board was that she'd taken the job to escape prosecution for killing an ex-husband. Holden liked her.

"Emergency signal," she said. "Picked it up two hours ago. The transponder verification just bounced back from *Callisto*. It's real."

"Ah," Holden said. And then: "Shit. Are we the closest?"

"Only ship in a few million klicks."

"Well. That figures," Holden said.

Becca turned her gaze to the captain. McDowell cracked his knuckles and stared at his display. The light from the screen gave him an odd greenish cast.

"It's next to a charted non-Belt asteroid," McDowell said.

"Really?" Holden said in disbelief. "Did they run into it? There's nothing else out here for millions of kilometers."

"Maybe they pulled over because someone had to go potty. All we have is that some knucklehead is out there, blasting an emergency signal, and we're the closest. Assuming…"

The law of the solar system was unequivocal. In an environment as hostile to life as space, the aid and goodwill of your fellow humans wasn't optional. The emergency signal, just by existing, obligated the nearest ship to stop and render aid—which didn't mean the law was universally followed.

The *Canterbury* was fully loaded. Well over a million tons of ice had been gently accelerated for the past month. Just like the little glacier that had crushed Paj's arm, it was going to be hard to slow down. The temptation to have an unexplained comm failure, erase the logs, and let the great god Darwin have his way was always there.

But if McDowell had really intended that, he wouldn't have called Holden up. Or made the suggestion where the crew could hear him. Holden understood the dance. The captain was going to be the one who would have blown it off except for Holden. The grunts would respect the captain for not wanting to cut into the ship's profit. They'd respect Holden for insisting that they follow the rule. No matter what happened, the captain and Holden would both be hated for what they were required by law and mere human decency to do.

"We have to stop," Holden said. Then, gamely: "There may be salvage."

McDowell tapped his screen. Ade's voice came from the console, as low and warm as if she'd been in the room.

"Captain?"

"I need numbers on stopping this crate," he said.

"Sir?"

"How hard is it going to be to put us alongside CA-2216862?"

"We're stopping at an asteroid?"

"I'll tell you when you've followed my order, Navigator Tukunbo."

"Yes, sir," she said. Holden heard a series of clicks. "If we flip the ship right now and burn like hell for most of two days, I can get us within fifty thousand kilometers, sir."

"Can you define 'burn like hell'?" McDowell said.

"We'll need everyone in crash couches."

"Of course we will," McDowell sighed, and scratched his scruffy beard. "And shifting ice is only going to do a couple million bucks' worth of banging up the hull, if we're lucky. I'm getting old for this, Holden. I really am."

"Yes, sir. You are. And I've always liked your chair," Holden said. McDowell scowled and made an obscene gesture. Rebecca snorted in laughter. McDowell turned to her.

"Send a message to the beacon that we're on our way. And let Ceres know we're going to be late. Holden, where does the *Knight* stand?"

"No flying in atmosphere until we get some parts, but she'll do fine for fifty thousand klicks in vacuum."

"You're sure of that?"

"Naomi said it. That makes it true."

McDowell rose, unfolding to almost two and a quarter meters and thinner than a teenager back on Earth. Between his age and never having lived in a gravity well, the coming burn was likely to be hell on the old man. Holden felt a pang of sympathy that he would never embarrass McDowell by expressing.

"Here's the thing, Jim," McDowell said, his voice quiet enough that only Holden could hear him. "We're required to stop and make an attempt, but we don't have to go out of our way, if you see what I mean."

"We'll already have stopped," Holden said, and McDowell patted at the air with his wide, spidery hands. One of the many Belter gestures that had evolved to be visible when wearing an environment suit.

"I can't avoid that," he said. "But if you see anything out there that seems off, don't play hero again. Just pack up the toys and come home."

"And leave it for the next ship that comes through?"

"And keep yourself safe," McDowell said. "Order. Understood?"

"Understood," Holden said.

As the shipwide comm system clicked to life and McDowell began explaining the situation to the crew, Holden imagined he could hear a chorus of groans coming up through the decks. He went over to Rebecca.

"Okay," he said, "what have we got on the broken ship?"

"Light freighter. Martian registry. Shows Eros as home port. Calls itself *Scopuli*…"

Chapter Two: Miller

Detective Miller sat back on the foam-core chair, smiling gentle encouragement while he scrambled to make sense of the girl's story.

"And then it was all pow! Room full up with bladeboys howling and humping shank," the girl said, waving a hand. "Look like a dance number, 'cept that Bomie's got this look he didn't know nothing never and ever amen. You know, que?"

Havelock, standing by the door, blinked twice. The squat man's face twitched with impatience. It was why Havelock was never going to make senior detective. And why he sucked at poker.

Miller was very good at poker.

"I totally," Miller said. His voice had taken on the twang of an inner level resident. He waved his hand in the same lazy arc the girl used. "Bomie, he didn't see. Forgotten arm."

"Forgotten fucking arm, yeah," the girl said as if Miller had spoken a line of gospel. Miller nodded, and the girl nodded back like they were two birds doing a mating dance.

The rent hole was three cream-and-black-fleck-painted rooms—bathroom, kitchen, living room. The struts of a pull-down sleeping loft in the living room had been broken and repaired so many times they didn't retract anymore. This near the center of Ceres' spin, that wasn't from gravity so much as mass in motion. The air smelled beery with old protein yeast and mushrooms. Local food, so whoever had bounced the girl hard enough to break her bed hadn't paid enough for dinner. Or maybe they did, and the girl had chosen to spend it on heroin or malta or MCK.

Her business, either way.

"Follow que?" Miller asked.

"Bomie vacuate like losing air," the girl said with a chuckle. "Bang-head hops, kennis tu?"

"Ken," Miller said.

"Now, all new bladeboys. Overhead. I'm out."

"And Bomie?"

The girl's eyes made a slow track up Miller, shoes to knees to porkpie hat. Miller chuckled. He gave the chair a light push, sloping up to his feet in the low gravity.

"He shows, and I asked, que si?" Miller said.

"Como no?" the girl said. *Why not?*

The tunnel outside was white where it wasn't grimy. Ten meters wide, and gently sloping up in both directions. The white LED lights didn't pretend to mimic sunlight. About half a kilometer down, someone had rammed into the wall so hard the native rock showed through, and it still hadn't been repaired. Maybe it wouldn't be. This was the deep dig, way up near the center of spin. Tourists never came here.

Havelock led the way to their cart, bouncing too high with every step. He didn't come up to the low gravity levels very often, and it made him awkward. Miller had lived on Ceres his whole life, and truth to tell, the Coriolis effect up this high could make him a little unsteady sometimes too.

"So," Havelock said as he punched in their destination code, "did you have fun?"

"Don't know what you mean," Miller said.

The electrical motors hummed to life, and the cart lurched forward into the tunnel, squishy foam tires faintly squeaking.

"Having your outworld conversation in front of the Earth guy?" Havelock said. "I couldn't follow even half of that."

"That wasn't Belters keeping the Earth guy out," Miller said. "That was poor folks keeping the educated guy out. And it was kind of fun, now you mention it."

Havelock laughed. He could take being teased and keep on moving. It was what made him good at team sports: soccer, basketball, politics.

Miller wasn't much good at those.

Ceres, the port city of the Belt and the outer planets, boasted two hundred fifty kilometers in diameter, tens of thousands of kilometers of tunnels in layer on layer on layer. Spinning it up to 0.3 g had taken the best minds at Tycho Manufacturing half a generation, and they were still pretty smug about it. Now Ceres had more than six million permanent residents, and as many as a thousand ships docking in any given day meant upping the population to as high as seven million.

Platinum, iron, and titanium from the Belt. Water from Saturn, vegetables and beef from the big mirror-fed greenhouses on Ganymede and Europa, organics from Earth and Mars. Power cells from Io, Helium-3 from the refineries on Rhea and Iapetus. A river of wealth and power unrivaled in human history came through Ceres. Where there was commerce on that level, there was also crime. Where there was crime, there were security forces to keep it in check. Men like Miller and Havelock, whose business it was to track the electric carts up the wide ramps, feel the false gravity of spin fall away beneath them, and ask low-rent glitz whores about what happened the night Bomie Chatterjee stopped collecting protection money for the Golden Bough Society.

The primary station house for Star Helix Security, police force and military garrison for the Ceres Station, was on the third level from the asteroid's skin, two kilometers square and dug into the rock so high Miller could walk from his desk up five levels without ever leaving the offices. Havelock turned in the cart while Miller went to his cubicle, downloaded the recording of their interview with the girl, and reran it. He was halfway through when his partner lumbered up behind him.

"Learn anything?" Havelock asked.

"Not much," Miller said. "Bomie got jumped by a bunch of unaffiliated local thugs. Sometimes a low-level guy like Bomie will hire people to pretend to attack him so he can heroically fight them off. Ups his reputation. That's what she meant when she called it a dance number. The guys that went after him were that caliber, only instead of turning into a ninja badass, Bomie ran away and hasn't come back."

"And now?"

"And now nothing," Miller said. "That's what I don't get. Someone took out a Golden Bough purse boy, and there's no payback. I mean, okay, Bomie's a bottom-feeder, but..."

"But once they start eating the little guys, there's less money coming up to the big guys," Havelock said. "So why hasn't the Golden Bough meted out some gangster justice?"

"I don't like this," Miller said.

Havelock laughed. "Belters," he said. "One thing goes weird and you think the whole ecosystem's crashing. If the Golden Bough's too weak to keep its claims, that's a good thing. They're the bad guys, remember?"

"Yeah, well," Miller said. "Say what you will about organized crime, at least it's organized."

Havelock sat on the small plastic chair beside Miller's desk and craned to watch the playback.

"Okay," Havelock said. "What the hell is the 'forgotten arm'?"

"Boxing term," Miller said. "It's the hit you didn't see coming."

The computer chimed and Captain Shaddid's voice came from the speakers.

"Miller? Are you there?"

"Mmm," Havelock said. "Bad omen."

"What?" the captain asked, her voice sharp. She had never quite overcome her prejudice against Havelock's inner planet origins. Miller held up a hand to silence his partner.

"Here, Captain. What can I do for you?"

"Meet me in my office, please."

"On my way," he said.

Miller stood, and Havelock slid into his chair. They didn't speak. Both of them knew that Captain Shaddid would have called them in together if she'd wanted Havelock to be there. Another reason the man would never make senior detective. Miller left him alone with the playback, trying to parse the fine points of class and station, origin and race. Lifetime's work, that.

Captain Shaddid's office was decorated in a soft, feminine style. Real cloth tapestries hung from the walls, and the scent of coffee and cinnamon came from an insert in her air filter that cost about a tenth of what the real foodstuffs would have. She wore her uniform casually, her hair down around her shoulders in violation of corporate regulations. If Miller had ever been called upon to describe her, the phrase *deceptive coloration* would have figured in. She nodded to a chair, and he sat.

"What have you found?" she asked, but her gaze was on the wall behind him. This wasn't a pop quiz; she was just making conversation.

"Golden Bough's looking the same as Sohiro's crew and the Loca Greiga. Still on station, but…distracted, I guess I'd call it. They're letting little things slide. Fewer thugs on the ground, less enforcement. I've got half a dozen mid-level guys who've gone dark."

He'd caught her attention.

"Killed?" she asked. "An OPA advance?"

An advance by the Outer Planets Alliance was the constant bogeyman of Ceres security. Living in the tradition of Al Capone and Hamas, the IRA and the Red Martials, the OPA was beloved by the people it helped and feared by the ones who got in its way.

Part social movement, part wannabe nation, and part terrorist network, it totally lacked an institutional conscience. Captain Shaddid might not like Havelock because he was from down a gravity well, but she'd work with him. The OPA would have put him in an airlock. People like Miller would only rate getting a bullet in the skull, and a nice plastic one at that. Nothing that might get shrapnel in the ductwork.

"I don't think so," he said. "It doesn't smell like a war. It's... Honestly, sir, I don't know what the hell it is. The numbers are great. Protection's down, unlicensed gambling's down. Cooper and Hariri shut down the underage whorehouse up on six, and as far as anyone can tell, it hasn't started up again. There's a little more action by independents, but that aside, it's all looking great. It just smells funny."

She nodded, but her gaze was back on the wall. He'd lost her interest as quickly as he'd gotten it.

"Well, put it aside," she said. "I have something. New contract. Just you. Not Havelock."

Miller crossed his arms.

"New contract," he said slowly. "Meaning?"

"Meaning Star Helix Security has accepted a contract for services separate from the Ceres security assignment, and in my role as site manager for the corporation, I'm assigning you to it."

"I'm fired?" he said.

Captain Shaddid looked pained.

"It's additional duty," she said. "You'll still have the Ceres assignments you have now. It's just that, in addition...Look, Miller, I think this is as shitty as you do. I'm not pulling you off station. I'm not taking you off the main contract. This is a favor someone down on Earth is doing for a shareholder."

"We're doing favors for shareholders now?" Miller asked.

"You are, yes," Captain Shaddid said. The softness was gone; the conciliatory tone was gone. Her eyes were dark as wet stone.

"Right, then," Miller said. "I guess I am."

Captain Shaddid held up her hand terminal. Miller fumbled at his side, pulled out his own, and accepted the narrow-beam transfer. Whatever this was, Shaddid was keeping it off the common network. A new file tree, labeled JMAO, appeared on his readout.

"It's a little-lost-daughter case," Captain Shaddid said. "Ariadne and Jules-Pierre Mao."

The names rang a bell. Miller pressed his fingertips onto the screen of his hand terminal.

"Mao-Kwikowski Mercantile?" he asked.

"The one."

Miller whistled low.

Maokwik might not have been one of the top ten corporations in the Belt, but it was certainly in the upper fifty. Originally, it had been a legal firm involved in the epic failure of the Venusian cloud cities. They'd used the money from that decades-long lawsuit to diversify and expand, mostly into interplanetary transport. Now the corporate station was independent, floating between the Belt and the inner planets with the regal majesty of an ocean liner on ancient seas. The simple fact that Miller knew that much about them meant they had enough money to buy and sell men like him on open exchange.

He'd just been bought.

"They're Luna-based," Captain Shaddid said. "All the rights and privileges of Earth citizenship. But they do a lot of shipping business out here."

"And they misplaced a daughter?"

"Black sheep," the captain said. "Went off to college, got involved with a group called the Far Horizons Foundation. Student activists."

"OPA front," Miller said.

"Associated," Shaddid corrected him. Miller let it pass, but a flicker of curiosity troubled him. He wondered which side Captain Shaddid would be on if the OPA attacked. "The family put it down to a phase. They've got two older children with controlling interest, so if Julie wanted to bounce around vacuum calling herself a freedom fighter, there was no real harm."

"But now they want her found," Miller said.

"They do."

"What changed?"

"They didn't see fit to share that information."

"Right."

"Last records show she was employed on Tycho Station but maintained an apartment here. I've found her partition on the network and locked it down. The password is in your files."

"Okay," Miller said. "What's my contract?"

"Find Julie Mao, detain her, and ship her home."

"A kidnap job, then," he said.

"Yes."

Miller stared down at his hand terminal, flicking the files open without particularly looking at them. A strange knot had tied itself in his guts. He'd been working Ceres security for thirty years, and he hadn't started with many illusions in place. The joke was that Ceres didn't have laws — it had police. His hands weren't any cleaner than Captain Shaddid's. Sometimes people fell out airlocks. Sometimes evidence vanished from the lockers. It wasn't so much that it was right or wrong as that it was justified. You spent your life in a stone bubble with your food, your water, your *air* shipped in from places so distant you could barely find them with a telescope, and a certain moral flexibility was necessary. But he'd never had to take a kidnap job before.

"Problem, Detective?" Captain Shaddid asked.

"No, sir," he said. "I'll take care of it."

"Don't spend too much time on it," she said.

"Yes, sir. Anything else?"

Captain Shaddid's hard eyes softened, like she was putting on a mask. She smiled.

"Everything going well with your partner?"

"Havelock's all right," Miller said. "Having him around makes people like me better by contrast. That's nice."

Her smile's only change was to become half a degree more gen-uine. Nothing like a little shared racism to build ties with the boss. Miller nodded respectfully and headed out.

His hole was on the eighth level, off a residential tunnel a hundred meters wide with fifty meters of carefully cultivated green park running down the center. The main corridor's vaulted ceiling was lit by recessed lights and painted a blue that Havelock assured him matched the Earth's summer sky. Living on the surface of a planet, mass sucking at every bone and muscle, and nothing but gravity to keep your air close, seemed like a fast path to crazy. The blue was nice, though.

Some people followed Captain Shaddid's lead by perfuming their air. Not always with coffee and cinnamon scents, of course. Havelock's hole smelled of baking bread. Others opted for floral scents or semipheromones. Candace, Miller's ex-wife, had pre-ferred something called EarthLily, which had always made him think of the waste recycling levels. These days, he left it at the vaguely astringent smell of the station itself. Recycled air that had passed through a million lungs. Water from the tap so clean it could be used for lab work, but it had been piss and shit and tears and blood and would be again. The circle of life on Ceres was so small you could see the curve. He liked it that way.

He poured a glass of moss whiskey, a native Ceres liquor made from engineered yeast, then took off his shoes and settled onto the foam bed. He could still see Candace's disapproving scowl and hear her sigh. He shrugged apology to her memory and turned back to work.

Juliette Andromeda Mao. He read through her work history, her academic records. Talented pinnace pilot. There was a picture of her at eighteen in a tailored vac suit with the helmet off: pretty girl with a thin, lunar citizen's frame and long black hair. She was grinning like the universe had given her a kiss. The linked text said she'd won first place in something called the Parrish/Dorn

500K. He searched briefly. Some kind of race only really rich people could afford to fly in. Her pinnace—the *Razorback*—had beaten the previous record and held it for two years.

Miller sipped his whiskey and wondered what had happened to the girl with enough wealth and power to own a private ship that would bring her here. It was a long way from competing in expensive space races to being hog-tied and sent home in a pod. Or maybe it wasn't.

"Poor little rich girl," Miller said to the screen. "Sucks to be you, I guess."

He closed the files and drank quietly and seriously, staring at the blank ceiling above him. The chair where Candace used to sit and ask him about his day stood empty, but he could see her there anyway. Now that she wasn't here to make him talk, it was easier to respect the impulse. She'd been lonely. He could see that now. In his imagination, she rolled her eyes.

An hour later, his blood warm with drink, he heated up a bowl of real rice and fake beans—yeast and fungus could mimic anything if you had enough whiskey first—opened the door of his hole, and ate dinner looking out at the traffic gently curving by. The second shift streamed into the tube stations and then out of them. The kids who lived two holes down—a girl of eight and her brother of four—met their father with hugs, squeals, mutual accusations, and tears. The blue ceiling glowed in its reflected light, unchanging, static, reassuring. A sparrow fluttered down the tunnel, hovering in a way that Havelock assured him they couldn't on Earth. Miller threw it a fake bean.

He tried to think about the Mao girl, but in truth he didn't much care. Something was happening to the organized crime families of Ceres, and it made him jumpy as hell.

This thing with Julie Mao? It was a sideshow.

Chapter Three: Holden

After nearly two full days in high gravity, Holden's knees and back and neck ached. And his head. Hell, his feet. He walked in the crew hatch of the *Knight* just as Naomi was climbing up the ladder from its cargo bay. She smiled and gave him a thumbs-up.

"The salvage mech is locked down," she said. "Reactor is warming up. We're ready to fly."

"Good."

"We got a pilot yet?" she asked.

"Alex Kamal is on the ready rotation today, so he's our man. I kind of wish Valka had been up. He's not the pilot Alex is, but he's quieter, and my head hurts."

"I like Alex. He's ebullient," Naomi said.

"I don't know what *ebullient* means, but if it means Alex, it makes me tired."

Holden started up the ladder to ops and the cockpit. In the

shiny black surface of a deactivated wall panel, Naomi's reflection smirked at his back. He couldn't understand how Belters, thin as pencils, bounced back from high g so quickly. Decades of practice and selective breeding, he assumed.

In ops, Holden strapped into the command console, the crash couch material silently conforming to his body. At the half g Ade put them on for the final approach, the foam felt good. He let a small groan slip out. The switches, plastic and metal made to withstand hard g and hundreds of years, clicked sharply. The *Knight* responded with an array of glowing diagnostic indicators and a near-subliminal hum.

A few minutes later, Holden glanced over to see Alex Kamal's thinning black hair appear, followed by his round cheerful face, a deep brown that years of shipboard life couldn't pale. Martian-raised, Alex had a frame that was thicker than a Belter's. He was slender compared to Holden, and even so, his flight suit stretched tight against his spreading waistline. Alex had flown in the Martian navy, but he'd clearly given up on the military-style fitness routine.

"Howdy, XO," he drawled. The old west affectation common to everyone from the Mariner Valley annoyed Holden. There hadn't been a cowboy on Earth in a hundred years, and Mars didn't have a blade of grass that wasn't under a dome, or a horse that wasn't in a zoo. Mariner Valley had been settled by East Indians, Chinese, and a small contingent of Texans. Apparently, the drawl was viral. They all had it now. "How's the old warhorse today?"

"Smooth so far. We need a flight plan. Ade will be bringing us to relative stop in"—he checked the time readout—"forty, so work fast. I want to get out, get it done, and get the *Cant* back on course to Ceres before she starts rusting."

"Roger that," Alex said, climbing up to the *Knight*'s cockpit.

Holden's headset clicked; then Naomi's voice said, "Amos and Shed are aboard. We're all ready down here."

"Thanks. Just waiting on flight numbers from Alex and we'll be ready to go."

The crew was the minimum necessary: Holden as command,

Alex to get them there and back, Shed in case there were survivors to treat, Naomi and Amos for salvage if there weren't.

It wasn't long before Alex called down, "Okay, Boss. It'll be about a four-hour trip flyin' teakettle. Total mass use at about thirty percent, but we've got a full tank. Total mission time: eleven hours."

"Copy that. Thanks, Alex," Holden said.

Flying teakettle was naval slang for flying on the maneuvering thrusters that used superheated steam for reaction mass. The *Knight*'s fusion torch would be dangerous to use this close to the *Canterbury* and wasteful on such a short trip. Torches were pre-Epstein fusion drives and far less efficient.

"Calling for permission to leave the barn," Holden said, and clicked from internal comm to the link with the *Canterbury*'s bridge. "Holden here. *Knight* is ready to fly."

"Okay, Jim, go ahead," McDowell said. "Ade's bringing her to a stop now. You kids be careful out there. That shuttle is expensive and I've always sort of had a thing for Naomi."

"Roger that, Captain," Holden said. Back on the internal comm, he buzzed Alex. "Go ahead and take us out."

Holden leaned back in his chair and listened to the creaks of the *Canterbury*'s final maneuvers, the steel and ceramics as loud and ominous as the wood planks of a sailing ship. Or an Earther's joints after high g. For a moment, Holden felt sympathy for the ship.

They weren't really stopping, of course. Nothing in space ever actually stopped; it only came into a matching orbit with some other object. They were now following CA-2216862 on its merry millennium-long trip around the sun.

Ade sent them the green light, and Holden emptied out the hangar bay air and popped the doors. Alex took them out of the dock on white cones of superheated steam.

They went to find the *Scopuli*.

CA-2216862 was a rock a half kilometer across that had wandered away from the Belt and been yanked around by Jupiter's enormous gravity. It had eventually found its own slow orbit around the sun in the vast expanse between Jupiter and the Belt, territory empty even for space.

The sight of the *Scopuli* resting gently against the asteroid's side, held in place by the rock's tiny gravity, gave Holden a chill. Even if it was flying blind, every instrument dead, its odds of hitting such an object by chance were infinitesimally low. It was a half-kilometer-wide roadblock on a highway millions of kilometers in diameter. It hadn't arrived there by accident. He scratched the hairs standing up on the back of his neck.

"Alex, hold us at two klicks out," Holden said. "Naomi, what can you tell me about that ship?"

"Hull configuration matches the registry information. It's definitely the *Scopuli*. She's not radiating in the electromagnetic or infrared. Just that little distress beacon. Looks like the reactor's shut down. Must have been manual and not damage, because we aren't getting any radiation leakage either," Naomi said.

Holden looked at the pictures they were getting from the *Knight*'s scopes, as well as the image the *Knight* created by bouncing a laser off the *Scopuli*'s hull. "What about that thing that looks like a hole in the side?"

"Uh," Naomi said. "Ladar says it's a hole in the side."

Holden frowned. "Okay, let's stay here for a minute and recheck the neighborhood. Anything on the scope, Naomi?"

"Nope. And the big array on the *Cant* can spot a kid throwing rocks on Luna. Becca says there's nobody within twenty million klicks right now," Naomi said.

Holden tapped out a complicated rhythm on the arm of his chair and drifted up in the straps. He felt hot, and reached over to aim the closest air-circulation nozzle at his face. His scalp tingled with evaporating sweat.

If you see anything out there that seems off, don't play hero again. Just pack up the toys and come home. Those were his orders. He looked at the image of the *Scopuli*, the hole in its side.

"Okay," he said. "Alex, take us in to a quarter klick, and hold station there. We'll ride to the surface on the mech. Oh, and keep the torch warmed up and ready. If something nasty is hiding in that ship, I want to be able to run away as fast as I can and melt anything behind us into slag while I do it. Roger?"

"Got it, Boss. *Knight*'s in run-like-a-bunny mode till you say otherwise," Alex replied.

Holden looked over the command console one more time, searching for the flashing red warning light that would give him permission to go back to the *Cant*. Everything remained a soft green. He popped open his buckles and shoved himself out of the chair. A push on the wall with one foot sent him over to the ladder, and he descended headfirst with gentle touches on the rungs.

In the crew area, Naomi, Amos, and Shed were still strapped into their crash couches. Holden caught the ladder and swung around so that his crew didn't look upside down. They started undoing their restraints.

"Okay, here's the situation. The *Scopuli* got holed, and someone left it floating next to this rock. No one is on the scopes, so maybe that means it happened a while ago and they left. Naomi, you'll be driving the salvage mech, and the three of us will tether on and catch a ride down to the wreck. Shed, you stay with the mech unless we find an injured person, which seems unlikely. Amos and I will go into the ship through that hole and poke around. If we find anything even remotely booby trap–like, we will come back to the mech, Naomi will fly us back to the *Knight,* and we will run away. Any questions?"

Amos raised one beefy hand. "Maybe we oughta be armed, XO. Case there's piratey types still lurking aboard."

Holden laughed. "Well, if there are, then their ride left without them. But if it makes you feel more comfortable, go ahead and bring a gun."

If the big, burly Earther mechanic was carrying a gun, it would make *him* feel better too, but better not to say it. Let them think the guy in charge felt confident.

Holden used his officer's key to open the weapon locker, and

Amos took a high-caliber automatic that fired self-propelled rounds, recoilless and designed for use in zero g. Old-fashioned slug throwers were more reliable, but in null gravity they were also maneuvering thrusters. A traditional handgun would impart enough thrust to achieve escape velocity from a rock the size of CA-2216862.

The crew drifted down to the cargo bay, where the egg-shaped, spider-legged open cage of Naomi's mech waited. Each of the four legs had a manipulator claw at the end and a variety of cutting and welding tools built into it. The back pair could grip on to a ship's hull or other structure for leverage, and the front two could be used to make repairs or chop salvage into portable pieces.

"Hats on," Holden said, and the crew helped each other put on and secure their helmets. Everyone checked their own suit and then someone else's. When the cargo doors opened, it would be too late to make sure they were buttoned up right.

While Naomi climbed into her mech, Amos, Holden, and Shed secured their suit tethers to the cockpit's metal cage. Naomi checked the mech and then hit the switch to cycle the cargo bay's atmosphere and open the doors. Sound inside Holden's suit faded to just the hiss of air and the faint static of the radio. The air had a slight medicine smell.

Naomi went first, taking the mech down toward the asteroid's surface on small jets of compressed nitrogen, the crew trailing her on three-meter-long tethers. As they flew, Holden looked back up at the *Knight:* a blocky gray wedge with a drive cone stuck on the wider end. Like everything else humans built for space travel, it was designed to be efficient, not pretty. That always made Holden a little sad. There should be room for aesthetics, even out here.

The *Knight* seemed to drift away from him, getting smaller and smaller, while he didn't move. The illusion vanished when he turned around to look at the asteroid and felt they were hurtling toward it. He opened a channel to Naomi, but she was humming to herself as she flew, which meant she, at least, wasn't worried. He didn't say anything, but he left the channel open to listen to her hum.

Up close, the *Scopuli* didn't look all that bad. Other than the gaping hole in its flank, it didn't have any damage. It clearly hadn't hit the asteroid; it had just been left close enough that the microgravity had slowly reeled it in. As they approached, he snapped pictures with his suit helmet and transmitted them to the *Canterbury*.

Naomi brought them to a stop, hovering three meters above the hole in the *Scopuli*'s side. Amos whistled across the general suit channel.

"That wasn't a torpedo did this, XO. This was a breaching charge. See how the metal's bent in all around the edges? That's shaped charges stuck right on her hull," Amos said.

In addition to being a fine mechanic, Amos was the one who used explosive surgery to crack open the icebergs floating around Saturn and turn them into more manageable chunks. Another reason to have him on the *Knight*.

"So," Holden said, "our friends here on the *Scopuli* stop, let someone climb onto their hull and plant a breaching charge, and then crack them open and let all the air out. Does that make sense to anyone?"

"Nope," Naomi said. "It doesn't. Still want to go inside?"

If you see anything out there that seems off, don't play hero again. Just pack up the toys and come home.

But what could he have expected? Of course the *Scopuli* wasn't up and running. Of course something had gone wrong. *Off* would have been not seeing anything strange.

"Amos," Holden said, "keep that gun out, just in case. Naomi, can you make us a bigger hole? And be careful. If anything looks wrong, back us off."

Naomi brought the mech in closer, nitrogen blasts no more than a white breath on a cold night. The mech's welding torch blazed to life, red hot, then white, then blue. In silence, the mech's arms unfurled—an insectile movement—and Naomi started cutting. Holden and Amos dropped to the ship's surface, clamping on with magnetic boots. He could feel the vibration in his feet when Naomi pulled a length of hull free. A moment later the torch turned off, and Naomi blasted the fresh edges of the hole with the mech's fire-suppression gear to cool them. Holden gave Amos the thumbs-up and dropped himself very slowly into the *Scopuli.*

The breaching charge had been placed almost exactly amid-ships, blasting a hole into the galley. When Holden landed and his boots grabbed on to the galley wall, he could feel flash-frozen bits of food crunch under them. There were no bodies in sight.

"Come on in, Amos. No crew visible yet," Holden called over the suit comm.

He moved off to the side and a moment later Amos dropped in, gun clutched in his right hand and a powerful light in his left. The white beam played across the walls of the destroyed galley.

"Which way first, XO?" Amos asked.

Holden tapped on his thigh with one hand and thought. "Engineering. I want to know why the reactor's off-line."

They took the crew ladder, climbing along it toward the aft of the ship. All the pressure doors between decks were open, which was a bad sign. They should all be closed by default, and certainly if the atmosphere-loss alarm had sounded. If they were open, that meant there were no decks with atmosphere left in the ship. Which meant no survivors. Not a surprise, but it still felt like a defeat. They passed through the small ship quickly, pausing in the machine shop. Expensive engine parts and tools were still in place.

"Guess it wasn't robbery," Amos said.

Holden didn't say, *Then what was it?* but the question hung between them anyway.

The engine room was neat as a pin, cold, and dead. Holden waited while Amos looked it over, spending at least ten minutes just floating around the reactor.

"Someone went through the shutdown procedures," Amos said. "The reactor wasn't killed by the blast, it was turned off afterward. No damage that I can see. Don't make sense. If everyone is dead from the attack, who shut it down? And if it's pirates, why not take the ship? She'll still fly."

"And before they turned off the power, they went through and opened every interior pressure door on the ship. Emptied out the air. I guess they wanted to make sure no one was hiding," Holden said. "Okay, let's head back up to ops and see if we can crack the computer core. Maybe it can tell us what happened."

They floated back toward the bow along the crew ladder, and up to the ops deck. It too was undamaged and empty. The lack of bodies was starting to bother Holden more than the presence of them would have. He floated over to the main computer console and hit a few keys to see if it might still be running on backup power. It wasn't.

"Amos, start cutting the core out. We'll take it with us. I'm going to check comms, see if I can find that beacon."

Amos moved to the computer and started taking out tools and sticking them to the bulkhead next to it. He began a profanity-laced mumble as he worked. It wasn't nearly as charming as Naomi's humming, so Holden turned off his link to Amos while he moved to the communications console. It was as dead as the rest of the ship. He found the ship's beacon.

No one had activated it. Something else had called them. Holden moved back, frowning.

He looked through the space, searching for something out of place. There, on the deck beneath the comm operator's console. A small black box not connected to anything else.

His heart took a long pause between beats. He called out to Amos, "Does that look like a bomb to you?"

Amos ignored him. Holden turned his radio link back on.

"Amos, does that look like a bomb to you?" He pointed at the box on the deck.

Amos left his work on the computer and floated over to look, then, in a move that made Holden's throat close, grabbed the box off the deck and held it up.

"Nope. It's a transmitter. See?" He held it up in front of Holden's helmet. "It's just got a battery taped to it. What's it doing there?"

"It's the beacon we followed. Jesus. The ship's beacon never even turned on. Someone made a fake one out of that transmitter and hooked it up to a battery," Holden said quietly, still fighting his panic.

"Why would they do that, XO? That don't make no kinda sense."

"It would if there's something about this transmitter that's different from standard," Holden said.

"Like?"

"Like if it had a second signal triggered to go when someone found it," Holden said, then switched to the general suit channel. "Okay, boys and girls, we've found something weird, and we're out of here. Everyone back to the *Knight,* and be very careful when you—"

His radio crackled to life on the outside channel, McDowell's voice filling his helmet. "Jim? We may have a problem out here."

Chapter Four: Miller

Miller was halfway through his evening meal when the system in his hole chirped. He glanced at the sending code. The Blue Frog. It was a port bar catering to the constant extra million noncitizens of Ceres that advertised itself as a near-exact replica of a famous Earth bar in Mumbai, only with licensed prostitutes and legal drugs. Miller took another forkful of fungal beans and vat-grown rice and debated whether to accept connection.

Should have seen this one coming, he thought.

"What?" he asked.

A screen popped open. Hasini, the assistant manager, was a dark-skinned man with eyes the color of ice. The near smirk on his face was the result of nerve damage. Miller had done him a favor when Hasini had had the poor judgment to take pity on an unlicensed prostitute. Since then, security detective and portside barman had traded favors. The unofficial, gray economics of civilization.

"Your partner's here again," Hasini said over the pulse and wail of bhangra music. "I think he's having a bad night. Should I keep serving him?"

"Yeah," Miller said. "Keep him happy for...Give me twenty minutes."

"He doesn't want to be kept happy. He very much wants a reason to get unhappy."

"Make it hard to find. I'll be there."

Hasini nodded, smirking his damaged smirk, and dropped the connection. Miller looked at his half-eaten meal, sighed, and shoved the remains into the recycling bin. He pulled on a clean shirt, then hesitated. The Blue Frog was always warmer than he liked, and he hated wearing a jacket. Instead, he put a compact plastic pistol in his ankle holster. Not as fast a draw, but if it got that far, he was screwed anyway.

Ceres at night was indistinguishable from Ceres in the daytime. There had been a move, back when the station first opened, to dim and brighten the lights through the traditional human twenty-four-hour cycle, mimicking the spin of Earth. The affectation had lasted four months before the council killed it.

On duty, Miller would have taken an electric cart down the wide tunnels and down to the port levels. He was tempted even though he was off duty, but a deep-seated superstition stopped him. If he took the cart, he was going as a cop, and the tubes ran just fine. Miller walked to the nearest station, checked the status, and sat on the low stone bench. A man about Miller's age and a girl no more than three came in a minute later and sat across from him. The girl's talk was as fast and meaningless as a leaking seal, and her father responded with grunts and nods at more or less appropriate moments.

Miller and the new man nodded to each other. The girl tugged at her father's sleeve, demanding his attention. Miller looked at her—dark eyes, pale hair, smooth skin. She was already too tall to be mistaken for an Earth child, her limbs longer and thinner. Her skin had the pink flush of Belter babies, which came with the pharmaceutical cocktail that assured that their muscles and bones would grow strong. Miller saw the father notice his attention. Miller smiled and nodded toward the kid.

"How old?" he asked.

"Two and a half," the father said.

"Good age."

The father shrugged, but he smiled.

"Kids?" he asked.

"No," Miller said. "But I've got a divorce about that old."

They chuckled together as if it was funny. In his imagination, Candace crossed her arms and looked away. The soft oil-and-ozone-scented breeze announced the tube's arrival. Miller let father and child go first, then chose a different compartment.

The tube cars were round, built to fit into the evacuated passages. There were no windows. The only view would have been stone humming by three centimeters from the car. Instead, broad screens advertised entertainment feeds or commented on inner planet political scandals or offered the chance to gamble away a week's pay at casinos so wonderful that your life would seem richer for the experience. Miller let the bright, empty colors dance and ignored their content. Mentally, he was holding up his problem, turning it one way and then the other, not even looking for an answer.

It was a simple mental exercise. Look at the facts without judgment: Havelock was an Earther. Havelock was in a portside bar again and looking for a fight. Havelock was his partner. Statement after statement, fact after fact, facet after facet. He didn't try to put them in order or make some kind of narrative out of them; that would all come later. Now it was enough to wash the day's cases out of his head and get ready for the immediate situation. By the time the tube reached his station, he felt centered. Like he was walking on his whole foot, was how he'd described it, back when he had anyone to describe it to.

The Blue Frog was crowded, the barn-heat of bodies adding to the fake-Mumbai temperature and artificial air pollution. Lights glittered and flashed in seizure-inducing display. Tables curved and undulated, the backlight making them seem darker than merely black. Music moved through the air with a physical presence, each beat a little concussion. Hasini, standing in a clot of steroid-enhanced bouncers and underdressed serving girls, caught Miller's eyes and nodded toward the back. Miller didn't acknowledge anything; he just turned and made his way through the crowd.

Port bars were always volatile. Miller was careful not to bump into anyone if he could help it. When he had to choose, he'd run into Belters before inner planet types, women before men. His face was a constant mild apology.

Havelock was sitting alone, with one thick hand wrapping a fluted glass. When Miller sat down beside him, Havelock turned toward him, ready to take offense, nostrils flared and eyes wide. Then the surprise registered. Then something like sullen shame.

"Miller," he said. In the tunnels outside, he would have been shouting. Here, it was barely enough to carry as far as Miller's chair. "What're you doing here?"

"Nothing much to do at the hole," Miller said. "Thought I'd come pick a fight."

"Good night for it," Havelock said.

It was true. Even in the bars that catered to inner planet types, the mix was rarely better than one Earther or Martian in ten. Squinting out at the crowd, Miller saw that the short, stocky men and women were nearer a third.

"Ship come in?" he asked.

"Yeah."

"EMCN?" he asked. The Earth-Mars Coalition Navy often passed through Ceres on its way to Saturn, Jupiter, and the stations of the Belt, but Miller hadn't been paying enough attention to the relative position of the planets to know where the orbits all stood. Havelock shook his head.

"Corporate security rotating out of Eros," he said. "Protogen, I think." A serving girl appeared at Miller's side, tattoos gliding over her skin, her teeth glowing in the black light. Miller took the drink she offered him, though he hadn't ordered. Soda water.

"You know," Miller said, leaning close enough to Havelock that even his normal conversational voice would reach the man, "it doesn't matter how many of their asses you kick. Shaddid's still not going to like you."

Havelock snapped to stare at Miller, the anger in his eyes barely covering the shame and hurt.

"It's true," Miller said.

Havelock rose lurching to his feet and headed for the door. He was trying to stomp, but in the Ceres spin gravity and his inebriated state, he misjudged. It looked like he was hopping. Miller, glass in hand, slid through the crowd in Havelock's wake, calming with a smile and a shrug the affronted faces that his partner left behind him.

The common tunnels down near the port had a layer of grime and grease to them that air scrubbers and astringent cleaners could never quite master. Havelock walked out, shoulders hunched, mouth tight, rage radiating from him like heat. But the doors of the Blue Frog closed behind them, the seal cutting off the music like someone hitting mute. The worst of the danger had passed.

"I'm not drunk," Havelock said, his voice too loud.

"Didn't say you were."

"And you," Havelock said, turning and stabbing an accusing finger at Miller's chest. "You are not my nanny."

"Also true."

They walked together for maybe a quarter of a kilometer. The bright LED signs beckoned. Brothels and shooting galleries, coffee bars and poetry clubs, casinos and show fights. The air smelled like piss and old food. Havelock began to slow, his shoulders coming down from around his ears.

"I worked homicide in Terrytown," Havelock said. "I did three years vice at L-5. Do you have any idea what that was like? They were shipping kids out of there, and I'm one of three guys that stopped it. I'm a good cop."

"Yes, you are."

"I'm damn good."

"You are."

They walked past a noodle bar. A coffin hotel. A public terminal, its displays running a free newsfeed: COMMUNICATION PROBLEMS PLAGUE PHOEBE SCIENCE STATION. NEW ANDREAS K GAME NETS 6 BILLION DOLLARS IN 4 HOURS. NO DEAL IN MARS, BELT TITANIUM CONTRACT. The screens glowed in Havelock's eyes, but he was staring past them.

"I'm a damn good cop," he said again. Then, a moment later: "So what the hell?"

"It's not about you," Miller said. "People look at you, they don't see Dmitri Havelock, good cop. They see Earth."

"That's crap. I was eight years in the orbitals and on Mars before I ever shipped out here. I worked on Earth maybe six months total."

"Earth. Mars. They're not that different," Miller said.

"Try telling that to a Martian," Havelock said with a bitter laugh. "They'll kick your ass for you."

"I didn't mean...Look, I'm sure there are all kinds of differences. Earth hates Mars for having a better fleet. Mars hates Earth for having a bigger one. Maybe soccer's better in full g; maybe it's worse. I don't know. I'm just saying anyone this far out from the sun? They don't care. From this distance, you can cover Earth and Mars with one thumb. And..."

"And I don't belong," Havelock said.

The door of the noodle bar behind them opened and four Belters in gray-green uniforms came out. One of them wore the split circle of the OPA on his sleeve. Miller tensed, but the Belters didn't come toward them, and Havelock didn't notice them. Near miss.

"I knew," Havelock said. "When I took the Star Helix contract, I knew I'd have to work to fit in. I thought it'd be the same as anywhere, you know? You go, you get your chops busted for a while.

Then, when they see you can take it, they treat you like one of the team. It's not like that here."

"It's not," Miller said.

Havelock shook his head, spat, and stared at the fluted glass in his hand.

"I think we just stole some glasses from the Blue Frog," Havelock said.

"We're also in a public corridor with unsealed alcohol," Miller said. "Well, you are, anyway. Mine's soda water."

Havelock chuckled, but there was despair in the sound. When Havelock spoke again, his voice was only rueful.

"You think I'm coming down here, picking fights with people from the inner planets so that Shaddid and Ramachandra and all the rest of them will think better of me."

"It occurred to me."

"You're wrong," Havelock said.

"Okay," Miller said. He knew he wasn't.

Havelock raised his fluted glass. "Take these back?" he asked.

"How about Distinguished Hyacinth?" Miller countered. "I'll buy."

The Distinguished Hyacinth Lounge was up three levels, far enough that foot traffic from the port levels was minimal. And it was a cop bar. Mostly Star Helix Security, but some of the minor corporate forces—Protogen, Pinkwater, Al Abbiq—hung out there too. Miller was more than half certain that his partner's latest breakdown had been averted, but if he was wrong, better to keep it in the family.

The décor was pure Belt—old-style ships' folding tables and chairs set into the wall and ceiling as if the gravity might shut off at any moment. Snake plant and devil's ivy—staples of first-generation air recycling—decorated the wall and freestanding columns. The music was soft enough to talk over, loud enough to keep private conversations private. The first owner, Javier Liu, was a structural engineer from Tycho who'd come out during the big spin and liked Ceres enough to stay. His grandchildren ran it now. Javier the Third was standing behind the bar, talking with half of the vice and exploitation team. Miller led the way to a back table, nodding to the men and women he knew as he passed. While he'd been careful and diplomatic at the Blue Frog, he chose a bluff masculinity here. It was just as much a pose.

"So," Havelock said as Javier's daughter Kate—a fourth generation for the same bar—left the table, Blue Frog glasses on her tray, "what is this supersecret private investigation Shaddid put you on? Or is the lowly Earther not supposed to know?"

"Is that what got to you?" Miller asked. "It's nothing. Some shareholders misplaced their daughter and want me to track her down, ship her home. It's a bullshit case."

"Sounds more like their backyard," Havelock said, nodding toward the V and E crowd.

"Kid's not a minor," Miller said. "It's a kidnap job."

"And you're good with that?"

Miller sat back. The ivy above them waved. Havelock waited, and Miller had the uncomfortable sense that a table had just been turned.

"It's my job," Miller said.

"Yeah, but we're talking about an adult here, right? It's not like she couldn't go back home if she wanted to be there. But instead her parents get security to take her home whether she wants to go or not. That's not law enforcement anymore. It's not even station security. It's just dysfunctional families playing power games."

Miller remembered the thin girl beside her racing pinnace. Her broad smile.

"I told you it was a bullshit case," Miller said.

Kate Liu returned to the table with a local beer and a glass of whiskey on her tray. Miller was glad for the distraction. The beer was his. Light and rich and just the faintest bit bitter. An ecology based on yeasts and fermentation meant subtle brews.

Havelock was nursing his whiskey. Miller took it as a sign that he was giving up on his bender. Nothing like being around the boys from the office to take the charm out of losing control.

"Hey, Miller! Havelock!" a familiar voice said. Yevgeny Cobb from homicide. Miller waved him over, and the conversation turned to homicide's bragging about the resolution of a particularly ugly case. Three months' work figuring out where the toxins came from ending with the corpse's wife awarded the full insurance settlement and a gray-market whore deported back to Eros.

By the end of the night, Havelock was laughing and trading jokes along with the rest of them. If there was occasionally a narrowed glance or a subtle dig, he took it in stride.

Miller was on his way up to the bar for another round when his terminal chimed. And then, slowly throughout the bar, fifty other chimes sounded. Miller felt his belly knot as he and every other security agent in the place pulled out their terminals.

Captain Shaddid was on the broadcast screen. Her eyes were bleary and filled with banked rage; she was the very picture of a woman of power wakened early from sleep.

"Ladies and gentlemen," she said. "Whatever you're doing, drop it and go to your stations for emergency orders. We have a situation.

"Ten minutes ago, an unencrypted, signed message came in from the rough direction of Saturn. We haven't confirmed it as true, but the signature matches the keys on record. I've put a hold on it, but we can assume some asshole's going to put it on the network, and the shit should hit the fan about five minutes after that. If you're in earshot of a civilian, turn off now. For the rest of you, here's what we're up against."

Shaddid moved to one side, tapping her system interface. The screen went black. A moment later a man's face and shoulders appeared. He was in an orange vacuum suit with the helmet off. An Earther, maybe in his early thirties. Pale skin, blue eyes, dark short-cropped hair. Even before the man opened his mouth, Miller saw the signs of shock and rage in his eyes and the way he held his head forward.

"My name," the man said, "is James Holden."

Chapter Five: Holden

Ten minutes at two g, and Holden's head was already starting to ache. But McDowell had called them home at all haste. The *Canterbury* was warming up its massive drive. Holden didn't want to miss his ride.

"*Jim? We may have a problem out here.*"
"*Talk to me.*"
"*Becca found something, and it is sufficiently weird to make my balls creep up. We're getting the hell out of here.*"

"Alex, how long?" Holden asked for the third time in ten minutes.
"We're over an hour out. Want to go on the juice?" Alex said.
Going on the juice was pilot-speak for a high-g burn that would

knock an unmedicated human unconscious. *The juice* was the cocktail of drugs the pilot's chair would inject into him to keep him conscious, alert, and hopefully stroke-free when his body weighed five hundred kilos. Holden had used the juice on multiple occasions in the navy, and coming down afterward was unpleasant.

"Not unless we have to," he said.

"What kind of weird?"

"Becca, link him up. Jim, I want you seeing what we're seeing."

Holden tongued a painkiller tab from his suit's helmet and reran Becca's sensor feed for the fifth time. The spot in space lay about two hundred thousand kilometers from the *Canterbury*. As the *Cant* had scanned it, the readout showed a fluctuation, the gray-black false color gradually developing a warm border. It was a small temperature climb, less than two degrees. Holden was amazed Becca had even spotted it. He reminded himself to give her a glowing review the next time she was up for promotion.

"Where did that come from?" Holden asked.

"No idea. It's just a spot faintly warmer than the background," Becca said. *"I'd say it was a cloud of gas, because we get no radar return from it, but there aren't supposed to be any gas clouds out here. I mean, where would it come from?"*

"Jim, any chance the Scopuli *killed the ship that killed it? Could it be a vapor cloud from a destroyed ship?"* McDowell asked.

"I don't think so, sir. The Scopuli *is totally unarmed. The hole in her side came from breaching charges, not torpedo fire, so I don't think they even fought back. It might be where the* Scopuli *vented, but..."*

"Or maybe not. Come back to the barn, Jim. Do it now."

"Naomi, what slowly gets hotter that gives no radar or ladar return when you scan it? Wild-ass guess here," Holden said.

"Hmmmm…" Naomi said, giving herself time to think. "Anything that was absorbing the energy from the sensor package wouldn't give a return. But it might get hotter when it shed the absorbed energy."

The infrared monitor on the sensor console next to Holden's chair flared like the sun. Alex swore loudly over the general comm.

"Are you seein' that?" he said.

Holden ignored him and opened a channel to McDowell.

"Captain, we just got a massive IR spike," Holden said.

For long seconds, there was no reply. When McDowell came on the channel, his voice was tight. Holden had never heard the old man sound afraid before.

"Jim, a ship just appeared in that warm spot. It's radiating heat like a bastard," McDowell said. "Where the hell did that thing come from?"

Holden started to answer but then heard Becca's voice coming faintly through the captain's headset. "No idea, sir. But it's smaller than its heat signature. Radar shows frigate-sized," she said.

"With what?" McDowell said. "Invisibility? Magical wormhole teleportation?"

"Sir," Holden said, "Naomi was speculating that the heat we picked up might have come from energy-absorbing materials. Stealth materials. Which means that ship was hiding on purpose. Which means its intentions are not good."

As if in answer, six new objects appeared on his radar, glowing yellow icons appearing and immediately shifting to orange as the system marked their acceleration. On the *Canterbury*, Becca yelled out, "Fast movers! We have six new high-speed contacts on a collision course!"

"Jesus H. Christ on a pogo stick, did that ship just fire a spread of torpedoes at us?" McDowell said. "They're trying to slap us down?"

"Yes, sir," Becca said.

"Time to contact."

"Just under eight minutes, sir," she replied.

McDowell cursed under his breath.

"We've got pirates, Jim."

"What do you need from us?" Holden said, trying to sound calm and professional.

"I need you to get off the radio and let my crew work. You're an hour out at best. The torpedoes are eight minutes. McDowell out," the captain said, his comm clicking off and leaving Holden listening to the faint hiss of static.

The general comm exploded with voices, Alex demanding to go on the juice and race the torpedoes to the *Cant,* Naomi chattering about missile-jamming strategies, Amos cursing at the stealth ship and questioning the parenting of its crew. Shed was the only quiet one.

"Everyone, shut up!" Holden yelled into his headset. The ship fell into shocked silence. "Alex, plot the fastest course to the *Cant* that won't kill us. Let me know when you have it. Naomi, set up a three-way channel with Becca, you, and me. We'll help however we can. Amos, keep cussing but turn your mic off."

He waited. The clock ticked toward impact.

"Link is up," Naomi said. Holden could hear two distinct sets of background noise over the comm channel.

"Becca, this is Jim. I've got Naomi on this channel too. Tell us what we can do to help. Naomi was talking about jamming techniques?"

"I'm doing everything I know to do," Becca said, her voice astonishingly calm. "They're painting us with a targeting laser. I'm broadcasting garbage to scramble it, but they've got really, really good shit. If we were any closer, that targeting laser would be burning a hole in our hull."

"What about physical chaff?" Naomi asked. "Can you drop snow?"

While Naomi and Becca talked, Jim opened a private channel to Ade. "Hey, this is Jim. I have Alex working on a fast-burn solution so we can get there before..."

"Before the missiles turn us into a flying brick? Good idea. Taken by pirates isn't something you want to miss," Ade said. He could hear the fear behind the mocking tone.

"Ade, please, I want to say something—"

"Jim, what do you think?" Naomi said on the other channel.

Holden cursed. To cover, he said, "Uh, about which thing?"

"Using the *Knight* to try and draw those missiles," Naomi said.

"Can we do that?" he asked.

"Maybe. Were you listening at all?"

"Ah...something happened here, drew my attention for a minute. Tell me again," Holden said.

"We try to match the frequency of the light scatter coming off the *Cant* and broadcast it with our comm array. Maybe the torpedoes will think we're the target instead," Naomi said like she was speaking to a child.

"And then they come blow us up?"

"I'm thinking we run away while pulling the torpedoes toward us. Then, when we get them far enough past the *Cant*, we kill the comm array and try to hide behind the asteroid," Naomi said.

"Won't work," Holden said with a sigh. "They follow the targeting laser's scatter for general guidance, but they also take telescope shots of the target on acquisition. They'll take one look at us and know we aren't their target."

"Isn't it worth a shot?"

"Even if we manage it, torpedoes designed to disable the *Cant* would make us into a greasy stretch of vacuum."

"All right," Naomi said. "What else have we got?"

"Nothing. Very smart boys in the naval labs have already thought of everything we are going to think of in the next eight minutes," Holden said. Saying it out loud meant admitting it to himself.

"Then what are we doing here, Jim?" Naomi asked.

"Seven minutes," Becca said, her voice still eerily calm.

"Let's get there. Maybe we can get some people off the ship

after it's hit. Help with damage control," Holden said. "Alex, got that plot figured out?"

"Roger that, XO. Bleeding-g burn-and-flip laid in. Angled approach course so our torch won't burn a hole in the *Cant*. Time to rock and roll?" Alex replied.

"Yeah. Naomi, get your people strapped in for high g," Holden said, then opened up a channel to Captain McDowell. "Captain, we're coming in hot. Try to survive, and we'll have the *Knight* on station for pickup or to help with damage control."

"Roger," McDowell said, and killed the line.

Holden opened up his channel to Ade again. "Ade, we're going to burn hard, so I won't be talking, but leave this channel open for me, okay? Tell me what's happening. Hell, hum. Humming is nice. I just really need to hear you're all right."

"Okay, Jim," Ade said. She didn't hum but she left the channel open. He could hear her breathing.

Alex began the countdown over the general comm. Holden checked the straps on his crash couch and palmed the button that started the juice. A dozen needles stuck into his back through membranes in his suit. His heart shuddered and chemical bands of iron gripped his brain. His spine went dead cold, and his face flushed like a radiation burn. He pounded a fist into the arm of the crash couch. He hated this part, but the next one was worse. On the general comm, Alex whooped as the drugs hit his system. Belowdecks, the others were getting the drugs that kept them from dying but kept them sedated through the worst of it.

Alex said, "One," and Holden weighed five hundred kilos. The nerves at the back of his eye sockets screamed at the massive load of his eyeballs. His testicles crushed themselves against his thighs. He concentrated on not swallowing his tongue. Around him, the ship creaked and groaned. There was a disconcerting bang from belowdecks, but nothing on his panel went red. The *Knight*'s torch drive could deliver a lot of thrust, but at the cost of a prodigious fuel-burn rate. But if they could save the *Cant*, it wouldn't matter.

Over the blood pounding in his ears, Holden could hear Ade's gentle breathing and the click of her keyboard. He wished he could just go to sleep to that sound, but the juice was singing and burning in his blood. He was more awake than he'd ever been.

"Yes, sir," Ade said over the comm.

It took Holden a second to realize she was talking to McDowell. He turned up the volume to hear what the captain was saying.

"—the mains online, full power."

"We're fully loaded, sir. If we try to burn that hard, we'll tear the drive right off the mounts," Ade replied. McDowell must have asked her to fire up the Epstein.

"Mr. Tukunbo," McDowell said, "we have…four minutes. If you break it, I won't bill you."

"Yes, sir. Bringing mains online. Setting for maximum burn," Ade said, and in the background Holden could hear the high-g warning Klaxon. There was a louder clicking as Ade strapped herself in.

"Mains online in three…two…one…execute," Ade said.

The *Canterbury* groaned so loud Holden had to turn the comm volume down. It moaned and shrieked like a banshee for several seconds, and then there was a shattering crash. He pulled up the exterior visual, fighting against the g-induced blackout at the edge of his vision. The *Canterbury* was in one piece.

"Ade, what the hell was that?" McDowell said, his speech slurred.

"The drive tearing a strut. Mains are off-line, sir," Ade replied, not saying *Exactly like I said would happen.*

"What did that buy us?" McDowell asked.

"Not much. The torpedoes are now at over forty klicks a second and accelerating. We're down to maneuvering thrusters," Ade said.

"Shit," McDowell said.

"They're going to hit us, sir," Ade said.

"Jim," McDowell said, his voice suddenly loud over the direct channel he'd opened. "We're going down, and there's no way around it. Click twice to acknowledge."

Jim clicked his radio twice.

"Okay, so, now we need to think about surviving after the hit. If they're looking to cripple us before boarding, they'll take out our drive and our comm array. Becca's been broadcasting an SOS ever since the torpedoes were fired, but I'd like you to keep yelling if we stop. If they know you're out there, they are less likely to toss everyone out an airlock. Witnesses, you know," McDowell said.

Jim clicked twice again.

"Turn around, Jim. Hide behind that asteroid. Call for help. Order."

Jim clicked twice, then signaled all-stop to Alex. In an instant, the giant sitting on his chest disappeared, replaced by weightlessness. The sudden transition would have made him throw up if his veins hadn't been coursing with antinausea drugs.

"What's up?" Alex said.

"New job," Holden said, teeth chattering from the juice. "We're calling for help and negotiating a release of prisoners once the bad guys have the *Cant*. Burn back to that asteroid, since it's the closest we can get to cover."

"Roger that, Boss," Alex said. He added in a lower voice, "I'd kill for a couple of tubes or a nice keel-mounted rail gun right now."

"I hear you."

"Wake up the kids downstairs?"

"Let them sleep."

"Roger that," Alex said, then clicked off.

Before the heavy g started up again, Holden turned on the *Knight*'s SOS. The channel to Ade was still open, and now that McDowell was off the line, he could hear her breathing again. He turned the volume all the way up and lay back in the straps, waiting to be crushed. Alex didn't disappoint him.

"One minute," Ade said, her voice loud enough to distort through his helmet's speakers. Holden didn't turn the volume down. Her voice was admirably calm as she called out the impact countdown.

"Thirty seconds."

Holden wanted desperately to talk, to say something comforting, to make ludicrous and untrue assertions of love. The giant standing on his chest just laughed with the deep rumble of their fusion torch.

"Ten seconds."

"Get ready to kill the reactor and play dead after the torpedoes hit. If we're not a threat, they won't hit us again," McDowell said.

"Five," Ade said.

"Four.

"Three.

"Two.

"One."

The *Canterbury* shuddered and the monitor went white. Ade took one sharp intake of breath, which cut off as the radio broke up. The static squeal almost ruptured Holden's eardrums. He chinned the volume down and clicked his radio at Alex.

The thrust suddenly dropped to a tolerable two g and all the ship's sensors flared into overload. A brilliant light poured through the small airlock porthole.

"Report, Alex, report! What happened?" Holden yelled.

"My God. They nuked her. They nuked the *Cant,*" Alex said, his voice low and dazed.

"What's her status? Give me a report on the *Canterbury*! I have zero sensors down here. Everything's just gone white!"

There was a long pause; then Alex said, "I have zero sensors up here too, Boss. But I can give you a status on the *Cant*. I can see her."

"See her? From here?"

"Yeah. She's a cloud of vapor the size of Olympus Mons. She's gone, Boss. She's gone."

That can't be right, Holden's mind protested. That doesn't happen. Pirates don't nuke water haulers. No one wins. No one gets paid. And if you just want to murder fifty people, walking into a restaurant with a machine gun is a *lot* easier.

He wanted to shout it, scream at Alex that he was wrong. But he had to keep it together. *I'm the old man now.*

"All right. New mission, Alex. Now we're witnesses to murder. Get us back to that asteroid. I'll start compiling a broadcast. Wake everyone up. They need to know," Holden said. "I'm rebooting the sensor package."

He methodically shut down the sensors and their software, waited two minutes, then slowly brought them back online. His hands were shaking. He was nauseated. His body felt like he was operating his flesh from a distance, and he didn't know how much was the juice and how much was shock.

The sensors came back up. Like any other ship that flew the space lanes, the *Knight* was hardened against radiation. You couldn't get anywhere near Jupiter's massive radiation belt unless you were. But Holden doubted the ship's designers had half a dozen nuclear weapons going off nearby in mind when they'd created the specs. They'd gotten lucky. Vacuum might protect them from an electromagnetic pulse, but the blast radiation could still have fried every sensor the ship had.

Once the array came back up, he scanned the space where the *Canterbury* had been. There was nothing larger than a softball. He switched over to the ship that killed it, which was flying off sunward at a leisurely one g. Heat bloomed in Holden's chest.

He wasn't scared. Aneurysm-inducing rage made his temples pound and his fists squeeze until his tendons hurt. He flipped on the comms and aimed a tightbeam at the retreating ship.

"This message is to whoever ordered the destruction of the *Canterbury*, the civilian ice freighter that you just blew into gas. You don't get to just fly away, you murderous son of a bitch. I don't care what your reasons are, but you just killed fifty friends of mine. You need to know who they were. I am sending to you the name and photograph of everyone who just died in that ship. Take a good look at what you did. Think about that while I work on finding out who you are."

He closed the voice channel, pulled up the *Canterbury*'s

personnel files, and began transmitting the crew dossiers to the other ship.

"What are you doing?" asked Naomi from behind him, not from his helmet speakers.

She was standing there with her helmet off. Sweat plastered her thick black hair to her head and neck. Her face was unreadable. Holden took off his helmet.

"I'm showing them the *Canterbury* was a real place where real people lived. People with names and families," he said, the juice making his voice less steady than he would have liked. "If there's something resembling a human being giving the orders on that ship, I hope it haunts him right up to the day they put him in the recycler for murder."

"I don't think they appreciate it," Naomi said, pointing at the panel behind him.

The enemy ship was now painting them with its targeting laser. Holden held his breath. No torpedoes launched, and after a few seconds, the stealth ship turned off its laser and the engine flared as it scooted off at high g. He heard Naomi let out a shuddering breath.

"So the *Canterbury*'s gone?" Naomi asked.

Holden nodded.

"Fuck me sideways," said Amos.

Amos and Shed stood together at the crew ladder. Amos' face was mottled red and white, and his big hands clenched and unclenched. Shed collapsed to his knees, slamming against the deck in the heavy two-g thrust. He didn't cry. He just looked at Holden and said, "Cameron's never going to get that arm, I guess," then buried his head in his hands and shook.

"Slow down, Alex. No need to run now," Holden said into the comm. The ship slowly dropped to one g.

"What now, Captain?" Naomi said, looking at him hard. *You're in charge now. Act like it.*

"Blowing them out of the sky would be my first choice, but since we don't have the weapons...follow them. Keep our eyes on

them until we know where they're going. Expose them to everyone," Holden replied.

"Fuckin' A," said Amos loudly.

"Amos," Naomi said over her shoulder, "take Shed below and
get him into a couch. If you need to, give him something to put
him to sleep."

"You got it, Boss." Amos put a thick arm around Shed's waist
and took him below.

When he was gone, Naomi turned back to Holden.

"No, sir. We are *not* chasing that ship. We are going to call for
help, and then go wherever the help tells us to go."

"I—" Holden started.

"Yes, you're in charge. That makes me XO, and it's the XO's
job to tell the captain when he's being an idiot. You're being an
idiot, sir. You already tried to goad them into killing us with that
broadcast. Now you want to chase them? And what will you do if
they let you catch them? Broadcast another emotional plea?" Naomi
said, moving closer to him. "You are going to get the remaining
four members of your crew to safety. And that's all. When we're
safe, you can go on your crusade. Sir."

Holden unbuckled the straps on his couch and stood up. The
juice was starting to burn out, leaving his body spent and sick-
ened. Naomi lifted her chin and didn't back up.

"Glad you're with me, Naomi," he said. "Go see to the crew.
McDowell gave me one last order."

Naomi looked him over critically; he could see her distrust.
He didn't defend himself; he just waited until she was done. She
nodded at him once and climbed down the ladder to the deck
below.

Once she was gone, he worked methodically, putting together a
broadcast package that included all the sensor data from the
Canterbury and the *Knight*. Alex climbed down from the cockpit
and sat down heavily in the next chair.

"You know, Captain, I've been thinkin'," he said. His voice had
the same post-juice shakes as Holden's own.

Holden bit back his irritation at the interruption and said, "What about?"

"That stealth ship."

Holden turned away from his work.

"Tell me."

"So, I don't know any pirates that have shit like that."

"Go on."

"In fact, the only time I've seen tech like that was back when I was in the navy," Alex said. "We were working on ships with energy-absorbing skins and internal heat sinks. More of a strategic weapon than a tactical one. You can't hide an active drive, but if you can get into position and shut the drive down, store all your waste heat internally, you can hide yourself pretty good. Add in the energy-absorbing skin, and radar, ladar, and passive sensors don't pick you up. Plus, pretty tough to get nuclear torpedoes outside of the military."

"You're saying the Martian navy did this?"

Alex took a long shuddering breath.

"If *we* had it, you know the Earthers were workin' on it too," he said.

They looked at each other across the narrow space, the implications heavier than a ten-g burn. Holden pulled the transmitter and battery they'd recovered from the *Scopuli* out of the thigh pocket of his suit. He started pulling it apart, looking for a stamp or an insignia. Alex watched, quiet for once. The transmitter was generic; it could have come from the radio room of any ship in the solar system. The battery was a nondescript gray block. Alex reached out and Holden handed it to him. Alex pried off the gray plastic cover and flipped the metal battery around in his hands. Without saying a word, he held the bottom up to Holden's face. Stamped in the black metal on the bottom of the battery was a serial number that began with the letters *MCRN*.

Martian Congressional Republic Navy.

The radio was set to broadcast on full power. The data package was ready to transmit. Holden stood in front of the camera, leaning a little forward.

"My name is James Holden," he said, "and my ship, the *Canterbury*, was just destroyed by a warship with stealth technology and what appear to be parts stamped with Martian navy serial numbers. Data stream to follow."

Chapter Six: Miller

The cart sped through the tunnel, siren masking the whine of motors. Behind them, they left curious civilians and the scent of overheated bearings. Miller leaned forward in his seat, willing the cart to go faster. They were three levels and maybe four kilometers from the station house.

"Okay," Havelock said. "I'm sorry, but I'm missing something here."

"What?" Miller said. He meant *What are you yammering about?* Havelock took it as *What are you missing?*

"A water hauler millions of klicks from here got vaporized. Why are we going to full alert? Our cisterns will last months without even going on rationing. There are a lot of other haulers out there. Why is this a crisis?"

Miller turned and looked at his partner straight on. The small, stocky build. The thick bones from a childhood in full g. Just like the asshole in the transmission. They didn't understand. If Have-lock had been in this James Holden's place, he might have done the same stupid, irresponsible, idiotic bullshit. For the space of a breath, they weren't security anymore. They weren't partners. They were a Belter and an Earther. Miller looked away before Havelock could see the change in his eyes.

"That prick Holden? The one in the broadcast?" Miller said. "He just declared war on Mars for us."

The cart swerved and bobbed, its internal computer adjusting for some virtual hiccup in the traffic flow half a kilometer ahead. Havelock shifted, grabbing for the support strut. They hit a ramp up to the next level, civilians on foot making a path for them.

"You grew up where the water's maybe dirty, but it falls out of the sky for you," Miller said. "The air's filthy, but it's not going away if your door seals fail. It's not like that out here."

"But we're not on the hauler. We don't need the ice. We aren't under threat," Havelock said.

Miller sighed, rubbing his eyes with thumb and knuckle until ghosts of false color bloomed.

"When I was homicide," Miller said, "there was this guy. Prop-erty management specialist working a contract out of Luna. Some-one burned half his skin off and dropped him out an airlock. Turned out he was responsible for maintenance on sixty holes up on level thirty. Lousy neighborhood. He'd been cutting corners. Hadn't replaced the air filters in three months. There was mold growing in three of the units. And you know what we found after that?"

"What?" Havelock asked.

"Not a goddamn thing, because we stopped looking. Some people need to die, and he was one. And the next guy that took the job cleaned the ducting and swapped the filters on schedule. That's what it's like in the Belt. Anyone who came out here and didn't put environmental systems above everything else died young. All us still out here are the ones that cared."

"Selective effect?" Havelock said. "You're seriously arguing in favor of selective effect? I never thought I'd hear that shit coming out of you."

"What's that?"

"Racist propaganda bullshit," Havelock said. "It's the one that says the difference in environment has changed the Belters so much that instead of just being a bunch of skinny obsessive-compulsives, they aren't really human anymore."

"I'm not saying that," Miller said, suspecting that it was exactly what he was saying. "It's just that Belters don't take the long view when you screw with basic resources. That water was future air, propellant mass, and potables for us. We have no sense of humor about that shit."

The cart hit a ramp of metalwork grate. The lower level fell away below them. Havelock was silent.

"This Holden guy didn't say it was Mars. Just that they found a Martian battery. You think people are going to...declare war?" Havelock said. "Just on the basis of this one guy's pictures of a battery?"

"The ones that wait to get the whole story aren't our problem."

At least not tonight, he thought. *Once the whole story gets out, we'll see where we stand.*

The station house was somewhere between one-half and three-quarters full. Security men stood in clumps, nodding to each other, eyes narrow and jaws tight. One of the vice cops laughed at something, his amusement loud, forced, smelling of fear. Miller saw the change in Havelock as they walked across the common area to their desks. Havelock had been able to put Miller's reaction down to one man's being oversensitive. A whole room, though. A whole station house. By the time they reached their chairs, Havelock's eyes were wide.

Captain Shaddid came in. The bleary look was gone. Her hair was pulled back, her uniform crisp and professional, her voice as calm as a surgeon in a battlefield hospital. She stepped up on the first desk she came to, improvising a pulpit.

"Ladies and gentlemen," she said. "You've seen the transmission. Any questions?"

"Who let that fucking Earther near a radio?" someone shouted. Miller saw Havelock laugh along with the crowd, but it didn't reach his eyes. Shaddid scowled and the crowd quieted.

"Here's the situation," she said. "No way we can control this information. It was broadcast everywhere. We have five sites on the internal network that have been mirroring it, and we have to assume it's public knowledge starting ten minutes ago. Our job now is to keep the rioting to a minimum and ensure station integrity around the port. Station houses fifty and two thirteen are helping on it too. The port authority has released all the ships with inner planet registry. That doesn't mean they're all gone. They still have to round up their crews. But it does mean they're going."

"The government offices?" Miller said, loud enough to carry.

"Not our problem, thank God," Shaddid said. "They have infrastructure in place. Blast doors are already down and sealed. They've broken off from the main environmental systems, so we aren't even breathing their air right now."

"Well, that's a relief," Yevgeny said from the cluster of homicide detectives.

"Now the bad news," Shaddid said. Miller heard the silence of a hundred and fifty cops holding their breath. "We've got eighty known OPA agents on the station. They're all employed and legal, and you know this is the kind of thing they've been waiting for. We have an order from the governor that we're not going to do any proactive detention. No one gets arrested until they do something."

Angry voices rose in chorus.

"Who does he think he is?" someone called from the back. Shaddid snapped at the comment like a shark.

"The governor is the one who contracted with us to keep this station in working order," Shaddid said. "We'll follow his directives."

In his peripheral vision, Miller saw Havelock nod. He wondered what the governor thought of the question of Belter independence. Maybe the OPA weren't the only ones who'd been waiting for something like this to happen. Shaddid went on, outlining the security response they were permitted. Miller listened with half an ear, so lost in speculating on the politics behind the situation he almost missed it when Shaddid called his name.

"Miller will take the second team to the port level and cover sectors thirteen through twenty-four. Kasagawa, team three, twenty-five through thirty-six, and so on. That's twenty men apiece, except for Miller."

"I can make it with nineteen," Miller said, then quietly to Havelock, "You're sitting this one out, partner. Having an Earther with a gun out there isn't going to make things better."

"Yeah," Havelock said. "Saw that coming."

"Okay," Shaddid said. "You all know the drill. Let's move."

Miller rounded up his riot squad. All the faces were familiar, all men and women he'd worked with over his years in security. He organized them in his mind with a nearly automatic efficiency. Brown and Gelbfish both had SWAT experience, so they would lead the wings if it came to crowd control. Aberforth had three write-ups for excessive violence since her kid had been busted for drug running on Ganymede, so she was second string. She could work out her anger-management issues another time. Around the station house, he heard the other squad commanders making similar decisions.

"Okay," Miller said. "Let's suit up."

They moved away in a group, heading for the equipment bay. Miller paused. Havelock remained leaning against his desk, arms folded, eyes locked on the middle distance. Miller was torn between sympathy for the man and impatience. It was hard being on the team but not on the team. On the other hand, what the hell had he expected, taking a contract in the Belt? Havelock looked up, meeting Miller's gaze. They nodded to each other. Miller was the first to turn away.

The equipment bay was part warehouse, part bank vault, designed by someone more concerned with conserving space than getting things out efficiently. The lights—recessed white LEDs—gave the gray walls a sterile cast. Bare stone echoed every voice and footfall. Banks of ammunition and firearms, evidence bags and test panels, spare servers and replacement uniforms lined the walls and filled most of the interior space. The riot gear was in a side room, in gray steel lockers with high-security electronic locks. The standard outfit consisted of high-impact plastic shields, electric batons, shin guards, bullet-resistant chest and thigh armor, and helmets with reinforced face guards—all of it designed to make a handful of station security into an intimidating, inhuman force.

Miller keyed in his access code. The seals released; the lockers opened.

"Well," Miller said conversationally. "Fuck me."

The lockers were empty, gray coffins with the corpses all gone. Across the room, he heard one of the other squads shouting in outrage. Miller systematically opened every riot control locker he could get to. All of them were the same. Shaddid appeared at his side, her face pale with rage.

"What's plan B?" Miller asked.

Shaddid spat on the floor, then closed her eyes. They shifted under her lids like she was dreaming. Two long breaths later, they opened.

"Check the SWAT lockers. There should be enough in there to outfit two people in each squad."

"Snipers?" Miller said.

"You have a better idea, Detective?" Shaddid said, leaning on the last word.

Miller raised his hands in surrender. Riot gear was meant to intimidate and control. SWAT gear was made to kill with the greatest efficiency possible. Seemed their mandate had just changed.

On any given day, a thousand ships might be docked on Ceres Station, and activity there rarely slowed and never stopped. Each sector could accommodate twenty ships, the traffic of humanity and cargo, transport vans, mesocranes, and industrial forklifts, and his squad was responsible for twenty sectors.

The air stank of refrigerant and oil. The gravity was slightly above 0.3 g, station spin alone lending the place a sense of oppression and danger. Miller didn't like the port. Having vacuum so close under his feet made him nervous. Passing the dockworkers and transport crews, he didn't know whether to scowl or smile. He was here to scare people into behaving and also to reassure them that everything was under control. After the first three sectors, he settled on the smile. It was the kind of lie he was better at.

They had just reached the junction of sectors nineteen and twenty when they heard screaming. Miller pulled his hand terminal out of his pocket, connected to the central surveillance network, and called up the security camera array. It took a few seconds to find it: a mob of fifty or sixty civilians stretching almost all the way across the tunnel, traffic blocked on both sides. There were weapons being waved over heads. Knives, clubs. At least two pistols. Fists pumped in the air. And at the center of the crowd, a huge shirtless man was beating someone to death.

"Showtime," Miller said, waving his squad forward at a run.

He was still a hundred meters from the turn that would take them to the clot of human violence when he saw the shirtless man knock his victim to the ground, then stomp on her neck. The head twisted sideways at an angle that didn't leave any question. Miller slowed his team to a brisk walk. Arresting the murderer while surrounded by a crowd of his friends would be tough enough without being winded.

There was blood in the water now. Miller could sense it. The mob was going to turn out. To the station, to the ships. If the people started joining the chaos...what path would it be likely to take? There was a brothel one level up from there and half a kilometer anti-spinward that catered to inner planet types. The tariff inspector for sector twenty-one was married to a girl from Luna and had bragged about it maybe once too often.

There were too many targets, Miller thought even as he motioned his snipers to spread out. He was trying to reason with a fire. Stop it here, and no one else got killed.

In his imagination, Candace crossed her arms and said, *What's plan B?*

The outer edge of the mob raised the alarm well before Miller reached it. The surge of bodies and threats shifted. Miller tipped back his hat. Men, women. Dark skin, pale, golden brown, and all with the long, thin build of Belters, all with the square-mouthed angry gape of chimpanzees at war.

"Let me take a couple of them down, sir," Gelbfish said from his terminal. "Put the fear of God into them."

"We'll get there," Miller said, smiling at the angry mob. "We'll get there."

The face he expected floated to the front. Shirtless. The big man, blood covering his hands and splattered on his cheek. The seed crystal of the riot.

"That one?" Gelbfish asked, and Miller knew that a tiny infrared dot was painting Shirtless' forehead even as he glowered at Miller and the uniforms behind him.

"No," Miller said. "That'll only set the rest of them off."

"So what do we do?" Brown said.

It was a hell of a question.

"Sir," Gelbfish said. "The big fucker's got an OPA tattoo on his left shoulder."

"Well," Miller said, "if you do have to shoot him, start there."

He stepped forward, tying his terminal into the local system, overriding the alert. When he spoke, his voice boomed from the overhead speakers.

"This is Detective Miller. Unless you all want to be locked up as accessories to murder, I suggest you disperse now." Muting the microphone in his terminal, he said to Shirtless, "Not you, big fella. Move a muscle and we shoot you."

Someone in the crowd threw a wrench, the silver metal arcing low through the air toward Miller's head. He almost stepped out of the way, but the handle caught him across the ear. His head filled with the deep sound of bells, and the wet of blood tracked down his neck.

"Hold fire," Miller shouted. "Hold your fire."

The crowd laughed, as if he'd been talking to them. Idiots. Shirtless, emboldened, strode forward. The steroids had distended his thighs so badly that he waddled. Miller turned the mic on his terminal back on. If the crowd was watching them face each other down, they weren't breaking things. It wasn't spreading. Not yet.

"So. Friend. You only kick helpless people to death, or can anybody join in?" Miller asked, his voice conversational but echoing out of the dock speakers like a pronouncement from God.

"The fuck you barking, Earth dog?" Shirtless said.

"Earth?" Miller said, chuckling. "I look like I grew up in a gravity well to you? I was born on this rock."

"Inners kibble you, bitch," Shirtless said. "You they dog."

"You think?"

"Fuckin' dui," Shirtless said. *Fucking true.* He flexed his pectorals. Miller suppressed the urge to laugh.

"So killing that poor bastard was for the good of the station?" Miller said. "The good of the Belt? Don't be a chump, kid. They're playing you. They want you to act like a bunch of stupid riotboys so they have a reason to shut this place down."

"*Schrauben sie sie weibchen,*" Shirtless said in Belter-inflected gutter German, leaning forward.

Okay, second time I've been called a bitch, Miller thought.

"Kneecap him," Miller said. Shirtless' legs blew out in twin sprays of crimson and he went down howling. Miller walked past his writhing body, stepping toward the mob.

"You're taking your orders from this *pendejo?*" he said. "Listen to me, we all know what's coming. We know dance starting, now, like pow, right? They fucked tu agua, and we all know the answer. Out an airlock, no?"

He could see it in their faces: the sudden fear of the snipers, then the confusion. He pressed on, not giving them time to think. He switched back to the lower-level lingo, the language of education, authority.

"You know what Mars wants? They want you, doing this. They want this piece of shit here to make sure that everyone looks at Belters and thinks we're a bunch of psychopaths who tear up their own station. They want to tell themselves we're just like them. Well, we aren't. We're Belters, and we take care of our own."

He picked a man at the edge of the mob. Not as pumped as Shirtless, but big. He had an OPA split circle on his arm.

"You," Miller said. "You want to fight for the Belt?"

"Dui," the man said.

"I bet you do. He did too," Miller said, jerking a thumb back at Shirtless. "But now he's a cripple, and he's going down for murder. So we've already lost one. You see? They're turning us against each other. Can't let them do that. Every one of you I have to arrest or cripple or kill, that's one less we have when the day comes. And it's coming. But it's not now. You understand?"

The OPA man scowled. The mob drew back from him, making space. Miller could feel it like a current against him. It was shifting.

"Day's coming, hombre," the OPA man said. "You know your side?"

The tone was a threat, but there was no power behind it. Miller took a slow breath. It was over.

"Always the side of the angels," he said. "Why don't you all go back to work? Show's over here, and we've all got plenty that needs doing."

Momentum broken, the mob fell apart. First one and two peeling off from the edges, and then the whole knot untying itself at once. Five minutes after Miller had arrived, the only signs that anything had happened were Shirtless mewling in a pool of his own blood, the wound on Miller's ear, and the body of the woman fifty good citizens had stood by and watched be beaten to death. She was short and wearing the flight suit of a Martian freight line.

Only one dead. Makes it a good night, Miller thought sourly.

He went to the fallen man. The OPA tattoo was smeared red. Miller knelt.

"Friend," he said. "You are under arrest for the murder of that lady over there, whoever the hell she is. You are not required to participate in questioning without the presence of an attorney or union representative, and if you so much as look at me wrong, I'll space you. Do we understand each other?"

From the look in the man's eyes, Miller knew they did.

Chapter Seven: Holden

Holden could drink coffee at half a g. Actually sit and hold a mug under his nose and let the aroma drift up. Sip it slowly and not burn his tongue. Drinking coffee was one of the activities that didn't make the transition to microgravity well, but at half a g, it was fine.

So he sat and tried very hard to think about coffee and gravity in the silence of the *Knight*'s tiny galley. Even the normally talkative Alex was quiet. Amos had set his big handgun on the table and was staring at it with frightening concentration. Shed was asleep. Naomi was sitting across the room, drinking tea and keeping one eye on the wall panel next to her. She'd routed ops to it.

As long as he kept his mind on his coffee, he didn't have to think about Ade giving one last gasp of fear and then turning into a glowing vapor.

Alex ruined it by speaking.

"At some point, we need to decide where we're goin'," he said.

Holden nodded, took a sip of his coffee, and closed his eyes. His muscles vibrated like plucked strings, and his peripheral vision was dappled with points of imaginary light. The first twinges of the post-juice crash were starting, and it was going to be a bad one. He wanted to enjoy these last few moments before the pain hit.

"He's right, Jim," Naomi said. "We can't just fly in a big circle at half a g forever."

Holden didn't open his eyes. The darkness behind his lids was bright and active and mildly nauseating.

"We aren't waiting forever," he said. "We're waiting fifty minutes for Saturn Station to call me back and tell me what to do with their ship. The *Knight* is still P and K property. We're still employees. You wanted me to call for help, I called for help. Now we are waiting to see what that looks like."

"Shouldn't we start flying toward Saturn Station, then, Boss?" Amos asked, directing his question at Naomi.

Alex snorted.

"Not on the *Knight*'s engine. Even if we had the fuel for that trip, which we don't, I don't want to sit in this can for the next three months," he said. "Naw, if we're goin' somewhere, it's gotta be the Belt or Jupiter. We're as close to exactly between 'em as you can get."

"I vote we continue on to Ceres," Naomi said. "P and K has offices there. We don't know anyone in the Jupiter complex."

Without opening his eyes, Holden shook his head.

"No, we wait for them to call us back."

Naomi made an exasperated sound. It was funny, he thought, how you could make someone's voice out from the smallest sounds. A cough or a sigh. Or the little gasp right before she died.

Holden sat up and opened his eyes. He placed his coffee mug on the table carefully, with hands that were starting to palsy.

"I don't want to fly sunward to Ceres, because that's the direction the torpedo ship went, and your point about chasing them is well taken, Naomi. I don't want to fly out to Jupiter, because we only have the fuel for one trip, and once we fly that direction for a while, we're locked in. We are sitting here and drinking coffee because I need to make a decision, and P and K gets a say in that decision. So we wait for them to answer, and then I decide."

Holden got up slowly, carefully, and began moving toward the crew ladder. "I'm going to crash for a few minutes, let the worst of the shakes wear off. If P and K calls, let me know."

Holden popped sedative tabs—thin, bitter pills with an aftertaste like bread mold—but he didn't sleep. Over and over, McDowell placed a hand on his arm and called him Jim. Becca laughed and cursed like a sailor. Cameron bragged about his prowess on the ice.

Ade gasped.

Holden had flown the Ceres-to-Saturn circuit on the *Canterbury* nine times. Two round-trips a year, for almost five years. Most of the crew had been there the entire time. Flying on the *Cant* might be the bottom of the barrel, but that meant there was nowhere else to go. People stayed, made the ship their home. After the near-constant duty transfers of the navy, he appreciated stability. Made it his home too. McDowell said something he couldn't quite make out. The *Cant* groaned like she was under a hard burn.

Ade smiled and winked at him.

The worst leg cramp in history hit every muscle in his body at once. Holden bit down hard on his rubber mouth guard, screaming. The pain brought an oblivion that was almost a relief. His mind shut off, drowned out by the needs of his body. Fortunately or not, the drugs started to kick in. His muscles unknotted. His nerves stopped screaming, and consciousness returned like a reluctant schoolboy. His jaw ached as he pulled out the guard. He'd worn toothmarks in the rubber.

In the dim blue cabin light, he thought about the kind of man who followed an order to kill a civilian ship.

He'd done some things in the navy that had kept him awake nights. He'd followed some orders he vehemently disagreed with. But to lock on to a civilian ship with fifty people aboard and press the button that launched six nuclear weapons? He would have refused. If his commanding officer had insisted, he'd have declared it an illegal order and demanded that the executive officer take control of the ship and arrest the captain. They'd have had to shoot him to get him away from the weapon post.

He'd known the sort of people who would have followed the order, though. He told himself that they were sociopaths and animals, no better than pirates who'd board your ship, strip your engine, and take your air. That they weren't human.

But even as he nursed his hatred, drug-hazed rage offering its nihilistic comforts, he couldn't believe they were idiots. The itch at the back of his head was still *Why? What does anyone gain from killing an ice hauler? Who gets paid? Someone always gets paid.*

I'm going to find you. I'm going to find you and end you. But before I do, I am going to make you explain.

The second wave of pharmaceuticals exploded in his bloodstream. He was hot and limp, his veins filled with syrup. Just before the tabs finally knocked him out, Ade smiled and winked.

And blew away like dust.

The comm beeped at him. Naomi's voice said, "Jim, the P and K response finally came in. Want me to send it down there?"

Holden struggled to make sense of the words. Blinked. Something was wrong with his bunk. With the ship. Slowly, he remembered.

"Jim?"

"No," he said. "I want to watch it up in ops with you. How long was I out?"

"Three hours," she said.

"Jesus. They took their sweet time getting back to us, didn't they?"

Holden rolled out of his couch and wiped off the crust that held his eyelashes together. He'd been weeping in his sleep. He told himself it was from the juice crash. The deep ache in his chest was only stressed cartilage.

What were you doing for three hours before you called us back? he wondered.

Naomi waited for him at the comm station, a man's face frozen mid-word on the screen in front of her. He seemed familiar.

"That isn't the operations manager."

"Nope. It's the P and K legal counsel on Saturn Station. The one who gave that speech after the crackdown on supply pilfering?" Naomi said. " 'Stealing from us is stealing from you.' That one."

"Lawyer," Holden said with a grimace. "This is going to be bad news, then."

Naomi restarted the message. The lawyer sprang into motion.

"James Holden, this is Wallace Fitz calling from Saturn Station. We've received your request for help, and your report of the incident. We've also received your broadcast accusing Mars of destroying the *Canterbury*. This was, to say the least, ill advised. The Martian representative on Saturn Station was in my office not five minutes after your broadcast was received, and the MCR is quite upset by what they view as unfounded accusations of piracy by their government.

"To further investigate this matter, and to aid in discovering the true wrongdoers, if any, the MCRN is dispatching one of their ships from the Jupiter system to pick you up. The MCRN *Donnager* is the name of this vessel. Your orders from P and K are as follows: You will fly at best possible speed to the Jupiter system. You will cooperate fully with instructions given you by the MCRN *Donnager*, or by any officer of the Martian Congressional Republic Navy. You will assist the MCRN in their investigation into the destruction of the *Canterbury*. You will *refrain* from any further broadcasting except to us or the *Donnager*.

"If you fail to follow these instructions from the company and from the government of Mars, your contract with P and K will be terminated, and you will be considered in illegal possession of a P and K shuttle craft. We will then prosecute you to the fullest extent of the law.

"Wallace Fitz out."

Holden frowned at the monitor, then shook his head.

"I never said Mars did it."

"You sort of did," Naomi replied.

"I didn't say anything that wasn't entirely factual and backed up by the data I transmitted, and I engaged in no speculation about those facts."

"So," Naomi said. "What do we do?"

"No fucking way," Amos said. "No *fucking* way."

The galley was a small space. The five of them filled it uncomfortably. The gray laminate walls showed whorls of bright scrapes where mold had grown once and been cleaned off with microwaves and steel wool. Shed sat with his back against the wall, Naomi across the table. Alex stood in the doorway. Amos had started pacing along the back — two fast paces, then a turn — before the lawyer had finished his first sentence.

"I'm not happy about it either. But that's the word from the home office," Holden said, pointing at the galley's display screen. "Didn't mean to get you guys in trouble."

"No problem, Holden. I still think you did the right thing," Shed replied, running one hand through his limp blond hair. "So what do you think the Martians will do with us?"

"I'm thinking pull our fucking toes off until Holden goes back on the radio and says it wasn't them," Amos said. "What in the holy hell is this? They attacked us, and now we're supposed to *cooperate?* They killed the captain!"

"Amos," Holden said.

"Sorry, Holden. Captain," Amos said. "But Jesus *wept*. We're getting fucked here and not the nice way. We're not gonna do this, are we?"

"I don't want to disappear into some Martian prison ship forever," Holden said. "The way I see it, we have two options. Either we go along with this, which is basically throwing ourselves on their mercy. Or we run, try to make it to the Belt and hide."

"I'm voting for the Belt," Naomi said, her arms crossed. Amos raised a hand, seconding the motion. Shed slowly raised his own.

Alex shook his head.

"I know the *Donnager,*" he said. "She's not some rock hopper. She's the flagship for the MCRN's Jupiter fleet. Battleship. Quarter million tons of bad news. You ever serve on a ship that size?"

"No. I wasn't on anything bigger than a destroyer," Holden replied.

"I served on the *Bandon,* with the home fleet. We can't go anywhere that a ship like that can't find us. She's got four main engines, each one bigger than our whole ship. She's designed for long periods at high g with every sailor on board juiced to the gills. We can't run, sir, and even if we did, her sensor package could track a golf ball and hit it with a torpedo from half the solar system away."

"Oh, fuck that, sir," Amos said, standing up. "These Martian needle dicks blew up the *Cant*! I say run. At least make it hard for them."

Naomi put one hand on Amos' forearm, and the big mechanic paused, shook his head, and sat down. The galley was silent. Holden wondered if McDowell had ever had to make a call like this, and what the old man would have done.

"Jim, this is your decision," she said, but her eyes were hard. *No, what you are going to do is get the remaining four members of your crew to safety. And that's all.*

Holden nodded and tapped his fingers against his lips.

"P and K doesn't have our back on this one. We probably can't get away, but I don't want to disappear either," Holden said. And then: "I think we go, but we don't go quietly. Why don't we go disobey the spirit of an order?"

Naomi finished working on the comm panel, her hair now float-ing around her like a black cloud in the zero g.

"Okay, Jim, I'm dumping every watt into the comm array. They'll be getting this loud and clear all the way out to Titania," she said.

Holden reached up to run one hand through his sweat-plastered hair. In the null gravity, that just made it stick straight out in every direction. He zipped up his flight suit and pressed the record button.

"This is James Holden, formerly of the *Canterbury,* now on the shuttle *Knight.* We are cooperating with an investigation into who destroyed the *Canterbury* and, as part of that cooperation, are agreeing to be taken aboard your ship, the MCRN *Donnager.* We hope that this cooperation means that we will not be held prisoner or harmed. Any such action would only serve to reinforce the idea that the *Canterbury* was destroyed by a Martian vessel. James Holden out."

Holden leaned back. "Naomi, send that out broadband."

"That's a dirty trick, Boss," said Alex. "Pretty hard to disap-pear us now."

"I believe in the ideal of the transparent society, Mr. Kamal," said Holden. Alex grinned, pushed off, and floated down the gangway. Naomi tapped the comm panel, making a small, satis-fied sound in the back of her throat.

"Naomi," Holden said. She turned, her hair waving lazily, like they were both drowning. "If this goes badly, I need you...I need you to..."

"Throw you to the wolves," she said. "Blame everything on you and get the others back to Saturn Station safely."

"Yeah," Holden said. "Don't play the hero."

She let the words hang in the air until the last of the irony leeched out of them.

"Hadn't crossed my mind, sir," she said.

"*Knight,* this is Captain Theresa Yao of the MCRN *Donnager,*" said the severe-looking woman on the comm screen. "Message received. Please refrain from further general broadcasts. My navigator will be sending course information shortly. Follow that course exactly. Yao out."

Alex laughed.

"I think you pissed her off," he said. "Got the course info. They'll be picking us up in thirteen days. Give her time to really stew on it."

"Thirteen days before I'm clapped in irons and have needles shoved under my fingernails," Holden sighed, leaning back in his couch. "Well, best begin our flight toward imprisonment and torture. You may lock in the transmitted course, Mr. Kamal."

"Roger that, Cap— Huh," said Alex.

"A problem?"

"Well, the *Knight* just did her pre-burn sweep for collision objects," Alex said. "And we have six Belt objects on an intercept course."

"Belt objects?"

"Fast contacts with no transponder signal," Alex replied. "Ships, but flyin' dark. They'll catch us just about two days before the *Donnager* does."

Holden pulled up the display. Six small signatures, yellow-orange shifting toward red. Heavy burn.

"Well," Holden said to the screen. "And who the hell are *you*?"

Chapter Eight: Miller

Aggression against the Belt is what Earth and Mars survive on. Our weakness is their strength," the masked woman said from Miller's terminal screen. The split circle of the OPA draped behind her, like something painted on a sheet. "Don't be afraid of them. Their only power is your fear."

"Well, that and a hundred or so gunships," Havelock said.

"From what I hear," Miller said, "if you clap your hands and say you believe, they can't shoot you."

"Have to try that sometime."

"We must rise up!" the woman said, her voice growing shrill. "We have to take our destiny before it is taken from us! Remember the *Canterbury*!"

Miller shut the viewer down and leaned back in his chair. The station was at its change-of-shift surge, voices raised one over the other as the previous round of cops brought the incoming

ones up to speed. The smell of fresh coffee competed with cigarette smoke.

"There's maybe a dozen like her," Havelock said, nodding
toward the dead terminal screen. "She's my favorite, though.
There're times I swear she's actually foaming at the mouth."

"How many more files?" Miller asked, and his partner shrugged.

"Two, three hundred," Havelock said, and took a drag on his
cigarette. He'd started smoking again. "Every few hours, there's a
new one. They aren't coming from one place. Sometimes they're
broadcast on the radio. Sometimes the files show up on public
partitions. Orlan found some guys at a portside bar passing out
those little VR squids like they were pamphlets."

"She bust them?"

"No," Havelock said as if it was no big deal.

A week had passed since James Holden, self-appointed martyr,
had proudly announced that he and his crew were going to go talk
to someone from the Martian navy instead of just slinging shit and
implications. The footage of the *Canterbury*'s death was everywhere, debates raging over every frame. The log files that documented the incident were perfectly legitimate, or they were
obviously doctored. The torpedoes that had slaughtered the hauler
were nukes or standard pirate fare that breached the drive by mistake, or it was all artifice lifted from old stock footage to cover up
what had really killed the *Cant*.

The riots had lasted for three days on and off, like a fire hot
enough to reignite every time the air pumped back in. The admin-
istrative offices reopened under heavy security, but they reopened.
The ports fell behind, but they were catching up. The shirtless
bastard who Miller had ordered shot was in the Star Helix detainment infirmary, getting new knees, filling out protests against
Miller, and preparing for his murder trial.

Six hundred cubic meters of nitrogen had gone missing from a
warehouse in sector fifteen. An unlicensed whore had been beaten
up and locked in a storage unit; as soon as she was done giving
evidence about her attackers, she'd be arrested. They'd caught the

kids who'd been breaking the surveillance cameras on level six-teen. Superficially, everything was business as usual.

Only superficially.

When Miller had started working homicide, one of the things that had struck him was the surreal calm of the victims' families. People who had just lost wives, husbands, children, and lovers. People whose lives had just been branded by violence. More often than not, they were calmly offering drinks and answering ques-tions, making the detectives feel welcome. A civilian coming in unaware might have mistaken them for whole. It was only in the careful way they held themselves and the extra quarter second it took their eyes to focus that Miller could see how deep the dam-age was.

Ceres Station was holding itself carefully. Its eyes were taking a quarter second longer to focus. Middle-class people—storekeepers, maintenance workers, computer techs—were avoiding him on the tube the way petty criminals did. Conversations died when Miller came near. In the station, the sense of being under siege was growing. A month earlier, Miller and Havelock, Cobb and Rich-ter, and the rest had been the steadying hand of the law. Now they were employees of an Earth-based security contractor.

The difference was subtle, but it was deep. It made him want to stand taller, to show with his body that he was a Belter. That he belonged there. It made him want to win people's good opinion back. Let by a bunch of guys passing out virtual reality propa-ganda with a warning, maybe.

It wasn't a smart impulse.

"What've we got on the board?" Miller asked.

"Two burglaries that look like that same ring," Havelock said. "That domestic dispute from last week still needs the report closed up. There was a pretty good assault over by Nakanesh Import Consortium, but Shaddid was talking to Dyson and Patel about that, so it's probably spoken for already."

"So you want..."

Havelock looked up and out to cover the fact that he was looking away. It was something he'd been doing more often since things had gone to shit.

"We've really got to get the reports done," Havelock said. "Not just the domestic. There're four or five folders that are only still open because they need to be crossed and dotted."

"Yeah," Miller said.

Since the riots, he'd watched everyone in a bar get served before Havelock. He'd seen how the other cops from Shaddid down went out of their way to reassure Miller that *he* was one of the good guys, a tacit apology for saddling him with an Earther. And he'd seen Havelock see it too.

It made Miller want to protect the man, to let Havelock spend his days in the safety of paperwork and station house coffee. Help the man pretend that he wasn't hated for the gravity he'd grown up in.

That wasn't a smart impulse either.

"What about your bullshit case?" Havelock asked.

"What?"

Havelock held up a folder. The Julie Mao case. The kidnap job. The sideshow. Miller nodded and rubbed his eyes. Someone at the front of the station house yelped. Someone else laughed.

"Yeah, no," Miller said. "Haven't touched it."

Havelock grinned and held it out to him. Miller accepted the file, flipped it open. The eighteen-year-old grinned out at him with perfect teeth.

"I don't want to saddle you with all the desk driving," Miller said.

"Hey, you're not the one that kept me off that one. That was Shaddid's call. And anyway…it's just paperwork. Never killed anyone. You feel guilty about it, you can buy me a beer after work."

Miller tapped the case against the corner of his desk, the small impacts settling the contents against the folder's spine.

"Right," he said. "I'll go do some follow-up on the bullshit. I'll be back by lunch, write something up to keep the boss happy."

"I'll be here," Havelock said. Then, as Miller rose: "Hey. Look.

I didn't want to say anything until I was sure, but I also don't want you to hear it someplace else..."

"Put in for a transfer?" Miller said.

"Yeah. Talked to some of those Protogen contractors that passed through. They say their Ganymede office is looking for a new lead investigator. And I thought..." Havelock shrugged.

"It's a good move," Miller said.

"Just want to go someplace with a sky, even if you look at it through domes," Havelock said, and all the bluff masculinity of police work couldn't keep the wistfulness out of his voice.

"It's a good move," Miller said again.

Juliette Andromeda Mao's hole was in the ninth level of a fourteen-tiered tunnel near the port. The great inverted V was almost half a kilometer wide at the top, and no more than a standard tube width at the bottom, the retrofit of one of a dozen reaction mass chambers from the years before the asteroid had been given its false gravity. Now thousands of cheap holes burrowed into the walls, hundreds on each level, heading straight back like shotgun shacks. Kids played on the terraced streets, shrieking and laughing at nothing. Someone at the bottom was flying a kite in the constant gentle spin breeze, the bright Mylar diamond swerving and bucking in the microturbulence. Miller checked his terminal against the numbers painted on the wall. *5151-I.* Home sweet home to the poor little rich girl.

He keyed his override, and the dirty green door popped its seals and let him pass.

The hole canted up into the body of the station. Three small rooms: general living space at the front, then a bedroom hardly larger than the cot it contained, then a stall with shower, toilet, and half sink all within elbow distance. It was a standard design. He'd seen it a thousand times.

Miller stood for a minute, not looking at anything in particular, listening to the reassuring hiss of air cycling through ductwork. He reserved judgment, waiting as the back of his head built an impression of the place and, through it, of the girl who'd lived there.

Spartan was the wrong word. The place was simple, yes. The only decorations were a small framed watercolor of a slightly abstracted woman's face over the table in the front room and a cluster of playing-card-sized plaques over the cot in the bedroom. He leaned close to read the small script. A formal award granting Julie Mao—not Juliette—purple belt status by the Ceres Center for Jiu Jitsu. Another stepping her up to brown belt. They were two years apart. Tough school, then. He put his fingers on the empty space on the wall where one for black could go. There was none of the affectation—no stylized throwing stars or imitation swords. Just a small acknowledgment that Julie Mao had done what she had done. He gave her points for that.

The drawers had two changes of clothes, one of heavy canvas and denim and one of blue linen with a silk scarf. One for work, one for play. It was less than Miller owned, and he was hardly a clotheshorse.

With her socks and underwear was a wide armband with the split circle of the OPA. Not a surprise, for a girl who'd turned her back on wealth and privilege to live in a dump like this. The refrigerator had two takeaway boxes filled with spoiled food and a bottle of local beer.

Miller hesitated, then took the beer. He sat at the table and pulled up the hole's built-in terminal. True to Shaddid's word, Julie's partition opened to Miller's password.

The custom background was a racing pinnace. The interface was customized in small, legible iconography. Communication, entertainment, work, personal. *Elegant.* That was the word. Not Spartan, but elegant.

He paged quickly through her professional files, letting his mind take in an overview, just as he had with the whole living space. There would be time for rigor, and a first impression was usually more useful than an encyclopedia. She had training videos on several different light transport craft. Some political archives, but nothing that raised a flag. A scanned volume of poetry by some of the first settlers in the Belt.

He shifted to her personal correspondence. It was all kept as neat and controlled as a Belter's. All incoming messages were filtered to subfolders. Work, Personal, Broadcast, Shopping. He popped open Broadcast. Two or three hundred political news-feeds, discussion group digests, bulletins and announcements. A few had been viewed here and there, but nothing with any sort of religious observation. Julie was the kind of woman who would sacrifice for a cause, but not the kind who'd take joy in reading the propaganda. Miller filed that away.

Shopping was a long tracking of simple merchant messages. Some receipts, some announcements, some requests for goods and services. A cancellation for a Belt-based singles circle caught his eye. Miller re-sorted for related correspondence. Julie had signed up for the "low g, low pressure" dating service in February of the previous year and canceled in June without having used it.

The Personal folder was more diverse. At a rough guess there were sixty or seventy subfolders broken down by name. Some were people—Sascha Lloyd-Navarro, Ehren Michaels. Others were private notations—Sparring Circle, OPA.

Bullshit Guilt Trips.

"Well, this could be interesting," he said to the empty hole.

Fifty messages dating back five years, all marked as originating at the Mao-Kwikowski Mercantile stations in the Belt and on Luna. Unlike the political tracts, all but one had been opened.

Miller took a pull from the beer and considered the most recent two messages. The most recent, still unread, was from JPM. Jules-Pierre Mao, at a guess. The one immediately before it showed three drafted replies, none of them sent. It was from Ariadne. The mother.

There was always an element of voyeurism in being a detective. It was legal for him to be here, poking through the private life of a woman he'd never met. It was part of his legitimate investigation to know that she was lonely, that the only toiletries in her bathroom were her own. That she was proud. No one would have any complaints to make, or at least any that carried repercussions for his job, if he read every private message on her partition. Drinking her beer was the most ethically suspect thing he'd done since he'd come in.

And still he hesitated for a few seconds before opening the second-to-last message.

The screen shifted. On better equipment, it would have been indistinguishable from ink on paper, but Julie's cheap system shuddered at the thinnest lines and leaked a soft glow at the left edge. The handwriting was delicate and legible, either done with a calligraphic software good enough to vary letter shape and line width, or else handwritten.

Sweetheart:

I hope everything's going well for you. I wish you would write to me on your own sometimes. I feel like I have to put in a request in triplicate just to hear how my own daughter is doing. I know this adventure of yours is all about freedom and self-reliance, but surely there's still room in there to be considerate.

I wanted to get in touch with you especially because your father is going through one of his consolidation phases again, and we're thinking of selling the Razorback. I know it was important to you once, but I suppose we've all given up on your racing again. It's just racking up storage fees now, and there's no call to be sentimental.

It was signed with the flowing initials *A M.*

Miller considered the words. Somehow he'd expected the parental extortions of the very rich to be more subtle. *If you don't do as we say, we'll get rid of your toys. If you don't write. If you don't come home. If you don't love us.*

Miller opened the first incomplete draft.

Mother, if that's what you call yourself:
Thank you so much for dropping yet another turd onto my
day. I can't believe how selfish and petty and crude you are.
I can't believe you sleep at night or that you ever thought I
could

Miller skimmed the rest. The tone seemed consistent. The second draft reply was dated two days later. He skipped to it.

Mom:
I'm sorry we've been so estranged these last few years. I
know it's been hard for you and for Daddy. I hope you can
see that the decisions I've made were never meant to hurt
either of you.
About the Razorback, I wish you'd reconsider. She's my
first boat, and I

It stopped there. Miller leaned back.

"Steady on, kid," he said to the imaginary Julie, then opened the last draft.

Ariadne:
Do what you have to.

Julie

Miller laughed and raised his bottle to the screen in toast. They'd known how to hit her where it hurt, and Julie had taken the blow. If he ever caught her and shipped her back, it was going to be a bad day for both of them. All of them.

He finished the beer, dropped the bottle into the recycling chute, and opened the last message. He more than half dreaded learning the final fate of the *Razorback,* but it was his job to know as much as he could.

Julie:

This is not a joke. This is not one of your mother's drama fits. I have solid information that the Belt is about to be a very unsafe place. Whatever differences we have we can work out later.

FOR YOUR OWN SAFETY COME HOME NOW.

Miller frowned. The air recycler hummed. Outside, the local kids whistled high and loud. He tapped the screen, closing the last Bullshit Guilt Trip message, then opened it again.

It had been sent from Luna, two weeks before James Holden and the *Canterbury* raised the specter of war between Mars and the Belt.

This sideshow was getting interesting.

Chapter Nine: Holden

The ships are still not responding," Naomi said, punching a key sequence on the comm panel.

"I didn't think they would. But I want to show the *Donnager* that we're worried about being followed. It's all covering our asses at this point," Holden said.

Naomi's spine popped as she stretched. Holden pulled a protein bar out of the box in his lap and threw it at her.

"Eat."

She peeled the wrapping off while Amos clambered up the ladder and threw himself into the couch next to her. His coverall was so filthy it shined. Just as with the others, three days on the cramped shuttle hadn't helped his personal hygiene. Holden reached up and scratched his own greasy hair with distaste. The *Knight* was too small for showers, and the zero-g sinks were too small to stick your head in. Amos had solved the hair-washing problem by shaving all of his off. Now he just had a ring of stubble around his bald spot. Somehow, Naomi's hair stayed shiny and mostly oil free. Holden wondered how she did that.

"Toss me some chow, XO," Amos said.

"Captain," Naomi corrected.

Holden threw a protein bar at him too. Amos snatched it from the air, then considered the long, thin package with distaste.

"Goddamn, Boss, I'd give my left nut for food that didn't look like a dildo," Amos said, then tapped his food against Naomi's in mock toast.

"Tell me about our water," Holden said.

"Well, I've been crawling around between hulls all day. I've tightened everything that can be tightened, and slapped epoxy on anything that can't, so we aren't dripping anywhere."

"It'll still be right down to the wire, Jim," Naomi said. "The *Knight*'s recycling systems are crap. She was never intended to process five people's worth of waste back into potables for two weeks."

"Down to the wire, I can handle. We'll just learn to live with each other's stink. I was worried about 'nowhere near enough.'"

"Speaking of which, I'm gonna head to my rack and spray on some more deodorant," Amos said. "After all day crawling in the ship's guts, my stink's even keeping me awake tonight."

Amos swallowed the last of his food and smacked his lips with mock relish, then climbed out of his couch and headed down the crew ladder. Holden took a bite of his own bar. It tasted like greased cardboard.

"What's Shed up to?" he asked. "He's been pretty quiet."

Naomi, frowning, put her half-eaten bar down on the comm panel.

"I wanted to talk to you about that. He's not doing well, Jim. Out of all of us, he's having the hardest time with…what's happened. You and Alex were both navy men. They train you to deal with losing shipmates. Amos has been flying so long this is actually the *third* ship that's gone down under him, if you can believe that."

"And you are made entirely of cast iron and titanium," Holden said, only pretending to joke.

"Not entirely. Eighty, ninety percent. Tops," Naomi said with a half smile. "Seriously, though. I think you should talk to him."

"And say what? I'm no psychiatrist. The navy version of this speech involves duty and honorable sacrifice and avenging fallen comrades. Doesn't work as well when your friends have been murdered for no apparent reason and there's essentially no chance you can do anything about it."

"I didn't say you had to fix him. I said you needed to talk to him."

Holden got up from his couch with a salute.

"Yes, sir," he said. At the ladder he paused. "Again, thank you, Naomi. I'd really—"

"I know. Go be the captain," she said, turning back to her panel and calling up the ship ops screen. "I'll keep waving at the neighbors."

Holden found Shed in the *Knight*'s tiny sick bay. Really more a sick closet. Other than a reinforced cot, the cabinets of supplies, and a half dozen pieces of wall-mounted equipment, there was just enough room for one stool stuck to the floor on magnetic feet. Shed was sitting on it.

"Hey, buddy, mind if I come in?" Holden asked. *Did I actually say "Hey, buddy"?*

Shed shrugged and pulled up an inventory screen on the wall panel, opening various drawers and staring at the contents. Pretending he'd been in the middle of something.

"Look, Shed. This thing with the *Canterbury* has really hit everyone hard, and you've—" Holden said. Shed turned, holding up a white squeeze tube.

"Three percent acetic acid solution. Didn't realize we had this out here. The *Cant*'s run out, and I've got three people with GW who could really use it. Why'd they put it on the *Knight*, I wonder," Shed said.

"GW?" was all Holden could think to reply.

"Genital warts. Acetic acid solution is the treatment for any visible warts. Burns 'em off. Hurts like hell, but it does the job. No reason to keep it on the shuttle. Medical inventory is always so messed up."

Holden opened his mouth to speak, found nothing to say, and closed it again.

"We've got acetic acid cream," Shed said, his voice increasingly shrill, "but no elemcet for pain. Which do you think you'd need more on a rescue shuttle? If we'd found anyone on that wreck with a bad case of GW, we'd have been set. A broken bone? You're out of luck. Just suck it up."

"Look, Shed," Holden said, trying to break in.

"Oh, and look at this. No coagulant booster. What the hell? Hey, no chance anyone on a rescue mission could, you know, start *bleeding.* Catch a case of red bumps on your crank, sure, but bleeding? No way! I mean, we've got four cases of syphilis on the *Cant* right now. One of the oldest diseases in the book, and we still can't get rid of it. I tell those guys, 'The hookers on Saturn Station are banging every ice bucker on the circuit, so put the glove on,' but do they listen? No. So here we are with syphilis and not enough ciprofloxacin."

Holden felt his jaw slide forward. He gripped the side of the hatch and leaned into the room.

"Everyone on the *Cant* is dead," Holden said, making each word clear and strong and brutal. "Everyone is dead. No one needs the antibiotics. No one needs wart cream."

Shed stopped talking, and all the air went out of him like he'd been gut punched. He closed the drawers in the supply cabinet and turned off the inventory screen with small precise movements.

"I know," he said in a quiet voice. "I'm not stupid. I just need some time."

"We all do. But we're stuck in this tiny can together. I'll be honest, I came down here because Naomi is worried about you, but now that I'm here, you're freaking me the hell out. That's okay, because I'm the captain now and it's my job. But I can't have you freaking Alex or Amos out. We're ten days from being grabbed by a Martian battleship, and that's scary enough without the doctor falling apart."

"I'm not a doctor, I'm just a tech," Shed said, his voice very small.

"You're *our* doctor, okay? To the four of us here with you on this ship, you're our doctor. If Alex starts having post-traumatic stress episodes and needs meds to keep it together, he'll come to you. If you're down here jabbering about warts, he'll turn around and go back up to the cockpit and just do a really bad job of flying. You want to cry? Do it with all of us. We'll sit together in the galley and get drunk and cry like babies, but we'll do it together where it's safe. No more hiding down here."

Shed nodded.

"Can we do that?" he said.

"Do what?" Holden asked.

"Get drunk and cry like babies?"

"Hell yes. That is officially on the schedule for tonight. Report to the galley at twenty hundred hours, Mr. Garvey. Bring a cup."

Shed started to reply when the general comm clicked on and Naomi said, "Jim, come back up to ops."

Holden gripped Shed's shoulder for a moment, then left.

In ops, Naomi had the comm screen up again and was speaking to Alex in low tones. The pilot was shaking his head and frowning. A map glowed on her screen.

"What's up?" Holden asked.

"We're getting a tightbeam, Jim. It locked on and started transmitting just a couple minutes ago," Naomi replied.

"From the *Donnager*?" The Martian battleship was the only thing he could think of that might be inside laser communications range.

"No. From the Belt," Naomi said. "And not from Ceres, or Eros, or Pallas either. None of the big stations."

She pointed at a small dot on her display.

"It's coming from here."

"That's empty space," Holden said.

"Nope. Alex checked. It's the site of a big construction project Tycho is working on. Not a lot of detail on it, but radar returns are pretty strong."

"Something out there has a comm array that'll put a dot the size of your anus on us from over three AU away," Alex said.

"Okay, wow, that's impressive. What is our anus-sized dot saying?" Holden asked.

"You'll never believe this," Naomi said, and turned on the playback.

A dark-skinned man with the heavy facial bones of an Earther appeared on the screen. His hair was graying, and his neck was ropy with old muscle. He smiled and said, "Hello, James Holden. My name is Fred Johnson."

Holden hit the pause button.

"This guy looks familiar. Search the ship's database for that name," he said.

Naomi didn't move; she just stared at him with a puzzled look on her face.

"What?" he said.

"That's *Frederick Johnson*," she said.

"Okay."

"Colonel Frederick Lucius Johnson."

The pause might have been a second; it might have been an hour.

"Jesus," was all Holden could think to say.

The man on the screen had once been among the most decorated officers in the UN military, and ended up one of its most embarrassing failures. To Belters, he was the Earther Sheriff of Nottingham who'd turned into Robin Hood. To Earth, he was the hero who'd fallen from grace.

Fred Johnson started his rise to fame with a series of high-profile captures of Belt pirates during one of the periods of tension between Earth and Mars that seemed to ramp up every few decades and then fade away again. Whenever the system's two superpowers rattled their sabers at each other, crime in the Belt rose. Colonel Johnson—Captain Johnson at the time—and his small wing of three missile frigates destroyed a dozen pirate ships and two major bases in a two-year span. By the time the Coalition had stopped bickering, piracy was actually *down* in the Belt, and Fred Johnson was the name on everyone's lips. He was promoted and given command over the Coalition marine division tasked with policing the Belt, where he continued to serve with distinction.

Until Anderson Station.

A tiny shipping depot almost on the opposite side of the Belt from the major port Ceres, most people, including most Belters, would not have been able to find Anderson Station on a map. Its only importance was as a minor distribution station for water and air in one of the sparsest stretches of the Belt. Fewer than a million Belters got their air from Anderson.

Gustav Marconi, a career Coalition bureaucrat on the station, decided to implement a 3-percent handling surcharge on shipments passing through the station in hopes of raising the bottom line. Less than 5 percent of the Belters buying their air from Anderson were living bottle to mouth, so just under fifty thousand Belters might have to spend one day of each month not breathing. Only a small percentage of those fifty thousand lacked the leeway in their recycling systems to cover this minor shortfall. Of those, only a small portion felt that armed revolt was the correct course.

Which was why of the million affected, only 170 armed Belters came to the station, took over, and threw Marconi out an airlock. They demanded a government guarantee that no further handling surcharges would be added to the price of air and water coming through the station.

The Coalition sent Colonel Johnson.

During the Massacre of Anderson Station, the Belters kept the station cameras rolling, broadcasting to the solar system the entire time. Everyone watched as Coalition marines fought a long, grue-some corridor-to-corridor battle against men with nothing to lose and no reason to surrender. The Coalition won—it was a fore-gone conclusion—but it took three days of broadcast slaughter. The iconic image of the video was not one of the fighting, but the last image the station cameras caught before they were cut off: Colonel Johnson in station ops, surrounded by the corpses of the Belters who'd made their last stand there, surveying the carnage with a flat stare and hands limp at his sides.

The UN tried to keep Colonel Johnson's resignation quiet, but he was too much a public figure. The video of the battle domi-nated the nets for weeks, only displaced when the former Colonel Johnson made a public statement apologizing for the massacre and announcing that the relationship between the Belt and the inner planets was untenable and heading toward ever greater tragedy.

Then he vanished. He was almost forgotten, a footnote in the history of human carnage, until the Pallas colony revolt four years later. This time refinery metalworkers kicked the Coalition gov-ernor off station. Instead of a tiny way station with 170 rebels, it was a major Belt rock with more than 150,000 people on it. When the Coalition ordered in the marines, everyone expected a blood-bath.

Colonel Johnson came out of nowhere and talked the metal-workers down; he talked the Coalition commanders into holding back the marines until the station could be handed over peace-fully. He spent more than a year negotiating with the Coalition governor to improve working conditions in the refineries. And suddenly, the Butcher of Anderson Station was a Belt hero and an icon.

An icon who was beaming private messages to the *Knight*.

Holden hit the play button, and *that* Fred Johnson said, "Mr. Holden, I think you're being played. Let me say straight out that I am speaking to you as an official representative of the Outer Planets Alliance. I don't know what you've heard, but we aren't all a bunch of cowboys itching for a chance to shoot our way to freedom. I've spent the last ten years working to make life for the Belters better without *anyone* getting shot. I believe in this idea so deeply that I gave up my Earth citizenship when I came out here.

"I tell you that so you'll know how invested I am. I may be the one person in the solar system who wants war the least, and my voice is loud in OPA councils.

"You may have heard some of the broadcasts beating on the war drums and calling for revenge against Mars for what happened to your ship. I've talked to every OPA cell leader I know, and no one's claiming responsibility.

"Someone is working very hard to start a war. If it's Mars, then when you get on that ship, you'll never say another word in public that isn't fed to you by Martian handlers. I don't want to think it *is* Mars. I can't see how they would get anything out of a war. So my hope is that even after the *Donnager* picks you up, you can still be a player in what follows.

"I am sending you a keyword. Next time you broadcast publicly, use the word *ubiquitous* within the first sentence of the broadcast to signal that you're not being coerced. Don't use it, and I'll assume you are. Either way, I want you to know you have allies in the Belt.

"I don't know who or what you were before, but your voice matters now. If you want to use that voice to make things better, I will do anything I can to help you do it. If you get free, contact me at the address that follows. I think maybe you and I have a lot to talk about.

"Johnson out."

The crew sat in the galley drinking a bottle of ersatz tequila Amos had scrounged from somewhere. Shed was politely sipping from a small cup of it and trying to hide his grimace each time. Alex and Amos drank like sailors: a finger full in the bottom of the cup, tossed back all at once. Alex had a habit of saying "Hooboy!" after each shot. Amos just used a different profanity each time.

He was up to his eleventh shot and so far had not repeated himself.

Holden stared at Naomi. She swirled the tequila in her cup and stared back. He found himself wondering what sort of genetic mashup had produced her features. Definitely some African and South American in there. Her last name hinted at Japanese ancestry, which was only barely visible, as a slight epicanthic fold. She'd never be conventionally pretty, but from the right angle she was actually fairly striking.

Shit, I'm drunker than I thought.

To cover, he said, "So…"

"So Colonel Johnson is calling you now. Quite the important man you've become, sir," Naomi replied.

Amos put down his cup with exaggerated care.

"Been meaning to ask about that, sir. Any chance we might take up his offer of help and just head back to the Belt?" he said. "Don't know about you, but with the Martian battleship in front, and the half dozen mystery ships behind, it's starting to feel pretty fuckin' crowded out here."

Alex snorted. "Are you kidding? If we flipped now, we'd be just about stopped by the time the *Donnager* caught up to us. She's burnin' the furniture to catch us before the Belter ships do. If we start headin' their direction, the *Donnie* might take that as a sign we've switched teams, frag the whole lot of us."

"I agree with Mr. Kamal," Holden said. "We've picked our course and we're going to see it through. I won't be losing Fred's contact information anytime soon. Speaking of which, have you deleted his message yet, Naomi?"

"Yes, sir. Scrubbed it from the ship's memory with steel wool. The Martians will never know he talked to us."

Holden nodded and unzipped his jumpsuit a little further. The galley was starting to feel very hot with five drunk people in it. Naomi raised an eyebrow at his days-old T-shirt. Embarrassed, he zipped back up.

"Those ships don't make any sense to me, Boss," Alex said. "A half dozen ships flyin' kamikaze missions with nukes strapped to their hulls *might* make a dent in a battlewagon like the *Donnie*, but not much else would. She opens up with her point defense network and rail guns, she can create a no-fly zone a thousand klicks across. They could be killin' those six ships with torpedoes already, 'cept I think they're as confused about who they are as we are."

"They'll know they can't catch us before the *Donnager* picks us up," Holden said. "And they can't take her in a fight. So I don't know what they're up to."

Amos poured the last of the tequila into everyone's cups and held his up in a toast.

"I guess we'll fucking find out."

Chapter Ten: Miller

Captain Shaddid tapped the tip of her middle finger against her thumb when she started getting annoyed. It was a small sound, soft as a cat's paws, but ever since Miller first noticed her habit, it had seemed louder. Quiet as it was, it could fill her office.

"Miller," she said, smiling as if she meant it. "We're all on edge these days. These have been hard, hard times."

"Yes, sir," Miller said, lowering his head like a fullback determined to muscle his way through all defenders, "but I think this is important enough to deserve closer—"

"It's a favor for a shareholder," Shaddid said. "Her father got jumpy. There's no reason to think he meant Mars blasting the *Canterbury*. Tariffs are going up again. There was a mine blowout on one of the Red Moon operations. Eros is having trouble with their yeast farm. We don't go through a day without something happening in the Belt that would make a daddy scared for his precious little flower."

"Yes, sir, but the timing—"

Her fingers upped tempo. Miller bit his lips. The cause was lost.

"Don't go chasing conspiracies," Shaddid said. "We've got a full board of crimes we know are real. Politics, war, system-wide cabals of inner planet bad guys searching for ways to screw us over? Not our mandate. Just get me a report that says you're looking, I'll send it back up the line, and we can get back to our jobs."

"Yes, sir."

"Anything else?"

"No, sir."

Shaddid nodded and turned back to her terminal. Miller plucked his hat from the corner of her desk and headed out. One of the station house air filters had gone bad over the weekend, and the replacement gave the rooms a reassuring smell of new plastic and ozone. Miller sat at his desk, fingers laced behind his head, and stared at the light fixture above him. The knot that had tied itself in his gut hadn't loosened up. That was too bad.

"Not so good, then?" Havelock asked.

"Could have gone better."

"She pull the job?"

Miller shook his head. "No, it's still mine. She just wants me to do it half-assed."

"Could be worse. At least you get to find out what happened. And if you maybe spend a little time after hours digging into it just for practice, you know?"

"Yeah," Miller said. "Practice."

Their desks were unnaturally clean, his and Havelock's both. The barrier of paperwork Havelock had created between himself and the station had eroded away, and Miller could tell from his partner's eyes and the way his hands moved that the cop in Havelock wanted to get back into the tunnels. He couldn't tell if it was to prove himself before his transfer went through, or just to break a few heads. Maybe those were two ways of saying the same thing.

Just don't get yourself killed before you get out of here, Miller thought. Aloud, he said, "What have we got?"

"Hardware shop. Sector eight, third level in," Havelock said. "Extortion complaint."

Miller sat for a moment, considering his own reluctance as if it belonged to someone else. It was like Shaddid had given a dog just one bite of fresh meat, then pointed it back toward kibble. The temptation to blow off the hardware shop bloomed, and for a moment he almost gave in. Then he sighed, swung his feet down to the decking, and stood.

"All right, then," he said. "Let's go make the station safe for commerce."

"Words to live by," Havelock said, checking his gun. He'd been doing that a lot more recently.

The shop was an entertainment franchise. Clean white fixtures offering up custom rigs for interactive environments: battle simulations, exploration games, sex. A woman's voice ululated on the sound system, somewhere between an Islamic call to prayer and orgasm with a drumbeat. Half the titles were in Hindi with Chinese and Spanish translations. The other half were English with Hindi as the second language. The clerk was hardly more than a boy. Sixteen, seventeen years old with a weedy black beard he wore like a badge.

"Can I help you?" the boy said, eyeing Havelock with disdain just short of contempt. Havelock pulled his ID, making sure the kid got a good long look at his gun when he did it.

"We'd like to talk to"—Miller glanced at the complaint form on his terminal screen—"Asher Kamamatsu. He here?"

The manager was a fat man, for a Belter. Taller than Havelock, the man carried fat around his belly and thick muscles through the shoulders, arms, and neck. If Miller squinted, he could see the seventeen-year-old boy he had been under the layers of time and disappointment, and it looked a lot like the clerk out front. The office was almost too small for the three of them and stacked with boxes of pornographic software.

"You catch them?" the manager said.

"No," Miller said. "Still trying to figure out who they are."

"Dammit, I already told you. There's pictures of them off the store camera. I gave you his fucking name."

Miller looked at his terminal. The suspect was named Mateo Judd, a dockworker with an unspectacular criminal record.

"You think it's just him, then," Miller said. "All right. We'll just go pick him up, throw him in the can. No reason for us to find out who he's working for. Probably no one who'll take it wrong, anyway. My experience with these protection rackets, the purse boys get replaced whenever one goes down. But since you're sure this guy's the *whole* problem..."

The manager's sour expression told Miller he'd made his point. Havelock, leaning against a stack of boxes marked сиротливые девушки, smiled.

"Why don't you tell me what he wanted," Miller said.

"I already told the last cop," the manager said.

"Tell me."

"He was selling us a private insurance plan. Hundred a month, same as the last guy."

"Last guy?" Havelock said. "So this happened before?"

"Sure," the manager said. "Everyone has to pay some, you know. Price of doing business."

Miller closed his terminal, frowning. "Philosophical. But if it's the price of doing business, what're we here for?"

"Because I thought you...you people had this shit under control. Ever since we stopped paying the Loca, I've been able to turn a decent profit. Now it's all starting up again."

"Hold on," Miller said. "You're telling me the Loca Greiga stopped charging protection?"

"Sure. Not just here. Half of the guys I know in the Bough just stopped showing up. We figured the cops had actually done something for once. Now we've got these new bastards, and it's the same damn thing all over again."

A crawling feeling made its way up Miller's neck. He looked up at Havelock, who shook his head. He hadn't heard of it either. The Golden Bough Society, Sohiro's crew, the Loca Greiga. All the organized crime on Ceres suffering the same ecological collapse, and now someone new moving into the evacuated niche. Might be opportunism. Might be something else. He almost didn't want to ask the next questions. Havelock was going to think he was paranoid.

"How long has it been since the old guys called on you for protection?" Miller asked.

"I don't know. Long time."

"Before or after Mars killed that water hauler?"

The manager folded his thick arms; his eyes narrowed.

"Before," he said. "Maybe a month or two. S'that got to do with anything?"

"Just trying to get the time scale right," Miller said. "The new guy. Mateo. He tell you who was backing his new insurance plan?"

"That's your job, figuring it. Right?"

The manager's expression had closed down so hard Miller imagined he could hear the click. Yes, Asher Kamamatsu knew who was shaking him down. He had balls enough to squeak about it but not to point the finger.

Interesting.

"Well, thanks for that," Miller said, standing up. "We'll let you know what we find."

"Glad you're on the case," the manager said, matching sarcasm for sarcasm.

In the exterior tunnel, Miller stopped. The neighborhood was at the friction point between sleazy and respectable. White marks showed where graffiti had been painted over. Men on bicycles swerved and weaved, foam wheels humming on the polished stone. Miller walked slowly, his eyes on the ceiling high above them until he found the security camera. He pulled up his terminal, navigated to the logs that matched the camera code, and cross-referenced the time code from the store's still frames. For a moment, he thumbed the controls, speeding people back and forth. And there was Mateo, coming out of the shop. A smug grin deformed the man's face. Miller froze the image and enhanced it. Havelock, watching over his shoulder, whistled low.

The split circle of the OPA was perfectly clear on the thug's armband—the same kind of armband he'd found in Julie Mao's hole.

What kind of company have you been keeping, kid? Miller thought. *You're better than this. You have to know you're better than this.*

"Hey, partner," he said aloud. "Think you can write up the report on that interview? I've got something I'd like to do. Might not be too smart to have you there. No offense."

Havelock's eyebrows crawled toward his hairline.

"You're going to question the OPA?"

"Shake some trees, is all," Miller said.

Miller would have thought that just being a security contractor in a known OPA-convivial bar would be enough to get him noticed. In the event, half the faces he recognized in the dim light of John Rock Gentlemen's Club were normal citizens. More than one of those were Star Helix, just like him, when they were on duty. The music was pure Belter, soft chimes accompanied by zither and guitar with lyrics in half a dozen languages. He was on his fourth beer, two hours past the end of his shift, and on the edge of giving up his plan as a losing scheme when a tall, thin man sat down at the bar next to him. Acne-pocked cheeks gave a sense of damage to a face that otherwise seemed on the verge of laughter. It wasn't the first OPA armband he'd seen that night, but it was worn with an air of defiance and authority. Miller nodded.

"I heard you've been asking about the OPA," the man said. "Interested in joining up?"

Miller smiled and lifted his glass, an intentionally noncommittal gesture.

"You who I'd talk to if I did?" he asked, his tone light.

"Might be able to help."

"Maybe you could tell me about a couple other things, then," he said, taking out his terminal and putting it on the fake bamboo bar with an audible click. Mateo Judd's picture glowed on the screen. The OPA man frowned, turning the screen to see it better.

"I'm a realist," Miller said. "When Chucky Snails was running protection, I wasn't above talking to his men. When the Hand took over and then the Golden Bough Society after them. My job isn't to stop people from bending the rules, it's to keep Ceres stable. You understand what I'm saying?"

"I can't say I do," the pock-marked man said. His accent made him sound more educated than Miller had expected. "Who is this man?"

"His name's Mateo Judd. He's been starting a protection business in sector eight. Says it's backed by the OPA."

"People say things, Detective. It is Detective, isn't it? But you were discussing realism."

"If the OPA's making a move on the Ceres black economy, it's going to be better all around if we can talk to each other. Communicate."

The man chuckled and pushed the terminal back. The bartender paced by, a question in his eyes that wasn't asking if they needed anything. It wasn't meant for Miller.

"I had heard that there was a certain level of corruption in Star Helix," the man said. "I admit I'm impressed by your straightforward manner. I'll clarify. The OPA isn't a criminal organization."

"Really? My mistake. I figured from the way it killed a lot of people..."

"You're baiting me. We defend ourselves against people who are perpetrating economic terrorism against the Belt. Earthers. Martians. We are in the business of protecting Belters," the man said. "Even you, Detective."

"Economic terrorism?" Miller said. "That seems a little overheated."

"You think so? The inner planets look on us as their labor force. They tax us. They direct what we do. They enforce their laws and ignore ours in the name of stability. In the last year, they've doubled the tariffs to Titania. Five thousand people on an ice ball orbiting Neptune, months from anywhere. The sun's just a bright star to them. Do you think they're in a position to get redress? They've blocked any Belter freighters from taking Europa contracts. They charge us twice as much to dock at Ganymede. The science station on Phoebe? We aren't even allowed to *orbit* it. There isn't a Belter in the place. Whatever they do there, we won't find out until they sell the technology back to us, ten years from now."

Miller sipped his beer and nodded toward his terminal.

"So this one isn't yours?"

"No. He isn't."

Miller nodded and put the terminal back in his pocket. Oddly, he believed the man. He didn't hold himself like a thug. The bravado wasn't there. The sense of trying to impress the world. No, this man was certain and amused and, underneath it all, profoundly tired. Miller had known soldiers like that, but not criminals.

"One other thing," Miller said. "I'm looking for someone."

"Another investigation?"

"Not exactly, no. Juliette Andromeda Mao. Goes by Julie."

"Should I know the name?"

"She's OPA," Miller said with a shrug.

"Do you know everyone in Star Helix?" the man said, and when Miller didn't answer, he added, "We are considerably larger than your corporation."

"Fair point," Miller said. "But if you could keep an ear out, I'd appreciate it."

"I don't know that you're in a position to expect favors."

"No harm asking."

The pock-faced man chuckled, put a hand on Miller's shoulder.

"Don't come back here, Detective," he said, and walked away into the crowd.

Miller took another drink of his beer, frowning. An uncomfortable feeling of having made the wrong step fidgeted in the back of his mind. He'd been sure that the OPA was making a move on Ceres, capitalizing on the death of the water hauler and the Belt's uptick in fear and hatred of the inner planets. But how did that fit with Julie Mao's father and his suspiciously well-timed anxiety? Or the disappearance of Ceres Station's supply of usual suspects in the first place? Thinking about it was like watching a video that was just out of focus. The sense of it was almost there, but only almost.

"Too many dots," Miller said. "Not enough lines."

"Excuse me?" the bartender said.

"Nothing," Miller said, pushing the half-empty bottle across the bar. "Thanks."

In his hole, Miller turned on some music. The lyrical chants that Candace had liked, back when they were young and, if not hopeful, at least more joyful in their fatalism. He set the lights to half power, hoping that if he relaxed, if for just a few minutes he let go of the gnawing sense that he had missed some critical detail, the missing piece might arrive on its own.

He'd half expected Candace to appear in his mind, sighing and looking crossly at him the way she had in life. Instead, he found himself talking with Julie Mao. In the half sleep of alcohol and exhaustion, he imagined her sitting at Havelock's desk. She was the wrong age, younger than the real woman would be. She was the age of the smiling kid in her picture. The girl who had raced in the *Razorback* and won. He had the sense of asking her questions, and her answers had the power of revelation. Everything made sense. Not only the change in the Golden Bough Society and her own abduction case, but Havelock's transfer, the dead ice hauler, Miller's own life and work. He dreamed of Julie Mao laughing, and he woke up late, with a headache.

Havelock was waiting at his desk. His broad, short Earther face seemed strangely alien, but Miller tried to shake it off.

"You look like crap," Havelock said. "Busy night?"

"Just getting old and drinking cheap beer," Miller said.

One of the vice squad shouted something angry about her files being locked again, and a computer tech scuttled across the station house like a nervous cockroach. Havelock leaned closer, his expression grave.

"Seriously, Miller," Havelock said. "We're still partners, and... honest to God, I think you may be the only friend I've got on this rock. You can trust me. If there's anything you want to tell me, I'm good."

"That's great," Miller said. "But I don't know what you're talking about. Last night was a bust."

"No OPA?"

"Sure, OPA. Anymore, you swing a dead cat in this station, you'll hit three OPA guys. Just no good information."

Havelock leaned back, lips pressed thin and bloodless. Miller's shrug asked a question, and the Earther nodded toward the board. A new homicide topped the list. At three in the morning, while Miller had been having inchoate dream conversations, someone had opened Mateo Judd's hole and fired a shotgun cartridge full of ballistic gel into his left eye.

"Well," Miller said, "called that one wrong."

"Which one?" Havelock said.

"OPA's not moving in on the criminals," Miller said. "They're moving in on the cops."

Chapter Eleven: Holden

The *Donnager* was ugly.

Holden had seen pictures and videos of the old oceangoing navies of Earth, and even in the age of steel, there had always been something beautiful about them. Long and sleek, they had the appearance of something leaning into the wind, a creature barely held on the leash. The *Donnager* had none of that. Like all long-flight spacecraft, it was built in the "office tower" configuration: each deck one floor of the building, ladders or elevators running down the axis. Constant thrust took the place of gravity.

But the *Donnager* actually *looked* like an office building on its side. Square and blocky, with small bulbous projections in seemingly random places. At nearly five hundred meters long, it was the size of a 130-story building. Alex had said it was 250,000 tons dry weight, and it looked heavier. Holden reflected, not for the first time, on how so much of the human sense of aesthetics had been formed in a time when sleek objects cut through the air. The *Donnager* would never move through anything thicker than inter-stellar gas, so curves and angles were a waste of space. The result was ugly.

It was also intimidating. As Holden watched from his seat next to Alex in the cockpit of the *Knight,* the massive battleship matched course with them, looming close and then seeming to stop above them. A docking bay opened, breaking up the *Donnager*'s flat black belly with a square of dim red light. The *Knight* beeped insistently, reminding him of the targeting lasers painting their hull. Holden looked for the point defense cannons aimed at him. He couldn't find them.

When Alex spoke, Holden jumped.

"Roger that, *Donnager,*" the pilot said. "We've got steering lock. I'm killing thrust."

The last shreds of weight vanished. Both ships were still moving at hundreds of kilometers a minute, but their matched courses felt like stillness.

"Got docking permission, Cap. Take her in?"

"It seems late to make a run for it, Mr. Kamal," Holden said. He imagined Alex making a mistake that the *Donnager* interpreted as threatening, and the point defense cannons throwing a couple hundred thousand Teflon-coated chunks of steel through them.

"Go slowly, Alex," he said.

"They say one of those can kill a planet," Naomi said over the comm. She was at the ops station a deck below.

"Anyone can kill a planet from orbit," Holden replied. "You don't even need bombs. Just push anvils out the airlock. That thing out there could kill...Shit. Anything."

Tiny touches shifted them as the maneuvering rockets fired. Holden knew that Alex was guiding them in, but he couldn't shake the feeling that the *Donnager* was swallowing them.

Docking took nearly an hour. Once the *Knight* was inside the bay, a massive manipulator arm grabbed *her* and put it down in an empty section of the deck. Clamps grabbed the ship, the *Knight*'s hull reverberating with a metallic bang that reminded Holden of a brig cell's maglocks.

The Martians ran a docking tube from one wall and mated up to the *Knight*'s airlock. Holden gathered the crew at the inner door.

"No guns, no knives, no anything that might look like a weapon," he said. "They'll probably be okay with hand terminals, but keep them turned off just in case. If they ask for it, hand it over without complaint. Our survival here may rest on them thinking we're very compliant."

"Yeah," Amos said. "Fuckers killed McDowell, but *we* have to act nice…"

Alex started to respond, but Holden cut him off.

"Alex, you did twenty flying with the MCRN. Anything else we should know?"

"Same stuff you said, Boss," Alex replied. "Yes sir, no sir, and snap to when given an order. The enlisted guys will be okay, but the officers get the sense of humor trained out of 'em."

Holden looked at his tiny crew, hoping he hadn't killed them all by bringing them here. He cycled open the lock, and they drifted down the short docking tube in the zero g. When they reached the airlock at the end—flat gray composites and immaculately clean—everyone pushed down to the floor. Their magnetic boots grabbed on. The airlock closed and hissed at them for several seconds before opening into a larger room with about a dozen people standing in it. Holden recognized Captain Theresa Yao. There were several others in naval officers' dress, who were part of her staff; one man in an enlisted uniform with a look of thinly veiled impatience; and six marines in heavy combat armor, carrying assault rifles. The rifles were pointed at him, so Holden put up his hands.

"We're not armed," he said, smiling and trying to look harmless.

The rifles didn't waver, but Captain Yao stepped forward.

"Welcome aboard the *Donnager*," she said. "Chief, check them."

The enlisted man clumped toward them and quickly and professionally patted them all down. He gave the thumbs-up to one of the marines. The rifles went down, and Holden worked hard not to sigh with relief.

"What now, Captain?" Holden asked, keeping his voice light.

Yao looked Holden over critically for several seconds before answering. Her hair was pulled tightly back, the few strands of gray making straight lines. In person, he could see the softening of age at her jaw and the corners of her eyes. Her stony expression had the same quiet arrogance that all the naval captains he'd known shared. He wondered what she saw, looking at him. He resisted the urge to straighten his greasy hair.

"Chief Gunderson will take you down to your rooms and get you settled in," she replied. "Someone will be along shortly to debrief you."

Chief Gunderson started to lead them from the room when Yao spoke again, her voice suddenly hard.

"Mr. Holden, if you know anything about the six ships that are following you, speak now," she said. "We gave them a two-hour deadline to change course about an hour ago. So far they haven't. In one hour I'm going to order a torpedo launch. If they're friends of yours, you could save them a great deal of pain."

Holden shook his head emphatically.

"All I know is they came out of the Belt when you started out to meet us, Captain," Holden said. "They haven't talked to us. Our best guess is they're concerned citizens of the Belt coming to watch what happens."

Yao nodded. If she found the thought of witnesses disconcerting, it didn't show.

"Take them below, Chief," she said, then turned away.

Chief Gunderson gave a soft whistle and pointed at one of the two doors. Holden's crew followed him out, the marines bringing up the rear. As they moved through the *Donnager,* Holden took his first really up-close look at a Martian capital ship. He'd never served on a battleship in the UN Navy, and he'd stepped foot on them maybe three times in seven years, always in dock, and usually for a party. Every inch of the *Donnager* was just a little sharper than any UN vessel he'd served on. *Mars really does build them better than we do.*

"Goddamn, XO, they sure do keep their shit squeaky clean," Amos said behind him.

"Ain't much to do on a long flight for most of the crew, Amos," Alex said. "So when you aren't doin' somethin' else, you clean."

"See, that's why I work haulers," Amos said. "Clean decks or get drunk and screw, and I've got a preference."

As they walked through a maze of corridors, the ship started a slight vibration, and gravity slowly reappeared. They were under thrust. Holden used his heels to touch his boots' slide controls, turning the magnets off.

They saw almost no one, and the few they did see moved fast and said little, barely sparing them a glance. With six ships closing on them, everyone would be at their duty stations. When Captain Yao had said she'd fire her torpedoes in an hour, there hadn't been a hint of threat in her voice. It was just a flat statement of fact. For most of the young sailors on this ship, it would probably be the first time they'd ever been in a live combat situation—if it came to that. Holden didn't believe it would.

He wondered what to make of the fact that Yao was prepared to take out a handful of Belt ships just because they were running quiet and close. It didn't suggest that they'd hesitate to kill a water hauler, like the *Cant,* if they thought there was reason to.

Gunderson brought them to a stop in front of a hatch with *OQ117* printed on it. He slid a card through the lock and gestured everyone inside.

"Better than I'd expected," Shed said, sounding impressed.

The compartment was large by ship standards. It had six high-g couches and a small table with four chairs stuck to the deck with magnetic feet. An open door in one bulkhead showed a smaller compartment with a toilet and sink. Gunderson and the marine lieutenant followed the crew inside.

"This is your rack for the time being," the chief said. "There's a comm panel on the wall. Two of Lieutenant Kelly's people will be stationed outside. Buzz them and they'll send for anything you need."

"How about some chow?" Amos said.

"We'll have some sent up. You are to remain here until called for," Gunderson said. "Lieutenant Kelly, you have anything to add, sir?"

The marine lieutenant looked them over.

"The men outside are there for your protection, but they will react unpleasantly if you make any trouble," he said. "You read me?"

"Loud and clear, Lieutenant," Holden said. "Don't worry. My people will be the easiest houseguests you've ever had."

Kelly nodded at Holden with what seemed like genuine gratitude. He was a professional doing an unpleasant job. Holden sympathized. Also, he'd known enough marines to know how unpleasant it could get if they felt challenged.

Gunderson said, "Can you take Mr. Holden here to his appointment on your way out, El Tee? I'd like to get these folks squared away."

Kelly nodded and took Holden's elbow.

"Come with me, sir," he said.

"Where am I going, Lieutenant?"

"Lieutenant Lopez asked to see you as soon as you landed. I'm taking you to him."

Shed looked nervously from the marine to Holden and back. Naomi nodded. They'd all see each other again, Holden told himself. He even thought it was likely to be true.

Kelly led Holden at a brisk pace through the ship. His rifle was no longer at the ready but hanging from his shoulder loosely. Either he'd decided Holden wasn't going to cause trouble, or that he could take him down easily if he did.

"Can I ask who Lieutenant Lopez is?"

"He's the guy who asked to see you," Kelly said.

Kelly stopped at a plain gray door, rapped once, then took Holden inside a small compartment with a table and two uncomfortable-looking chairs. A dark-haired man was setting up a recorder. He waved one hand vaguely in the direction of a chair. Holden sat. The chair was even less comfortable than it looked.

"You can go, Mr. Kelly," the man Holden assumed was Lopez said. Kelly left and closed the door.

When Lopez had finished, he sat down across the table from Holden and reached out one hand. Holden shook it.

"I'm Lieutenant Lopez. Kelly probably told you that. I work for naval intelligence, which he almost certainly didn't tell you. My job isn't secret, but they train jarheads to be tight-lipped."

Lopez reached into his pocket, took out a small packet of white lozenges, and popped one into his mouth. He didn't offer one to Holden. Lopez's pupils contracted to tiny points as he sucked the lozenge. Focus drugs. He'd be watching every tic of Holden's face during questioning. Tough to lie to.

"First Lieutenant James R. Holden, of Montana," he said. It wasn't a question.

"Yes, sir," Holden said anyway.

"Seven years in the UNN, last posting on the destroyer *Zhang Fei*."

"That's me."

"Your file says you were busted out for assaulting a superior officer," Lopez said. "That's pretty cliché, Holden. You punched the old man? Seriously?"

"No. I missed. Broke my hand on a bulkhead."

"How'd that happen?"

"He was quicker than I expected," Holden replied.

"Why'd you try?"

"I was projecting my self-loathing onto him. It's just a stroke of luck that I actually wound up hurting the right person," Holden said.

"Sounds like you've thought about it some since then," Lopez said, his pinprick pupils never moving from Holden's face. "Therapy?"

"Lots of time to think on the *Canterbury*," Holden replied.

Lopez ignored the obvious opening and said, "What did you come up with, during all that thinking?"

"The Coalition has been stepping on the necks of the people out here for over a hundred years now. I didn't like being the boot."

"An OPA sympathizer, then?" Lopez said, his expression not changing at all.

"No. I didn't switch sides. I stopped playing. I didn't renounce my citizenship. I like Montana. I'm out here because I like flying, and only a Belter rust trap like the *Canterbury* will hire me."

Lopez smiled for the first time. "You're an exceedingly honest man, Mr. Holden."

"Yes."

"Why did you claim that a Martian military vessel destroyed your ship?"

"I didn't. I explained all that in the broadcast. It had technology only available to inner planet fleets, and I found a piece of MCRN hardware in the device that tricked us into stopping."

"We'll want to see that."

"You're welcome to it."

"Your file says you were the only child of a family co-op," Lopez said, acting as though they'd never stopped talking about Holden's past.

"Yes, five fathers, three mothers."

"So many parents for only one child," Lopez said, slowly unwrapping another lozenge. The Martians had lots of space for traditional families.

"The tax break for eight adults only having one child allowed them to own twenty-two acres of decent farmland. There are over thirty billion people on Earth. Twenty-two acres is a national park," Holden said. "Also, the DNA mix is legit. They aren't parents in name only."

"How did they decide who carried you?"

"Mother Elise had the widest hips."

Lopez popped the second lozenge into his mouth and sucked on it a few moments. Before he could speak again, the deck shook. The video recorder jiggled on its arm.

"Torpedo launches?" Holden said. "Guess those Belt ships didn't change course."

"Any thoughts about that, Mr. Holden?"

"Just that you seem pretty willing to kill Belt ships."

"You've put us in a position where we can't afford to seem weak. After your accusations, there are a lot of people who don't think much of us."

Holden shrugged. If the man was watching for guilt or remorse from Holden, he was out of luck. The Belt ships had known what they were going toward. They hadn't turned away. But still, something bothered him.

"They might hate your living guts," Holden said. "But it's hard to find enough suicidal people to crew six ships. Maybe they think they can outrun torpedoes."

Lopez didn't move, his whole body preternaturally still with the focus drugs pouring through him.

"We—" Lopez began, and the general quarters Klaxon sounded. It was deafening in the small metal compartment.

"Holy shit, did they shoot *back*?" Holden asked.

Lopez shook himself, like a man waking up from a daydream. He got up and hit the comm button by the door. A marine came through seconds later.

"Take Mr. Holden back to his quarters," Lopez said, then left the room at a run.

The marine gestured at the corridor with the barrel of his rifle. His expression was hard.

It's all fun and games till someone shoots back, Holden thought.

Naomi patted the empty couch next to her and smiled.

"Did they put slivers under your fingernails?" she asked.

"No, actually, he was surprisingly human for a naval intelligence wonk," Holden replied. "Of course, he was just getting warmed up. Have you guys heard anything about the other ships?"

Alex said, "Nope. But that alarm means they're takin' them seriously all of a sudden."

"It's insane," Shed said quietly. "Flying around in these metal bubbles, and then trying to poke holes in each other. You ever seen what long-term decompression and cold exposure does? Breaks all the capillaries in your eyes and skin. Tissue damage to the lungs can cause massive pneumonia followed by emphysema-like scarring. I mean, if you don't just die."

"Well, that's awful fucking cheerful, Doc. Thanks for that," Amos said.

The ship suddenly vibrated in a syncopated but ultra-high-speed rhythm. Alex looked at Holden, his eyes wide.

"That's the point defense network openin' up. That means incoming torpedoes," he said. "Better strap in tight, kids. The ship might start doin' some violent maneuvering."

Everyone but Holden was already belted into the couches. He fastened his restraints too.

"This sucks. All the real action is happenin' thousands of klicks from here, and we got no instruments to look at," Alex said. "We won't know if somethin' slipped through the flack screen till it rips the hull open."

"Boy, everybody is just a fucking pile of fun right now," Amos said loudly.

Shed's eyes were wide, his face too pale. Holden shook his head.

"Not going to happen," he said. "This thing is unkillable. Whoever those ships are, they can put on a good show, but that's it."

"All respect, Captain," Naomi said. "But whoever those ships are, they should be dead already, and they aren't."

The distant noises of faraway combat kept up. The occasional rumble of a torpedo firing. The near-constant vibration of the high-speed point defense guns. Holden didn't realize he'd fallen asleep until he was jerked awake by an earsplitting roar. Amos and Alex were yelling. Shed was screaming.

"What happened?" Holden yelled over the noise.

"We're hit, Cap!" Alex said. "That was a torpedo hit!"

The gravity suddenly dropped away. The *Donnager* had stopped its engines. Or they'd been destroyed.

Amos was still yelling, "Shit shit shit," over everything. But at least Shed had stopped screaming. He was staring wide eyed out of his couch, his face white. Holden unbuckled his straps and pushed off toward the comm panel.

"Jim!" Naomi called out. "What are you doing?"

"We need to find out what's going on," Holden said over his shoulder.

When he reached the bulkhead by the hatch, he punched the comm panel call button. There was no reply. He hit it again, then started pounding on the hatch. No one came.

"Where are our damn marines?" he said.

The lights dimmed, came back up. Then again, and again, in a slow cadence.

"Gauss turrets firing. Shit. It's CQB," Alex said in awe.

In the history of the Coalition, no capital ship had ever gotten into a close-quarters battle. But here they were, firing the ship's big cannons, which meant that the range was sufficiently short that a nonguided weapon was viable. Hundreds or even dozens of kilometers, not thousands. Somehow the Belt ships had survived *Donnager*'s torpedo barrage.

"Anyone else think this is desperate fucking queer?" Amos asked, a touch of panic in his voice.

The *Donnager* began to ring like a gong struck over and over again by a massive hammer. Return fire.

The gauss round that killed Shed didn't even make a noise. Like a magic trick, two perfectly round holes appeared on either side of the room in a line that intersected Shed's couch. One moment, the medic was there; the next, his head was gone from the Adam's apple up. Arterial blood pumped out in a red cloud, pulled into two thin lines, and whirled to the holes in the walls of the room as the air rushed out.

Chapter Twelve: Miller

For thirty years, Miller had worked security. Violence and death were familiar companions to him. Men, women. Animals. Kids. Once he'd held a woman's hand while she bled to death. He'd killed two people, could still see them die if he closed his eyes and thought about it. If anyone had asked him, he'd have said there wasn't much left that would shake him.

But he'd never watched a war start before.

The Distinguished Hyacinth Lounge was in the shift-change rush. Men and women in security uniforms—mostly from Star Helix, but a few smaller companies too—were either drinking their after-work liquor and winding down or making trips to the breakfast buffet for coffee, textured fungi in sugar sauce, sausage with meat maybe one part in a thousand. Miller chewed the sausage and watched the display monitor on the wall. A Star Helix external relations head looked sincerely out, his demeanor radiating calm and certainty as he explained how everything was going to hell.

"Preliminary scans suggest that the explosion was the result of a failed attempt to connect a nuclear device to the docking station. Officials from the Martian government have referred to the incident only as an 'alleged terrorist action' and refused comment pending further investigation."

"Another one," Havelock said from behind him. "You know, eventually, one of those assholes is going to get it right."

Miller turned in his seat, then nodded to the chair beside him. Havelock sat.

"That'll be an interesting day," Miller said. "I was about to call you."

"Yeah, sorry," his partner said. "I was up kind of late."

"Any word on the transfer?"

"No," Havelock said. "Figure my paperwork's hung on a desk someplace in Olympus. What about you? Any word on your special-project girl?"

"Not yet," Miller said. "Look, the reason I wanted to meet up before we went in...I need to take a couple days, try to run down some leads on Julie. With all this other shit going on, Shaddid doesn't want me doing much more than phoning this one in."

"But you're ignoring that," Havelock said. It wasn't a question.

"I've got a feeling about this one."

"So how can I help?"

"I need you to cover for me."

"How am I going to do that?" Havelock asked. "It's not like I can tell them you're sick. They've got access to your medical records same as everyone else's."

"Tell 'em I've been getting drunk a lot," Miller said. "That Candace came by. She's my ex-wife."

Havelock chewed his sausage, brow furrowed. The Earther shook his head slowly—not a refusal, but the prelude to a question. Miller waited.

"You're telling me you'd rather have the boss think you're

missing work because you're on a dysfunctional, heartbroken bender than that you're doing the work she assigned you? I don't get it."

Miller licked his lips and leaned forward, elbows on the smooth off-white table. Someone had scratched a design into the plastic. A split circle. And this was a cop bar.

"I don't know what I'm looking at," Miller said. "There's a bunch of things that belong together somehow, and I'm not sure yet what it is. Until I know more, I need to stay low. A guy has a fling with his ex, hits the bottle for a few days? That's not going to light up anyone's panels."

Havelock shook his head again, this time in mild disbelief. If he'd been a Belter, he'd have made the gesture with his hands, so you could see it when he had an environment suit on. Another of the hundred small ways someone who hadn't grown up on the Belt betrayed himself. The wall monitor cut to the image of a blond woman in a severe uniform. The external relations head was talking about the Martian navy's tactical response and whether the OPA was behind the increased vandalism. That was what he called fumbling an overloaded fusion reactor while setting up a ship-killing booby trap: vandalism.

"That shit just doesn't follow," Havelock said, and for a moment Miller didn't know if he meant the Belter guerrilla actions, the Martian response, or the favor he'd asked. "Seriously. Where's Earth? All this shit's going on, and we don't hear a damn thing from them."

"Why would we?" Miller asked. "It's Mars and the Belt going at it."

"When was the last time Earth let anything major happen without them in the middle of it?" Havelock said, then sighed. "Okay. You're too drunk to come in. Your love life's a mess. I'm trying to cover for you."

"Just for a couple days."

"Make sure you get back before someone decides it's the perfect chance for a random shooting to take out the Earther cop."

"I'll do that," Miller said, rising from the table. "You watch your back."

"Don't need to tell me twice," Havelock said.

The Ceres Center for Jiu Jitsu was down near the port, where the spin gravity was strongest. The hole was a converted storage space from before the big spin. A cylinder flattened where flooring had been set in about a third of the way from the bottom. Racks bearing various lengths of staffs, bamboo swords, and dull plastic practice knives hung from the vaulted ceiling. The polished stone echoed with the grunting of men working a line of resistance machines and the soft thud of a woman at the back punishing a heavy bag. Three students stood on the central mat, speaking in low voices.

Pictures filled the front wall on either side of the door. Soldiers in uniform. Security agents for half a dozen Belter corporations. Not many inner planet types, but a few. Plaques commemorating placements in competitions. A page of small type outlining the history of the studio.

One of the students shouted and collapsed, carrying one of the others to the mat with her. The one still standing applauded and helped them back up. Miller searched through the wall of pictures, hoping to find Julie.

"Can I help you?"

The man was half a head shorter than Miller and easily twice as broad. It should have made him look like an Earther, but everything else about him said Belt. He wore pale sweats that made his skin seem even darker. His smile was curious and as serene as a well-fed predator. Miller nodded.

"Detective Miller," he said. "I'm with station security. There's one of your students I wanted to get some background on."

"This is an official investigation?" the man asked.

"Yeah," Miller said. "I'm afraid it is."

"Then you'll have a warrant."

Miller smiled. The man smiled back.

"We don't give out any information on our students without a warrant," he said. "Studio policy."

"I respect that," Miller said. "No, I really do. It's just that... parts of this particular investigation are maybe a little more official than others. The girl's not in trouble. She didn't do anything. But she has family on Luna who want her found."

"A kidnap job," the man said, folding his arms. The serene face had gone cool without any apparent movement.

"Only the official part," Miller said. "I can get a warrant, and we can do the whole thing through channels. But then I have to tell my boss. The more she knows, the less room I have to move."

The man didn't react. His stillness was unnerving. Miller struggled not to fidget. The woman working the heavy bag at the far end of the studio went through a flurry of strikes, shouting out with each one.

"Who?" the man asked.

"Julie Mao," Miller said. He could have said he was looking for the Buddha's mother for all the reaction he got. "I think she's in trouble."

"Why do you care if she is?"

"I don't know the answer to that one," Miller said. "I just do. If you don't want to help me, then you don't."

"And you'll go get your warrant. Do this through channels."

Miller took off his hat, rubbed a long, thin hand across his head, and put the hat back in place.

"Probably not," he said.

"Let me see your ID," the man said. Miller pulled up his terminal and let the man confirm who he was. The man handed it back and pointed to a small door behind the heavy bags. Miller did as he was told.

The office was cramped. A small laminate desk with a soft sphere behind it in lieu of a chair. Two stools that looked like they'd come out of a bar. A filing cabinet with a small fabricator that stank of ozone and oil that was probably where the plaques and certificates were made.

"Why does the family want her?" the man asked, lowering himself onto the sphere. It acted like a chair but required constant balance. A place to rest without actually resting.

"They think she's in harm's way. At least, that's what they're saying, and I don't have reason to disbelieve them yet."

"What kind of harm?"

"Don't know," Miller said. "I know she was on station. I know she shipped out for Tycho, and after that, I've got nothing."

"Her family want her back on their station?"

The man knew who her family was. Miller filed the information away without missing a beat.

"I don't think so," Miller said. "The last message she got from them routed through Luna."

"Down the well." The way he said it made it sound like a disease.

"I'm looking for anyone who knows who she was shipping with. If she's on a run, where she was going and when she was planning to get there. If she's in range of a tightbeam."

"I don't know any of that," the man said.

"You know anyone I should ask?"

There was a pause.

"Maybe. I'll find what I can for you."

"Anything else you can tell me about her?"

"She started at the studio five years ago. She was ... angry when she first came. Undisciplined."

"She got better," Miller said. "Brown belt, right?"

The man's eyebrows rose.

"I'm a cop," Miller said. "I find things out."

"She improved," her teacher said. "She'd been attacked. Just after she came to the Belt. She was seeing that it didn't happen twice."

"Attacked," Miller said, parsing the man's tone of voice. "Raped?"

"I didn't ask. She trained hard, even when she was off station.

You can tell when people let it slide. They come back weaker. She never did."

"Tough girl," Miller said. "Good for her. Did she have friends? People she sparred with?"

"A few. No lovers that I know of, since that's the next question."

"That's strange. Girl like that."

"Like what, Detective?"

"Pretty girl," Miller said. "Competent. Smart. Dedicated. Who wouldn't want to be with someone like that?"

"Perhaps she hadn't met the right person."

Something in the way he said it hinted at amusement. Miller shrugged, uncomfortable in his skin.

"What kind of work did she do?" he asked.

"Light freighter. I don't know of any particular cargo. I had the impression that she shipped wherever there was a need."

"Not a regular route, then?"

"That was my impression."

"Whose ships did she work? One particular freighter, or whatever came to hand? A particular company?"

"I'll find what I can for you," the man said.

"Courier for the OPA?"

"I'll find out," the man said, "what I can."

The news that afternoon was all about Phoebe. The science station there—the one that Belters weren't allowed even to dock at—had been hit. The official report stated that half the inhabitants of the base were dead, the other half missing. No one had claimed responsibility yet, but the common wisdom was that some Belter group—maybe the OPA, maybe someone else—had finally managed an act of "vandalism" with a body count. Miller sat in his hole, watching the broadcast feed and drinking.

It was all going to hell. The pirate casts from the OPA calling for war. The burgeoning guerrilla actions. All of it. The time was coming that Mars wasn't going to ignore them anymore. And when Mars took action, it wouldn't matter if Earth followed suit. It would be the first real war in the Belt. The catastrophe was coming, and neither side seemed to understand how vulnerable they were. And there was nothing—not one single goddamned thing—that he could do to stop it. He couldn't even slow it down.

Julie Mao grinned at him from the still frame, her pinnace behind her. Attacked, the man had said. There was nothing about it in her record. Might have been a mugging. Might have been something worse. Miller had known a lot of victims, and he put them into three categories. First there were the ones who pretended nothing had happened, or that whatever it was didn't really matter. That was well over half the people he talked to. Then there were the professionals, people who took their victimization as permission to act out any way they saw fit. That ate most of the rest.

Maybe 5 percent, maybe less, were the ones who sucked it up, learned the lesson, and moved on. The Julies. The good ones.

His door chimed three hours after his official shift was over. Miller stood up, less steady on his feet than he'd expected. He counted the bottles on the table. There were more than he'd thought. He hesitated for a moment, torn between answering the door and throwing the bottles into the recycler. The door chimed again. He went to open it. If it was someone from the station, they expected him to be drunk, anyway. No reason to disappoint.

The face was familiar. Acne-pocked, controlled. The OPA armband from the bar. The one who'd had Mateo Judd killed.

The cop.

"Evening," Miller said.

"Detective Miller," the pocked man said. "I think we've gotten off on the wrong foot. I was hoping we could try again."

"Right."

"May I come in?"

"I try not to take strange men home," Miller said. "I don't even know your name."

"Anderson Dawes," the pocked man said. "I'm the Ceres liaison for the Outer Planets Alliance. I think we can help each other. May I come in?"

Miller stood back, and the pocked man—Dawes—stepped inside. Dawes took in the hole for the space of two slow breaths, then sat as if the bottles and the stink of old beer were nothing to comment on. Silently cursing himself and willing a sobriety he didn't feel, Miller sat across from him.

"I need a favor from you," Dawes said. "I'm willing to pay for it. Not money, of course. Information."

"What do you want?" Miller asked.

"Stop looking for Juliette Mao."

"No sale."

"I'm trying to keep the peace, Detective," Dawes said. "You should hear me out."

Miller leaned forward, elbows on the table. Mr. Serene Jiu Jitsu Instructor was working for the OPA? The timing of Dawes' visit seemed to be saying so. Miller filed that possibility away but said nothing.

"Mao worked for us," Dawes said. "But you'd guessed that."

"More or less. You know where she is?"

"We don't. We are looking for her. And we need to be the ones to find her. Not you."

Miller shook his head. There was a response, the right thing to say. It was rattling in the back of his head, and if he just didn't feel quite so fuzzy...

"You're one of *them*, Detective. You may have lived your whole life out here, but your salary is paid by an inner planet corporation. No, wait. I don't blame you. I understand how it is. They were hiring and you needed the work. But...we're walking on a bubble right now. The *Canterbury*. The fringe elements in the Belt calling for war."

"Phoebe Station."

"Yes, they'll blame us for that too. Add a Luna corporation's prodigal daughter..."

"You think something's happened to her."

"She was on the *Scopuli*," Dawes said, and when Miller didn't immediately respond, he added, "The freighter that Mars used as bait when they killed the *Canterbury*."

Miller thought about that for a long moment, then whistled low.

"We don't know what happened," Dawes said. "Until we do, I can't have you stirring up the water. It's muddy enough now."

"And what information are you offering?" Miller asked. "That's the trade, right?"

"I'll tell you what we find. After we find her," Dawes said. Miller chuckled, and the OPA man went on. "It's a generous offer, considering who you are. Employee of Earth. Partner of an Earther. Some people would think that was enough to make you the enemy too."

"But not you," Miller said.

"I think we've got the same basic goals, you and I. Stability. Safety. Strange times make for strange alliances."

"Two questions."

Dawes spread his arms, welcoming them.

"Who took the riot gear?" Miller asked.

"Riot gear?"

"Before the *Canterbury* died, someone took our riot gear. Maybe they wanted to arm soldiers for crowd control. Maybe they didn't want our crowds controlled. Who took it? Why?"

"It wasn't us," Dawes said.

"That's not an answer. Try this one. What happened to the Golden Bough Society?"

Dawes looked blank.

"Loca Greiga?" Miller asked. "Sohiro?"

Dawes opened his mouth, closed it. Miller dropped his beer bottle into the recycler.

"Nothing personal, friend," he said, "but your investigative techniques aren't impressing me. What makes you think you can find her?"

"It's not a fair test," Dawes said. "Give me a few days, I'll get answers for you."

"Talk to me then. I'll try not to start an all-out war while you do, but I'm not letting go of Julie. You can go now."

Dawes rose. He looked sour.

"You're making a mistake," he said.

"Won't be my first."

After the man left, Miller sat at his table. He'd been stupid. Worse, he'd been self-indulgent. Drinking himself into a stupor instead of doing the work. Instead of finding Julie. But he knew more now. The *Scopuli*. The *Canterbury*. More lines between the dots.

He cleaned away his bottles, took a shower, and pulled up his terminal, searching what there was about Julie's ship. After an hour, a new thought occurred to him, a small fear that grew the more he looked at it. Near midnight, he put a call through to Havelock's hole.

His partner took two full minutes to answer. When he did, his image was wild-haired and bleary-eyed.

"Miller?"

"Havelock. You have any vacation time saved up?"

"A little."

"Sick leave?"

"Sure," Havelock said.

"Take it," Miller said. "Take it now. Get off station. Someplace safe if you can find it. Someplace they're not going to start killing Earthers for shits and giggles if things go pear-shaped."

"I don't understand. What are you talking about?"

"I had a little visit with an OPA agent tonight. He was trying to talk me into dropping my kidnap job. I think...I think he's nervous. I think he's scared."

Havelock was silent for a moment while the words filtered into his sleep-drunk mind.

"Jesus," he said. "What scares the OPA?"

Chapter Thirteen: Holden

Holden froze, watching the blood pump from Shed's neck, then whip away like smoke into an exhaust fan. The sounds of combat began to fade as the air was sucked out of the room. His ears throbbed and then hurt like someone had put ice picks in them. As he fought with his couch restraints, he glanced over at Alex. The pilot was yelling something, but it didn't carry through the thin air. Naomi and Amos had gotten out of their couches already, kicked off, and were flying across the room to the two holes. Amos had a plastic dinner tray in one hand. Naomi, a white three-ring binder. Holden stared at them for the half second it took to understand what they were doing. The world narrowed, his peripheral vision all stars and darkness.

By the time he'd gotten free, Amos and Naomi had already covered the holes with their makeshift patches. The room was filled with a high-pitched whistle as the air tried to force its way out through the imperfect seals. Holden's sight began to return as the air pressure started to rise. He was panting hard, gasping for breath. Someone slowly turned the room's volume knob back up and Naomi's yells for help became audible.

"Jim, open the emergency locker!" she screamed.

She was pointing at a small red-and-yellow panel on the bulkhead near his crash couch. Years of shipboard training made a path through the anoxia and depressurization, and he yanked the tab on the locker's seal and pulled the door open. Inside were a white first aid kit marked with the ancient red-cross symbol, half a dozen oxygen masks, and a sealed bag of hardened plastic disks attached to a glue gun. The emergency-seal kit. He snatched it.

"Just the gun," Naomi yelled at him. He wasn't sure if her voice sounded distant because of the thin air or because the pressure drop had blown his eardrums.

Holden yanked the gun free from the bag of patches and threw it at her. She ran a bead of instant sealing glue around the edge of her three-ring binder. She tossed the gun to Amos, who caught it with an effortless backhand motion and put a seal around his dinner tray. The whistling stopped, replaced by the hiss of the atmosphere system as it labored to bring the pressure back up to normal. Fifteen seconds.

Everyone looked at Shed. Without the vacuum, his blood was pouring out into a floating red sphere just above his neck, like a hideous cartoon replacement for his head.

"Jesus Christ, Boss," Amos said, looking away from Shed to Naomi. He snapped his teeth closed with an audible click and shook his head. "What..."

"Gauss round," Alex said. "Those ships have rail guns."

"*Belt* ships with *rail* guns?" Amos said. "Did they get a fucking navy and no one told me?"

"Jim, the hallway outside and the cabin on the other side are both in vacuum," Naomi said. "The ship's compromised."

Holden started to respond, then caught a good look at the binder Naomi had glued over the breach. The white cover was stamped with black letters that read MCRN EMERGENCY PROCEDURES. He had to suppress a laugh that would almost certainly go manic on him.

"Jim," Naomi said, her voice worried.

"I'm okay, Naomi," Holden replied, then took a deep breath. "How long do those patches hold?"

Naomi shrugged with her hands, then started pulling her hair behind her head and tying it up with a red elastic band.

"Longer than the air will last. If everything around us is in vacuum, that means the cabin's running on emergency bottles. No recycling. I don't know how much each room has, but it won't be more than a couple hours."

"Kinda makes you wish we'd worn our fucking suits, don't it?" Amos asked.

"Wouldn't have mattered," Alex said. "We'd come over here in our enviro suits, they'd just have taken 'em away."

"Could have tried," Amos said.

"Well, if you'd like to go back in time and do it over, be my guest, partner."

Naomi sharply said, "Hey," but then nothing more.

No one was talking about Shed. They were working hard not to look at the body. Holden cleared his throat to get everyone's attention, then floated to Shed's couch, drawing their eyes with him. He paused a moment, letting everyone get a good look at the decapitated body, then pulled a blanket from the storage drawer beneath the couch and strapped it down over Shed's body with the couch's restraints.

"Shed's been killed. We're in deep peril. Arguing won't extend our lives one second," Holden said, looking at each member of his crew in turn. "What will?"

No one spoke. Holden turned to Naomi first.

"Naomi, what will keep us alive longer that we can do right now?" he asked.

"I'll see if I can find the emergency air. The room's built for six, and there're only . . . there are four of us. I might be able to turn the flow down and stretch it longer."

"Good. Thank you. Alex?"

"If there's anyone other than us, they'll be lookin' for survivors. I'll start poundin' on the bulkhead. They won't hear it in the vacuum, but if there're cabins with air, the sound'll travel down the metal."

"Good plan. I refuse to believe we're the only ones left on this ship," Holden said, then turned to Amos. "Amos?"

"Lemme check on that comm panel. Might be able to get the bridge or damage control or . . . shit, *something*," Amos replied.

"Thanks. I'd love to let someone know we're still here," Holden said.

People moved off to work while Holden floated in the air next to Shed. Naomi began yanking access panels off the bulkheads. Alex, hands pressed against a couch for leverage, lay on the deck and began to kick the bulkhead with his boots. The room vibrated slightly with each booming kick. Amos pulled a multi-tool out of his pocket and began taking the comm panel apart.

When Holden was sure everyone was busy, he put one hand on Shed's shoulder, just below the blanket's spreading red stain.

"I'm sorry," he whispered to the body. His eyes burned and he pressed them into the back of his thumbs.

The comm unit was hanging out of the bulkhead on wires when it buzzed once, loudly. Amos yelped and pushed off hard enough to fly across the room. Holden caught him, wrenching his shoulder by trying to arrest the momentum of 120 kilos of Earther mechanic. The comm buzzed again. Holden let Amos go and floated to it. A yellow LED glowed next to the unit's white button. Holden pressed the button. The comm crackled to life with Lieutenant Kelly's voice.

"Move away from the hatch, we're coming in," he said.

"Grab something!" Holden yelled to the crew, then grabbed a couch restraint and wrapped it around his hand and forearm.

When the hatch opened, Holden expected all the air to rush out. Instead, there was a loud crack and the pressure dropped slightly for a second. Outside in the corridor, thick sheets of plastic had been sealed to the walls, creating an ad hoc airlock. The walls of the new chamber bowed out dangerously with the air pressure, but they held. Inside the newly created lock, Lieutenant Kelly and three of his marines wore heavy vacuum-rated armor and carried enough weaponry to fight several minor wars.

The marines moved quickly into the room, weapons ready, and then sealed the hatch behind them. One of them tossed a large bag at Holden.

"Five vac suits. Get them on," Kelly said. His eyes moved to the bloody blanket covering Shed, then to the two improvised patches. "Casualty?"

"Our medic, Shed Garvey," Holden replied.

"Yeah. What the fuck?" Amos said loudly. "Who's out there shooting the shit out of your fancy boat?"

Naomi and Alex said nothing but started pulling the suits from the bag and handing them out.

"I don't know," Kelly said. "But we're leaving right now. I've been ordered to get you off this ship in an escape craft. We've got less than ten minutes to make it to the hangar bay, take possession of a ship, and get out of this combat area. Dress fast."

Holden put on his suit, the implications of their evacuation racing through his mind.

"Lieutenant, is the ship coming apart?" he asked.

"Not yet. But we're being boarded."

"Then why are we leaving?"

"We're losing."

Kelly didn't tap his foot while waiting for them to seal into their suits; Holden guessed this was only because the marines had their magnetic boots turned on. As soon as everyone had given the thumbs-up, Kelly did a quick radio check on each suit, then headed back into the corridor. With eight people in it, four of them in powered armor, the mini-airlock was tight. Kelly pulled a heavy knife from a sheath on his chest and slashed the plastic barrier open in one quick movement. The hatch behind them slammed shut, and the air in the corridor vanished in a soundless ripple of plastic flaps. Kelly charged into the corridor with the crew scrambling to keep up.

"We are moving with all speed to the keel elevator banks," Kelly said through the radio link. "They're locked down because of the boarding alarm, but I can get the doors open on one and we'll float down the shaft to the hangar bay. Everything is on the double. If you see boarders, do not stop. Keep moving at all times. We'll handle the hostiles. Roger that?"

"Roger, Lieutenant," Holden gasped out. "Why board you?"

"The command information center," Alex said. "It's the holy grail. Codes, deployments, computer cores, the works. Takin' a flagship's CIC is a strategist's wet dream."

"Cut the chatter," Kelly said. Holden ignored him.

"That means they'll blow the core rather than let that happen, right?"

"Yep," Alex replied. "Standard ops for boarders. Marines hold the bridge, CIC, and engineering. If any of the three is breached, the other two flip the switch. The ship turns into a star for a few seconds."

"Standard ops," Kelly growled. "Those are my friends."

"Sorry, El Tee," Alex replied. "I served on the *Bandon*. Don't mean to make light."

They turned a corner and the elevator bank came into view. All eight elevators were closed and sealed. The heavy pressure doors had slammed shut when the ship was holed.

"Gomez, run the bypass," Kelly said. "Mole, Dookie, watch those corridors."

Two of the marines spread out, watching the hallways through their gun sights. The third moved to one of the elevator doors and started doing something complicated to the controls. Holden motioned his crew to the wall, out of the firing lines. The deck vibrated slightly from time to time beneath his feet. The enemy ships wouldn't still be firing, not with their boarders inside. It must be small-arms fire and light explosives. But as they stood there in the perfect quiet of vacuum, everything that was happening took on a distant and surreal feeling. Holden recognized that his mind wasn't working the way it should be. Trauma reaction. The destruction of the *Canterbury*, the deaths of Ade and McDowell. And now someone had killed Shed in his bunk. It was too much; he couldn't process it. He felt the scene around him grow more and more distant.

Holden looked behind him at Naomi, Alex, and Amos. His crew. They stared back, faces ashen and ghostly in the green light of their suit displays. Gomez pumped his fist in triumph as the outer pressure door slid open, revealing the elevator doors. Kelly gestured to his men.

The one called Mole turned around and started to walk to the elevator when his face disintegrated in a spray of pebble-shaped bits of armored glass and blood. His armored torso and the corridor bulkhead beside him bloomed in a hundred small detonations and puffs of smoke. His body jerked and swayed, attached to the floor by magnetic boots.

Holden's sense of unreality washed away in adrenaline. The fire spraying across the wall and Mole's body was high-explosive rounds from a rapid-fire weapon. The comm channel filled with yelling from the marines and Holden's own crew. To Holden's left, Gomez yanked the elevator doors open using the augmented strength of his powered armor, exposing the empty shaft behind them.

"Inside!" Kelly shouted. "Everybody inside!"

Holden held back, pushing Naomi in, and then Alex. The last marine—the one Kelly had called Dookie—fired his rifle on full auto at some target around the corner from Holden. When the weapon ran dry, the marine dropped to one knee and ejected the clip in the same motion. Almost faster than Holden could follow, he pulled a new magazine from his harness and slapped it into his weapon. He was firing again less than two seconds after he'd run out.

Naomi yelled at Holden to get into the elevator shaft, and then a viselike hand grabbed his shoulder, yanked him off his magnetic grip on the floor, and hurled him through the open elevator doors.

"Get killed when I'm not babysitting," Lieutenant Kelly barked.

They shoved off the walls of the elevator shaft and flew down the long tunnel toward the aft of the ship. Holden kept looking back at the open door, receding into the distance behind them.

"Dookie isn't following us," he said.

"He's covering our exit," Kelly replied.

"So we better get away," Gomez added. "Make it mean something."

Kelly, at the head of the group, grabbed at a rung on the wall of the shaft and came to a jerking stop. Everyone else followed suit.

"Here's our exit. Gomez, go check it out," Kelly said. "Holden, here's the plan. We'll be taking one of the corvettes from the hangar bay."

That made sense to Holden. The corvette class was a light frigate. A fleet escort vessel, it was the smallest naval ship equipped with an Epstein drive. It would be fast enough to travel anywhere in the system and outrun most threats. Its secondary role was as a torpedo bomber, so it would also have teeth. Holden nodded inside his helmet at Kelly, then gestured for him to continue. Kelly waited until Gomez had finished opening the elevator doors and gone into the hangar bay.

"Okay, I've got the key card and activation code to get us inside and the ship fired up. I'll be heading straight for it, so all of you stick right on my ass. Make sure your boot mags are off. We're going to push off the wall and fly to it, so aim straight or you miss your ride. Everyone with me?"

Affirmative replies all around.

"Outstanding. Gomez, what's it look like out there?"

"Trouble, El Tee. Half a dozen boarders looking over the ships in the hangar. Powered armor, zero-g maneuvering packs, and heavy weapons. Loaded for bear," Gomez whispered back. People always whispered when they were hiding. Wrapped in a space suit and surrounded by vacuum, Gomez could have been lighting fireworks inside his armor and no one would have heard it, but he whispered.

"We run for the ship and shoot our way through," Kelly said. "Gomez, I'm bringing the civvies in ten seconds. You're covering fire. Shoot and displace. Try and make them think you're a small platoon."

"You callin' me small, sir?" Gomez said. "Six dead assholes coming up."

Holden, Amos, Alex, and Naomi followed Kelly out of the elevator shaft and into the hangar bay and stopped behind a stack of military-green crates. Holden peeked over them, spotting the boarders immediately. They were in two groups of three near the *Knight,* one group walking on top of it and the other on the deck below it. Their armor was flat black. Holden hadn't seen the design before.

Kelly pointed at them and looked at Holden. Holden nodded back. Kelly pointed across the hangar at a squat black frigate about twenty-five meters away, halfway between them and the *Knight.* He held up his left hand and began counting down from five on his fingers. At two, the room strobed like a disco: Gomez opening fire from a position ten meters from their own. The first barrage hit two of the boarders on top of the *Knight* and hurled them spinning off. A heartbeat later, a second burst was fired five meters from where Holden had seen the first. He would have sworn it was two different men.

Kelly folded up the last finger on his hand, planted his feet on the wall, and pushed off toward their corvette. Holden waited for Alex, Amos, and Naomi, then shoved off last. By the time he was in motion, Gomez was firing from a new location. One of the boarders on the deck pointed a large weapon toward the muzzle flash from Gomez's gun. Gomez and the crate he'd been taking cover behind disappeared in fire and shrapnel.

They were halfway to the ship and Holden was starting to think they might make it when a line of smoke crossed the room and intersected with Kelly, and the lieutenant disappeared in a flash of light.

Chapter Fourteen: Miller

The *Xinglong* died stupid. Afterward, everyone knew she was
one of thousands of small-time rock-hopping prospector
ships. The Belt was lousy with them: five- or six-family operations that had scraped together enough for a down payment and
set up operations. When it happened, they'd been three payments
behind, and their bank—Consolidated Holdings and Invest-
ments—had put a lien on the ship. Which, common wisdom had
it, was why they had disabled her transponder. Just honest folks
with a rust bucket to call their own trying to keep flying.

If you were going to make a poster of the Belter's dream, it
would have been the *Xinglong*.

The *Scipio Africanus*, a patrol destroyer, was due to head back
down toward Mars at the end of its two-year tour of the Belt.
They both headed for a captured cometary body a few hundred
thousand kilometers from Chiron to top off their water.

When the prospecting ship first came in range, the *Scipio* saw a fast-moving ship running dark and headed more or less in their direction. The official Martian press releases all said that the *Scipio* had tried repeatedly to hail her. The OPA pirate casts all said it was crap and that no listening station in the Belt had heard anything like that. Everyone agreed that the *Scipio* had opened its point defense cannons and turned the prospecting ship into glowing slag.

The reaction had been as predictable as elementary physics. The Martians were diverting another couple dozen ships to help "maintain order." The OPA's shriller talking heads called for open war, and fewer and fewer of the independent sites and casts were disagreeing with them. The great, implacable clockwork of war ticked one step closer to open fighting.

And someone on Ceres had put a Martian-born citizen named Enrique Dos Santos through eight or nine hours of torture and nailed the remains to a wall near sector eleven's water reclamation works. They identified him by the terminal that had been left on the floor along with the man's wedding ring and a thin faux-leather wallet with his credit access data and thirty thousand Europa-script new yen. The dead Martian had been affixed to the wall with a single-charge prospector's spike. Five hours afterward, the air recyclers were still laboring to get the acid smell out. The forensics team had taken their samples. They were about ready to cut the poor bastard down.

It always surprised Miller how peaceful dead people looked. However godawful the circumstances, the slack calm that came at the end looked like sleep. It made him wonder if when his turn came, he'd actually feel that last relaxation.

"Surveillance cameras?" he said.

"Been out for three days," his new partner said. "Kids busted 'em."

Octavia Muss was originally from crimes against persons, back before Star Helix split violence up into smaller specialties. From there, she'd been on the rape squad. Then a couple of months of crimes against children. If the woman still had a soul, it had been pressed thin enough to see through. Her eyes never registered anything more than mild surprise.

"We know which kids?"

"Some punks from upstairs," she said. "Booked, fined, released into the wild."

"We should round 'em back up," Miller said. "It'd be interesting to know whether someone paid them to take out these particular cameras."

"I'd bet against it."

"Then whoever did this had to know that these cameras were busted."

"Someone in maintenance?"

"Or a cop."

Muss smacked her lips and shrugged. She'd come from three generations in the Belt. She had family on ships like the one the *Scipio* had killed. The skin and bone and gristle hanging in front of them were no surprise to her. You dropped a hammer under thrust, and it fell to the deck. Your government slaughtered six families of ethnic Chinese prospectors, someone pinned you to the living rock of Ceres with a three-foot titanium alloy spike. Same same.

"There's going to be consequences," Miller said, meaning *This isn't a corpse, it's a billboard. It's a call to war.*

"There ain't," Muss said. *The war is here anyway, banner or no.*

"Yeah," Miller said. "You're right. There ain't."

"You want to do next of kin? I'll go take a look at outlying video. They didn't burn his fingers off here in the corridor, so they had to haul him in from somewhere."

"Yeah," Miller said. "I've got a sympathy form letter I can fire off. Wife?"

"Don't know," she said. "Haven't looked."

Back at the station house, Miller sat alone at his desk. Muss already had her own desk, two cubicles over and customized the way she liked it. Havelock's desk was empty and cleaned twice over, as if the custodial services had wanted the smell of Earth off their good Belter chair. Miller pulled up the dead man's file, found the next of kin. Jun-Yee Dos Santos, working on Ganymede. Married six years. No kids. Well, there was something to be glad of, at least. If you were going to die, at least you shouldn't leave a mark.

He navigated to the form letter, dropped in the new widow's name and contact address. *Dear Mrs. Dos Santos, I am very sorry to have to tell you* blah blah blah. *Your* [he spun through the menu] *husband was a valued and respected member of the Ceres community, and I assure you that everything possible will be done to see that her* [Miller toggled that] *his killer or killers will be brought to answer for this. Yours...*

It was inhuman. It was impersonal and cold and as empty as vacuum. The hunk of flesh on that corridor wall had been a real man with passions and fears, just like anyone else. Miller wanted to wonder what it said about him that he could ignore that fact so easily, but the truth was he knew. He sent the message and tried not to dwell on the pain it was about to cause.

The board was thick. The incident count was twice what it should have been. *This is what it looks like,* he thought. No riots. No hole-by-hole military action or marines in the corridors. Just a lot of unsolved homicides.

Then he corrected himself: *This is what it looks like so far.*

It didn't make his next task any easier.

Shaddid was in her office.

"What can I do for you?" she asked.

"I need to make some requisitions for interrogation transcripts," he said. "But it's a little irregular. I was thinking it might be better if it came through you."

Shaddid sat back in her chair.

"I'll look at it," she said. "What are we trying to get?"

Miller nodded, as if by signaling *yes* himself, he could get her to say the same.

"Jim Holden. The Earther from the *Canterbury*. Mars should

be picking his people up around now, and I need to petition for the debriefing transcripts."

"You have a case that goes back to the *Canterbury*?"

"Yeah," he said. "Seems like I do."

"Tell me," she said. "Tell me now."

"It's the side job. Julie Mao. I've been looking into it…"

"I saw your report."

"So you know she's associated with the OPA. From what I've found, it looks like she was on a freighter that was doing courier runs for them."

"You have proof of that?"

"I have an OPA guy that said as much."

"On the record?"

"No," Miller said. "It was informal."

"And it tied into the Martian navy killing the *Canterbury* how?"

"She was on the *Scopuli*," Miller said. "It was used as bait to stop the *Canterbury*. The thing is, you look at the broadcasts Holden makes, he talks about finding it with a Mars Navy beacon and no crew."

"And you think there's something in there that'll help you?"

"Won't know until I see it," Miller said. "But if Julie wasn't on that freighter, then someone had to take her off."

Shaddid's smile didn't reach her eyes.

"And you would like to ask the Martian navy to please hand over whatever they got from Holden."

"If he saw something on that boat, something that'll give us an idea what happened to Julie and the other—"

"You aren't thinking this through," Shaddid said. "The Mars Navy killed the *Canterbury*. They did it to provoke a reaction from the Belt so they'd have an excuse to roll in and take us over. The only reason they're 'debriefing' the survivors is so that no one could get to the poor bastards first. Holden and his crew are either dead or getting their minds cored out by Martian interrogation specialists right now."

"We can't be sure…"

"And even if I could get a full record of what they said as each toenail got ripped off, it would do you exactly no good, Miller. The Martian navy isn't going to ask about the *Scopuli*. They know good and well what happened to the crew. They planted the *Scopuli*."

"Is that Star Helix's official stand?" Miller asked. The words were barely out of his mouth before he saw they'd been a mistake. Shaddid's face closed down like a light going out. Now that he'd said it, he saw the implied threat he'd just made.

"I'm just pointing out the source reliability issue," Shaddid said. "You don't go to the suspect and ask where they think you should look next. And the Juliette Mao retrieval isn't your first priority."

"I'm not saying it is," Miller said, chagrined to hear the defensiveness in his voice.

"We have a board out there that's full and getting fuller. Our first priorities are safety and continuity of services. If what you're doing isn't directly related to that, there are better things for you to be doing."

"This war—"

"Isn't our job," Shaddid said. "Our job is Ceres. Get me a final report on Juliette Mao. I'll send it through channels. We've done what we could."

"I don't think—"

"I do," Shaddid said. "We've done what we could. Now stop being a pussy, get your ass out there, and catch bad guys. Detective."

"Yes, Captain," Miller said.

Muss was sitting at Miller's desk when he got back to it, a cup in her hand that was either strong tea or weak coffee. She nodded toward his desktop monitor. On it, three Belters—two men and one woman—were coming out of a warehouse door, an orange plastic shipping container carried between them. Miller raised his eyebrows.

"Employed by an independent gas-hauling company. Nitrogen, oxygen. Basic atmospherics. Nothing exotic. Looks like they had the poor bastard in one of the company warehouses. I've sent forensics over to see if we can get any blood splatters for confirmation."

"Good work," Miller said.

Muss shrugged. *Adequate work,* she seemed to say.

"Where are the perps?" Miller asked.

"Shipped out yesterday," she said. "Flight plan logs them as headed for Io."

"Io?"

"Earth-Mars Coalition central," Muss said. "Want to put any money on whether they actually show up there?"

"Sure," Miller said. "I'll lay you fifty that they don't."

Muss actually laughed.

"I've put them on the alert system," she said. "Anyplace they land, the locals will have a heads-up and a tracking number for the Dos Santos thing."

"So case closed," Miller said.

"Chalk another one up for the good guys," Muss agreed.

The rest of the day was hectic. Three assaults, two of them overtly political and one domestic. Muss and Miller cleared all three from the board before the end of shift. There would be more by tomorrow.

After he clocked out, Miller stopped at a food cart near one of the tube stations for a bowl of vat rice and textured protein that approximated teriyaki chicken. All around him on the tube, normal citizens of Ceres read their newsfeeds and listened to music. A young couple half a car up from him leaned close to each other, murmuring and giggling. They might have been sixteen. Seventeen. He saw the boy's wrist snake up under the girl's shirt. She didn't protest. An old woman directly across from Miller slept, her head lolling against the wall of the car, her snores almost delicate.

These people were what it was all about, Miller told himself. Normal people living small lives in a bubble of rock surrounded by hard vacuum. If they let the station turn into a riot zone, let order fail, all these lives would get turned into kibble like a kitten in a meat grinder. Making sure it didn't happen was for people like him, Muss, even Shaddid.

So, a small voice said in the back of his mind, *why isn't it your job to stop Mars from dropping a nuke and cracking Ceres like an egg? What's the bigger threat to that guy standing over there, a few unlicensed whores or a Belt at war with Mars?*

What was the harm that could come from knowing what happened to the *Scopuli*?

But of course he knew the answer to that. He couldn't judge how dangerous the truth was until he knew it—which was itself a fine reason to keep going.

The OPA man, Anderson Dawes, was sitting on a cloth folding chair outside Miller's hole, reading a book. It was a real book— onionskin pages bound in what might have been actual leather. Miller had seen pictures of them before; the idea of that much weight for a single megabyte of data struck him as decadent.

"Detective."

"Mr. Dawes."

"I was hoping we could talk."

Miller was glad, as they went inside together, that he'd cleaned up a little. All the beer bottles had gone to the recycler. The tables and cabinets were dusted. The cushions on the chairs had all been mended or replaced. As Dawes took his seat, Miller realized he'd done the housework in anticipation of this meeting. He hadn't realized it until now.

Dawes put his book on the table, dug in his jacket pocket, and slid a thin black filmdrive across the table. Miller picked it up.

"What am I going to see on this?" he asked.

"Nothing you can't confirm in the records," Dawes answered.

"Anything fabricated?"

"Yes," Dawes said. His grin did nothing to improve his appearance. "But not by us. You asked about the police riot gear. It was signed for by a Sergeant Pauline Trikoloski for transfer to special services unit twenty-three."

"Special services twenty-three?"

"Yes," Dawes said. "It doesn't exist. Nor does Trikoloski. The equipment was all boxed up, signed for, and delivered to a dock. The freighter in the berth at the time was registered to the Corporaçõ do Gato Preto."

"Black Cat?"

"You know them?"

"Import-export, same as everyone else," Miller said with a shrug. "We investigated them as a possible front for the Loca Greiga. Never tied them down, though."

"You were right."

"You prove it?"

"Not my job," Dawes said. "But this might interest you. Automated docking logs for the ship when she left here and when she arrived on Ganymede. She's three tons lighter, not even counting reaction mass consumption. And the transit time is longer than the orbital mechanics projections."

"Someone met her," Miller said. "Transferred the gear to another ship."

"There's your answer," Dawes said. "Both of them. The riot gear was taken off the station by local organized crime. There aren't records to support it, but I think it's safe to assume that they also shipped out the personnel to use that gear."

"Where to?"

Dawes lifted his hands. Miller nodded. They were off station. Case closed. Another one for the good guys.

Damn.

"I've kept my part of our bargain," Dawes said. "You asked for information. I've gotten it. Now, are you going to keep your end?"

"Drop the Mao investigation," Miller said. It wasn't a question, and Dawes didn't act is if it were. Miller leaned back in his chair.

Juliette Andromeda Mao. Inner system heiress turned OPA courier. Pinnace racer. Brown belt, aiming for black.

"Sure, what the hell," he said. "It's not like I would have shipped her back home if I'd found her."

"No?"

Miller shifted his hands in a gesture that meant *Of course not.*

"She's a good kid," Miller said. "How would you feel if you were all grown up and Mommy could still pull you back home by your ear? It was a bullshit job from the start."

Dawes smiled again. This time it actually did help a little.

"I'm glad to hear you say that, Detective. And I won't forget the rest of our agreement. When we find her, I *will* tell you. You've got my word on it."

"I appreciate that," Miller said.

There was a moment of silence. Miller couldn't decide if it was companionable or awkward. Maybe there was room for both. Dawes rose, put out his hand. Miller shook it. Dawes left. Two cops working for different sides. Maybe they had something in common.

Didn't mean Miller was uncomfortable lying to the man.

He opened his terminal's encryption program, routed it to his communication suite, and started talking into the camera.

"We haven't met, sir, but I hope you'll find a few minutes to help me out. I'm Detective Miller with Star Helix Security. I'm on the Ceres security contract, and I've been tasked with finding your daughter. I've got a couple questions."

Chapter Fifteen: Holden

Holden grabbed for Naomi. He struggled to orient himself as the two of them spun across the bay with nothing to push off of and nothing to arrest their flight. They were in the middle of the room with no cover.

The blast had hurled Kelly five meters through the air and into the side of a packing crate, where he was floating now, one magnetic boot connected to the side of the container, the other struggling to connect with the deck. Amos had been blown down, and lay flat on the floor, his lower leg stuck out at an impossible angle. Alex crouched at his side.

Holden craned his neck, looking toward the attackers. There was the boarder with the grenade launcher who had blasted Kelly, lining up on them for the killing shot. *We're dead*, Holden thought. Naomi made an obscene gesture.

The man with the grenade launcher shuddered and dissolved in a spray of blood and small detonations.

"Get to the ship!" Gomez screamed from the radio. His voice was grating and high, half shrieking pain and half battle ecstasy.

Holden pulled the tether line off Naomi's suit.

"What are you...?" she began.

"Trust me," he said, then put his feet into her stomach and shoved off, hard. He hit the deck while she spun toward the ceiling. He kicked on his boot mags and then yanked the tether to pull her down to him.

The room strobed with sustained machine gun fire. Holden said, "Stay low," and ran as quickly as his magnetic boots would allow toward Alex and Amos. The mechanic moved his limbs feebly, so he was still alive. Holden realized he still had the end of Naomi's tether in his hand, so he clipped it on to a loop on his suit. No more getting separated.

Holden lifted Amos off the deck, then checked the inertia. The mechanic grunted and muttered something obscene. Holden attached Amos' tether to his suit too. He'd carry the whole crew if that was what it took. Without saying a word, Alex clipped his tether to Holden and gave him a weary thumbs-up.

"That was...I mean, *fuck*," Alex said.

"Yeah," Holden said.

"Jim," Naomi said. "Look!"

Holden followed her gaze. Kelly was staggering toward them. His armor was visibly crushed on the left side of his torso, and hydraulic fluid leaked from his suit into a trail of droplets floating behind him, but he was moving—toward the frigate.

"Okay," Holden said. "Let's go."

The five of them moved as a group to the ship, the air around them filled with pieces of packing crates blown apart by the ongoing battle. A wasp stung Holden's arm, and his suit's head-up display informed him that it had sealed a minor breach. He felt something warm trickle down his bicep.

Gomez shouted like a madman over the radio as he dashed

around the outer edge of the bay, firing wildly. The return fire was constant. Holden saw the marine hit again and again, small explosions and ablative clouds coming off his suit until Holden could hardly believe that there could be anything inside it still living. But Gomez kept the enemy's attention, and Holden and the crew were able to limp up to the half cover of the corvette's airlock.

Kelly pulled a small metal card from a pocket on his armor. A swipe of the card opened the outer door, and Holden pulled Amos' floating body inside. Naomi, Alex, and the wounded marine came in after, staring at each other in shocked disbelief as the airlock cycled and the inner doors opened.

"I can't believe we…" Alex said; then his voice trailed off.

"Talk about it later," Kelly barked. "Alex Kamal, you served on MCRN ships. Can you fly this thing?"

"Sure, El Tee," Alex replied, then visibly straightened. "Why me?"

"Our other pilot's outside getting killed. Take this," Kelly said, handing him the metal card. "The rest of you, get strapped in. We've lost a lot of time."

Up close, the damage to Kelly's armor was even more apparent. He had to have severe injuries to his chest. And not all the liquid coming out of the suit was hydraulic fluid. There was definitely blood as well.

"Let me help you," Holden said, reaching for him.

"Don't touch me," Kelly said, with an anger that took Holden by surprise. "You get strapped in, and you shut the fuck up. Now."

Holden didn't argue. He unhooked the tethers from his suit and helped Naomi maneuver Amos to the crash couches and strap him in. Kelly stayed on the deck above, but his voice came over the ship's comm.

"Mr. Kamal, are we ready to fly?" he said.

"Roger that, El Tee. The reactor was already hot when we got here."

"The *Tachi* was the ready standby. That's why we're taking her. Now go. As soon as we clear the hangar, full throttle."

"Roger," Alex said.

Gravity returned in tiny bursts at random directions as Alex lifted the ship off the deck and spun it toward the hangar door. Holden finished putting on his straps and checked to see that Naomi and Amos were squared away. The mechanic was moaning and holding on to the edge of the couch with a death grip.

"You still with us, Amos?" Holden said.

"Fan-fucking-tastic, Cap."

"Oh shit, I can see Gomez," Alex said over the comm. "He's down. Aw, you goddammed bastards! They're shootin' him while he's down! Son of a bitch!"

The ship stopped moving, and Alex said in a quiet voice, "Suck on this, asshole."

The ship vibrated for half a second, then paused before continuing toward the lock.

"Point defense cannons?" Holden asked.

"Summary roadside justice," Alex grunted back.

Holden was imagining what several hundred rounds of Teflon-coated tungsten steel going five thousand meters per second would do to human bodies when Alex threw down the throttle and a roomful of elephants swan dived onto his chest.

Holden woke in zero g. His eye sockets and testicles ached, so they'd been at high thrust for a while. The wall terminal next to him said it had been almost half an hour. Naomi was moving in her couch, but Amos was unconscious, and blood was coming out of a hole in his suit at an alarming rate.

"Naomi, check Amos," Holden croaked, his throat aching with the effort. "Alex, report."

"The *Donnie* went up behind us, Cap. Guess the marines didn't hold. She's gone," Alex said in a subdued voice.

"The six attacking ships?"

"I haven't seen any sign of them since the explosion. I'd guess they're toast."

Holden nodded to himself. Summary roadside justice, indeed. Boarding a ship was one of the riskiest maneuvers in naval combat. It was basically a race between the boarders rushing to the engine room and the collective will of those who had their fingers on the self-destruct button. After even one look at Captain Yao, Holden could have told them who'd lose *that* race.

Still. Someone had thought it was worth the risk.

Holden pulled his straps off and floated over to Amos. Naomi had opened an emergency kit and was cutting the mechanic's suit off with a pair of heavy scissors. The hole had been punched out by a jagged end of Amos' broken tibia when the suit had pushed against it at twelve g.

When she'd finished cutting the suit away, Naomi blanched at the mass of blood and gore that Amos' lower leg had turned into.

"What do we do?" Holden asked.

Naomi just stared at him, then barked out a harsh laugh.

"I have no idea," she said.

"But you—" Holden started. She talked right over him.

"If he were made of metal, I'd just hammer him straight and then weld everything into place," she said.

"I—"

"But he *isn't* made out of ship parts," she continued, her voice rising into a yell, "so why are you asking *me* what to do?"

Holden held up his hands in a placating gesture.

"Okay, got it. Let's just stop the bleeding for now, all right?"

"If Alex gets killed, are you going to ask me to fly the ship too?"

Holden started to answer and then stopped. She was right. Whenever he didn't know what to do, he handed off to Naomi. He'd been doing it for years. She was smart, capable, usually unflappable. She'd become a crutch, and she'd been through all the same trauma he had. If he didn't start paying attention, he'd break her, and he needed not to do that.

"You're right. I'll take care of Amos," he said. "You go up and check on Kelly. I'll be there in a few minutes."

Naomi stared at him until her breathing slowed, then said, "Okay," and headed to the crew ladder.

Holden sprayed Amos' leg with coagulant booster and wrapped it in gauze from the first aid kit. Then he called up the ship's database on the wall terminal and did a search on compound fractures. He was reading it with growing dismay when Naomi called.

"Kelly's dead," she said, her voice flat.

Holden's stomach dropped, and he gave himself three breaths to get the panic out of his voice.

"Okay. I'll need your help setting this bone. Come on back down. Alex? Give me half a g of thrust while we work on Amos."

"Any particular direction, Cap?" Alex asked.

"I don't care, just give me half a g and stay off the radio till I say so."

Naomi dropped back down the ladder well as the gravity started to come up.

"It looks like every rib on the left side of Kelly's body was broken," she said. "Thrust g probably punctured all his organs."

"He had to know that was going to happen," Holden said.

"Yeah."

It was easy to make fun of the marines when they weren't listening. In Holden's navy days, making fun of jarheads was as natural as cussing. But four marines had died getting him off the *Donnager,* and three of them had made a conscious decision to do so. Holden promised himself that he'd never make fun of them again.

"We need to pull the bone straight before we set it. Hold him still, and I'll pull on his foot. Let me know when the bone has retracted and lined up again."

Naomi started to protest.

"I know you're not a doctor. Just best guess," Holden said.

It was one of the most horrible things Holden had ever done. Amos woke up screaming during the procedure. He had to pull the leg out twice, because the first time the bones didn't line up, and when he let go, the jagged end of the tibia popped back out the hole in a spray of blood. Fortunately, Amos passed out after that and they were able to make the second attempt without the screaming. It seemed to work. Holden sprayed the wound down with antiseptics and coagulants. He stapled the hole closed and slapped a growth-stimulating bandage over it, then finished up with a quick-form air-cast and an antibiotic patch on the mechanic's thigh.

Afterward he collapsed onto the deck and gave in to the shakes. Naomi climbed into her couch and sobbed. It was the first time Holden had ever seen her cry.

Holden, Alex, and Naomi floated in a loose triangle around the crash couch where Lieutenant Kelly's body lay. Below, Amos was in a heavily sedated sleep. The *Tachi* drifted through space toward no particular destination. For the first time in a long time, no one followed.

Holden knew the other two were waiting for him. Waiting to hear how he was going to save them. They looked at him expectantly. He tried to appear calm and thoughtful. Inside, he panicked. He had no idea where to go. No idea what to do. Ever since they'd found the *Scopuli*, everywhere that should have been safe had turned into a death trap. The *Canterbury*, the *Donnager*. Holden was terrified of going *anywhere*, for fear that it would be blown up moments later.

Do something, a mentor of a decade earlier said to his young officers. *It doesn't have to be right, it just has to be something.*

"Someone is going to investigate what happened to the *Donnager*," Holden said. "Martian ships are speeding to that spot as we speak. They'll already know the *Tachi* got away, because our transponder is blabbing our survival to the solar system at large."

"No it ain't," Alex said.

"Explain that, Mr. Kamal."

"This is a torpedo bomber. You think they want a nice transponder signal to lock on to when they're makin' runs on an enemy capital ship? Naw, there's a handy switch up in the cockpit that says 'transponder off.' I flipped it before we flew out. We're just another moving object out of a million like us."

Holden was silent for two long breaths.

"Alex, that may be the single greatest thing anyone has ever done, in the history of the universe," he said.

"But we can't land, Jim," Naomi said. "One, no port is going to let a ship with no transponder signal anywhere near them, and two, as soon as they make us out visually, the fact that we're a Martian warship will be hard to hide."

"Yep, that's the downside," Alex agreed.

"Fred Johnson," Holden said, "gave us the network address to get in touch with him. I'm thinking that the OPA might be the one group that would let us land our stolen Martian warship somewhere."

"It ain't stolen," Alex said. "It's legitimate salvage now."

"Yeah, you make that argument to the MCRN if they catch us, but let's try and make sure they don't."

"So, we just wait here till Colonel Johnson gets back to us?" Alex asked.

"No, I wait. You two prep Lieutenant Kelly for burial. Alex, you were MCRN. You know the traditions. Do it with full honors and record it in the log. He died to get us off that ship, and we're going to accord him every respect. As soon as we land anywhere, we'll bounce the full record to MCRN command so they can do it officially."

Alex nodded. "We'll do it right, sir."

Fred Johnson replied to his message so fast that Holden wondered if he'd been sitting at his terminal waiting for it. Johnson's message consisted only of coordinates and the word *tightbeam*. Holden aimed the laser array at the specified location—it was the same one Fred had beamed his first message from—then turned on his mic and said, "Fred?"

The coordinates given were more than eleven light-minutes

away. Holden prepared to wait twenty-two minutes for his answer. Just to have something to do, he fed the location up to the cockpit and told Alex to fly in that direction at one g as soon as they'd finished with Lieutenant Kelly.

Twenty minutes later the thrust came up and Naomi climbed the ladder. She'd stripped off her vacuum suit and was wearing a red Martian jumpsuit that was half a foot too short for her and three times too big around. Her hair and face looked clean.

"This ship has a head with a shower. Can we keep it?" she said.

"How'd it go?"

"We took care of him. There's a decent-sized cargo bay down by engineering. We put him there until we can find some way to send him home. I turned off the environment in there, so he'll stay preserved."

She held out her hand and dropped a small black cube into his lap.

"That was in a pocket under his armor," she said.

Holden held up the object. It looked like some sort of data-storage device.

"Can you find out what's on it?" he asked.

"Sure. Give me some time."

"And Amos?"

"Blood pressure's steady," Naomi said. "That's got to be a good thing."

The comm console beeped at them, and Holden started the playback.

"Jim, news of the *Donnager* has just started hitting the net. I admit I am extremely surprised to be hearing from you," said Fred's voice. "What can I do for you?"

Holden paused a moment while he mentally prepared his response. Fred's suspicion was palpable, but he'd sent Holden a keyword to use for exactly that reason.

"Fred. While our enemies have become *ubiquitous,* our list of friends has grown kind of short. In fact, you're pretty much it. I am in a stolen—"

Alex cleared his throat.

"A *salvaged* MCRN gunboat," Holden went on. "I need a way to hide that fact. I need somewhere to go where they won't just shoot me down for showing up. Help me do that."

It was half an hour before the reply came.

"I've attached a datafile on a subchannel," Fred said. "It's got your new transponder code and directions on how to install it. The code will check out in all the registries. It's legitimate. It's also got coordinates that will get you to a safe harbor. I'll meet you there. We have a lot to talk about."

"New transponder code?" Naomi said. "How does the OPA get new transponder codes?"

"Hack the Earth-Mars Coalition's security protocols or get a mole in the registry office," Holden said. "Either way, I think we're playing in the big league now."

Chapter Sixteen: Miller

Miller watched the feed from Mars along with the rest of the station. The podium was draped in black, which was a bad sign. The single star and thirty stripes of the Martian Congressional Republic hung in the background not once, but eight times. That was worse.

"This cannot happen without careful planning," the Martian president said. "The information they sought to steal would have compromised Martian fleet security in a profound and fundamental way. They failed, but at the price of two thousand and eighty-six Martian lives. This aggression is something the Belt has been preparing for years at the least."

The Belt, Miller noticed. Not the OPA—the Belt.

"In the week since first news of that attack, we have seen thirty incursions into the security radius of Martian ships and bases, including Pallas Station. If those refineries were to be lost, the economy of Mars could suffer irreversible damage. In the face of an armed, organized guerrilla force, we have no choice but to enforce a military cordon on the stations, bases, and ships of the Belt. Congress has delivered new orders to all naval elements not presently involved in active Coalition duty, and it is our hope that our brothers and sisters of Earth will approve joint Coalition maneuvers with the greatest possible speed.

"The new mandate of the Martian navy is to secure the safety of all honest citizens, to dismantle the infrastructures of evil presently hiding in the Belt, and bring to justice those responsible for these attacks. I am pleased to say that our initial actions have resulted in the destruction of eighteen illegal warships and—"

Miller turned off the feed. That was it, then. The secret war was out of the closet. Papa Mao had been right to want Julie out, but it was too late. His darling daughter was going to have to take her chances, just like everyone else.

At the very least, it was going to mean curfews and personnel tracking all through Ceres Station. Officially, the station was neutral. The OPA didn't own it or anything else. And Star Helix was an Earth corporation, not under contractual or treaty obligation to Mars. At best, Mars and the OPA would keep their fight outside the station. At worst, there would more riots on Ceres. More death.

No, that wasn't true. At worst, Mars or the OPA would make a statement by throwing a rock or a handful of nuclear warheads at the station. Or by blowing a fusion drive on a docked ship. If things got out of hand, it would mean six or seven million dead people and the end of everything Miller had ever known.

Odd that it should feel almost like relief.

For weeks, Miller had known. Everyone had known. But it hadn't actually happened, so every conversation, every joke, every chance interaction and semi-anonymous nod and polite moment of light banter on the tube had seemed like an evasion. He couldn't fix the cancer of war, couldn't even slow down the spread, but at least he could admit it was happening. He stretched, ate his last bite of fungal curds, drank the dregs of something not entirely unlike coffee, and headed out to keep peace in wartime.

Muss greeted him with a vague nod when he got to the station house. The board was filled with cases—crimes to be investigated, documented, and dismissed. Twice as many entries as the day before.

"Bad night," Miller said.

"Could be worse," Muss said.

"Yeah?"

"Star Helix could be a Mars corporation. As long as Earth stays neutral, we don't have to actually be the Gestapo."

"And how long you figure that'll last?"

"What time is it?" she asked. "Tell you what, though. When it does come down, I need to make a stop up toward the core. There was this one guy back when I was rape squad we could never quite nail."

"Why wait?" Miller asked. "We could go up, put a bullet in him, be back by lunch."

"Yeah, but you know how it is," she said. "Trying to stay professional. Anyway, if we did that, we'd have to investigate it, and there's no room on the board."

Miller sat at his desk. It was just shoptalk. The kind of over-the-top deadpan you did when your day was filled with underage whores and tainted drugs. And still, there was a tension in the station. It was in the way people laughed, the way they held themselves. There were more holsters visible than usual, as if by showing their weapons they might be made safe.

"You think it's the OPA?" Muss asked. Her voice was lower now.

"That killed the *Donnager,* you mean? Who else could? Plus which, they're taking credit for it."

"Some of them are. From what I heard, there's more than one OPA these days. The old-school guys don't know a goddamn thing about any of this. All shitting their pants and trying to track down the pirate casts that are claiming credit."

"So they can do what?" Miller asked. "You can shut down every loudmouth caster in the Belt, it won't change a thing."

"If there's a schism in the OPA, though..." Muss looked at the board.

If there was a schism within the OPA, the board as they saw it now was nothing. Miller had lived through two major gang wars. First when the Loca Greiga displaced and destroyed the Aryan Flyers, and then when the Golden Bough split. The OPA was bigger, and meaner, and more professional than any of them. That would be civil war in the Belt.

"Might not happen," Miller said.

Shaddid stepped out of her office, her gaze sweeping the station house. Conversations dimmed. Shaddid caught Miller's eye. She made a sharp gesture. *Get in the office.*

"Busted," Muss said.

In the office, Anderson Dawes sat at ease on one of the chairs. Miller felt his body twitch as that information fell into place. Mars and the Belt in open, armed conflict. The OPA's face on Ceres sitting with the captain of the security force.

So that's how it is, he thought.

"You're working the Mao job," Shaddid said as she took her seat. Miller hadn't been offered the option of sitting, so he clasped his hands behind him.

"You assigned it to me," he said.

"And I told you it wasn't a priority," she said.

"I disagreed," Miller said.

Dawes smiled. It was a surprisingly warm expression, especially compared to Shaddid's.

"Detective Miller," Dawes said. "You don't understand what's happening here. We are sitting on a pressure vessel, and you keep swinging a pickax at it. You need to stop that."

"You're off the Mao case," Shaddid said. "Do you understand that? I am officially removing you from that investigation as of right now. Any further investigation you do, I will have you disciplined for working outside your caseload and misappropriating

Star Helix resources. You will return any material on the case to me. You will wipe any data you have in your personal partition. And you'll do it before the end of shift."

Miller's brain spun, but he kept his face impassive. She was taking Julie away. He wasn't going to let her. That was a given. But it wasn't the first issue.

"I have some inquiries in process…" he began.

"No, you don't," Shaddid said. "Your little letter to the parents was a breach of policy. Any contact with the shareholders should have come through me."

"You're telling me it didn't go out," Miller said. Meaning *You've been monitoring me.*

"It did not," Shaddid said. *Yes, I have. What are you going to do about it?*

And there wasn't anything he could do.

"And the transcripts of the James Holden interrogation?" Miller said. "Did those get out before…"

Before the *Donnager* was destroyed, taking with it the only living witnesses to the *Scopuli* and plunging the system into war? Miller knew the question sounded like a whine. Shaddid's jaw tensed. He wouldn't have been surprised to hear teeth cracking. Dawes broke the silence.

"I think we can make this a little easier," he said. "Detective, if I'm hearing you right, you think we're burying the issue. We aren't. But it's not in anyone's interests that Star Helix be the one to find the answers you're looking for. Think about it. You may be a Belter, but you're working for an Earth corporation. Right now, Earth is the only major power without an oar in the water. The only one who can possibly negotiate with all sides."

"And so why wouldn't they want to know the truth?" Miller said.

"That isn't the problem," Dawes said. "The problem is that Star Helix and Earth can't appear to be involved one way or the other. Their hands need to stay clean. And this issue leads outside your contract. Juliette Mao isn't on Ceres, and maybe there was a time you could have jumped a ship to wherever you found her and done the abduction. Extradition. Extraction. Whatever you want to call it. But that time has passed. Star Helix is Ceres, part of Ganymede, and a few dozen warehouse asteroids. If you leave that, you're going into enemy territory."

"But the OPA isn't," Miller said.

"We have the resources to do this right," Dawes said with a nod. "Mao is one of ours. The *Scopuli* was one of ours."

"And the *Scopuli* was the bait that killed the *Canterbury*," Miller said. "And the *Canterbury* was the bait that killed the *Donnager.* So why exactly would anyone be better off having you be the only ones looking into something you might have done?"

"You think we nuked the *Canterbury*," Dawes said. "The OPA, with its state-of-the-art Martian warships?"

"It got the *Donnager* out where it could be attacked. As long as it was with the fleet, it couldn't have been boarded."

Dawes looked sour.

"Conspiracy theories, Mr. Miller," he said. "If we had cloaked Martian warships, we wouldn't be losing."

"You had enough to kill the *Donnager* with just six ships."

"No. We didn't. Our version of blowing up the *Donnager* is a whole bunch of tramp prospectors loaded with nukes going on a suicide mission. We have many, many resources. What happened to the *Donnager* wasn't part of them."

The silence was broken only by the hum of the air recycler. Miller crossed his arms.

"But...I don't understand," he said. "If the OPA didn't start this, who did?"

"That is what Juliette Mao and the crew of the *Scopuli* can tell us," Shaddid said. "Those are the stakes, Miller. Who and why and please Christ some idea of how to stop it."

"And you don't want to find them?" Miller said.

"I don't want *you* to," Dawes said. "Not when someone else can do it better."

Miller shook his head. It was going too far, and he knew it. On the other hand, sometimes going too far could tell you something too.

"I'm not sold," he said.

"You don't have to be *sold*," Shaddid said. "This isn't a negotiation. We aren't bringing you in to ask you for a goddamn favor. I am your boss. I am telling you. Do you know those words? Telling. You."

"We have Holden," Dawes said.

"What?" Miller said at the same time Shaddid said, "You're not supposed to talk about that."

Dawes raised an arm toward Shaddid in the Belt's physical idiom of telling someone to be quiet. To Miller's surprise, she did as the OPA man said.

"We have Holden. He and his crew didn't die, and they are or are about to be in OPA custody. Do you understand what I'm saying, Detective? Do you see my point? I can do this investigation because I have the resources to do it. *You* can't even find out what happened to your own riot gear."

It was a slap. Miller looked at his shoes. He'd broken his word to Dawes about dropping the case, and the man hadn't brought it up until now. He had to give the OPA operative points for that. Added to that, if Dawes really did have James Holden, there was no chance of Miller's getting access to the interrogation.

When Shaddid spoke, her voice was surprisingly gentle.

"There were three murders yesterday. Eight warehouses got broken into, probably by the same bunch of people. We've got six people in hospital wards around the station with their nerves falling apart from a bad batch of bathtub pseudoheroin. The whole station's jumpy," she said. "There's a lot of good you can do out there, Miller. Go catch some bad guys."

"Sure, Captain," Miller said. "You bet."

Muss leaned against his desk, waiting for him. Her arms were crossed, her eyes as bored looking at him as they had been looking at the corpse of Dos Santos pinned to the corridor wall.

"New asshole?" she asked.

"Yeah."

"It'll grow closed. Give it time. I got us one of the murders. Mid-level accountant for Naobi-Shears got his head blown off outside a bar. It looked fun."

Miller pulled up his hand terminal and took in the basics. His heart wasn't in it.

"Hey, Muss," he said. "I got a question."

"Fire away."

"You've got a case you don't want solved. What do you do?"

His new partner frowned, tilted her head, and shrugged.

"I hand it to a fish," she said. "There was a guy back in crimes against children. If we knew the perp was one of our informants, we'd always give it to him. None of our guys ever got in trouble."

"Yeah," Miller said.

"For that matter, I need someone to take the shitty partner, I do the same thing," Muss went on. "You know. Someone no one else wants to work with? Got bad breath or a shitty personality or whatever, but he needs a partner. So I pick the guy who maybe he used to be good, but then he got a divorce. Started hitting the bottle. Guy still thinks he's a hotshot. Acts like it. Only his numbers aren't better than anyone else's. Give him the shit cases. The shit partner."

Miller closed his eyes. His stomach felt uneasy.

"What did you do?" he asked.

"To get assigned to you?" Muss said. "One of the seniors made the moves on me and I shot him down."

"So you got stuck."

"Pretty much. Come on, Miller. You aren't stupid," Muss said. "You had to know."

He'd had to know that he was the station house joke. The guy who used to be good. The one who'd lost it.

No, actually he hadn't known that. He opened his eyes. Muss didn't look happy or sad, pleased at his pain or particularly distressed by it. It was just work to her. The dead, the wounded, the injured. She didn't care. Not caring was how she got through the day.

"Maybe you shouldn't have turned him down," Miller said.

"Ah, you're not that bad," Muss said. "And he had back hair. I hate back hair."

"Glad to hear it," Miller said. "Let's go make some justice."

"You're drunk," the asshole said.

"'M a cop," Miller said, stabbing the air with his finger. "Don't fuck with me."

"I know you're a cop. You've been coming to my bar for three years. It's me. Hasini. And you're drunk, my friend. Seriously, dangerously drunk."

Miller looked around him. He was indeed at the Blue Frog. He didn't remember having come here, and yet here he was. And the asshole was Hasini after all.

"I..." Miller began, then lost his train of thought.

"Come on," Hasini said, looping an arm around him. "It's not that far. I'll get you home."

"What time is it?" Miller asked.

"Late."

The word had a depth to it. *Late.* It was late. All the chances to make things right had somehow passed him. The system was at war, and no one was even sure why. Miller himself was turning fifty years old the next June. It was late. Late to start again. Late to realize how many years he'd spent running down the wrong road. Hasini steered him toward an electric cart the bar kept for occasions like this one. The smell of hot grease came out of the kitchen.

"Hold on," Miller said.

"You going to puke?" Hasini asked.

Miller considered for a moment. No, it was too late to puke. He stumbled forward. Hasini laid him back in the cart and engaged the motors, and with a whine they steered out into the corridor. The lights high above them were dimmed. The cart vibrated as they passed intersection after intersection. Or maybe it didn't. Maybe that was just his body.

"I thought I was good," he said. "You know, all this time, I thought I was at least good."

"You do fine," Hasini said. "You've just got a shitty job."

"That I was good at."

"You do fine," Hasini repeated, as if saying it would make it true.

Miller lay on the bed of the cart. The formed plastic arch of the wheel well dug into his side. It ached, but moving was too much effort. Thinking was too much effort. He'd made it through his day, Muss at his side. He'd turned in the data and materials on Julie. He had nothing worth going back to his hole for, and no place else to be.

The lights shifted into and out of his field of view. He wondered if that was what it would be like to look at stars. He'd never looked up at a sky. The thought inspired a certain vertigo. A sense of terror of the infinite that was almost pleasant.

"There anyone who can take care of you?" Hasini said when they reached Miller's hole.

"I'll be fine. I just...I had a bad day."

"Julie," Hasini said, nodding.

"How do you know about Julie?" Miller asked.

"You've been talking about her all night," Hasini said. "She's a girl you fell for, right?"

Frowning, Miller kept a hand on the cart. Julie. He'd been talking about Julie. That was what this was about. Not his job. Not his reputation. They'd taken away Julie. The special case. The one that mattered.

"You're in love with her," Hasini said.

"Yeah, sort of," Miller said, something like revelation forcing its way through the alcohol. "I think I am."

"Too bad for you," Hasini said.

Chapter Seventeen: Holden

The *Tachi*'s galley had a full kitchen and a table with room for twelve. It also had a full-size coffeepot that could brew forty cups of coffee in less than five minutes whether the ship was in zero g or under a five-g burn. Holden said a silent prayer of thanks for bloated military budgets and pressed the brew button. He had to restrain himself from stroking the stainless steel cover while it made gentle percolating noises.

The aroma of coffee began to fill the air, competing with the baking-bread smell of whatever Alex had put in the oven. Amos was thumping around the table in his new cast, laying out plastic plates and actual honest-to-god metal silverware. In a bowl Naomi was mixing something that had the garlic scent of good hummus. Watching the crew work at these domestic tasks, Holden had a sense of peace and safety deep enough to leave him light-headed.

They'd been on the run for weeks now, pursued the entire time by one mysterious ship or another. For the first time since the *Canterbury* was destroyed, no one knew where they were. No one was demanding anything of them. As far as the solar system was concerned, they were a few casualties out of thousands on the *Donnager*. A brief vision of Shed's head disappearing like a grisly magic trick reminded him that at least one of his crew *was* a casualty. And still, it felt so good to once again be master of his own destiny that even regret couldn't entirely rob him of it.

A timer rang, and Alex pulled out a tray covered with thin, flat bread. He began cutting it into slices, onto which Naomi slathered a paste that did in fact look like hummus. Amos put them on the plates around the table. Holden drew fresh coffee into mugs that had the ship's name on the side. He passed them around. There was an awkward moment when everyone stared at the neatly set table without moving, as if afraid to destroy the perfection of the scene.

Amos solved this by saying, "I'm hungry as a fucking bear," and then sitting down with a thump. "Somebody pass me that pepper, wouldja?"

For several minutes, no one spoke; they only ate. Holden took a small bite of the flat bread and hummus, the strong flavors making him dizzy after weeks of tasteless protein bars. Then he was stuffing it into his mouth so fast it made his salivary glands flare with exquisite agony. He looked around the table, embarrassed, but everyone else was eating just as fast, so he gave up on propriety and concentrated on food. When he'd finished off the last scraps from his plate, he leaned back with a sigh, hoping to make the contentment last as long as possible. Alex sipped coffee with his eyes closed. Amos ate the last bits of the hummus right out of the serving bowl with his spoon. Naomi gave Holden a sleepy look through half-lidded eyes that was suddenly sexy as hell. Holden quashed that thought and raised his mug.

"To Kelly's marines. Heroes to the last, may they rest in peace," he said.

"To the marines," everyone at the table echoed, then clinked mugs and drank.

Alex raised his mug and said, "To Shed."

"Yeah, to Shed, and to the assholes who killed him roasting in hell," Amos said in a quiet voice. "Right beside the fucker who killed the *Cant*."

The mood at the table got somber. Holden felt the peaceful moment slipping away as quietly as it had come.

"So," he said. "Tell me about our new ship. Alex?"

"She's a beaut, Cap. I ran her at twelve g for most of half an hour when we left the *Donnie*, and she purred like a kitten the whole time. The pilot's chair is comfy too."

Holden nodded.

"Amos? Get a chance to look at her engine room yet?" he asked.

"Yep. Clean as a whistle. This is going to be a boring gig for a grease monkey like me," the mechanic replied.

"Boring would be nice," Holden said. "Naomi? What do you think?"

She smiled. "I love it. It's got the nicest showers I've ever seen on a ship this size. Plus, there's a truly amazing medical bay with a computerized expert system that knows how to fix broken marines. We should have found it rather than fix Amos on our own."

Amos thumped his cast with one knuckle.

"You guys did a good job, Boss."

Holden looked around at his clean crew and ran a hand through his own hair, not pulling it away covered in grease for the first time in weeks.

"Yeah, a shower and not having to fix broken legs sounds good. Anything else?"

Naomi tilted her head back, her eyes moving as though she was running through a mental checklist.

"We've got a full tank of water, the injectors have enough fuel pellets to run the reactor for about thirty years, and the galley is fully stocked. You'll have to tie me up if you plan to give her back to the navy. I love her."

"She is a cunning little boat," Holden said with a smile. "Have a chance to look at the weapons?"

"Two tubes and twenty long-range torpedoes with high-yield plasma warheads," Naomi said. "Or at least that's what the manifest says. They load those from the outside, so I can't physically verify without climbing around on the hull."

"The weapons panel is sayin' the same thing, Cap," Alex said. "And full loads in all the point defense cannons. You know, except..."

Except the burst you fired into the men who killed Gomez.

"Oh, and, Captain, when we put Kelly in the cargo hold, I found a big crate with the letters MAP on the side. According to the manifest, it stands for 'Mobile Assault Package.' Apparently navy-speak for a big box of guns," Naomi said.

"Yeah," Alex said. "It's full kit for eight marines."

"Okay," Holden said. "So with the fleet-quality Epstein, we've got legs. And if you guys are right about the weapons load out, we've also got teeth. The next question is what do we do with it? I'm inclined to take Colonel Johnson's offer of refuge. Any thoughts?"

"I'm all for that, Captain," Amos said. "I always did think the Belters were getting the short end of the stick. I'll go be a revolutionary for a while, I guess."

"Earthman's burden, Amos?" Naomi asked with a grin.

"What the fuck does that even mean?"

"Nothing, just teasing," she said. "I know you like our side because you just want to steal our women."

Amos grinned back, suddenly in on the joke.

"Well, you ladies do have the legs that go *all* the way up," he said.

"Okay, enough," Holden said, raising his hand. "So, two votes for Fred. Anyone else?"

Naomi raised her hand.

"I vote for Fred," she said.

"Alex? What do you think?" Holden asked.

The Martian pilot leaned back in his chair and scratched his head.

"I got nowhere in particular to be, so I'll stick with you guys, I guess," he said. "But I hope this don't turn into another round of bein' told what to do."

"It won't," Holden replied. "I have a ship with guns on it now, and the next time someone orders me to do something, I'm using them."

After dinner, Holden took a long, slow tour of his new ship. He opened every door, looked in every closet, turned on every panel, and read every readout. He stood in engineering next to the fusion reactor and closed his eyes, getting used to the almost subliminal vibration she made. If something ever went wrong with it, he wanted to feel it in his bones before any warning ever sounded. He stopped and touched all the tools in the well-stocked machine shop, and he climbed up to the personnel deck and wandered through the crew cabins until he found one he liked, and messed up the bed to show it was taken. He found a bunch of jumpsuits in what looked like his size, then moved them to the closet in his new room. He took a second shower and let the hot water massage knots in his back that were three weeks old. As he wandered back to his cabin, he trailed his fingers along the wall, feeling the soft give of the fire-retardant foam and anti-spalling webbing over the top of the armored steel bulkheads. When he arrived at his cabin, Alex and Amos were both getting settled into theirs.

"Which cabin did Naomi take?" he asked.

Amos shrugged. "She's still up in ops, fiddling with something."

Holden decided to put off sleep for a while and rode the keel ladder-lift—*we have a lift!*—up to the operations deck. Naomi was sitting on the floor, an open bulkhead panel in front of her and what looked like a hundred small parts and wires laid out around her in precise patterns. She was staring at something inside the open compartment.

"Hey, Naomi, you should really get some sleep. What are you working on?"

She gestured vaguely at the compartment.

"Transponder," she said.

Holden moved over and sat down on the floor next to her.

"Tell me how to help."

She handed him her hand terminal; Fred's instructions for changing the transponder signal were open on the screen.

"It's ready to go. I've got the console hooked up to the transponder's data port just like he says. I've got the computer program set up to run the override he describes. The new transponder code and ship registry data are ready to be entered. I put in the new name. Did Fred pick it?"

"No, that was me."

"Oh. All right, then. But…" Her voice trailed off, and she waved at the transponder again.

"What's the problem?" Holden asked.

"Jim, they make these things *not* to be fiddled with. The civilian version of this device fuses itself into a solid lump of silicon if it thinks it's being tampered with. Who knows what the military version of the fail-safe is? Drop the magnetic bottle in the reactor? Turn us into a supernova?"

Naomi turned to look at him.

"I've got it all set up and ready to go, but now I don't think we should throw the switch," she said. "We don't know the consequences of failure."

Holden got up off the floor and moved over to the computer console. A program Naomi had named Trans01 was waiting to be run. He hesitated for one second, then pressed the button to execute. The ship failed to vaporize.

"I guess Fred wants us alive, then," he said.

Naomi slumped down with a noisy, extended exhale.

"See, this is why I can't ever be in command," she said.

"Don't like making tough calls with incomplete information?"

"More I'm not suicidally irresponsible," she replied, and began slowly reassembling the transponder housing.

Holden punched the comm system on the wall. "Well, crew, welcome aboard the gas freighter *Rocinante*."

"What does that name even mean?" Naomi said after he let go of the comm button.

"It means we need to go find some windmills," Holden said over his shoulder as he headed to the lift.

Tycho Manufacturing and Engineering Concern was one of the first major corporations to move into the Belt. In the early days of expansion, Tycho engineers and a fleet of ships had captured a small comet and parked it in stable orbit as a water resupply point decades before ships like the *Canterbury* began bringing ice in from the nearly limitless fields in Saturn's rings. It had been the most complex, difficult feat of mass-scale engineering humanity had ever accomplished until the next thing they did.

As an encore, Tycho had built the massive reaction drives into the rock of Ceres and Eros and spent more than a decade teaching the asteroids to spin. They had been slated to create a network of high-atmosphere floating cities above Venus before the development rights fell into a labyrinth of lawsuits now entering its eighth decade. There was some discussion of space elevators for Mars and Earth, but nothing solid had come of it yet. If you had an impossible engineering job that needed to be done in the Belt, and you could afford it, you hired Tycho.

Tycho Station, the Belt headquarters of the company, was a massive ring station built around a sphere half a kilometer across, with more than sixty-five million cubic meters of manufacturing and storage space inside. The two counter-rotating habitation rings that circled the sphere had enough space for fifteen thousand workers and their families. The top of the manufacturing sphere was festooned with half a dozen massive construction waldoes that looked like they could rip a heavy freighter in half. The bottom of the sphere had a bulbous projection fifty meters across, which housed a capital-ship-class fusion reactor and drive system, making Tycho Station the largest mobile construction platform in the solar system. Each compartment within the massive rings was built on a swivel system that allowed the chambers to reorient to thrust gravity when the rings stopped spinning and the station flew to its next work location.

Holden knew all this, and his first sight of the station still took his breath away. It wasn't just the size of it. It was the idea that four generations of the smartest people in the solar system had been living and working here as they helped drag humanity into the outer planets almost through sheer force of will.

Amos said, "It looks like a big bug."

Holden started to protest, but it did resemble some kind of giant spider: fat bulbous body and all its legs sprouting from the top of its head.

Alex said, "Forget the station, look at *that* monster."

The vessel it was constructing dwarfed the station. Ladar returns told Holden the ship was just over two kilometers long and half a kilometer wide. Round and stubby, it looked like a cigarette butt made of steel. Framework girders exposed internal compartments and machinery at various stages of construction, but the engines looked complete, and the hull had been assembled over the bow. The name *Nauvoo* was painted in massive white letters across it.

"So the Mormons are going to ride that thing all the way to Tau Ceti, huh?" Amos asked, following it up with a long whistle. "Ballsy bastards. No guarantee there's even a planet worth a damn on the other end of that hundred-year trip."

"They seem pretty sure," Holden replied. "And you don't make the money to build a ship like that by being stupid. I, for one, wish them nothing but luck."

"They'll get the stars," Naomi said. "How can you not envy them that?"

"Their great-grandkids'll get maybe *a* star if they don't all starve to death orbiting a rock they can't use," Amos said. "Let's not get grandiose here."

He pointed at the impressively large comm array jutting from the *Nauvoo's* flank.

"Want to bet that's what threw our anus-sized tightbeam message?" Amos said.

Alex nodded. "If you want to send private messages home from a couple light-years away, you need serious beam coherence. They probably had the volume turned down to avoid cuttin' a hole in us."

Holden got up from the copilot's couch and pushed past Amos. "Alex, see if they'll let us land."

Landing was surprisingly easy. The station control directed them to a docking port on the side of the sphere and stayed on the line, guiding them in, until Alex had married the docking tube to the airlock door. The tower control never pointed out that they had a lot of armaments for a transport and no tanks for carrying compressed gas. She got them docked, then wished them a pleasant day.

Holden put on his atmosphere suit and made a quick trip to the cargo bay, then met the others just inside the *Rocinante's* inner airlock door with a large duffel.

"Put your suits on, that's now standard ops for this crew anytime we go someplace new. And take one of these," he said, pulling handguns and cartridge magazines from the bag. "Hide it in a pocket or your bag if you like, but I will be wearing mine openly."

Naomi frowned at him.

"Seems a bit…confrontational, doesn't it?"

"I'm tired of being kicked around," Holden said. "The *Roci's* a good start toward independence, and I'm taking a little piece of her with me. Call it a good luck charm."

"Fuckin' A," said Amos, and strapped one of the guns to his thigh.

Alex stuffed his into the pocket of his flight suit. Naomi wrinkled her nose and waved off the last gun. Holden put it back into his duffel, led the crew into the *Rocinante*'s airlock, and cycled it. An older, dark-skinned man with a heavy build waited for them on the other side. As they came in, he smiled.

"Welcome to Tycho Station," said the Butcher of Anderson Station. "Call me Fred."

Chapter Eighteen: Miller

The death of the *Donnager* hit Ceres like a hammer striking a gong. Newsfeeds clogged themselves with high-power telescopic footage of the battle, most if not all of it faked. The Belt chatter swam with speculation about a secret OPA fleet. The six ships that had taken down the Martian flagship were hailed as heroes and martyrs. Slogans like *We did it once and we can do it again* and *Drop some rocks* cropped up even in apparently innocuous settings.

The *Canterbury* had stripped away the complacency of the Belt, but the *Donnager* had done something worse. It had taken away the fear. The Belters had gotten a sudden, decisive, and unexpected win. Anything seemed possible, and the hope seduced them.

It would have scared Miller more if he'd been sober.

Miller's alarm had been going off for the past ten minutes. The grating buzz took on subtones and overtones when he listened to it long enough. A constant rising tone, fluttering percussion throbbing under it, even soft music hiding underneath the blare. Illusions. Aural hallucinations. The voice of the whirlwind.

The previous night's bottle of fungal faux bourbon sat on the bedside table where a carafe of water usually waited. It still had a couple fingers at the bottom. Miller considered the soft brown of the liquid, thought about how it would feel on his tongue.

The beautiful thing about losing your illusions, he thought, was that you got to stop pretending. All the years he'd told himself that he was respected, that he was good at his job, that all his sacrifices had been made for a reason fell away and left him with the clear, unmuddied knowledge that he was a functional alcoholic who had pared away everything good in his own life to make room for anesthetic. Shaddid thought he was a joke. Muss thought he was the price she paid not to sleep with someone she didn't like. The only one who might have any respect for him at all was Havelock, an Earther. It was peaceful, in its way. He could stop making the effort to keep up appearances. If he stayed in bed listening to the alarm drone, he was just living up to expectations. No shame in that.

And still there was work to be done. He reached over and turned off the alarm. Just before it cut off, he heard a voice in it, soft but insistent. A woman's voice. He didn't know what she'd been saying. But since she was just in his head, she'd get another chance later.

He levered himself out of bed, sucked down some painkillers and rehydration goo, stalked to the shower, and burned a day and a half's ration of hot water just standing there, watching his legs get pink. He dressed in his last set of clean clothes. Breakfast was a bar of pressed yeast and grape sweetener. He dropped the bourbon from the bedside table into the recycler without finishing it, just to prove to himself that he still could.

Muss was waiting at the desk. She looked up when he sat.

"Still waiting for the labs on the rape up on eighteen," she said. "They promised them by lunch."

"We'll see," Miller said.

"I've got a possible witness. Girl who was with the vic earlier in the evening. Her deposition said she left before anything happened, but the security cameras aren't backing her up."

"Want me in the questioning?" Miller asked.

"Not yet. But if I need some theater, I'll pull you in."

"Fair enough."

Miller didn't watch her walk away. After a long moment staring at nothing, he pulled up his disk partition, reviewed what still needed doing, and started cleaning the place up.

As he worked, his mind replayed for the millionth time the slow, humiliating interview with Shaddid and Dawes. *We have Holden,* Dawes said. *You can't even find out what happened to your own riot gear.* Miller poked at the words like a tongue at the gap of a missing tooth. It rang true. Again.

Still, it might have been bullshit. It might have been a story concocted just to make him feel small. There wasn't any proof, after all, that Holden and his crew had survived. What proof could there be? The *Donnager* was gone, and all its logs along with it. There would have to have been a ship that made it out. Either a rescue vessel or one of the Martian escort ships. There was no way a ship could have gotten out and not been the singular darling of every newsfeed and pirate cast since. You couldn't keep something like that quiet.

Or sure you could. It just wouldn't be easy. He squinted at the empty air of the station house. Now. How *would* you cover up a surviving ship?

Miller pulled up a cheap navigation plotter he'd bought five years before—transit times had figured in a smuggling case—and plotted the date and position of the *Donnager*'s demise. Anything running under non-Epstein thrust would still have been out there, and Martian warships would have either picked it up or blasted it into background radiation by now. So if Dawes wasn't just handing him bullshit, that meant an Epstein drive. He ran a couple quick calculations. With a good drive, someone could have made Ceres in just less than a month. Call it three weeks to be safe.

He looked at the data for almost ten minutes, but the next step didn't come to him, so he stepped away, got some coffee, and pulled up the interview he and Muss had done with a Belter ground-crew grunt. The man's face was long and cadaverous and subtly cruel. The recorder hadn't had a good fix on him, so the picture kept bouncing around. Muss asked the man what he'd seen, and Miller leaned forward to read the transcribed answers, checking for incorrectly recognized words. Thirty seconds later, the grunt said *clip whore* and the transcript read *clipper.* Miller corrected it, but the back of his mind kept churning.

Probably eight or nine hundred ships came into Ceres in a given day. Call it a thousand to be safe. Give it a couple days on either side of the three-week mark, that was only four thousand entries. Pain in the ass, sure, but not impossible. Ganymede would be the other real bitch. With its agriculture, there would be hundreds of transports a day there. Still, it wouldn't double the workload. Eros. Tycho. Pallas. How many ships docked on Pallas every day?

He'd missed almost two minutes of the recording. He started again, forcing himself to pay attention this time, and half an hour later, he gave up.

The ten busiest ports with two days to either side of an estimated arrival of an Epstein-drive ship that originated when and where the *Donnager* died totaled twenty-eight thousand docking records, more or less. But he could cut that down to seventeen thousand if he excluded stations and ports explicitly run by Martian military and research stations with all or nearly all inner planet inhabitants. So how long would it take him to check all the porting records by hand, pretending for a minute that he was stupid enough to do it? Call it 118 days — if he didn't eat or sleep. Just working ten-hour days, doing nothing else, he could almost get through it in less than a year. A little less.

Except no. Because there were ways to narrow it. He was only looking for Epstein drive ships. Most of the traffic at any of the ports would be local. Torch drive ships flown by prospectors and short-hop couriers. The economics of spaceflight made relatively few and relatively large ships the right answer for long flights. So take it down by, conservatively, three-quarters, and he was back in the close-to-four-thousand range again. Still hundreds of hours of work, but if he could think of some other filter that would just feed him the likely suspects…For instance, if the ship couldn't have filed a flight plan before the *Donnager* got killed.

The request interface for the port logs was ancient, uncomfortable, and subtly different from Eros to Ganymede to Pallas and on and on. Miller tacked the information requests on to seven different cases, including a month-old cold case on which he was only a consultant. Port logs were public and open, so he didn't particularly need his detective status to hide his actions. With any luck Shaddid's monitoring of him wouldn't extend to low-level, public-record poking around. And even if it did, he might get the replies before she caught on.

Never knew if you had any luck left unless you pushed it. Besides, there wasn't a lot to lose.

When the connection from the lab opened on his terminal, he almost jumped. The technician was a gray-haired woman with an unnaturally young face.

"Miller? Muss with you?"

"Nope," Miller said. "She's got an interrogation."

He was pretty sure that was what she'd said. The tech shrugged.

"Well, her system's not answering. I wanted to tell you we got a match off the rape you sent us. It wasn't the boyfriend. Her boss did it."

Miller nodded. "You put in for the warrant?" he asked.

"Yep," she said. "It's already in the file."

Miller pulled it up: STAR HELIX ON BEHALF OF CERES STATION AUTHORIZES AND MANDATES THE DETENTION OF IMMANUEL CORVUS DOWD PENDING ADJUDICATION OF SECURITY INCIDENT CCS-4949231. The judge's digital signature was listed in green. He felt a slow smile on his lips.

"Thanks," he said.

On the way out of the station, one of the vice squads asked him where he was headed. He said lunch.

The Arranha Accountancy Group had their offices in the nice part of the governmental quarter in sector seven. It wasn't Miller's usual stomping grounds, but the warrant was good on the whole station. Miller went to the secretary at the front desk—a good-looking Belter with a starburst pattern embroidered on his vest—and explained that he needed to speak with Immanuel Corvus Dowd. The secretary's deep-brown skin took on an ashy tone. Miller stood back, not blocking the exit, but keeping close.

Twenty minutes later, an older man in a good suit came through the front door, stopped in front of Miller, and looked him up and down.

"Detective Miller?" the man said.

"You'd be Dowd's lawyer," Miller said cheerfully.

"I am, and I would like to—"

"Really," Miller said. "We should do this now."

The office was clean and spare with light blue walls that lit themselves from within. Dowd sat at the table. He was young enough that he still looked arrogant, but old enough to be scared. Miller nodded to him.

"You're Immanuel Corvus Dowd?" he said.

"Before you continue, Detective," the lawyer said, "my client is involved with very high-level negotiations. His client base includes some of the most important people in the war effort. Before you make any accusations, you should be aware that I can and will have everything you've done reviewed, and if there is one mistake, you will be held responsible."

"Mr. Dowd," Miller said. "What I am about to do to you is literally the only bright spot in my day. If you could see your way clear to resisting arrest, I'd really appreciate it."

"Harry?" Dowd said, looking to his lawyer. His voice cracked a little.

The lawyer shook his head.

Back at the police cart, Miller took a long moment. Dowd,

handcuffed in the back, where everyone walking by could see him, was silent. Miller pulled up his hand terminal, noted the time of arrest, the objections of the lawyer, and a few other minor comments. A young woman in professional dress of cream-colored linen hesitated at the door of the accountancy. Miller didn't recognize her; she was no one involved with the rape case, or at least not the one he was working. Her face had the expressionless calm of a fighter. He turned, craning his neck to look at Dowd, humiliated and not looking back. The woman shifted her gaze to Miller. She nodded once. *Thank you.*

He nodded back. *Just doing my job.*

She went through the door.

Two hours later, Miller finished the last of the paperwork and sent Dowd off to the cells.

Three and a half hours later, the first of his docking log requests came in.

Five hours later, the government of Ceres collapsed.

Despite being full, the station house was silent. Detectives and junior investigators, patrolmen and desk workers, the high and the low, they all gathered before Shaddid. She stood at her podium, her hair pulled back tight. She wore her Star Helix uniform, but the insignia had been removed. Her voice was shaky.

"You've all heard this by now, but starting now, it's official. The United Nations, responding to requests from Mars, is withdrawing from its oversight and ... protection of Ceres Station. This is a peaceful transition. This is not a coup. I'm going to say that again. This isn't a coup. Earth is pulling out of here, we aren't pushing."

"That's bullshit, sir," someone shouted. Shaddid raised her hand.

"There's a lot of loose talk," Shaddid said. "I don't want to hear any of it from you. The governor's going to make the formal announcement at the start of the next shift, and we'll get more details then. Until we hear otherwise, the Star Helix contract is still in place. A provisional government is being formed with members drawn from local business and union representation. We are still the law on Ceres, and I expect you to behave appropriately. You will all be here for your shifts. You will be here on time. You will act professionally and within the scope of standard practice."

Miller looked over at Muss. His partner's hair was still unkempt from the pillow. It was pushing midnight for them both.

"Any questions?" Shaddid said in a voice that implied there ought not be.

Who's going to pay Star Helix? Miller thought. *What laws are we enforcing? What does Earth know that makes walking away from the biggest port in the Belt the smart move?*

Who's going to negotiate your peace treaty now?

Muss, seeing Miller's gaze, smiled.

"Guess we're hosed," Miller said.

"Had to happen," Muss agreed. "I better go. Got a stop to make."

"Up at the core?"

Muss didn't answer, because she didn't have to. Ceres didn't have laws. It had police. Miller headed back to his hole. The station hummed, the stone beneath him vibrating from the countless docking clamps and reactor cores, tubes and recyclers and pneumatics. The stone was alive, and he'd forgotten the small signs that proved it. Six million people lived here, breathed this air. Fewer than in a middle-sized city on Earth. He wondered if they were expendable.

Had it really gone so far that the inner planets would be willing to lose a major station? It seemed like it had if Earth was abandoning Ceres. The OPA would step in, whether it wanted to or not. The power vacuum was too great. Then Mars would call it an OPA coup. Then…Then what? Board it and put it under martial law? That was the good answer. Nuke it into dust? He couldn't quite bring himself to believe that either. There was just too much money involved. Docking fees alone would fuel a small national economy. And Shaddid and Dawes—much as he hated it—were right. Ceres under Earth contract had been the best hope for a negotiated peace.

Was there someone on Earth who didn't *want* that peace? Someone or something powerful enough to move the glacial bureaucracy of the United Nations to take action?

"What am I looking at, Julie?" he said to the empty air. "What did you see out there that's worth Mars and the Belt killing each other?"

The station hummed to itself, a quiet, constant sound too soft for him to hear the voices within it.

Muss didn't come to work in the morning, but there was a message on his system telling him she'd be in late. "Cleanup" was her only explanation.

To look at it, nothing about the station house had changed. The same people coming to the same place to do the same thing. No, that wasn't true. The energy was high. People were smiling, laughing, clowning around. It was a manic high, panic pressed through a cheesecloth mask of normalcy. It wasn't going to last.

They were all that separated Ceres from anarchy. They were the law, and the difference between the survival of six million people and some mad bastard forcing open all the airlocks or poisoning the recyclers rested on maybe thirty thousand people. People like him. Maybe he should have rallied, risen to the occasion like the rest of them. The truth was the thought made him tired.

Shaddid marched by and tapped him on the shoulder. He sighed, rose from his chair, and followed her. Dawes was in her office again, looking shaken and sleep deprived. Miller nodded to him. Shaddid crossed her arms, her eyes softer and less accusing than he'd become used to.

"This is going to be tough," she said. "We're facing something harder than anything we've had to do before. I need a team I can trust with my life. Extraordinary circumstances. You understand that?"

"Yeah," he said. "I got it. I'll stop drinking, get myself together."

"Miller. You're not a bad person at heart. There was a time you were a pretty good cop. But I don't trust you, and we don't have time to start over," Shaddid said, her voice as near to gentle as he had ever heard it. "You're fired."

Chapter Nineteen: Holden

Fred stood alone, hand outstretched, a warm and open smile on his broad face. There were no guards with assault rifles behind him. Holden shook Fred's hand and then started laughing. Fred smiled and looked confused but let Holden keep a grip on his hand, waiting for Holden to explain what was so funny.

"I'm sorry, but you have no idea how pleasant this is," Holden said. "This is *literally* the first time in over a month that I've gotten off a ship without it blowing up behind me."

Fred laughed with him now, an honest laugh that seemed to originate somewhere in his belly.

After a moment the man said, "You're quite safe here. We are the most protected station in the outer planets."

"Because you're OPA?" Holden asked.

Fred shook his head.

"No. We make campaign contributions to Earth and Mars

politicians in amounts that would make a Hilton blush," he said. "If anyone blows us up, half the UN assembly and all of the Martian Congress will be howling for blood. It's the problem with politics. Your enemies are often your allies. And vice versa."

Fred gestured to a doorway behind him and motioned for everyone to follow. The ride was short, but halfway through, gravity reappeared, shifting in a disorienting swoop. Holden stumbled. Fred looked chagrined.

"I'm sorry. I should have warned you about that. The central hub's null g. Moving into the ring's rotational gravity can be awkward the first time."

"I'm fine," Holden said. Naomi's brief smile might only have been his imagination.

A moment later the elevator door opened onto a wide carpeted corridor with walls of pale green. It had the reassuring smell of air scrubbers and fresh carpet glue. Holden wouldn't have been surprised to find they were piping "new space station" scent into the air. The doors that led off the corridor were made of faux wood distinguishable from the real thing only because nobody had that much money. Of all his crew, Holden was almost certainly the only one who had grown up in a house with real wooden furniture and fixtures. Amos had grown up in Baltimore. They hadn't seen a tree there in more than a century.

Holden pulled off his helmet and turned around to tell his crew to do the same, but theirs were already off. Amos looked up and down the corridor and whistled.

"Nice digs, Fred," he said.

"Follow me, I'll get you settled in," Fred replied, leading them down the corridor. As he walked, he spoke. "Tycho Station has undergone a number of refurbishments over the last hundred years, as you might guess, but the basics haven't changed much. It was a brilliant design to begin with; Malthus Tycho was an engineering genius. His grandson, Bredon, runs the company now. He isn't on station at the moment. Down the well at Luna negotiating the next big deal."

Holden said, "Seems like you have a lot on your plate already, with that monster parked outside. And, you know, a war going on."

A group of people in jumpsuits of various colors walked past, talking animatedly. The corridor was so wide that no one had to give way. Fred gestured at them as they went by.

"First shift's just ending, so this is rush hour," he said. "It's actually time to start drumming up new work. The *Nauvoo* is almost done. They'll be loading colonists on her in six months. Always have to have the next project lined up. The Tycho spends eleven million UN dollars every day she's in operation, whether we make money that day or not. It's a big nut to cover. And the war...well, we're hoping that's temporary."

"And now you're taking in refugees. That won't help," Holden said.

Fred just laughed and said, "Four more people won't put us in the poorhouse anytime soon."

Holden stopped, forcing the others to pull up short behind him. It was several steps before Fred noticed, then turned around with a confused look.

"You're dodging," Holden said. "Other than a couple billion dollars' worth of stolen Martian warship, we haven't got anything of value. Everyone thinks we're dead. Any access of our accounts ruins that, and I just don't live in a universe where Daddy War-bucks swoops in and makes everything okay out of the goodness of his heart. So either tell us why you're taking the risk of putting us up, or we go get back on our ship and try our hand at piracy."

"Scourge of the Martian merchant fleet, they'll call us," Amos growled from somewhere behind him. He sounded pleased.

Fred held up his hands. There was a hardness in his eyes, but also an amused respect.

"Nothing underhanded, you have my word," he said. "You're armed, and station security will allow you to carry guns when-ever you like. That alone should reassure you that I'm not plan-ning foul play. But let me get you settled in before we do much more talking, okay?"

Holden didn't move. Another group of returning workers was going by in the corridor, and they watched the scene curiously as they passed. Someone from the knot of people called out, "Everything okay, Fred?"

Fred nodded and waved them by impatiently. "Let's get out of the corridor at least."

"We aren't unpacking until we get some answers," Holden replied.

"Fine. We're almost there," Fred said, and then led them off again at a somewhat faster pace. He stopped at a small inset in the corridor wall with two doors in it. Opening one with the swipe of a card, he led the four of them into a large residential suite with a roomy living space and lots of seating.

"Bathroom is that door back there on the left. The bedroom is the one on the right. There's even a small kitchen space over here," Fred said, pointing to each thing as he spoke.

Holden sat down in a large brown faux-leather recliner and leaned it back. A remote control was in a pocket of the armrest. He assumed it controlled the impressively large screen that took up most of one wall. Naomi and Amos sat on a couch that matched his chair, and Alex draped himself over a loveseat in a nice contrasting cream color.

"Comfortable?" Fred asked, pulling a chair away from the six-seat dining area and sitting down across from Holden.

"It's all right," Holden said defensively. "My ship has a really nice coffeemaker."

"I suppose bribes won't work. You are all comfortable, though? We have two suites set aside for you, both this basic layout, though the other suite has two rooms. I wasn't sure of the, ah, sleeping arrangements..." Fred trailed off uncomfortably.

"Don't worry, Boss, you can bunk with me," Amos said with a wink at Naomi.

Naomi just smiled faintly.

"Okay, Fred, we're off the street," she said. "Now answer the captain's questions."

Fred nodded, then stood up and cleared his throat. He seemed to review something. When he spoke, the conversational facade was gone. His voice carried a grim authority.

"War between the Belt and Mars is suicide. Even if every rock hopper in the Belt were armed, we still couldn't compete with the Martian navy. We might kill a few with tricks and suicide runs. Mars might feel forced to nuke one of our stations to prove a point. But we can strap chemical rockets onto a couple hundred rocks the size of bunk beds and rain Armageddon down on Martian dome cities."

Fred paused, as if looking for words, then sat back down on his chair.

"All of the war drums ignore that. It's the elephant in the room. Anyone who doesn't live on a spaceship is structurally vulnerable. Tycho, Eros, Pallas, Ceres. Stations can't evade incoming missiles. And with all of the enemy's citizens living at the bottom of huge gravity wells, we don't even have to aim particularly well. Einstein was right. We will be fighting the next war with rocks. But the Belt has rocks that will turn the surface of Mars into a molten sea.

"Right now everyone is still playing nice, and only shooting at ships. Very gentlemanly. But sooner or later, one side or the other will be pressed to do something desperate."

Holden leaned forward, the slick surface of his environment suit making an embarrassing squeak on the leather textured chair. No one laughed.

"I agree. What does that have to do with us?" he asked.

"Too much blood has already been shed," Fred said.

Shed.

Holden winced at the bleak, unintentional pun but said nothing.

"The *Canterbury*," Fred continued. "The *Donnager.* People aren't just going to forget about those ships, and those thousands of innocent people."

"Seems like you just crossed off the only two options, Chief," Alex said. "No war, no peace."

"There's a third alternative. Civilized society has another way of dealing with things like this," Fred said. "A criminal trial."

Amos' snort shook the air. Holden had to fight not to smile himself.

"Are you fucking serious?" Amos asked. "And how do you put a goddamn Martian stealth ship on trial? Do we go question all the stealth ships about their whereabouts, double-check their alibis?"

Fred held up a hand.

"Stop thinking of the *Canterbury*'s destruction as an act of war," he said. "It was a crime. Right now, people are overreacting, but once the situation sinks in, heads will cool. People on both sides will see where this road goes and look for another way out. There is a window where the saner elements can investigate events, negotiate jurisdiction, and assign blame to some party or parties that both sides can agree to. A trial. It's the only outcome that doesn't involve millions of deaths and the collapse of human infrastucture."

Holden shrugged, a gesture barely visible in his heavy environment suit.

"So it goes to a trial. You still aren't answering my question."

Fred pointed at Holden, then at each of the crew in turn.

"You're the ace in the hole. You four people are the only eyewitnesses to the destruction of *both* ships. When the trial comes, I need you and your depositions. I have influence already through our political contacts, but you can buy me a seat at the table. It will be a whole new set of treaties between the Belt and the inner planets. We can do in months what I'd dreamed of doing in decades."

"And you want to use our value as witnesses to force your way into the process so you can make those treaties look the way you want them to," Holden said.

"Yes. And I'm willing to give you protection, shelter, and run of my station for as long as it takes to get there."

Holden took a long, deep breath, got up, and started unzipping his suit.

"Yeah, okay. That's just self-serving enough I believe it," he said. "Let's get settled in."

Naomi was singing karaoke. Just thinking about it made Holden's head spin. Naomi. Karaoke. Even considering everything that had happened to them over the past month, Naomi up onstage with a mic in one hand and some sort of fuchsia martini in the other, screaming out an angry Belt-punk anthem by the Moldy Filters, was the strangest thing he'd ever seen. She finished to scattered applause and a few catcalls, then staggered off the stage and collapsed across from him in the booth.

She held up her drink, sloshing a good half of it onto the table, then threw the other half back all at once.

"Whadja think?" Naomi asked, waving at the bartender for another.

"It was terrible," Holden replied.

"No, really."

"It was truly one of the most awful renditions of one of the most awful songs I've ever heard."

Naomi shook her head, blowing an exasperated raspberry at him. Her dark hair fell across her face and, when the bartender brought her a second brightly colored martini, foiled all her attempts at drinking. She finally grabbed her hair and held it above her head in a clump while she drank.

"You don't get it," she said. "It's *supposed* to be awful. That's the point."

"Then it was the best version of that song I've ever heard," Holden said.

"Damn straight." Naomi looked around the bar. "Where're Amos and Alex?"

"Amos found what I'm pretty sure was the most expensive hooker I've ever seen. Alex is in the back playing darts. He made some claims about the superiority of Martian darts players. I assume they're going to kill him and throw him out an airlock."

A second singer was onstage, crooning out some sort of Vietnamese power ballad. Naomi watched the singer for a while, sipping her drink, then said, "Maybe we should go save him."

"Which one?"

"Alex. Why would Amos need saving?"

"Because I'm pretty sure he told the expensive hooker he was on Fred's expense account."

"Let's mount a rescue mission; we can save them both," Naomi said, then drank the rest of her cocktail. "I need more rescue fuel, though."

She started waving at the bartender again, but Holden reached out and grabbed her hand and held it on the table.

"Maybe we should take a breather instead," he said.

A flush of anger as intense as it was brief lit her face. She pulled back her hand.

"You take a breather. I've just had two ships and a bunch of friends shot out from underneath me, and spent three weeks of dead time flying to get here. So, no. I'm getting another drink, and then doing another set. The crowd loves me," Naomi said.

"What about our rescue mission?"

"Lost cause. Amos will be murdered by space hookers, but at least he'll die the way he lived."

Naomi pushed her way up from the table, grabbed her martini off the bar, and headed toward the karaoke stage. Holden watched her go, then finished off the scotch he'd been nursing for the past two hours and got up.

For a moment there, he'd had a vision of the two of them staggering back to the room together, then falling into bed. He'd have hated himself in the morning for taking advantage, but he'd still have done it. Naomi was looking at him from the stage, and he realized he'd been staring. He gave a little wave, then headed out the door with only ghosts—Ade, Captain McDowell, Gomez and Kelly and Shed—to keep him company.

The suite was comfortable and huge and depressing. He'd lain on the bed less than five minutes before he was up and out the door again. He walked the corridor for half an hour, finding the big intersections that led to other parts of the ring. He found an electronics store and a teahouse and what on closer inspection turned out to be a very expensive brothel. He declined the video menu of services the desk clerk offered and wandered out again, wondering if Amos was somewhere inside.

He was halfway down a corridor he hadn't seen before when a small knot of teenage girls passed him. Their faces looked no older than fourteen, but they were already as tall as he was. They got quiet as he walked by, then burst out laughing when he was behind them, and hurried away. Tycho was a city, and he suddenly felt very much like a foreigner, unsure of where to go or what to do.

It was no surprise to him when he looked up from his wanderings and discovered he'd come to the elevator to the docking area. He punched the button and climbed inside, remembering to turn on his boot mags just in time to avoid being flung off his feet when the gravity twisted sideways and vanished.

Even though he'd only had possession of the ship for three weeks, climbing back onto the *Rocinante* felt like going home. Using gentle touches on the keel ladder, he made his way up to the cockpit. He pulled himself into the copilot's couch, strapped in, and closed his eyes.

The ship was silent. With the reactor off-line, and no one aboard, nothing was moving at all. The flexible docking tube that connected the *Roci* to the station transmitted very little vibration to the ship. Holden could close his eyes and drift in the straps and disconnect from everything around him.

It would have been peaceful except that every time he'd closed his eyes for the past month, the fading ghost lights behind his eyelids had been Ade winking and blowing away like dust. The voice at the back of his head was McDowell's as he tried to save his ship right up to the very last second. He wondered if he'd have them for the rest of his life, coming out to haunt him every time he found a moment of quiet.

He remembered the old-timers from his navy days. Grizzled lifers who could soundly sleep while two meters away their shipmates played a raucous game of poker or watched the vids with the volume all the way up. Back then he'd assumed it was just learned behavior, the body adapting so it could get enough rest in an environment that never really had downtime. Now he wondered if those vets found the constant noise preferable. A way to keep their lost shipmates away. They probably went home after their twenty and never slept again. He opened his eyes and watched a small green telltale blink on the pilot's console.

It was the only light in the room, and it illuminated nothing. But its slow fade in and out was somehow comforting. A quiet heartbeat for the ship.

He told himself that Fred was right; a trial was the right thing to hope for. But he wanted that stealth ship in Alex's gun sights. He wanted that unknown crew to live through the terrifying moment when all the countermeasures have failed, the torpedoes are seconds from impact, and absolutely nothing can stop them.

He wanted them to have that same last gasp of fear he'd heard through Ade's mic.

For a time, he displaced the ghosts in his head with violent vengeance fantasies. When they stopped working, he floated down to the personnel deck, strapped into his cot, and tried to sleep. The *Rocinante* sang him a lullaby of air recyclers and silence.

Chapter Twenty: Miller

Miller sat at an open café, the tunnel wide above him. Grass grew tall and pale in the public commons, and the ceiling glowed full-spectrum white. Ceres Station had come unmoored. Orbital mechanics and inertia kept it physically where it had always been, but the stories about it had changed. The point defenses were the same. The tensile strength of the port blast doors was the same. The ephemeral shield of political status was all they'd lost, and it was everything.

Miller leaned forward and sipped his coffee.

There were children playing on the commons. He thought of them as children, though he remembered thinking of himself as an adult at that age. Fifteen, sixteen years old. They wore OPA armbands. The boys spoke in loud, angry voices about tyranny and freedom. The girls watched the boys strut. The ancient, animal story, the same whether it was on a spinning rock surrounded by hard vacuum or the stamp-sized chimpanzee preserves on Earth. Even in the Belt, youth brought invulnerability, immortality, the unshakable conviction that for you, things would be different. The laws of physics would cut you a break, the missiles would never hit, the air would never hiss out into nothing. Maybe for other people—the patched-together fighting ships of the OPA, the water haulers, the Martian gunships, the *Scopuli*, the *Canterbury*, the *Donnager,* the hundred other ships that had died in small actions since the system had turned itself into a battlefield—but not you. And when youth was lucky enough to survive its optimism, all Miller had left was a little fear, a little envy, and the overwhelming sense of life's fragility. But he had three month's worth of company script in his account and a lot of free time, and the coffee wasn't bad.

"You need anything, sir?" the waiter asked. He didn't look any older than the kids on the grass. Miller shook his head.

Five days had passed since Star Helix pulled its contract. The governor of Ceres was gone, smuggled out on a transport before the news had gone wide. The Outer Planets Alliance had announced the inclusion of Ceres among official OPA-held real estate, and no one had said otherwise. Miller had spent the first day of his unemployment drunk, but his bender had an oddly pro forma feel. He'd descended into the bottle because it was familiar, because it was what you did when you'd lost the career that defined you.

The second day, he'd gotten through the hangover. The third, he'd gotten bored. All through the station, security forces were making the kind of display he'd expected, preemptive peacekeeping. The few political rallies and protests ended fast and hard, and the citizens of Ceres didn't much care. Their eyes were on their monitors, on the war. A few locals with busted heads getting thrown into prison without charges were beneath notice. And Miller was personally responsible for none of it.

The fourth day, he'd checked his terminal and discovered that 80 percent of his docking log requests had come through before

Shaddid had shut his access down. Over a thousand entries, any one of which could be the only remaining lead to Julie Mao. So far, no Martian nukes were on their way to crack Ceres. No demands of surrender. No boarding forces. It could all change in a moment, but until it did, Miller was drinking coffee and auditing ship records, about one every fifteen minutes. Miller figured that if Holden was the last ship in the log, he'd find him in about six weeks.

The *Adrianopole*, a third-gen prospector, had docked at Pallas within the arrival window. Miller checked the open registration, frustrated again at how little information was there compared to the security databases. Owned by Strego Anthony Abramowitz. Eight citations for substandard maintenance, banned from Eros and Ceres as a danger to the port. An idiot and an accident waiting to happen, but the flight plan seemed legitimate, and the history of the ship was deep enough not to smell new-minted. Miller deleted the entry.

The *Badass Motherfucker*, a freight hauler doing a triangle between Luna, Ganymede, and the Belt. Owned by MYOFB Corporation out of Luna. A query to the public bases at Ganymede showed it had left the port there at the listed time and just hadn't bothered to file a flight plan. Miller tapped the screen with a fingernail. Not exactly how he'd fly under the radar. Anyone with authority would roust that ship just for the joy of doing it. He deleted the entry.

His terminal chimed. An incoming message. Miller flipped over to it. One of the girls on the commons shrieked and the others laughed. A sparrow flew past, its wings humming in the constant recycler-driven breeze.

Havelock looked better than when he'd been on Ceres. Happier. The dark circles were gone from his eyes, and the shape of his face had subtly softened, as if the need to prove himself in the Belt had changed his bones and now he was falling back into his natural form.

"Miller!" the recording said. "I heard about Earth cutting Ceres just before I got your message. Bad luck. I'm sorry to hear Shad-did fired you. Between the two of us, she's a pompous idiot. The rumor I've heard is Earth is doing everything it can to stay out of the war, including giving up any station that it's expecting to be a point of contention. You know how it is. You've got a pit bull on one side of you and a rottweiler on the other, first thing you do is drop your steak."

Miller chuckled.

"I've signed on with Protogen security, big-company private army bullshit. But the pay is worth putting up with their delusions of grandeur. The contract's supposed to be on Ganymede, but with the crap going on right now, who knows how it'll really play out? Turns out Protogen's got a training base in the Belt. I'd never heard about it, but it's supposed to be quite the gymnasium. I know they're hiring on, and I'd be happy to put in a word for you. Just let me know, and I'll get you together with the induction recruiter, get you off that damned rock."

Havelock smiled.

"Take care of yourself, partner," the Earther said. "Keep in touch."

Protogen. Pinkwater. Al Abbiq. Small corporate security forces that the big transorbital companies used as private armies and mercenary forces to rent out as needed. AnnanSec had the Pallas security contract, and had for years, but it was Mars-based. The OPA was probably hiring, but probably not him.

It had been years since he'd tried to find work. He'd assumed that particular struggle was behind him, that he was going to die working the Ceres Station security contract. Now that events had thrown him out, everything had an odd floating feeling. Like the gap between getting hit and feeling the pain. He needed to find another job. He needed to do more than send a couple messages out to his old partners. There were employment firms. There were bars on Ceres that would hire an ex-cop for a bouncer. There were gray markets that would take anyone capable of giving them a veneer of legality.

The last thing that made sense was to sit around, ogling girls in the park and chasing down leads on a case that he hadn't been meant to follow up on in the first place.

The *Dagon* had come into Ceres just a little ahead of the arrival window. Owned by the Glapion Collective, who were, he was pretty sure, an OPA front. That made it a good fit. Except the flight plan had been put in just a few hours after the *Donnager* blew, and the exit record from Io looked solid. Miller shifted it into a file he was keeping for ships that earned a second look.

The *Rocinante,* owned by Silencieux Courant Holdings out of Luna, was a gas hauler that had landed at Tycho just hours before the end of the arrival window. Silencieux Courant was a medium-sized corporate entity with no obvious ties to the OPA, and the flight plan from Pallas was plausible. Miller put his fingertip over the delete key, then paused. He sat back.

Why was a gas hauler going between Pallas and Tycho? Both stations were gas *consumers.* Flying from consumer to consumer without hitting a supply in the middle was a good way to not cover your docking fees. He put in a request for the flight plan that had taken the *Rocinante* to Pallas from wherever it had been before, then sat back to wait. If the records were cached in the Ceres servers, the request shouldn't take more than a minute or two. The notification bar estimated an hour and a half, so that meant the request was getting forwarded to the docking systems at Pallas. It hadn't been in the local backup.

Miller stroked his chin; five days of stubble had almost reached the beginning of a beard. He felt a smile starting. He did a definition search on *Rocinante.* Literally meaning "no longer a workhorse," its first entry was as the name of Don Quixote's horse.

"That you, Holden?" Miller said to the screen. "You out tilting at windmills?"

"Sir?" the waiter said, but Miller waved him away.

There were hundreds of entries still to be looked at and dozens at least in his second-look folder. Miller ignored them, staring at the entry from Tycho as if by sheer force of will he could make more information appear on the screen. Then, slowly, he pulled up the message from Havelock, hit the respond key, and looked into the tiny black pinprick of the terminal's camera.

"Hey, partner," he said. "Thanks for the offer. I may take you up on it, but I've got some kinks I need to work out before I jump. You know how it is. If you can do me a favor, though . . . I need to keep track of a ship, and I've only got the public databases to work from, plus which Ceres may be at war with Mars by now. Who knows, you know? Anyway, if you can put a level one watch on any flight plans for her, drop me a note if anything comes up . . . I'd buy you a drink sometime."

He paused. There had to be something more to say.

"Take care of yourself, partner."

He reviewed the message. On-screen, he looked tired, the smile a little fake, the voice a little higher than it sounded in his head. But it said what it needed to say. He sent it.

This was what he'd been reduced to. Access gone, service gun confiscated—though he still had a couple of drops in his hole—money running out. He had to play the angles, call in favors for things that should have been routine, outthink the system for any scrap. He'd been a cop, and they'd turned him into a mouse. *Still*, he thought, sitting back in the chair. *Pretty good work for a mouse.*

The sound of detonation came from spinward, then voices raised in anger. The kids on the commons stopped their games of touch-me touch-you and stared. Miller stood up. There was smoke, but he couldn't see flames. The breeze picked up as the station air cleaners raised the flow to suck away particulates so the sensors didn't think there was a risk of fanning a fire. Three gunshots rang out in fast succession, and the voices came together in a rough chant. Miller couldn't make words out of it, but the rhythm told him all he needed to know. Not a disaster, not a fire, not a breach. Just a riot.

The kids were walking toward the commotion. Miller caught one by the elbow. She couldn't have been more than sixteen, her eyes near black, her face a perfect heart shape.

"Don't go over there," he said. "Get your friends together and walk the other way."

The girl looked at him, his hand on her arm, the distant commotion.

"You can't help," he said.

She pulled her arm free.

"Gotta try, yeah?" she said. "Podría intentar, you know." *You could too.*

"Just did," Miller said as he put his terminal in its case and walked away. Behind him, the sounds of the riot grew. But he figured the police could take care of it.

Over the next fourteen hours, the system net reported five riots on the station, some minor structural damage. Someone he'd never heard of announced a tri-phase curfew; people out of their holes more than two hours before or after their work shifts would be subject to arrest. Whoever was running the show now thought they could lock down six million people and create stability and peace. He wondered what Shaddid thought about that.

Outside Ceres, things were getting worse. The deep astronomy labs on Triton had been occupied by a band of prospectors sympathetic to the OPA. They'd turned the array in-system and had been broadcasting the location of every Martian ship in the system along with high-definition images of the surface of Mars, down to the topless sunbathers in the dome parks. The story was that a volley of nukes was on its way to the station, and the array would be bright dust within a week. Earth's imitation of a snail was picking up the pace as Earth- and Luna-based companies pulled back down the gravity well. Not all of them, not even half, but enough to send the Terran message: *Count us out.* Mars appealed for solidarity; the Belt appealed for justice or, more often, told the birthplace of humanity to go fuck itself.

It wasn't out of control yet, but it was ramping up. Another few incidents and it wouldn't matter how it had started. It wouldn't matter what the stakes were. Mars knew the Belt couldn't win, and the Belt knew it had nothing to lose. It was a recipe for death on a scale humanity had never seen.

And, like Ceres, there wasn't much Miller could do about that either. But he could find James Holden, find out what had happened to the *Scopuli,* follow the leads back to Julie Mao. He was a detective. It was what he did.

As he packed up his hole, throwing out the collected detritus that grew over decades like a crust, he talked to her. He tried to explain why he'd given up everything to find her. After his discovery of the *Rocinante,* he could hardly avoid the word *quixotic.*

His imaginary Julie laughed or was touched. She thought he was a sad, pathetic little man, since just tracking her down was the nearest to a purpose in life he could find. She dressed him down as being a tool of her parents. She wept and put her arms around him. She sat with him in some almost unimaginable observation lounge and watched the stars.

He fit everything he had into a shoulder bag. Two changes of clothes, his papers, his hand terminal. A picture of Candace from back in better days. All the hard copy of Julie's case he'd made before Shaddid wiped his partition, including three pictures of Julie. He thought that everything he'd lived through should have added up to more, and then changed his mind. It was probably about right.

He spent one last day ignoring the curfew, making his rounds of the station, saying goodbye to the few people he felt he might miss or might miss him. To his surprise, Muss, who he found at a tense and uncomfortable police bar, actually teared up and hugged him until his ribs ached from it.

He booked passage on a transport to Tycho. His bunk ran him a quarter of his remaining funds. It occurred to him, not for the first time, that he had to find Julie pretty damn quick or find a job to support him through the investigation. But it hadn't happened yet, and the universe wasn't stable enough anymore to make long-range planning more than a sour joke.

As if to prove the point, his terminal chimed as he was in the line to board the transport.

"Hey, partner," Havelock said. "That favor you needed? I got a bite. Your package just put in a flight plan for Eros. I'm sending the public-access data attached. I'd get you the good stuff, but these Protogen guys are tight. I mentioned you to the recruiter and she seemed interested. So let me know, right? Talk to you soon."

Eros.

Great.

Miller nodded at the woman behind him, stepped out of line, and walked to the kiosk. By the time a screen was open, they were calling final boarding for the Tycho transport. Miller turned in his ticket, got a nominal refund, and spent a third of what he still had in his account for a ticket to Eros. Still, it could have been worse. He could have been on the way before he got word. He had to start thinking about it as good luck, not bad.

The passage confirmation came through with a chime like a gently struck triangle.

"I hope I'm right about this," he said to Julie. "If Holden's not there, I'm gonna feel pretty stupid."

In his mind, she smiled ruefully.

Life is risk, she said.

Chapter Twenty-One: Holden

Ships were small. Space was always at a premium, and even on a monster like the *Donnager,* the corridors and compartments were cramped and uncomfortable. On the *Rocinante,* the only rooms where Holden could spread out his arms without touching two walls were the galley and the cargo bay. No one who flew for a living was claustrophobic, but even the most hardened Belt prospector could recognize the rising tension of being ship-bound. It was the ancient stress response of the trapped animal, the subconscious knowledge that there was literally nowhere to go that you couldn't see from where you were already standing. Getting off the ship at port was a sudden and sometimes giddying release of tension.

It often took the form of a drinking game.

Like all professional sailors, Holden had sometimes ended long flights by drinking himself into a stupor. More than once he'd wandered into a brothel and left only when they threw him out with an emptied account, a sore groin, and a prostate as dry as the Sahara desert. So when Amos staggered into his room after three days on station, Holden knew exactly what the big mechanic felt like.

Holden and Alex were sharing the couch and watching a newsfeed. Two talking heads were discussing the Belter actions with words like *criminal, terrorist,* and *sabotage.* The Martians were "peacekeepers." It was a Martian news channel. Amos snorted and collapsed on the couch. Holden muted the screen.

"Having a good shore leave, sailor?" Holden asked with a grin.

"I'll never drink again," Amos groaned.

"Naomi's comin' over with some chow she got at that sushi place," Alex said. "Nice raw fish wrapped in fake seaweed."

Amos groaned again.

"That's not nice, Alex," Holden said. "Let the man's liver die in peace."

The door to the suite slid open again, and Naomi came in carrying a tall stack of white boxes.

"Food's here," she said.

Alex opened all the boxes and started handing around small disposable plates.

"Every time it's your turn to get food, you get salmon rolls. It shows a lack of imagination," Holden said as he began putting food on his plate.

"I like salmon," Naomi replied.

The room got quiet as people ate; the only sounds were the clack of plastic chopsticks and the wet squish of things being dipped in wasabi and soy. When the food was gone, Holden wiped his eyes, made runny by the heat in his sinuses, and leaned his chair all the way back. Amos used one of his chopsticks to scratch under the cast on his leg.

"You guys did a pretty good job setting this," he said. "It's the thing on my body that hurts the least right now."

Naomi grabbed the remote off Holden's armrest and turned

the volume back on. She began spooling through the different feeds. Alex closed his eyes and slid down on the loveseat, lacing his fingers across his belly and sighing contentedly. Holden felt a sudden and irrational annoyance at his crew for being so comfortable.

"Everyone had enough of sucking on Fred's teat yet?" he said. "I know I have."

"What the fuck are you talking about?" Amos said, shaking his head. "I'm just getting started."

"I mean," Holden said, "how long are we going to hang around on Tycho, drinking and whoring and eating sushi on Fred's expense account?"

"As long as I can?" Alex said.

"You have a better plan, then," Naomi said.

"I don't have a plan, but I want to get back in the game. We were full of righteous anger and dreams of vengeance when we got here, and a couple of blowjobs and hangovers later, it's like nothing ever happened."

"Uh, vengeance kinda requires someone to avenge upon, Cap," Alex said. "Case you ain't noticed, we're lackin' in that department."

"That ship is still out there, somewhere. The people who ordered it to shoot are, too," Holden said.

"So," Alex replied slowly, "we take off and start flyin' in a spiral until we run into it?"

Naomi laughed and threw a soy packet at him.

"I don't know what we do," Holden said, "but sitting here while the people who killed our ship keep doing whatever it is *they're* doing is making me nuts."

"We've been here three days," Naomi said. "We deserve some comfortable beds and decent food and a chance to blow off steam. Don't try to make us feel bad for taking it."

"Besides, Fred said we'll get those bastards at the trial," Amos said.

"If there's a trial," Holden replied. "*If.* It won't happen for months, or maybe even years. And even then, Fred's looking at those treaties. Amnesty might be another bargaining chip, right?"

"You were quick enough to agree to his terms, Jim," Naomi said. "Changed your mind?"

"If Fred wants depositions in exchange for letting us patch up and rest, the price was cheap. That doesn't mean I think a trial will fix everything, or that I want to be sidelined until it happens."

He gestured at the faux-leather couch and huge wall screen around them.

"Besides, this can be a prison. It's a nice one, but as long as Fred controls the purse strings, he owns us. Make no mistake."

Naomi's brow crinkled; her eyes grew serious.

"What's the option, sir?" she asked. "Leave?"

Holden folded his arms, his mind turning over everything he'd said as if he was hearing it for the first time. Saying things out loud actually made them clearer.

"I'm thinking we look for work," he said. "We've got a good ship. More importantly, we have a sneaky ship. It's fast. We can run without a transponder if we need to. Lots of people will need things moved from place to place with a war on. Gives us something to do while we wait for Fred's trial, and a way to put money in our pockets so we can get off the dole. And, as we fly from place to place, we can keep our ears and eyes open. Never know what we'll find. And seriously, how long can you three stand to be station rats?"

There was a moment's silence.

"I could station rat for another...week?" Amos said.

"It ain't a bad idea, Cap," Alex said with a nod.

"It's your decision, Captain," Naomi said. "I'll stick with you, and I like the idea of getting my own money again. But I hope you're not in a hurry. I could really use a few more days off."

Holden clapped his hands and jumped to his feet.

"Nope," he said. "Having a plan makes all the difference. Downtime's easier to enjoy when I know it'll end."

Alex and Amos got up together and headed for the door. Alex

had won a few dollars playing darts, and now he and Amos were in the process of turning it into even more money at the card tables.

"Don't wait up, Boss," Amos said to Naomi. "I'm feeling lucky today."

They left, and Holden went to the small kitchen nook to make coffee. Naomi followed him in.

"One other thing," she said.

Holden tore open the sealed coffee packet, the strong odor filling the room.

"Shoot," he said.

"Fred is taking care of all the arrangements for Kelly's body. He'll hold it here in state until we go public with our survival. Then he'll ship it back to Mars."

Holden filled the coffeemaker with water from the tap and started the machine. It made soft gurgling sounds.

"Good. Lieutenant Kelly deserves all the respect and dignity we can give him."

"It got me thinking about that data cube he had. I haven't been able to hack it. It's some kind of military über-encryption that makes my head hurt. So..."

"Just say it," Holden said with a frown.

"I want to give it to Fred. I know it's a risk. We have no idea what's on it, and for all his charm and hospitality, Fred's still OPA. But he was also high-ranking UN military. And he's got a serious brain trust here on the station. He might be able to open it up."

Holden thought for a moment, then nodded.

"Okay, let me sit with that. I want to know what Yao was trying to get off the ship, but—"

"Yeah."

They shared a companionable silence as the coffee brewed. When it was finished, Holden poured two mugs and handed one to Naomi.

"Captain," she said, then paused. "Jim. I've been a pain-in-the-

ass XO so far. I've been stressed out and scared shitless about eighty percent of the time."

"You do an amazing job of hiding that fact," Holden replied.

Naomi nodded the compliment away.

"Anyway, I've been pushy about some things that I probably shouldn't have been."

"Not a big deal."

"Okay, let me finish," she said. "I want you to know I think you've done a great job of keeping us alive. You keep us focused on the problems we can solve instead of feeling sorry for ourselves. You keep everyone in orbit around you. Not everyone can do that, I couldn't do it, and we've needed that stability."

Holden felt a glow of pride. He hadn't expected it, and he didn't trust it, but it felt good all the same.

"Thank you," Holden said.

"I can't speak for Amos and Alex, but I plan to stick it out. You're not just the captain because McDowell is dead. You're *our* captain, as far as I'm concerned. Just so you know."

She looked down, blushing as if she'd just confessed something. Maybe she had.

"I'll try not to blow it," he said.

"I'd appreciate that, sir."

Fred Johnson's office was like its occupant: big, intimidating, and overflowing with things that needed to be done. The room was easily two and a half square meters, making it larger than any single compartment on the *Rocinante*. His desk was made of actual wood, looked at least a hundred years old, and smelled of lemon oil. Holden sat in a chair that was just a little lower than Fred's, and looked at the mounds of file folders and papers covering every flat surface.

Fred had sent for him and then spent the first ten minutes after he'd arrived speaking on the phone. Whatever he was talking about, it sounded technical. Holden assumed it was related to the giant generation ship outside. It didn't bother him to be ignored for a few minutes, since the wall behind Fred was entirely covered by a bleedingly high-definition screen pretending to be a window. It was showing a spectacular view of the *Nauvoo* moving past as the station spun. Fred spoiled the scene by putting the phone down.

"Sorry about that," he said. "The atmosphere processing system has been a nightmare from day one. When you're going a hundred plus years on only the air you can bring with you, the loss tolerances are...stricter than usual. Sometimes it's difficult to impress the importance of fine details on the contractors."

"I was enjoying the view," Holden said, gesturing at the screen.

"I'm starting to wonder if we'll be able to get it done on schedule."

"Why?"

Fred sighed and leaned his chair back with a squeak.

"It's the war between Mars and the Belt."

"Material shortages, then?"

"Not just that. Pirate casts claiming to speak for the OPA are working into a frenzy. Belt prospectors with homemade torpedo launchers are firing on Martian warships. They get wiped out in response, but every now and then one of those torpedoes hits and kills a few Martians."

"Which means Mars starts shooting first."

Fred nodded and then got up and started pacing the room.

"And then even honest citizens on legitimate business start getting worried about going out of the house," he said. "We've had over a dozen late shipments so far this month, and I'm worried it will stop being delays and start being cancellations."

"You know, I've been thinking about the same thing," Holden said.

Fred acted as though he hadn't heard.

"I've been on that bridge," Fred said. "Unidentified ship coming on you, and a decision to make? No one wants to press the button. I've watched a ship get bigger and bigger on the scope while my finger was on the trigger. I remember begging them to stop."

Holden said nothing. He'd seen it too. There was nothing to say. Fred let silence hang in the air for a moment, then shook his head and straightened up.

"I need to ask you a favor," Fred said.

"You can always ask, Fred. You've paid for that much," Holden replied.

"I need to borrow your ship."

"The *Roci*?" Holden said. "Why?"

"I need to have something picked up and delivered here, and I need a ship that can stay quiet and run past Martian picket ships if it needs to."

"The *Rocinante* is definitely the right ship, then, but that didn't answer my question. Why?"

Fred turned his back to Holden and looked at the view screen. The nose of the *Nauvoo* was just vanishing from sight. The view turned to the flat, star-speckled black of forever.

"I need to pick someone up on Eros," he said. "Someone important. I've got people who can do it, but the only ships we've got are light freighters and a couple of small shuttles. Nothing that can make the trip quickly enough or have a hope of running away if trouble starts."

"Does this person have a name? I mean, you keep saying you don't want to fight, but the other unique thing about my ship is that it's the only one here with guns. I'm sure the OPA has a whole list of things they'd like blown up."

"You don't trust me."

"Nope."

Fred turned back around and gripped the back of his chair. His knuckles were white. Holden wondered if he'd gone too far.

"Look," Holden said, "you talk a good game about peace and trials and all that. You disavow the pirate casts. You have a nice station filled with nice people. I have every reason to believe you are what you say you are. But we've been here three days, and the first time you tell me about your plans, you ask to borrow my ship for a secret mission. Sorry. If I'm part of this, I get full access; no secrets. Even if I knew for a fact, which I don't, that you had nothing but good intentions, I still wouldn't go along with the cloak-and-dagger bullshit."

Fred stared at him for a few seconds, then came around his chair and sat down. Holden found he was tapping his fingers on his thigh nervously and forced himself to stop. Fred's eyes flicked down at Holden's hand and then back up. He continued to stare.

Holden cleared his throat.

"Look, you're the big dog here. Even if I didn't know who you used to be, you'd scare the shit out of me, so don't feel the need to prove it. But no matter how scared I am, I'm not backing down on this."

Fred's hoped-for laughter didn't come. Holden tried to swallow without gulping.

"I bet every captain you ever flew under thought you were a gigantic pain in the ass," Fred said finally.

"I believe my record reflects that," Holden said, trying to hide his relief.

"I need to fly to Eros and find a man named Lionel Polanski, and then bring him back to Tycho."

"That's only a week out if we push," Holden said, doing the math in his head.

"The fact that Lionel doesn't actually exist complicates the mission."

"Yeah, okay. Now I'm confused," Holden agreed.

"You wanted in?" Fred said, the words taking on a quiet ferocity. "Now you're in. Lionel Polanski exists only on paper, and owns things that Mr. Tycho doesn't want to own. Including a courier ship called the *Scopuli*."

Holden leaned forward in his chair, his face intense.

"You now have my undivided attention," he said.

"The nonexistent owner of the *Scopuli* checked into a flophouse on one of the shit levels of Eros. We only just got the message. We have to work on the assumption that whoever got the room knows our operations intimately, needs help, and can't ask for it openly."

"We can leave in an hour," Holden said breathlessly.

Fred held up his hands in a gesture that was surprisingly Belter for an Earth man.

"When," Fred asked, "did this turn into *you* leaving?"

"I won't loan my ship, but I'll definitely rent it out. My crew and I were talking about getting jobs, actually. Hire us. Deduct whatever's fair for services you've already rendered."

"No," Fred said. "I need *you*."

"You don't," Holden replied. "You need our depositions. And we're not going to sit here waiting a year or two for sanity to reign. We'll all do video depositions, sign whatever affidavits you want us to as to their authenticity, but we're leaving to find work one way or the other. You might as well make use of it."

"No," Fred said. "You're too valuable to take risks with your lives."

"What if I throw in the data cube the captain of the *Donnager* was trying to liberate?"

The silence was back, but it had a different feel to it.

"Look," Holden said, pressing on. "You need a ship like the *Roci*. I've got one. You need a crew for her. I've got that too. And you're as hungry to know what's on that cube as I am."

"I don't like the risk."

"Your other option is to throw us in the brig and commandeer the ship. There's some risks in that too."

Fred laughed. Holden felt himself relax.

"You'll still have the same problem that brought you here," Fred said. "Your ship looks like a gunship, no matter what its transponder is saying."

Holden jumped up and grabbed a piece of paper from Fred's desk. He started writing on it with a pen snatched from a decorative pen set.

"I've been thinking about that. You've got full manufacturing facilities here. And we're supposed to be a light gas freighter. So," he said as he sketched a rough outline of the ship, "we weld on a bunch of empty compressed-gas storage tanks in two bands around the hull. Use them to hide the tubes. Repaint the whole thing. Weld on a few projections to break up the hull profile and hide us from ship-recognition software. It'll look like shit and screw up the aerodynamics, but we won't be near atmo anytime soon. It'll look exactly like what it is: something a bunch of Belters slapped together in a hurry."

He handed the paper to Fred. Fred began laughing in earnest, either at the terrible drawing or at the absurdity of the whole thing.

"You could give a pirate a hell of a surprise," he said. "If I do this, you and your crew will record my depositions and hire on as an independent contractor for errands like the Eros run and appear on my behalf when the peace negotiations start."

"Yes."

"I want the right to outbid anyone else who tries to hire you. No contracts without my counteroffer."

Holden held out his hand, and Fred shook it.

"Nice doing business with you, Fred."

As Holden left the office, Fred was already on the comm with his machine-shop people. Holden pulled out his portable terminal and called up Naomi.

"Yeah," she said.

"Pack up the kids, we're going to Eros."

"They don't. Not officially. But after a few decades, you come to a place where you realize that there's really no difference between trying and not trying. I still travel. I still talk to people. Sometimes we talk about Jesus Christ. Sometimes we talk about cooking. If someone is ready to accept Christ, it doesn't take much effort on my part to help them. If they aren't, no amount of hectoring them does any good. So why try?"

"Do people talk about the war?" Miller asked.

"Often," the missionary said.

"Anyone make sense of it?"

"No. I don't believe war ever does. It's a madness that's in our nature. Sometimes it recurs; sometimes it subsides."

"Sounds like a disease."

"The herpes simplex of the species?" the missionary said with a laugh. "I suppose there are worse ways to think of it. I'm afraid that as long as we're human, it will be with us."

Miller looked over at the wide, moon-round face.

"As long as we're human?" he said.

"Some of us believe that we shall all eventually become angels," the missionary said.

"Not the Methodists."

"Even them, eventually," the man said, "but they probably won't go first. And what brings you to Our Lady of Sleeping Through It?"

Miller sighed, sitting back against the unyielding chair. Two rows down, a young woman shouted at two boys to stop jumping on the seats and was ignored. A man behind them coughed. Miller took a long breath and let it out slowly.

"I was a cop on Ceres," he said.

"Ah. The change of contract."

"That," Miller said.

"Taking up work on Eros, then?"

"More looking up an old friend," Miller said. Then, to his own surprise, he went on. "I was born on Ceres. Lived there my whole life. This is the...fifth? Yeah, fifth time I've been off station."

"Do you plan to go back?"

"No," Miller said. He sounded more certain than he'd known. "No, I think that part of my life is pretty much over."

"That must be painful," the missionary said.

Miller paused, letting the comment settle. The man was right; it should have been painful. Everything he'd ever had was gone. His job, his community. He wasn't even a cop anymore, his checked-in-luggage handgun notwithstanding. He would never eat at the little East Indian cart at the edge of sector nine again. The receptionist at the station would never nod her greeting to him as he headed in for his desk again. No more nights at the bar with the other cops, no more off-color stories about busts gone weird, no more kids flying kites in the high tunnels. He probed himself like a doctor searching for inflammation. Did it hurt here? Did he feel the loss there?

He didn't. There was only a sense of relief so profound it approached giddiness.

"I'm sorry," the missionary said, confused. "Did I say something funny?"

Eros supported a population of one and a half million, a little more than Ceres had in visitors at any given time. Roughly the shape of a potato, it had been much more difficult to spin up, and its surface velocity was considerably higher than Ceres' for the same internal g. The old shipyards protruded from the asteroid, great spiderwebs of steel and carbon mesh studded with warning lights and sensor arrays to wave off any ships that might come in too tight. The internal caverns of Eros had been the birthplace of the Belt. From raw ore to smelting furnace to annealing platform and then into the spines of water haulers and gas harvesters and prospecting ships. Eros had been a port of call in the first generation of humanity's expansion. From there, the sun itself was only a bright star among billions.

The economics of the Belt had moved on. Ceres Station had

spun up with newer docks, more industrial backing, more people. The commerce of shipping moved to Ceres, while Eros remained a center of ship manufacture and repair. The results were as predictable as physics. On Ceres, a longer time in dock meant lost money, and the berth fee structure reflected that. On Eros, a ship might wait for weeks or months without impeding the flow of traffic. If a crew wanted a place to relax, to stretch, to get away from one another for a while, Eros was the port of call. And with the lower docking fees, Eros Station found other ways to soak money from its visitors: Casinos. Brothels. Shooting galleries. Vice in all its commercial forms found a home in Eros, its local economy blooming like a fungus fed by the desires of Belters.

A happy accident of orbital mechanics put Miller there half a day ahead of the *Rocinante*. He walked through the cheap casinos, the opioid bars and sex clubs, the show fight areas where men or women pretended to beat one another senseless for the pleasure of the crowds. Miller imagined Julie walking with him, her sly smile matching his own as he read the great animated displays. RANDOLPH MAK, HOLDER OF THE BELT FREEFIGHT CHAMPION-SHIP FOR SIX YEARS, AGAINST MARTIAN KIVRIN CARMICHAEL IN A FIGHT TO THE DEATH!

Surely not fixed, Julie said drily in his mind.

Wonder which one's going to win, he thought, and imagined her laughing.

He'd stopped at a noodle cart, two new yens' worth of egg noodles in black sauce steaming in their cone, when a hand clapped on his shoulder.

"Detective Miller," a familiar voice said. "I think you're outside your jurisdiction."

"Why, Inspector Sematimba," Miller said. "As I live and breathe. You give a girl the shakes, sneaking up like that."

Sematimba laughed. He was a tall man, even among Belters, with the darkest skin Miller had ever seen. Years before, Sematimba and Miller had coordinated on a particularly ugly case. A smuggler with a cargo of designer euphorics had broken with his supplier. Three people on Ceres had been caught in the crossfire, and the smuggler had shipped out for Eros. The traditional competitiveness and insularity of the stations' respective security forces had almost let the perp slip away. Only Miller and Sematimba had been willing to coordinate outside the corporate channels.

"What brings you," Sematimba said, leaning against a thin steel railing and gesturing at the tunnel, "to the navel of the Belt, the glory and power that is Eros?"

"Following up on a lead," Miller said.

"There's nothing good here," Sematimba said. "Ever since Protogen pulled out, things have been going from bad to worse."

Miller sucked up a noodle.

"Who's the new contract?" he asked.

"CPM," Sematimba said.

"Never heard of them."

"*Carne Por la Machina*," Sematimba said, and pulled a face: exaggerated bluff masculinity. He thumped his breast and growled, then let the imitation go and shook his head. "New corporation out of Luna. Mostly Belters on the ground. Make themselves out to be all hard core, but they're mostly amateurs. All bluster, no balls. Protogen was inner planets, and that was a problem, but they were serious as hell. They broke heads, but they kept the peace. These new assholes? Most corrupt bunch of thugs I've ever worked for. I don't think the board of governors is going to renew when the contract's up. I didn't say that, but it's true."

"I've got an old partner signed up with Protogen," Miller said.

"They're not bad," Sematimba said. "Almost wish I'd picked them in the divorce, you know?"

"Why didn't you?" Miller asked.

"You know how it is. I'm from here."

"Yeah," Miller said.

"So. You didn't know who was running the playhouse? You aren't here looking for work."

"Nope," Miller said. "I'm on sabbatical. Doing some travel for myself these days."

"You've got money for that?"

"Not really. But I don't mind going on the cheap. For a while, you know. You heard anything about a Juliette Mao? Goes by Julie?"

Sematimba shook his head.

"Mao-Kwikowski Mercantile," Miller said. "Came up the well and went native. OPA. It was an abduction case."

"Was?"

Miller leaned back. His imagined Julie raised her eyebrows.

"It's changed a little since I got it," Miller said. "May be connected to something. Kind of big."

"How big are we talking about?" Sematimba said. All trace of jocularity had vanished from his expression. He was all cop now. Anyone but Miller would have found the man's empty, almost angry face intimidating.

"The war," Miller said. Sematimba folded his arms.

"Bad joke," he said.

"Not joking."

"I consider us friends, old man," Sematimba said. "But I don't want any trouble around here. Things are unsettled as it stands."

"I'll try to stay low-profile."

Sematimba nodded. Down the tunnel, an alarm blared. Only security, not the earsplitting ditone of an environmental alert. Sematimba looked down the tunnel as if squinting would let him see through the press of people, bicycles, and food carts.

"I'd better go look," he said with an air of resignation. "Probably some of my fellow officers of the peace breaking windows for the fun of it."

"Great to be part of a team like that," Miller said.

"How would you know?" Sematimba said with a smile. "If you need something…"

"Likewise," Miller said, and watched the cop wade into the sea of chaos and humanity. He was a large man, but something about the passing crowd's universal deafness to the alarm's blare made him seem smaller. *A stone in the ocean,* the phrase went. One star among millions.

Miller checked the time, then pulled up the public docking records. The *Rocinante* showed as on schedule. The docking berth was listed. Miller sucked down the last of his noodles, tossed the foam cone with the thin smear of black sauce into a public recycler, found the nearest men's room, and when he was done there, trotted toward the casino level.

The architecture of Eros had changed since its birth. Where once it had been like Ceres—webworked tunnels leading along the path of widest connection—Eros had learned from the flow of money: All paths led to the casino level. If you wanted to go anywhere, you passed through the wide whale belly of lights and displays. Poker, blackjack, roulette, tall fish tanks filled with prize trout to be caught and gutted, mechanical slots, electronic slots, cricket races, craps, rigged tests of skill. Flashing lights, dancing neon clowns, and video screen advertisements blasted the eyes. Loud artificial laughter and merry whistles and bells assured you that you were having the time of your life. All while the smell of thousands of people packed into too small a space competed with the scent of heavily spiced vat-grown meat being hawked from carts rolling down the corridor. Greed and casino design had turned Eros into an architectural cattle run.

Which was exactly what Miller needed.

The tube station that arrived from the port had six wide doors, which emptied to the casino floor. Miller accepted a drink from a tired-looking woman in a G-string and bared breasts and found a screen to stand at that afforded him a view of all six doors. The crew of the *Rocinante* had no choice but to come through one of those. He checked his hand terminal. The docking logs showed the ship had arrived ten minutes earlier. Miller pretended to sip his drink and settled in to wait.

Chapter Twenty-Three: Holden

The casino level of Eros was an all-out assault on the senses. Holden hated it.

"I love this place," Amos said, grinning.

Holden pushed his way through a knot of drunk middle-aged gamblers, who were laughing and yelling, to a small open space near a row of pay-by-the-minute wall terminals.

"Amos," he said, "we'll be going to a less touristy level, so watch our backs. The flophouse we're looking for is in a rough neighborhood."

Amos nodded. "Gotcha, Cap."

While Naomi, Alex, and Amos blocked him from view, Holden reached behind his back to adjust the pistol that pulled uncomfortably on his waistband. The cops on Eros were pretty uptight about people walking around with guns, but there was no way he was going to "Lionel Polanski" unarmed. Amos and Alex were both carrying too, though Amos kept his in the right pocket of his jacket and his hand never left it. Only Naomi flatly refused to carry a gun.

Holden led the group toward the nearest escalators, with Amos, casting the occasional glance behind, in the rear. The casinos of Eros stretched for three seemingly endless levels, and even though they moved as quickly as possible, it took half an hour to get away from the noise and crowds. The first level above was a residential neighborhood and disorientingly quiet and neat after the casino's chaos and noise. Holden sat down on the edge of a planter with a nice array of ferns in it and caught his breath.

"I'm with you, Captain. Five minutes in that place gives me a headache," Naomi said, and sat down next to him.

"You kidding me?" Amos said. "I wish we had more time. Alex and I took almost a grand off those fish at the Tycho card tables. We'd probably walk out of here fucking millionaires."

"You know it," Alex said, and punched the big mechanic on the shoulder.

"Well, if this Polanski thing turns out to be nothing, you have my permission to go make us a million dollars at the card tables. I'll wait for you on the ship," Holden said.

The tube system ended at the first casino level and didn't start again until the level they were on. You could choose not to spend your money at the tables, but they made sure you were punished for doing so. Once the crew had climbed into a car and started the ride to Lionel's hotel, Amos sat down next to Holden.

"Somebody's following us, Cap," he said conversationally. "Wasn't sure till he climbed on a couple cars down. Behind us all through the casinos too."

Holden sighed and put his face in his hands.

"Okay, what's he look like?" he said.

"Belter. Fifties, or maybe forties with a lot of mileage. White shirt and dark pants. Goofy hat."

"Cop?"

"Oh yeah. But no holster I can see," Amos said.

"All right. Keep an eye on him, but no need to get too worried. Nothing we're doing here is illegal," Holden said.

"You mean, other than arriving in our stolen Martian warship, sir?" Naomi asked.

"You mean our *perfectly legitimate* gas freighter that all the paperwork and registry data says is *perfectly legitimate*?" Holden replied with a thin smile. "Yeah, well, if they'd seen through that, they would have stopped us at the dock, not followed us around."

An advertising screen on the wall displayed a stunning view of multicolored clouds rippling with flashes of lightning, and encouraged Holden to take a trip to the amazing dome resorts on Titan. He'd never been to Titan. Suddenly he wanted to go there very much. A few weeks of sleeping late, eating in fine restaurants, and lying on a hammock, watching Titan's colorful atmosphere storm above him sounded like heaven. Hell, as long as he was fantasizing, he threw in Naomi walking over to his hammock with a couple of fruity-looking drinks in her hands.

She ruined it by talking.

"This is our stop," she said.

"Amos, watch our friend, see if he gets off the train with us," Holden said as he got up and headed to the door.

After they got off and walked a dozen steps down the corridor, Amos whispered, "Yep," at his back. *Shit.* Well, definitely a tail, but there wasn't really any reason not to go ahead and check up on Lionel. Fred hadn't asked them to do anything *with* whoever was pretending to be the *Scopuli*'s owner. They couldn't very well be arrested for knocking on a door. Holden whistled a loud and jaunty tune as he walked, to let his crew and whoever was following them know he wasn't worried about a thing.

He stopped when he saw the flophouse.

It was dark and dingy and exactly the sort of place where people got mugged or worse. Broken lights created dark corners, and there wasn't a tourist in sight. He turned to give Alex and Amos meaningful looks, and Amos shifted his hand in his pocket. Alex reached under his coat.

The lobby was mostly empty space, with a pair of couches at one end next to a table covered with magazines. A sleepy-looking older woman sat reading one. Elevators were recessed into the wall at the far end, next to a door marked STAIRS. In the middle was the check-in desk, where, in lieu of a human clerk, a touch screen terminal let guests pay for their rooms.

Holden stopped next to the desk and turned around to look at the woman sitting on the couch. Graying hair, but good features and an athletic build. In a flophouse like this, that probably meant a prostitute reaching the end of her shelf life. She pointedly ignored his stare.

"Is our tail still with us?" Holden asked in a quiet voice.

"Stopped outside somewhere. Probably just watching the door now," Amos replied.

Holden nodded and hit the inquiry button on the check-in screen. A simple menu would let him send a message to Lionel Polanski's room, but Holden exited the system. They knew Lionel was still checked in, and Fred had given them the room number. If it was someone playing games, no reason to give him a heads-up before Holden knocked on the door.

"Okay, he's still here, so let's—" Holden said, and then stopped when he saw the woman from the couch standing right behind Alex. He hadn't heard or seen her approach.

"You need to come with me," she said in a hard voice. "Walk to the stairwell slowly, stay at least three meters ahead of me the entire time. Do it now."

"Are you a cop?" Holden asked, not moving.

"I'm the person with the gun," she said, a small weapon appearing like magic in her right hand. She pointed it at Alex's head. "So do what I say."

Her weapon was small and plastic and had some kind of battery pack. Amos pulled his heavy slug thrower out and aimed it at her face.

"Mine's bigger," he said.

"Amos, don't—" was all Naomi had time to say before the

stairwell door burst open and half a dozen men and women armed with compact automatic weapons came into the room, yelling at them to drop their guns.

Holden started to put his hands up when one of them opened fire, the weapon coughing out rounds so fast it sounded like someone ripping construction paper; it was impossible to hear the separate shots. Amos threw himself to the floor. A line of bullet holes stitched across the chest of the woman with the taser, and she fell backward with a soft, final sound.

Holden grabbed Naomi by one hand and dragged her behind the check-in desk. Someone in the other group was yelling, "Cease fire! Cease fire!" but Amos was already shooting back from his position, prone on the floor. A yelp of pain and a curse told Holden he'd probably hit someone. Amos rolled sideways to the desk, just in time to avoid a hail of slugs that tore up the floor and wall and made the desk shudder.

Holden reached for his gun, but the front sight caught in his waistband. He yanked it out, tearing his underwear, then crawled on his knees to the edge of the desk and looked out. Alex was lying on the floor on the other side of one of the couches, gun drawn and face white. As Holden looked, a burst of gunfire hit the couch, blowing stuffing into the air and making a line of holes in the back of the couch not more than twenty centimeters above Alex's head. The pilot reached his pistol around the corner of the couch and blindly fired off half a dozen shots, yelling at the same time.

"Fucking assholes!" Amos yelled, then rolled out and fired a couple more shots and rolled back before the return fire started.

"Where are they?" Holden yelled at him.

"Two are down, the rest in the stairwell!" Amos yelled back over the sound of return fire.

Out of nowhere a burst of rounds bounced off the floor past Holden's knee. "Shit, someone's flanking us!" Amos cried out, then moved farther behind the desk and away from the shots.

Holden crawled to the other side of the desk and peeked out.

Someone was moving low and fast toward the hotel entrance. Holden leaned out and took a couple shots at him, but three guns opened up from the stairwell doorway and forced him back behind the desk.

"Alex, someone's moving to the entrance!" Holden screamed at the top of his lungs, hoping the pilot might be able to get off a shot before they were all chopped to pieces by crossfire.

A pistol barked three times by the entrance. Holden risked a look. Their tail with the goofy hat crouched by the door, a gun in his hand, the machine gun–toting flanker lying still at his feet. Instead of looking at them, the tail was pointing his gun toward the stairwell.

"No one shoot the guy with the hat!" Holden yelled, then moved back to the edge of the desk.

Amos put his back to the desk and popped the magazine from his gun. As he fumbled around in his pocket for another, he said, "Guy is probably a cop."

"Extra especially do *not* shoot any cops," Holden said, then fired a few shots at the stairwell door.

Naomi, who'd spent the entire gunfight so far on the floor with her arms over her head, said, "They might all be cops."

Holden squeezed off a few more shots and shook his head.

"Cops don't carry small, easily concealable machine guns and ambush people from stairwells. We call those death squads," he said, though most of his words were drowned out by a barrage of gunfire from the stairwell. Afterward came a few seconds of silence.

Holden leaned back out in time to see the door swing shut.

"I think they're bugging out," he said, keeping his gun trained on the door anyway. "Must have another exit somewhere. Amos, keep your eye on that door. If it opens, start shooting." He patted Naomi on the shoulder. "Stay down."

Holden rose from behind the now ruined check-in kiosk. The desk facade had splintered and the underlying stone showed through. Holden held his gun barrel-up, his hands open. The man in the hat stood, considering the corpse at his feet, then looked up as Holden came near.

"Thanks. My name is Jim Holden. You are?"

The man didn't speak for a second. When he did, his voice was calm. Almost weary. "Cops will be here soon. I need to make a call or we're all going to jail."

"Aren't you the cops?" Holden asked.

The other man laughed; it was a bitter, short sound, but with some real humor behind it. Apparently Holden had said something funny.

"Nope. Name's Miller."

Chapter Twenty-Four: Miller

Miller looked at the dead man—the man he'd just killed—and tried to feel something. There was the trailing adrenaline rush still ramping up his heartbeat. There was a sense of surprise that came from walking into an unexpected firefight. Past that, though, his mind had already fallen into the long habit of analysis. One plant in the main room so Holden and his crew wouldn't see anything too threatening. A bunch of trigger-happy yahoos in the stairwell to back her up. *That* had gone well.

It was a slapdash effort. The ambush had been set by people who either didn't know what they were doing or didn't have the time or resources to do it right. If it hadn't been improvised, Holden and his three buddies would have been taken or killed. And him along with them.

The four survivors of the *Canterbury* stood in the remains of the firefight like rookies at their first bust. Miller felt his mind shift back half a step as he watched everything without watching anything in particular. Holden was smaller than he'd expected from the video feeds. It shouldn't have been surprising; he was an Earther. The man had the kind of face that was bad at hiding things.

"Thanks. My name is Jim Holden. You are?"

Miller thought of six different answers and turned them all aside. One of the others—a big man, solid, with a bare scalp—was pacing out the room, his eyes unfocused the same way Miller's were. Of Holden's four, that was the only guy who'd seen serious gunplay before.

"Cops will be here soon," Miller said. "I need to make a call or we're all going to jail."

The other man—thinner, taller, East Indian by the look of him—had been hiding behind a couch. He was sitting on his haunches now, his eyes wide and panicky. Holden had some of the same look, but he was doing a better job of keeping control. The burdens, Miller thought, of leadership.

"Aren't you the cops?"

Miller laughed.

"Nope," he said. "Name's Miller."

"Okay," the woman said. "Those people just tried to kill us. Why did they do that?"

Holden took a half step toward her voice even before he turned to look at her. Her face was flushed, full lips pressed thin and pale. Her features showed a far-flung racial mix that was unusual even in the melting pot of the Belt. Her hands weren't shaking. The big one had the most experience, but Miller put the woman down as having the best instincts.

"Yeah," Miller said. "I noticed."

He pulled out his hand terminal and opened a link to Sematimba. The cop accepted a few seconds later.

"Semi," Miller said. "I'm really sorry about this, but you know how I was going to stay low-profile?"

"Yes?" the local cop said, drawing the word out to three syllables.

"Didn't work out. I was heading to a meeting with a friend..."

"A meeting with a friend," Sematimba echoed. Miller could imagine the man's crossed arms even though they didn't show in the frame.

"And I happened to see a bunch of tourists in the wrong place at the wrong time. It got out of hand."

"Where are you?" Sematimba asked. Miller gave him the station level and address. There was a long pause while Sematimba consulted with some internal communication software that would have been part of Miller's tool set once. The man's sigh was percussive. "I don't see anything. Were there shots fired?"

Miller looked at the chaos and ruin around them. About a thousand different alerts should have gone out with the first weapon fired. Security should have been swarming toward them.

"A few," he said.

"Strange," Sematimba said. "Stay put. I'll be there."

"Will do," Miller said, and dropped the connection.

"Okay," Holden said. "Who was that?"

"The real cops," Miller said. "They'll be here soon. It'll be fine."

I think it'll be fine. It occurred to him that he was treating the situation like he was still on the inside, a part of the machine. That wasn't true anymore, and pretending it was might have consequences.

"He was following us," the woman said to Holden. And then, to Miller, she said, "You were following us."

"I was," Miller said. He didn't think he sounded rueful, but the big guy shook his head.

"It was the hat," the big one said. "Stood out some."

Miller swept off his porkpie and considered it. Of course the big one had been the one to make him. The other three were competent amateurs, and Miller knew that Holden had done some time in the UN Navy. But Miller gave it better than even money that the big one's background check would be interesting reading.

"Why were you following us?" Holden asked. "I mean, I appreciate the part where you shot the people who were shooting at us, but I'd still like to know that first part."

"I wanted to talk to you," Miller said. "I'm looking for someone."

There was a pause. Holden smiled.

"Anyone in particular?" he asked.

"A crew member of the *Scopuli*," Miller said.

"The *Scopuli*?" Holden said. He started to glance at the woman and stopped himself. There was something there. The *Scopuli* meant something to him beyond what Miller had seen on the news.

"There was nobody on her when we got there," the woman said.

"Holy shit," the shaky one behind the couch said. It was the first thing he'd said since the firefight ended, and he repeated it five or six more times in quick succession.

"What about you?" Miller asked. "*Donnager* blew you to Tycho, and now here. What's that about?"

"How did you know that?" Holden said.

"It's my job," Miller said. "Well, it used to be."

The answer didn't appear to satisfy the Earther. The big guy had fallen in behind Holden, his face a friendly cipher: No trouble, unless there was trouble, and then maybe a whole lot of trouble. Miller nodded, half to the big guy, half to himself.

"I had a contact in the OPA who told me you didn't die on the *Donnager*," Miller said.

"They just *told* you that?" the woman asked, banked outrage in her voice.

"He was making a point at the time," Miller said. "Anyway, he said it, and I took it from there. And in about ten minutes, I'm going to make sure Eros security doesn't throw all of you in a hole, and me with you. So if there's anything at all you want to tell me—like what you're doing here, for instance—this would be the right time."

The silence was broken only by the sound of recyclers laboring to clear the smoke and particulate dust of gunfire. The shaky one stood. Something about the way he held himself looked military. Ex-something, Miller assumed, but not a ground pounder. Navy, maybe; Martian at a guess. He had the vocal twang some of them affected.

"Ah, fuck it, Cap'n," the big one said. "He shot the flank guy for us. He may be an asshole, but he's okay by me."

"Thank you, Amos," Holden said. Miller filed that. The big one was Amos. Holden put his hands behind his back, returning his gun to his waistband.

"We're here to look for someone too," he said. "Probably someone from the *Scopuli*. We were just double-checking the room when everyone decided to start shooting at us."

"Here?" Miller said. Something like emotion trickled into his veins. Not hope, but dread. "Someone off the *Scopuli* is in this flop right now?"

"We think so," Holden said.

Miller looked out the flophouse lobby's front doors. A small, curious crowd had started to gather in the tunnel. Crossed arms, nervous glances. He knew how they felt. Sematimba and his police were on the way. The gunmen who'd attacked Holden and his crew weren't mounting another attack, but that didn't mean they were gone. There might be another wave. They could have fallen back to a better position to wait for Holden to advance.

But what if Julie was here right now? How could he come this far and stop in the lobby? To his surprise, he still had his gun drawn. That was unprofessional. He should have holstered it. The only other one still drawn was the Martian's. Miller shook his head. Sloppy. He needed to stop that.

Still, he had more than half a magazine left in the pistol.

"What room?" he asked.

The flophouse corridors were thin and cramped. The walls had the impervious gloss of warehouse paint, and the carpet was carbon-silicate weave that would wear out more slowly than bare stone. Miller and Holden went first, then the woman and the Martian—Naomi and Alex, their names were—then Amos, trailing and looking back over his shoulder. Miller wondered if anyone but he and Amos understood how they were keeping the others safe. Holden seemed to know and be irritated by it; he kept edging ahead.

The doors of the rooms were identical fiberglass laminates, thin enough to be churned out by the thousands. Miller had kicked in a hundred like them in his career. A few here and there were decorated by longtime residents—with a painting of improbably red flowers, a whiteboard with a string where a pen had once been attached, a cheap reproduction of an obscene cartoon acting out its punch line in a dimly glowing infinite loop.

Tactically, it was a nightmare. If the ambushing forces stepped out of doors in front of and behind them, all five could be slaughtered in seconds. But no slugs flew, and the only door that opened disgorged an emaciated, long-bearded man with imperfect eyes and a slack mouth. Miller nodded at the man as they passed, and he nodded back, possibly more surprised by someone's acknowledging his presence than by the drawn pistols. Holden stopped.

"This is it," he murmured. "This is the room."

Miller nodded. The others came up in a clump, Amos casually hanging back, his eyes on the corridor retreating behind them. Miller considered the door. It would be easy to kick in. One strong blow just above the latch mechanism. Then he could go in low and to the left, Amos high and to the right. He wished Havelock were there. Tactics were simpler for people who'd trained together. He motioned Amos to come up close.

Holden knocked on the door.

"What are you...?" Miller whispered fiercely, but Holden ignored him.

"Hello?" Holden called. "Anyone there?"

Miller tensed. Nothing happened. No voice, no gunfire. Nothing. Holden seemed perfectly at ease with the risk he'd just taken.

From the expression on Naomi's face, Miller took it this wasn't the first time he'd done things this way.

"You want that open?" Amos said.

"Kinda do," Miller said at the same moment Holden said, "Yeah, kick it down."

Amos looked from one to the other, not moving until Holden nodded at him. Then Amos shifted past them, kicked the door open in one blow, and staggered back, cussing.

"You okay?" Miller asked.

The big man nodded once through a pale grimace.

"Yeah, busted my leg a while back. Cast just came off. Keep forgetting about that," he said.

Miller turned back to the room. Inside, it was as black as a cave. No lights came on, not even the dim glow of monitors and sensory devices. Miller stepped in, pistol drawn. Holden was close behind him. The floor made the crunching sound of gravel under their feet, and there was an odd astringent smell that Miller associated with broken screens. Behind it was another smell, much less pleasant. He chose not to think about that one.

"Hello?" Miller said. "Anyone here?"

"Turn on the lights," Naomi said from behind them. Miller heard Holden patting the wall panel, but no light came up.

"They're not working," Holden said.

The dim spill from the corridor gave almost nothing. Miller kept his gun steady in his right hand, ready to empty it toward muzzle flash if anyone opened fire from the darkness. With his left, he took out his hand terminal, thumbed on the backlight, and opened a blank white writing tablet. The room came into monochrome. Beside him, Holden did the same.

A thin bed pressed against one wall, a narrow tray beside it. The bedding was knotted like the remnant of a bad night's sleep. A closet stood open, empty. The hulking form of an empty vacuum suit lay on the floor like a mannequin with a misplaced head. An old entertainment console hung on the wall across from the cot, its screen shattered by half a dozen blows. The wall was dimpled where blows intended to break the LED sconces had missed. Another hand terminal added its glow, and another. Hints of color started to come into the room—the cheap gold of the walls, the green of the blankets and sheet. Under the cot, something glimmered. An older-model hand terminal. Miller crouched as the others stepped in.

"Shit," Amos said.

"Okay," Holden said. "Nobody touches anything. Period. Nothing." It was the most sensible thing Miller had heard the man say.

"Someone put up a bitch of a fight," Amos muttered.

"No," Miller said. It had been vandalism, maybe. It hadn't been a struggle. He pulled a thin-film evidence bag out of his pocket and turned it inside out over his hand like a glove before picking up the terminal, flipping the plastic over it, and setting off the sealing charge.

"Is that…blood?" Naomi asked, pointing to the cheap foam mattress. Wet streaks pooled on the sheet and pillow, not more than a fingers' width, but dark. Too dark even for blood.

"No," Miller said, shoving the terminal into his pocket.

The fluid marked a thin path toward the bathroom. Miller raised a hand, pushing the others back as he crept toward the half-open door. Inside the bathroom, the nasty background smell was much stronger. Something deep, organic, and intimate. Manure in a hothouse, or the aftermath of sex, or a slaughterhouse. All of them. The toilet was brushed steel, the same model they used in prisons. The sink matched. The LED above it and the one in the ceiling had both been destroyed. In the light of his terminal, like the glow of a single candle, black tendrils reached from the shower stall toward the ruined lights, bent and branching like skeletal leaves.

In the shower stall, Juliette Andromeda Mao lay dead.

Her eyes were closed, and that was a mercy. She'd cut her hair differently since she'd taken the pictures Miller had seen, and it changed the shape of her face, but she was unmistakable. She was nude, and barely human. Coils of complex growth spilled from her mouth, ears, and vulva. Her ribs and spine had grown spurs like knives that stretched pale skin, ready to cut themselves free of her. Tubes stretched from her back and throat, crawling up the walls behind her. A deep brown slush had leaked from her, filling the shower pan almost three centimeters high. He sat silently, willing the thing before him not to be true, trying to force himself awake.

What did they do to you? he thought. *Oh, kid. What did they do?*

"Ohmygod," Naomi said behind him.

"Don't touch anything," he said. "Get out of the room. Into the hall. Do it now."

The light in the next room faded as the hand terminals retreated. The twisting shadows momentarily gave her body the illusion of movement. Miller waited, but no breath lifted the bent rib cage. No flicker touched her eyelids. There was nothing. He rose, carefully checking his cuffs and shoes, and walked out to the corridor.

They'd all seen it. He could tell from the expressions, they'd all seen. And they didn't know any better than he did what it was. Gently, he pulled the splintered door closed and waited for Sematimba. It wasn't long.

Five men in police riot armor with shotguns made their way down the hall. Miller walked forward to meet them, his posture better than a badge. He could see them relax. Sematimba came up behind them.

"Miller?" he said. "The hell is this? I thought you said you were staying put."

"I didn't leave," he said. "Those are the civilians back there. The dead guys downstairs jumped them in the lobby."

"Why?" Sematimba demanded.

"Who knows?" Miller said. "Roll them for spare change. That's not the problem."

Sematimba's eyebrows rose. "I've got four corpses down there, and they're not the problem."

Miller nodded down the corridor.

"Fifth one's up here," he said. "It's the girl I was looking for."

Sematimba's expression softened. "I'm sorry," he said.

"Nah," Miller said. He couldn't accept sympathy. He couldn't accept comfort. A gentle touch would shatter him, so he stayed hard instead. "But you're going to want the coroner on this one."

"It's bad, then?"

"You've got no idea," Miller said. "Listen, Semi. I'm in over my head here. Seriously. Those boys down there with the guns? If they weren't hooked in with your security force, there would have been alarms as soon as the first shot was fired. You know this was a setup. They were waiting for these four. And the squat fella with the dark hair? That's James Holden. He's not even supposed to be alive."

"Holden that started the war?" Sematimba said.

"That's the one," Miller said. "This is deep. Drowning deep. And you know what they say about going in after a drowning man, right?"

Sematimba looked down the corridor. He nodded.

"Let me help you," Sematimba said, but Miller shook his head.

"I'm too far gone. Forget me. What happened was you got a call. You found the place. You don't know me, you don't know them, you've got no clue what happened. Or you come along and drown with me. Your pick."

"You don't leave the station without telling me?"

"Okay," Miller said.

"I can live with that," Sematimba said. Then, a moment later: "That's really Holden?"

"Call the coroner," Miller said. "Trust me."

Chapter Twenty-Five: Holden

Miller gestured at Holden and headed for the elevator without waiting to see if he was following. The presumption irritated him, but he went anyway.

"So," Holden said, "we were just in a gunfight where we killed at least three people, and now we're just leaving? No getting questioned or giving a statement? How exactly does that happen?" Holden asked.

"Professional courtesy," Miller said, and Holden couldn't tell if he was joking.

The elevator door opened with a muffled ding, and Holden and the others followed Miller inside. Naomi was closest to the panel, so she reached out to press the lobby button, but her hand was shaking so badly that she had to stop and clench it into a fist. After a deep breath, she reached out a now steady finger and pressed the button.

"This is bullshit. Being an ex-cop doesn't give you a license to get in gunfights," Holden said to Miller's back.

Miller didn't move, but he seemed to shrink a little bit. His sigh was heavy and unforced. His skin seemed grayer than before.

"Sematimba knows the score. Half the job is knowing when to look the other way. Besides, I promised we wouldn't leave the station without letting him know."

"Fuck that," Amos said. "You don't make promises for us, pal."

The elevator came to a stop and opened onto the bloody scene of the gunfight. A dozen cops were in the room. Miller nodded at them and they nodded back. He led the crew out of the lobby to the corridor, then turned around.

"We can work that out later," Miller said. "Right now, let's get someplace we can talk."

Holden agreed with a shrug. "Okay, but you're paying."

Miller headed off down the corridor toward the tube station.

As they followed, Naomi put a hand on Holden's arm and slowed him down a bit so that Miller could get ahead. When he was far enough away, she said, "He knew her."

"Who knew who?"

"He," Naomi said, nodding at Miller, "knew her." She jerked her head back toward the crime scene behind them.

"How do you know?" Holden said.

"He wasn't expecting to find her there, but he knew who she was. Seeing her like that was a shock."

"Huh, I didn't get that at all. He's seemed like Mr. Cool all through this."

"No, they were friends or something. He's having trouble dealing with it, so maybe don't push him too hard," she said. "We might need him."

The hotel room Miller got was only slightly better than the one they'd found the body in. Alex immediately headed for the bathroom and locked the door. The sound of water running in the sink wasn't quite loud enough to cover the pilot's retching.

Holden plopped down on the small bed's dingy comforter, forcing Miller to take the room's one uncomfortable-looking chair. Naomi sat next to Holden on the bed, but Amos stayed on his feet, prowling around the room like a nervous animal.

"So, talk," Holden said to Miller.

"Let's wait for the rest of the gang to finish up," Miller replied with a nod toward the bathroom.

Alex came out a few moments later, his face still white, but now freshly washed.

"Are you all right, Alex?" Naomi asked in a soft voice.

"Five by five, XO," Alex said, then sat down on the floor and put his head in his hands.

Holden stared at Miller and waited. The older man sat and played with his hat for a minute, then tossed it onto the cheap plastic desk that cantilevered out from the wall.

"You knew Julie was in that room. How?" Miller said.

"We didn't even know her name was Julie," Holden replied. "We just knew that it was someone from the *Scopuli*."

"You should tell me how you knew that," Miller said, a frightening intensity in his eyes.

Holden paused a moment. Miller had killed someone who had been trying to kill them, and that certainly helped make the case that he was a friend, but Holden wasn't about to sell out Fred and his group on a hunch. He hesitated, then went halfway.

"The fictional owner of the *Scopuli* had checked into that flophouse," he said. "It made sense that it was a member of the crew raising a flag."

Miller nodded. "Who told you?" he said.

"I'm not comfortable telling you that. We believed the information was accurate," Holden replied. "The *Scopuli* was the bait that someone used to kill the *Canterbury*. We thought someone from the *Scopuli* might know why everyone keeps trying to kill us."

Miller said, "Shit," and then leaned back in his chair and stared at the ceiling.

"You've been looking for Julie. You'd hoped we were looking for her too. That we knew something," Naomi said, not making it a question.

"Yeah," Miller said.

It was Holden's turn to ask why.

"Parents sent a contract to Ceres looking for her to be sent home. It was my case," Miller said.

"So you work for Ceres security?"

"Not anymore."

"So what are you doing here?" Holden asked.

"Her family was connected to something," Miller replied. "I just naturally hate a mystery."

"And how did you know it was bigger than just a missing girl?"

Talking to Miller felt like digging through granite with a rubber chisel. Miller grinned humorlessly.

"They fired me for looking too hard."

Holden consciously decided not to be annoyed by Miller's nonanswer. "So let's talk about the death squad in the hotel."

"Yeah, seriously, what the fuck?" Amos said, finally pausing in his pacing. Alex took his head out of his hands and looked up with interest for the first time. Even Naomi leaned forward on the edge of the bed.

"No idea," Miller replied. "But someone knew you were coming."

"Yeah, thanks for the brilliant police work," Amos said with a snort. "No way we woulda figured that out on our own."

Holden ignored him. "But they didn't know why, or they would have already gone up to Julie's room and gotten whatever they wanted."

"Does that mean Fred's been compromised?" Naomi said.

"Fred?" Miller asked.

"Or maybe someone figured out the Polanski thing too, but didn't have a room number," Holden said.

"But why come out guns blazing like that?" Amos said. "Doesn't make any sense to shoot us."

"*That* was a mistake," Miller said. "I saw it happen. Amos here drew his gun. Somebody overreacted. They were yelling cease-fire right up until you folks started shooting back."

Holden began ticking off points on his fingers.

"So someone finds out we're headed to Eros, and that it is related to the *Scopuli*. They even know the hotel, but not the room."

"They don't know it's Lionel Polanski either," Naomi said. "They could have looked it up at the desk, just like we did."

"Right. So they wait for us to show, and have a squad of gunmen ready to take us in. But that goes to shit and it turns into a gunfight in the lobby. They absolutely *don't* see you coming, Detective, so they aren't omniscient."

"Right," Miller said. "The whole thing screams last minute. Grab you guys and find out what you're looking for. If they'd had more time, they could have just searched the hotel. Might have taken two or three days, but it could have been done. They didn't, so that means grabbing you was easier."

Holden nodded. "Yes," he said. "But that means that they already had teams here. Those didn't seem like locals to me."

Miller paused, looking disconcerted.

"Now you say it, me either," he agreed.

"So whoever it is, they already have teams of gunmen on Eros, and they can redeploy them to come at a moment's notice to pick us up," Holden said.

"And enough pull with security that they could have a firefight and nobody came," Miller said. "Police didn't know anything was happening until I called them."

Holden cocked his head to one side, then said, "Shit, we really need to get out of here."

"Wait a minute," Alex said loudly. "Just wait a goddamn minute here. How come no one is talkin' about the *mutant horror show* in that room? Was I the only one that saw that?"

"Yeah, Jesus, what was that all about?" Amos said quietly.

Miller reached into his coat pocket and took out the evidence bag with Julie's hand terminal in it.

"Any of you guys a techie?" he asked. "Maybe we could find out."

"I could probably hack it," Naomi said. "But there's no way I'm touching that thing until we know what did that to her and that it isn't catching. I'm not pushing my luck by handling anything she's touched."

"You don't have to touch it. Keep the bag sealed. Just use it right through the plastic. The touch screen should still work."

Naomi paused for a second, then reached out and took the bag.

"Okay, give me a minute," she said, then set to work on it.

Miller leaned back in his chair again, letting out another heavy sigh.

"So," Holden said. "Did you know Julie before this? Naomi seems to think finding her dead like that really knocked you for a loop."

Miller shook his head slowly. "You get a case like that, you look into whoever it is. You know, personal stuff. Read their e-mail. Talk to the people they know. You get a picture."

Miller stopped talking and rubbed his eyes with his thumbs. Holden didn't push him, but he started talking again anyway.

"Julie was a good kid," Miller said as if he were confessing something. "She flew a mean racing ship. I just...I wanted to get her back alive."

"It's got a password," Naomi said, holding up the terminal. "I could hack the hardware, but I'd have to open the case."

Miller reached out and said, "Let me give it a try."

Naomi handed the terminal to him, and he tapped a few characters on the screen and handed it back.

"*Razorback,*" Naomi said. "What's that?"

"It's a sled," Miller replied.

"Is he talking to us?" Amos said, pointing his chin at Miller. " 'Cause there's no one else here, but I swear half the time I don't know what the fuck he's on about."

"Sorry," Miller said. "I've been working more or less solo. Makes for bad habits."

Naomi shrugged and went back to work with Holden and Miller now looking over her shoulders.

"She's got a lot of stuff on here," Naomi said. "Where to start?"

Miller pointed at a text file simply labeled NOTES sitting on the terminal's desktop.

"Start there," he said. "She's a fanatic about putting things in the right folders. If she left that on the desktop, it means she wasn't sure where it went."

Naomi tapped on the document to open it up. It expanded into a loosely organized collection of text that read like someone's diary.

First off, get your shit together. Panic doesn't help. It never helps. Deep breaths, figure this out, make the right moves. Fear is the mind-killer. Ha. Geek.

Shuttle Pros:
No reactor, just batteries. V. low radiation.
Supplies for eight
Lots of reaction mass

Shuttle Cons:
No Epstein, no torch
Comm not just disabled, but physically removed *(feeling a little paranoid about leaks, guys?)*

Closest transit is Eros. Is that where we were going? Maybe go someplace else? On just teakettle, this is gonna be a **slow** *boat. Another transit adds seven more weeks. Eros, then.*

I've got the Phoebe bug, no way around it. Not sure how, but that brown shit was everywhere. It's anaerobic, must

*have touched some. Doesn't matter how, just work the
problem.*

*I just slept for THREE WEEKS. Didn't even get up to pee.
What does that?*

I'm so fucked.

Things you need to remember:

* BA834024112
** Radiation kills. No reactor on this shuttle, but keep the
lights off. Keep the e-suit on. Video asshat said this thing eats
radiation. Don't feed it.*
** Send up a flag. Get some help. You work for the smartest
people in the system. They'll figure something out.*
** Stay away from people. Don't spread the bug. Not
coughing up the brown goo yet. No idea when that starts.*
** Keep away from bad guys—as if you know who they are.
Fine. So keep away from everyone. Incognito is my name.
Hmm. Polanski?*

*Damn. I can feel it. I'm hot all the time, and I'm starving.
Don't eat. Don't feed it. Feed a cold, starve a flu? Other way
around? Eros is a day out, and then help is on the way. Keep
fighting.*

*Safe on Eros. Sent up the flag. Hope the home office is
watching. Head hurts. Something's happening on my back.
Lump over my kidneys. Darren turned into goo. Am I going
to be a suit full of jelly?*

*Sick now. Things coming out of my back and leaking that
brown stuff everywhere. Have to take the suit off. If you*

read this, don't let anyone touch the brown stuff. Burn me. I'm burning up.

Naomi put the terminal down, but no one spoke for a moment. Finally, Holden said, "Phoebe bug. Anyone have an idea?"

"There was a science station on Phoebe," Miller said. "Inner planets place, no Belters allowed. It got hit. Lots of dead people, but…"

"She talks about being on a shuttle," Naomi said. "The *Scopuli* didn't have a shuttle."

"There had to be another ship," Alex said. "Maybe she got the shuttle off it."

"Right," Holden said. "They got on another ship, they got infected with this Phoebe bug, and the rest of the crew…I don't know. Dies?"

"She gets out, not realizing she's infected till she's on the shuttle," Naomi continued. "She comes here, she sends up the flag to Fred, and she dies in that hotel room of the infection."

"Not, however, turned to goo," Holden said. "Just really badly…I don't know. Those tubes and bone spurs. What kind of disease does that?"

The question hung in the air. Again no one spoke. Holden knew they were all thinking the same thing. They hadn't touched anything in the flophouse room. Did that mean they were safe from it? Or did they have the Phoebe bug, whatever the hell it was? But she'd said anaerobic. Holden was pretty sure that meant you couldn't get it by breathing it in the air. *Pretty* sure…

"Where do we go from here, Jim?" Naomi asked.

"How about Venus?" Holden said, his voice higher and tighter than he'd expected. "Nothing interesting happening on Venus."

"Seriously," Naomi said.

"Okay. Seriously, I think Miller there lets his cop friend know the story, and then we get the hell off of this rock. It's got to be a bioweapon, right? Someone steals it off a Martian science lab, seeds this shit in a dome, a month later every human being in the city is dead."

Amos interrupted with a grunt.

"There's some holes in that, Cap'n," Amos said. "Like what the fuck does that have to do with taking down the *Cant* and the *Donnager*?"

Holden looked Naomi in the eye and said, "We have a place to look now, don't we?"

"Yeah, we do," she said. "BA834024112. That's a rock designation."

"What do you think is out there?" Alex asked.

"If I was a betting man, I'd say it's whatever ship she stole that shuttle from," Holden replied.

"Makes sense," Naomi said. "Every rock in the Belt is mapped. You want to hide something, put it in a stable orbit next to one and you can always find it later."

Miller turned toward Holden, his face even more drawn.

"If you're going there, I want in," he said.

"Why?" Holden asked. "No offense, but you found your girl. Your job's over, right?"

Miller looked at him, his lips a thin line.

"Different case," Miller said. "Now it's about who killed her."

Chapter Twenty-Six: Miller

Your police friend put a lockdown order on my ship," Holden said. He sounded outraged.

Around them, the hotel restaurant was busy. Last shift's prostitutes mixed with the next shift's tourists and businessmen at the cheap pink-lit buffet. The pilot and the big guy—Alex and Amos—were vying for the last bagel. Naomi sat at Holden's side, her arms crossed, a cup of bad coffee cooling before her.

"We did kill some people," Miller said gently.

"I thought you got us out of that with your secret police handshake," Holden said. "So why's my ship in lockdown?"

"You remember when Sematimba said we shouldn't leave the station without telling him?" Miller said.

"I remember you making some kind of deal," Holden said. "I don't remember agreeing to it."

"Look, he's going to keep us here until he's sure he won't get fired for letting us go. Once he knows his ass is covered, the lock goes down. So let's talk about the part where I rent a berth on your ship."

Jim Holden and his XO exchanged a glance, one of those tiny human burst communications that said more than words could have. Miller didn't know either of them well enough to decode all of it, but he guessed they were skeptical.

They had reason to be. Miller had checked his credit balance before he'd called them. He had enough left for another night in the hotel or a good dinner, but not both. He was spending it on a cheap breakfast that Holden and his crew didn't need and probably wouldn't enjoy, buying goodwill.

"I need to make very, very sure I understand what you're saying," Holden said as the big one—Amos—returned and sat at his other side holding the bagel. "Are you saying that unless I let you on my ship, your friend is going to keep us here? Because that's blackmail."

"Extortion," Amos said.

"What?" Holden said.

"It's not blackmail," Naomi said. "That would be if he threatened to expose information we didn't want known. If it's just a threat, that's extortion."

"And it's not what I'm talking about," Miller said. "Freedom of the station while the investigation rolls? That's no trouble. Leaving jurisdiction's another thing. I can't hold you here any more than I can cut you loose. I'm just looking for a ride when you go."

"Why?" Holden said.

"Because you're going to Julie's asteroid," Miller said.

"I'm willing to bet there's no port there," Holden said. "Did you plan on going anyplace after that?"

"I'm kind of low on solid plans. Haven't had one yet that actually happened."

"I hear that," Amos said. "We've been fucked eighteen different ways since we got into this."

Holden folded his hands on the table, one finger tapping a

complicated rhythm on the wood-textured concrete top. It wasn't a good sign.

"You seem like a...well, like an angry, bitter old man, actually. But I've been working water haulers for the past five years. That just means you'd fit in."

"But," Miller said, and let the word hang there.

"But I've been shot at a lot recently, and the machine guns yesterday were the least lethal thing I've had to deal with," Holden said. "I'm not letting anyone on my ship that I wouldn't trust with my life, and I don't actually know you."

"I can get the money," Miller said, his belly sinking. "If it's money, I can cover it."

"It's not about negotiating a price," Holden said.

"Get the money?" Naomi said, her eyes narrowing. " 'Get the money,' as in you don't have it now?"

"I'm a little short," Miller said. "It's temporary."

"You have an income?" Naomi said.

"More like a strategy," Miller said. "There's some independent rackets down on the docks. There always are at any port. Side games. Fights. Things like that. Most of them, the fix is in. It's how you bribe cops without actually bribing cops."

"That's your plan?" Holden said, incredulity in his voice. "Go collect some police bribes?"

Across the restaurant, a prostitute in a red nightgown yawned prodigiously; the john across the table from her frowned.

"No," Miller said reluctantly. "I play the side bets. A cop goes in, I make a side bet that he's going to win. I know who the cops are mostly. The house, they know because they're bribing them. The side bets are with fish looking to feel edgy because they're playing unlicensed."

Even as he said it, Miller knew how weak it sounded. Alex, the pilot, came and sat beside Miller. His coffee smelled bright and acidic.

"What's the deal?" Alex asked.

"There isn't one," Holden said. "There wasn't one before and there still isn't."

"It works better than you'd think," Miller said gamely, and four hand terminals chimed at once. Holden and Naomi exchanged another, less complicit glance and pulled up their terminals. Amos and Alex already had theirs up. Miller caught the red-and-green border that meant either a priority message or an early Christmas card. There was a moment's silence as they all read something; then Amos whistled low.

"Stage three?" Naomi said.

"Can't say as I like the sound of that," Alex said.

"You mind if I ask?" Miller said.

Holden slid his terminal across the table. The message was plaintext, encoded from Tycho.

CAUGHT MOLE IN TYCHO COMM STATION.
YOUR PRESENCE AND DESTINATION LEAKED TO
UNKNOWN PERSONS ON EROS. BE CAREFUL.

"Little late on that," Miller said.

"Keep reading," Holden said.

MOLE'S ENCRYPTION CODE ALLOWED INTERCEPT
OF SUBSIGNAL BROADCAST FROM EROS FIVE
HOURS AGO.
    INTERCEPTED MESSAGE FOLLOWS:
HOLDEN ESCAPED BUT PAYLOAD SAMPLE
RECOVERED. REPEAT: SAMPLE RECOVERED.
PROCEEDING TO STAGE THREE.

"Any idea what that means?" Holden asked.

"I don't," Miller said, pushing the terminal back. "Except...if the payload sample is Julie's body."

"Which I think we can assume it is," Holden said.

Miller tapped his fingertips on the tabletop, unconsciously copying Holden's rhythm, his mind working through the combinations.

"This thing," Miller said. "The bioweapon or whatever. They were shipping it here. So now it's here. Okay. There's no reason to take out Eros. It's not particularly important to the war when you hold it up to Ceres or Ganymede or the shipyard at Callisto. And if you wanted it dead, there're easier ways. Blow a big fusion bomb on the surface, and crack it like an egg."

"It's not a military base, but it is a shipping hub," Naomi said. "And, unlike Ceres, it's not under OPA control."

"They're shipping her out, then," Holden said. "They're taking their sample out to infect whatever their original target was, and once they're off the station, there's no way we're going to stop it."

Miller shook his head. Something about the chain of logic felt wrong. He was missing something. His imaginary Julie appeared across the room, but her eyes were dark, black filaments pouring down her cheeks like tears.

What am I looking at here, Julie? he thought. *I'm seeing something here, but I don't know what it is.*

The vibration was a slight, small thing, less than a transport tube's braking stutter. A few plates rattled; the coffee in Naomi's cup danced in a series of concentric circles. Everyone in the hotel went silent with the sudden shared dread of thousands of people made aware of their fragility in the same moment.

"Oh-kay," Amos said. "The fuck was that?" and the emergency Klaxons started blaring.

"Or possibly stage three is something else," Miller said over the noise.

The public-address system was muddy by its nature. The same voice spoke from consoles and speakers that might have been as close as a meter from each other or as far out as earshot would take them. It made every word reverberate, a false echo. Because of that, the voice of the emergency broadcast system enunciated very carefully, each word bitten off separately.

"Attention, please. Eros Station is in emergency lockdown. Proceed immediately to the casino level for radiological safety confinement. Cooperate with all emergency personnel. Attention, please. Eros station is in emergency lockdown..."

And on in a loop that would continue, if no one coded in the override, until every man, woman, child, animal, and insect on the station had been reduced to dust and humidity. It was the nightmare scenario, and Miller did what a lifetime on pressurized rocks had trained him to do. He was up from the table, in the corridor, and heading down toward the wider passages, already clogged with bodies. Holden and his crew were on his heels.

"That was an explosion," Alex said. "Ship drive at the least. Maybe a nuke."

"They are going to kill the station," Holden said. There was a kind of awe in his voice. "I never thought I'd miss the part where they just blew up the ships I was on. But now it's stations."

"They didn't crack it," Miller said.

"You're sure of that?" Naomi asked.

"I can hear you talking," Miller said. "That tells me there's air."

"There are airlocks," Holden said. "If the station got holed and the locks closed down..."

A woman pushed hard against Miller's shoulder, forcing her way forward. If they weren't damn careful, there was going to be a stampede. This was too much fear and not enough space. It hadn't happened yet, but the impatient movement of the crowd, vibrating like molecules in water just shy of boiling, made Miller very uncomfortable.

"This isn't a ship," Miller said. "It's a station. This is rock we're on. Anything big enough to get to the parts of the station with atmosphere would crack the place like an egg. A great big pressurized egg."

The crowd was stopped, the tunnel full. They were going to

need crowd control, and they were going to need it fast. For the first time since he'd left Ceres, Miller wished he had a badge. Someone pushed into Amos' side, then backed away through the press when the big guy growled.

"Besides," Miller said, "it's a rad hazard. You don't need air loss to kill everyone in the station. Just burn a few quadrillion spare neutrons through the place at C, and there won't be any trouble with the oxygen supply."

"Cheerful fucker," Amos said.

"They build stations inside of rocks for a reason," Naomi said. "Not so easy to force radiation through this many meters of rock."

"I spent a month in a rad shelter once," Alex said as they pushed through the thickening crowd. "Ship I was on had magnetic containment drop. Automatic cutoffs failed, and the reactor kept runnin' for almost a second. Melted the engine room. Killed five of the crew on the next deck up before they knew we had a problem, and it took them three days to carve the bodies free of the melted decking for burial. The rest of us wound up eighteen to a shelter for thirty-six days while a tug flew to get us."

"Sounds great," Holden said.

"End of it, six of 'em got married, and the rest of us never spoke to each other again," Alex said.

Ahead of them, someone shouted. It wasn't in alarm or even anger, really. Frustration. Fear. Exactly the things Miller didn't want to hear.

"That may not be our big problem," Miller said, but before he could explain, a new voice cut in, drowning out the emergency-response loop.

"Okay, everybody! We're Eros security, *que no*? We got an emergency, so you do what we tell you and nobody gets hurt."

About time, Miller thought.

"So here's the rule," the new voice said. "Next asshole who pushes anyone, I'm going to shoot them. Move in an orderly fashion. First priority: orderly. Second priority is *move*! Go, go, go!"

At first nothing happened. The knot of human bodies was tied too tightly for even the most heavy-handed crowd control to free quickly, but a minute later, Miller saw some heads far ahead of him in the tunnel start to shift, then move away. The air in the tunnel was thickening and the hot plastic smell of overloaded recyclers reached him just as the clot came free. Miller's breath started coming easier.

"Do they have hard shelters?" a woman behind them asked her companion, and then was swept away by the currents. Naomi plucked Miller's sleeve.

"Do they?" she asked.

"They should, yes," Miller said. "Enough for maybe a quarter million, and essential personnel and medical crews would get first crack at them."

"And everyone else?" Amos said.

"If they survive the event," Holden said, "station personnel will save as many people as they can."

"Ah," Amos said. Then: "Well, fuck that. We're going for the *Roci*, right?"

"Oh, hell yes," Holden said.

Ahead of them, the fast-shuffling crowd in their tunnel was merging with another flow of people from a lower level. Five thick-necked men in riot gear were waving people on. Two of them were pointing guns at the crowd. Miller was more than half tempted to go up and slap the little idiots. Pointing guns at people was a lousy way to avoid panic. One of the security men was also far too wide for his gear, the Velcro fasteners at his belly reaching out for each other like lovers at the moment of separation.

Miller looked down at the floor and slowed his steps, the back of his mind suddenly and powerfully busy. One of the cops swung his gun out over the crowd. Another one—the fat guy—laughed and said something in Korean.

What had Sematimba said about the new security force? All bluster, no balls. A new corporation out of Luna. Belters on the ground. Corrupt.

The name. They'd had a name. CPM. *Carne Por la Machina.* Meat for the machine. One of the gun-wielding cops lowered his weapon, swept off his helmet, and scratched violently behind one ear. He had wild black hair, a tattooed neck, and a scar that went from one eyelid down almost to the joint of his jaw.

Miller knew him. A year and a half ago, he'd arrested him for assault and racketeering. And the equipment—armor, batons, riot guns—also looked hauntingly familiar. Dawes had been wrong. Miller had been able to find his own missing equipment after all.

Whatever this was, it had been going on a long time before the *Canterbury* had picked up a distress call from the *Scopuli.* A long time before Julie had vanished. And putting a bunch of Ceres Station thugs in charge of Eros crowd control using stolen Ceres Station equipment had been part of the plan. The third phase.

Ah, he thought. *Well. That can't be good.*

Miller slid to the side, letting as many bodies as he plausibly could fill the space between him and the gunmen dressed as police.

"Get down to the casino level," one of the gunmen shouted over the crowd. "We'll get you into the radiation shelters from there, but you've got to get to the casino level!"

Holden and his crew hadn't noticed anything odd. They were talking among themselves, strategizing about how to get to their ship and what to do once they got there, speculating about who might have attacked the station and where Julie Mao's twisted, infected corpse might be headed. Miller fought the impulse to interrupt them. He needed to stay calm, to think things through. They couldn't attract attention. He needed the right moment.

The corridor turned and widened. The press of bodies lightened a little bit. Miller waited for a dead zone in the crowd control, a space where none of the fake security men could see them. He took Holden by the elbow.

"Don't go," he said.

Chapter Twenty-Seven: Holden

What do you mean, don't go?" Holden asked, yanking his elbow out of Miller's grasp. "Somebody just nuked the station. This has escalated beyond our capacity to respond. If we can't get to the *Roci*, we're doing whatever they tell us to until we can."

Miller took a step back and put up his hands; he was clearly doing his best to look nonthreatening, which just pissed Holden off even more. Behind him, the riot cops were motioning the people milling in the corridors toward the casinos. The air echoed with the electronically amplified voices of the police directing the crowds and the buzz of anxious citizens. Over it all, the public-address system told everyone to remain calm and cooperate with emergency personnel.

"See that bruiser over there in the police riot gear?" Miller said. "His name is Gabby Smalls. He supervises a chunk of the Golden Bough protection racket on Ceres. He also runs a little dust on the side, and I suspect he's tossed more than a few people out airlocks."

Holden looked at the guy. Wide shoulders, thick gut. Now that Miller pointed him out, there was something about him that didn't seem right for a cop.

"I don't get it," Holden said.

"A couple months ago, when you started a bunch of riots by saying Mars blew up your water hauler, we found out—"

"I never said—"

"—*found out* that most of the police riot gear on Ceres was missing. A few months before that, a bunch of our underworld muscle went missing. I just found out where both of them are."

Miller pointed at the riot-gear-equipped Gabby Smalls.

"I wouldn't go wherever he's sending people," he said. "I really wouldn't."

A thin stream of people bumped past.

"Then where?" Naomi asked.

"Yeah, I mean, if the choice is radiation or mobsters, I gotta go with the mobsters," Alex said, nodding emphatically at Naomi.

Miller pulled out his hand terminal and held it up so everyone could see the screen.

"I've got no radiation warnings," he said. "Whatever happened outside isn't a danger on this level. Not right now. So let's just calm down and make the smart move."

Holden turned his back on Miller and motioned to Naomi. He pulled her aside and said in a quiet voice, "I still think we go back to the ship and get out of here. Take our chances getting past these mobsters."

"If there's no radiation danger, then I agree," she said with a nod.

"I disagree," Miller said, not even pretending he hadn't been eavesdropping. "To do that we have to walk through three levels of casino filled with riot gear and thugs. They're going to tell us to get in one of those casinos for our own protection. When we don't, they'll beat us unconscious and throw us in anyway. For our own protection."

Another crowd of people poured out of a branch corridor, heading for the reassuring presence of the police and the bright casino lights. Holden found it difficult not to be swept along with the crowd. A man with two enormous suitcases bumped into Naomi, almost knocking her down. Holden grabbed her hand.

"What's the alternative?" he asked Miller.

Miller glanced up and down the corridor, seeming to measure the flow of people. He nodded at a yellow-and-black-striped hatch down a small maintenance corridor.

"That one," he said. "It's marked HIGH VOLTAGE, so the guys sweeping for stragglers won't bother with it. It's not the kind of place citizens hide."

"Can you get that door open quickly?" Holden said, looking at Amos.

"Can I break it?"

"If you need to."

"Then sure," Amos said, and began pushing his way through the crowd toward the maintenance hatch. At the door, he pulled out his multi-tool and popped off the cheap plastic housing for the card reader. After he twisted a couple of wires together, the hatch slid open with a hydraulic hiss.

"Ta-da," Amos said. "The reader won't work anymore, so anyone who wants in comes in."

"Let's worry about that if it happens," Miller replied, then led them into the dimly lit passageway beyond.

The service corridor was filled with electrical cable held together with plastic ties. It stretched through the dim red light for thirty or forty feet before falling into gloom. The light came from LEDs mounted on the metal bracing that sprouted from the wall every five feet or so to hold the cable up. Naomi had to duck to enter, her frame about four centimeters too tall for the ceiling. She put her back to the wall and slid down onto her haunches.

"You'd think they'd make the maintenance corridors tall enough for Belters to work in," she said irritably.

Holden touched the wall almost reverently, tracing a corridor identification number carved right into the stone.

"The Belters who built this place weren't tall," he said. "These are some of the main power lines. This tunnel goes back to the first Belt colony. The people who carved it grew up in gravity."

Miller, who also had to duck his head, sat on the floor with a grunt and popping knees.

"History lesson later," he said. "Let's figure a way off this rock."

Amos, studying the bundles of cable intently, said over his shoulder, "If you see a frayed spot, don't touch it. This thick fucker right here is a couple million volts. That'd melt your shit down real good."

Alex sat down next to Naomi, grimacing when his butt hit the cold stone floor.

"You know," he said, "if they decide to seal up the station, they might pump all the air outta these maintenance corridors."

"I get it," Holden said loudly. "It's a shitty and uncomfortable hiding spot. You have my permission to now shut up about that."

He squatted down across the corridor from Miller and said, "Okay, Detective. Now what?"

"Now," Miller said, "we wait for the sweep to pass us by, and get behind it, try to get to the docks. The folks in the shelters are easy to avoid. Shelters are up deep. Trick's going to be getting through the casino levels."

"Can't we just use these maintenance passages to move around?" Alex asked.

Amos shook his head. "Not without a map, we won't. You get lost in here, you're in trouble," he said.

Ignoring them, Holden said, "Okay, so we wait for everyone to move to the radiation shelters and then we leave."

Miller nodded at him, and then the two men sat staring at each other for a moment. The air between them seemed to thicken, the silence taking on a meaning of its own. Miller shrugged like his jacket itched.

"Why do you think a bunch of Ceres mobsters are moving everyone to radiation shelters when there's no actual radiation danger?" Holden finally said. "And why are the Eros cops letting them?"

"Good questions," Miller said.

"If they were using these yahoos, it helps explain why their attempted kidnapping at the hotel went so poorly. They don't seem like pros."

"Nope," Miller said. "That's not their usual area of expertise."

"Would you two be quiet?" Naomi said.

For almost a minute they were.

"It'd be really stupid," Holden said, "to go take a look at what's going on, wouldn't it?"

"Yes. Whatever's going on at those shelters, you know that's where all the guards and patrols will be," Miller said.

"Yeah," Holden said.

"Captain," Naomi said, a warning in her voice.

"Still," Holden said, talking to Miller, "you hate a mystery."

"I do at that," Miller replied with a nod and a faint smile. "And you, my friend, are a damn busybody."

"It's been said."

"Goddamn it," Naomi said quietly.

"What is it, Boss?" Amos asked.

"These two just broke our getaway plan," Naomi replied. Then she said to Holden, "You guys are going to be very bad for each other and, by extension, us."

"No," Holden replied. "You aren't coming along. You stay here with Amos and Alex. Give us"—he looked at his terminal—"three hours to go look and come back. If we aren't here—"

"We leave you to the gangsters and the three of us get jobs on Tycho and live happily ever after," Naomi said.

"Yeah," Holden said with a grin. "Don't be a hero."

"Wouldn't even consider it, sir."

Holden crouched in the shadows outside the maintenance hatch and watched as Ceres mobsters dressed in police riot gear led the citizens of Eros away in small groups. The PA system continued to declare the possibility of radiological danger and exhorted the citizens and guests of Eros to cooperate fully with emergency personnel. Holden had selected a group to follow and was getting ready to move when Miller placed a hand on his shoulder.

"Wait," Miller said. "I want to make a call."

He quickly dialed up a number on his hand terminal, and after a few moments, a flat gray *Network Not Available* message appeared.

"Phone is down?" Holden asked.

"That's the first thing I'd do, too," Miller replied.

"I see," Holden said even though he really didn't.

"Well, I guess it's just you and me," Miller said, then took the magazine out of his gun and began reloading it with cartridges he pulled out of his coat pocket.

Even though he'd had enough of gunfights to last him the rest of his life, Holden took out his gun and checked the magazine as well. He'd replaced it after the shoot-out in the hotel, and it was full. He racked it and put it back in the waistband of his pants. Miller, he noticed, kept his out, holding it close to his thigh, where his coat mostly covered it.

It wasn't difficult following the groups up through the station toward the inner sections where the radiation shelters were. As long as they kept moving in the same direction as the crowds, no one gave them a second look. Holden made a mental note of the many corridor intersections where men in riot gear stood guard. It would be much tougher coming back down.

When the group they were following eventually stopped outside a large metal door marked with the ancient radiation symbol, Holden and Miller slipped off to the side and hid behind a large planter filled with ferns and a couple of stunted trees. Holden watched the fake riot cops order everyone into the shelter and then seal the door behind them with the swipe of a card. All but one of them left, the remaining one standing guard outside the door.

Miller whispered, "Let's ask him to let us in."

"Follow my lead," Holden replied, then stood up and began walking toward the guard.

"Hey, shithead, you supposed to be in a shelter or in the casino, so get the fuck back to your group," the guard said, his hand on the butt of his gun.

Holden held up his hands placatingly, smiled, and kept walking. "Hey, I lost my group. Got mixed up somehow. I'm not from here, you know," he said.

The guard pointed down the corridor with the stun baton in his left hand.

"Go that way till you hit the ramps down," he said.

Miller seemed to appear out of nowhere in the dimly lit corridor, his gun already out and pointed at the guard's head. He thumbed off the safety with an audible click.

"How about we just join the group already inside?" he said. "Open it up."

The guard looked at Miller out of the corners of his eyes, not turning his head at all. His hands went up, and he dropped the baton.

"You don't want to do that, man," the fake cop said.

"I kind of think he does," Holden said. "You should do what he says. He's not a very nice person."

Miller pushed the barrel of his gun against the guard's head and said, "You know what we used to call a 'no-brainer' back at the station house? It's when a shot to the head actually blows the entire brain out of someone's skull. It usually happens when a gun is pressed to the victim's head right about here. The gas's got nowhere to go. Pops the brain right out through the exit wound."

"They said not to open these up once they'd been sealed, man," the guard said, speaking so fast he ran all the words together. "They were pretty serious about that."

"This is the last time I ask," Miller said. "Next time I just use the card I took off your body."

Holden turned the guard around to face the door and pulled the handgun out of the man's belt holster. He hoped all Miller's threats were just threats. He suspected they weren't.

"Just open the door, and we'll let you go, I promise," Holden said to the guard.

The guard nodded and moved up to the door, then slid his card through it and punched in a number on the keypad. The heavy blast door slid open. Beyond it, the room was even darker than the corridor outside. A few emergency LEDs glowed a sullen red. In the faint illumination, Holden could see dozens...*hundreds* of bodies scattered across the floor, unmoving.

"Are they dead?" Holden asked.

"I don't know nothing about—" the guard said, but Miller cut him off.

"You go in first," Miller said, and pushed the guard forward.

"Hold on," Holden said. "I don't think it's a good idea to just charge in here."

Three things happened at once. The guard took four steps forward and then collapsed on the floor. Miller sneezed once, loudly, and then started to sway drunkenly. And both Holden's and Miller's hand terminals began an angry electric buzzing.

Miller staggered back and said, "The door..."

Holden hit the button and the door slid shut again.

"Gas," Miller said, then coughed. "There's gas in there."

While the ex-cop leaned against the corridor wall and coughed, Holden took out his terminal to shut off the buzzing. But the alarm flashing on its screen wasn't an air-contamination alert. It was the venerable three wedge shapes pointing inward. Radiation. As he watched, the symbol, which should have been white, shifted through an angry orange color to dark red.

Miller was looking at his too, his expression unreadable.

"We've been dosed," Holden said.

"I've never actually seen the detector activate," Miller said, his voice rough and faint after his coughing fit. "What does it mean when the thing is red?"

"It means we'll be bleeding from our rectums in about six hours," Holden said. "We have to get to the ship. It'll have the meds we need."

"What," Miller said, "the *fuck*...is going on?"

Holden grabbed Miller by the arm and led him back down the

corridor toward the ramps. Holden's skin felt warm and itchy. He didn't know if it was radiation burn or psychosomatic. With the amount of radiation he'd just taken, it was a good thing he had sperm tucked away in Montana and on Europa.

Thinking that made his balls itch.

"They nuke the station," Holden said. "Hell, maybe they just *pretend* to nuke it. Then they drag everyone down here and toss them into radiation shelters that are only radioactive on the inside. Gas them to keep them quiet."

"There are easier ways to kill people," Miller said, his breathing coming in ragged gasps as they ran down the corridor.

"So it has to be more than that," Holden said. "The bug, right? The one that killed that girl. It…fed on radiation."

"Incubators," Miller said, nodding in agreement.

They arrived at one of the ramps to the lower levels, but a group of citizens led by two fake riot cops were coming up. Holden grabbed Miller and pulled him to one side, where they could hide in the shadow of a closed noodle shop.

"So they infected them, right?" Holden said in a whisper, waiting for the group to pass. "Maybe fake radiation meds with the bug in it. Maybe that brown goo just spread around on the floor. Then whatever was in the girl, Julie—"

He stopped when Miller walked away from him straight at the group that had just come up the ramp.

"Officer," said Miller to one of the fake cops.

They both stopped, and one of them said, "You supposed to be—"

Miller shot him in the throat, right below his helmet's faceplate. Then he swiveled smoothly and shot the other guard in the inside of the thigh, just below the groin. When the man fell backward, yelling in pain, Miller walked up and shot him again, this time in the neck.

A couple of the citizens started screaming. Miller pointed his gun at them and they got quiet.

"Go down a level or two and find someplace to hide," he said.

"Do not cooperate with these men, even though they're dressed like police. They do not have your best interests at heart. Go."

The citizens hesitated, then ran. Miller took a few cartridges out of his pocket and began replacing the three he'd fired. Holden started to speak, but Miller cut him off.

"Take the throat shot if you can. Most people, the faceplate and chest armor don't quite cover that gap. If the neck is covered, then shoot the inside of the thigh. Very thin armor there. Mobility issue. Takes most people down in one shot."

Holden nodded, as though that all made sense.

"Okay," Holden said. "Say, let's get back to the ship before we bleed to death, right? No more shooting people if we can help it." His voice sounded calmer than he felt.

Miller slapped the magazine back into his gun and chambered a round.

"I'm guessing there's a lot more people need to be shot before this is over," he said. "But sure. First things first."

Chapter Twenty-Eight: Miller

The first time Miller killed anyone was in his third year working security. He'd been twenty-two, just married, talking about having kids. As the new guy on the contract, he'd gotten the shit jobs: patrolling levels so high the Coriolis made him seasick, taking domestic disturbance calls in holes no wider than a storage bin, standing guard on the drunk tank to keep predators from raping the unconscious. The normal hazing. He'd known to expect it. He'd thought he could take it.

The call had been from an illegal restaurant almost at the mass center. At less than a tenth of a g, gravity had been little more than a suggestion, and his inner ear had been confused and angered by the change in spin. If he thought about it, he could still remember the sound of raised voices, too fast and slurred for words. The smell of bathtub cheese. The thin haze of smoke from the cheap electric griddle.

It had happened fast. The perp had come out of the hole with a gun in one hand, dragging a woman by the hair with the other. Miller's partner, a ten-year veteran named Carson, had shouted out the warning. The perp had turned, swinging the gun out at arm's length like a stuntman in a video.

All through training, the instructors had said that you couldn't know what you'd do until the moment came. Killing another human being was hard. Some people couldn't. The perp's gun came around; the gunman dropped the woman and shouted. It turned out that, for Miller at least, it wasn't all that hard.

Afterward, he'd been through mandatory counseling. He'd cried. He'd suffered the nightmares and the shakes and all the things that cops suffered quietly and didn't talk about. But even then, it seemed to be happening at a distance, like he'd gotten too drunk and was watching himself throw up. It was just a physical reaction. It would pass.

The important thing was he knew the answer to the question. Yes, if he needed to, he could take a life.

It wasn't until now, walking through the corridors of Eros, that he'd taken joy in it. Even taking down the poor bastard in that first firefight had felt like the sad necessity of work. Pleasure in killing hadn't come until after Julie, and it wasn't really pleasure as much as a brief cessation of pain.

He held the gun low. Holden started down the ramp, and Miller followed, letting the Earther take point. Holden walked faster than he did and with the uncommented athleticism of someone who lived in a wide variety of gravities. Miller had the feeling he'd made Holden nervous, and he regretted that a little. He hadn't intended to, and he really needed to get aboard Holden's ship if he was going to find Julie's secrets.

Or, for that matter, not die of radiation sickness in the next few hours. That seemed a finer point than it probably was.

"Okay," Holden said at the bottom of the ramp. "We need to get back down, and there are a lot of guards between us and Naomi that are going to be really confused by two guys walking the wrong direction."

"That's a problem," Miller agreed.

"Any thoughts?"

Miller frowned and considered the flooring. The Eros floors were different than Ceres'. Laminate with flecks of gold.

"Tubes aren't going to be running," he said. "If they are, it'll be in lockdown mode, where it only stops at the holding pen down in the casino. So that's out."

"Maintenance corridor again?"

"If we can find one that goes between levels," Miller said. "Might be a little tricky, but it seems like a better bet than shooting our way past a couple dozen assholes in armor. How long have we got before your friend takes off?"

Holden looked at his hand terminal. The radiation alarm was still deep red. Miller wondered how long those took to reset.

"A little more than two hours," Holden said. "Shouldn't be a problem."

"Let's see what we can find," Miller said.

The corridors nearest the radiation shelters—the death traps, the incubators—had been emptied. Wide passages built to accommodate the ancient construction equipment that had carved Eros into a human habitation were eerie with only Holden's and Miller's footsteps and the hum of the air recyclers. Miller hadn't noticed when the emergency announcements had stopped, but the absence of them now seemed ominous.

If it had been Ceres, he would have known where to go, where everything led, how to move gracefully from one stage to another. On Eros, all he had was an educated guess. That wasn't so bad.

But he could tell it was taking too long, and worse than that—they weren't talking about it; neither one spoke—they were walking more slowly than normal. It wasn't up to the threshold of consciousness, but Miller knew that both of their bodies were starting to feel the radiation damage. It wasn't going to get better.

"Okay," Holden said. "Somewhere around here there has to be a maintenance shaft."

"Could also try the tube station," Miller said. "The cars run in vacuum, but there might be some service tunnels running parallel."

"Don't you think they'd have shut those down as part of the big roundup?"

"Probably," Miller said.

"Hey! You two! What the fuck you think you're doing up here?"

Miller looked back over his shoulder. Two men in riot gear were waving at them menacingly. Holden said something sharp under his breath. Miller narrowed his eyes.

The thing was these men were amateurs. The beginning of an idea moved in the back of Miller's mind as he watched the two approach. Killing them and taking their gear wouldn't work. There was nothing like scorch marks and blood to make it clear something had happened. But...

"Miller," Holden said, a warning in his voice.

"Yeah," Miller said. "I know."

"I said what the fuck are you two doing here?" one of the security men said. "The station's on lockdown. Everyone goes down to the casino level or up to the radiation shelters."

"We were just looking for a way to...ah...get down to the casino level," Holden said, smiling and being nonthreatening. "We're not from around here, and—"

The closer of the two guards jabbed the butt of his rifle neatly into Holden's leg. The Earther staggered, and Miller shot the guard just below the faceplate, then turned to the one still standing, mouth agape.

"You're Mikey Ko, right?" Miller said.

The man's face went even paler, but he nodded. Holden groaned and stood.

"Detective Miller," Miller said. "Busted you on Ceres about four years ago. You got a little happy in a bar. Tappan's, I think? Hit a girl with a pool cue?"

"Oh, hey," the man said with a frightened smile. "Yeah, I remember you. How you been doing?"

"Good and bad," Miller said. "You know how it is. Give the Earther your gun."

Ko looked from Miller to Holden and back, licking his lips and judging his chances. Miller shook his head.

"Seriously," Miller said. "Give him the gun."

"Sure, yeah. No problem."

This was the kind of man who'd killed Julie, Miller thought. Stupid. Shortsighted. A man born with a sense for raw opportunity where his soul should have been. Miller's mental Julie shook her head in disgust and sorrow, and Miller found himself wondering if she meant the thug now handing his rifle to Holden or himself. Maybe both.

"What's the deal here, Mikey?" Miller asked.

"What do you mean?" the guard said, playing stupid, like they were in an interrogation cell. Stalling for time. Walking through the old script of cop and criminal as if it still made sense. As if everything hadn't changed. Miller was surprised by a tightness in his throat. He didn't know what it was there for.

"The job," he said. "What's the job?"

"I don't know—"

"Hey," Miller said gently. "I just killed your buddy."

"And that's his third today," Holden said. "I saw him."

Miller could see it in the man's eyes: the cunning, the shift, the move from one strategy to another. It was old and familiar and as predictable as water moving down.

"Hey," Ko said, "it's just a job. They told us about a year ago how we were making a big move, right? But no one knows what it is. So a few months back, they start moving guys over. Training us up like we were cops, you know?"

"Who was training you?" Miller said.

"The last guys. The ones who were working the contract before us," Ko said.

"Protogen?"

"Something like that, yeah," he said. "Then they took off, and we took over. Just muscle, you know. Some smuggling."

"Smuggling what?"

"All kinds of shit," Ko said. He was starting to feel safe, and it showed in the way he held himself and the way he spoke. "Surveillance equipment, communication arrays, serious-as-fuck servers with their own little gel software wonks already built in. Scientific equipment too. Stuff for checking the water and the air and shit. And these ancient remote-access robots like you'd use in a vacuum dig. All sorts of shit."

"Where was it going to?" Holden asked.

"Here," Ko said, gesturing to the air, the stone, the station. "It's all here. They were like months installing it all. And then for weeks, nothing."

"What do you mean, nothing?" Miller asked.

"Nothing nothing. All this buildup and then we sat around with our thumbs up our butts."

Something had gone wrong. The Phoebe bug hadn't made its rendezvous, but then Julie had come, Miller thought, and the game had turned back on. He saw her again as if he were in her apartment. The long, spreading tendrils of whatever the hell it was, the bone spurs pressing out against her skin, the black froth of filament pouring from her eyes.

"The pay's good, though," Ko said philosophically. "And it was kind of nice taking some time off."

Miller nodded in agreement, leaned close, tucking the barrel of his gun through the interleaving of armor at Ko's belly, and shot him.

"What the fuck!" Holden said as Miller put his gun into his jacket pocket.

"What did you think was going to happen?" Miller said, squatting down beside the gut-shot man. "It's not like he was going to let us go."

"Yeah, okay," Holden said. "But..."

"Help me get him up," Miller said, hooking an arm behind Ko's shoulder. Ko shrieked when Miller lifted him.

"What?"

"Get his other side," Miller said. "Man needs medical attention, right?"

"Um. Yes," Holden said.

"So get his other side."

It wasn't as far back to the radiation shelters as Miller had expected, which had its good points and its bad ones. On the upside, Ko was still alive and screaming. The chances were better that he'd be lucid, which wasn't what Miller had intended. But as they came near the first group of guards, Ko's babbling seemed scattered enough to work.

"Hey!" Miller shouted. "Some help over here!"

At the head of the ramp, four of the guards looked at one another and then started moving toward them, curiosity winning out over basic operating procedures. Holden was breathing hard. Miller was too. Ko wasn't that heavy. It was a bad sign.

"What the hell is this?" one of the guards said.

"There's a bunch of people holed up back there," Miller said. "Resistance. I thought you people swept this level."

"That wasn't our job," the guy said. "We're just making sure the groups from the casino get to the shelters."

"Well, someone screwed up," Miller snapped. "You have transport?"

The guards looked at each other again.

"We can call for one," a guy at the back said.

"Never mind," Miller said. "You boys go find the shooters."

"Wait a minute," the first guy said. "Exactly who the hell are you?"

"The installers from Protogen," Holden said. "We're replacing the sensors that failed. This guy was supposed to help us."

"I didn't hear about that," the leader said.

Miller dug a finger under Ko's armor and squeezed. Ko shrieked and tried to writhe away from him.

"Talk to your boss about it on your own time," Miller said. "Come on. Let's get this asshole to a medic."

"Hold on!" the first guard said, and Miller sighed. Four of them. If he dropped Ko and jumped for cover...but there wasn't much cover. And who the hell knew what Holden would do?

"Where are the shooters?" the guard asked. Miller kept himself from smiling.

"There's a hole about a quarter klick anti-spinward," Miller said. "The other one's body's still there. You can't miss it."

Miller turned down the ramp. Behind him, the guards were talking among themselves, debating what to do, who to call, who to send.

"You're completely insane," Holden said over Ko's semiconscious weeping.

Maybe he was right.

When, Miller wondered, *does someone stop being human?* There had to be a moment, some decision that you made, and before it, you were one person, and after it, someone else. Walking down through the levels of Eros, Ko's bleeding body slung between him and Holden, Miller reflected. He was probably dying of radiation damage. He was lying his way past half a dozen men who were only letting him by because they were used to people being scared of them and he wasn't. He had killed three people in the last two hours. Four if he counted Ko. Probably safer to say four, then.

The analytical part of his mind, the small, still voice he had cultivated for years, watched him move and replayed all his decisions. Everything he'd done had made perfect sense at the time. Shooting Ko. Shooting the other three. Leaving the safety of the crew's hideout to investigate the evacuation. Emotionally, it had all been obvious at the time. It was only when he considered it from outside that it seemed dangerous. If he'd seen it in someone else — Muss, Havelock, Sematimba — he wouldn't have taken more than a minute to realize they'd gone off the rails. Since it was him, he had taken longer to notice. But Holden was right. Somewhere along the line, he'd lost himself.

He wanted to think it had been finding Julie, seeing what had happened to her body, knowing he hadn't been able to save her, but that was only because it seemed like the sentimental moment. The truth was his decisions before then — leaving Ceres to go on a wild hunt for Julie, drinking himself out of a career, remaining a cop for even a day after that first kill all those years earlier — none of them seemed to make sense, viewed objectively. He'd lost a marriage to a woman he'd loved once. He'd lived hip deep in the worst humanity had to offer. He'd learned firsthand that he was capable of killing another human being. And nowhere along the line could he say that there, at that moment, he had been a sane, whole man, and that afterward, he hadn't.

Maybe it was a cumulative process, like smoking cigarettes. One didn't do much. Five didn't do much more. Every emotion he'd shut down, every human contact he'd spurned, every love and friendship and moment of compassion from which he'd turned had taken him a degree away from himself. Until now, he'd been able to kill men with impunity. To face his impending death with a denial that let him make plans and take action.

In his mind, Julie Mao tilted her head, listening to his thoughts. In his mind, she held him, her body against his in a way that was more comforting than erotic. Consoling. Forgiving.

This was why he had searched for her. Julie had become the part of him that was capable of human feeling. The symbol of what he could have been if he hadn't been this. There was no reason to think his imagined Julie had anything in common with the real woman. Meeting her would have been a disappointment for them both.

He had to believe that, the same way he'd had to believe everything that had cut him off from love before.

Holden stopped, the body — corpse now — of Ko tugging Miller back to himself.

"What?" Miller said.

Holden nodded at the access panel in front of them. Miller looked at it, uncomprehending, and then recognized it. They'd made it. They were back at the hideout.

"Are you all right?" Holden said.

"Yeah," Miller said. "Just woolgathering. Sorry."

He dropped Ko, and the thug slid to the floor with a sad thud. Miller's arm had fallen asleep. He shook it, but the tingling didn't go away. A wave of vertigo and nausea passed through him. *Symptoms,* he thought.

"How'd we do for time?" Miller asked.

"We're a little past deadline. Five minutes. It'll be fine," Holden said, and slid the door open.

The space beyond, where Naomi and Alex and Amos had been, was empty.

"Fuck me," Holden said.

Chapter Twenty-Nine: Holden

F uck me," Holden said. And a moment later: "They left us."

No. *She* had left *him*. Naomi had said she would, but confronted with the reality of it, Holden realized that he hadn't really believed her. But here it was—the proof. The empty space where she used to be. His heart hammered and his throat tightened, breath coming in gasps. The sick feeling in his gut was either despair or his colon sloughing off its lining. He was going to die sitting outside a cheap hotel on Eros because Naomi had done exactly what she'd said she would. What he himself had ordered her to do. His resentment refused to listen to reason.

"We're dead," he said, and sat down on the edge of a fern-filled planter.

"How long do we have?" Miller asked, looking up and down the corridor while he fidgeted with his gun.

"No idea," Holden replied, gesturing vaguely at his terminal's flashing red radiation symbol. "Hours before we really start to feel it, I think, but I don't know. God, I wish Shed was still here."

"Shed?"

"Friend of mine," Holden said, not feeling up to elaborating. "Good med tech."

"Call her," Miller said.

Holden looked at his terminal and tapped the screen a few times.

"Network's still down," he said.

"All right," Miller said. "Let's go to your ship. See if it's still in dock."

"They'll be gone. Naomi's keeping the crew alive. She warned me, but I—"

"So let's go anyway," Miller said. He was shifting from one foot to the other and looking down the corridor as he spoke.

"Miller," Holden said, then stopped. Miller was clearly on edge, and he'd shot four people. Holden was increasingly frightened of the former cop. As if reading his mind, Miller stepped close, the two-meter man towering over him where he sat. Miller smiled ruefully, his eyes unnervingly gentle. Holden would almost have preferred they be threatening.

"Way I see it, there's three ways this can go," Miller said. "One, we find your ship still in dock, get the meds we need, and maybe we live. Two, we try to get to the ship, and along the way we run into a bunch of mafia thugs. Die gloriously in a hail of bullets. Three, we sit here and leak out of our eyes and assholes."

Holden said nothing; he just stared up at the cop and frowned.

"I'm liking the first two better than the last one," Miller said. His voice made it sound like an apology. "How about you come with?"

Holden laughed before he could catch himself, but Miller didn't look like he was taking offense.

"Sure," Holden said. "I just needed to feel sorry for myself for a minute. Let's go get killed by the mafia."

He said it with much more bravado than he felt. The truth was he didn't want to die. Even during his time in the navy, the idea of dying in the line of duty had always seemed distant and unreal. *His* ship would never be destroyed, and if it was, *he* would make it to the escape shuttle. The universe without him in it didn't make any sense at all. He'd taken risks; he'd seen other people die. Even people he loved. Now, for the first time, his own death was a real thing.

He looked at the cop. He'd known the man less than a day, didn't trust him, and wasn't sure he much liked him. And this was who he'd die with. Holden shuddered and stood up, pulling his gun out of his waistband. Under the panic and fear, there was a deep feeling of calm. He hoped it would last.

"After you," Holden said. "If we make it, remind me to call my mothers."

The casinos were a powder keg waiting for a match. If the evacuation sweeps had been even moderately successful, there were probably a million or more people crammed into three levels of the station. Hard-looking men in riot gear moved through the crowds, telling everyone to stay put until they were taken to the radiation shelters, keeping the crowd frightened. Every now and then, a small group of citizens would be led away. Knowing where they were going made Holden's stomach burn. He wanted to yell out that the cops were fake, that they were killing people. But a riot with this many people in such a confined space would be a meat grinder. Maybe that was inevitable but he wasn't going to be the one to start it.

Someone else did.

Holden could hear raised voices, the angry rumble of the mob, followed by the electronically amplified voice of someone in a riot helmet yelling for people to get back. And then a gunshot, a brief pause, then a fusillade. People screamed. The entire crowd around Holden and Miller surged in two opposing directions, some of the people rushing toward the sound of the conflict, but many more of them running away from it. Holden spun in the current of bodies; Miller reached out and grabbed the back of his shirt, gripping it in his fist and yelling for Holden to stay close.

About a dozen meters down the corridor, in a coffee shop seating area separated by a waist-high black iron fence, one of the mafia thugs had been cut off from his group by a dozen citizens. Gun drawn, he was backing up and yelling at them to move aside. They kept advancing, their faces wild with the drunken frenzy of mob violence.

The mafia thug fired once, and one small body staggered forward, then fell to the ground at the thug's feet. Holden couldn't tell if it was a boy or a girl, but they couldn't be more than thirteen or fourteen years old. The thug moved forward, looking down at the small thin figure at his feet, and pointed his gun at them again.

It was too much.

Holden found himself running down the corridor toward the thug, gun drawn and screaming for people to get out of the way. When he was about seven meters away, the crowd split apart enough for him to begin firing. Half his shots went wild, hitting the coffee shop counter and walls, one round blowing a stack of ceramic plates into the air. But a few of them hit the thug, staggering him back.

Holden vaulted the waist-high metal fence and came to a sliding halt about three meters from the fake cop and his victim. Holden's gun fired one last time and then the slide locked in the open position to let him know it was empty.

The thug didn't fall down. He straightened up, looked down at his torso, and then looked up and pointed his gun at Holden's face. Holden had time to count the three bullets that were smashed against the heavy chest armor of the thug's riot gear. *Die gloriously in a hail of bullets,* he thought.

The thug said, "Stupid mother fu—" and his head snapped back in a spray of red. He slumped to the floor.

"Gap at the neck, remember?" Miller said from behind him. "Chest armor's too thick for a pistol."

Suddenly dizzy, Holden bent over at the waist, gasping for air. He tasted lemon at the back of his throat and swallowed twice to stop himself from throwing up. He was afraid it would be full of blood and stomach lining. He didn't need to see that.

"Thanks," he gasped out, turning his head toward Miller.

Miller just nodded vaguely in his direction, then walked over to the guard and nudged him with one foot. Holden stood up and looked around the corridor, waiting for the inevitable wave of vengeful mafia enforcers to come crashing down on them. He didn't see any. He and Miller were standing in a quiet island of calm in the midst of Armageddon. All around them, tendrils of violence were whipping into high gear. People were running in every direction; the mafia goons were yelling in booming amplified voices and punctuating the threats with periodic gunfire. But there were only hundreds of them, and there were many thousands of angry and panicked civilians. Miller gestured at the chaos.

"This is what happens," he said. "Give a bunch of yahoos the equipment, and they think they know what they're doing."

Holden crouched beside the fallen child. It was a boy, maybe thirteen, with Asian features and dark hair. His chest had a gaping wound in it, blood trickling out instead of gushing. He didn't have a pulse that Holden could find. Holden picked him up anyway, looking around for someplace to take him.

"He's dead," Miller said as he replaced the cartridge he'd fired.

"Go to hell. We don't know. If we can get him to the ship, maybe..."

Miller shook his head, a sad but distant expression on his face as he looked at the child in Holden's arms.

"He took high-caliber round to the center of mass," Miller said. "He's gone."

"Fuck me," Holden said.

"You keep saying that."

A bright neon sign flashed above the corridor that led out of the

casino l̶ and onto the ramps down to the docks. THANK YOU
FOR PLAYING, it read. And YOU'RE ALWAYS A WINNER ON EROS.
Below it, two ranks of men in heavy combat armor blocked the
way. They might have given up on crowd control in the casinos,
but they weren't letting anyone go.

Holden and Miller crouched behind an overturned coffee cart a
hundred meters from the soldiers. As they watched, a dozen or so
people made a dash toward the guards and were summarily
mowed down by machine gun fire, then fell to the deck beside
those who had tried before.

"I count thirty-four of them," Miller said. "How many can you
handle?"

Holden spun to look at him in surprise, but Miller's face told
him the former cop was joking.

"Kidding aside, how *do* we get past that?" Holden said.

"Thirty men with machine guns and a clear line of sight. No
cover to speak of for the last twenty meters or so," Miller said.
"We don't get past that."

Chapter Thirty: Miller

They sat on the floor with their backs to a bank of pachinko machines no one was playing, watching the ebb and flow of the violence around them like it was a soccer game. Miller's hat was perched on his bent knee. He felt the vibration against his back when one of the displays cycled through its dupe-call. The lights glittered and glowed. Holden, beside him, was breathing hard, like he'd run a race. Out beyond them, like something from Hieronymus Bosch, the casino levels of Eros prepared for death.

The riot's momentum had spent itself for now. Men and women gathered together in small groups. Guards strode through, threatening and scattering any bunch that got too large or unruly. Something was burning fast enough that the air scrubbers couldn't get out the smell of melting plastic. The bhangra Muzak mixed with weeping and screaming and wails of despair. Some idiot was shouting at one of the so-called cops: he was a lawyer; he was getting all of this on video; whoever was responsible was going to be in big trouble. Miller watched a bunch of people start to gather around the confrontation. The guy in the riot gear listened, nodded, and shot the lawyer once in the kneecap. The crowd dispersed except for one woman, the lawyer's wife or girlfriend, bent down over him screaming. And in the privacy of Miller's skull, everything slowly fell apart.

He was aware of having two different minds. One was the Miller he was used to, familiar with. The one who was thinking about what was going to happen when he got out, what the next step would be in connecting the dots between Phoebe Station, Ceres, Eros, and Juliette Mao, how to work the case. That version of him was scanning the crowd the way he might have watched the line at a crime scene, waiting for some detail, some change to catch his attention. Send him in the right direction to solve the mystery. It was the shortsighted, idiotic part of him that couldn't conceive of his own personal extinction, and it thought surely, *surely* there was going to be an after.

The other Miller was different. Quieter. Sad, maybe, but at peace. He'd read a poem many years before called "The Death-Self," and he hadn't understood the term until now. A knot at the middle of his psyche was untying. All the energy he'd put into holding things together—Ceres, his marriage, his career, himself—was coming free. He'd shot and killed more men in the past day than in his whole career as a cop. He'd started—only started—to realize that he'd actually fallen in love with the object of his search after he knew for certain that he'd lost her. He'd seen unequivocally that the chaos he'd dedicated his life to holding at bay was stronger and wider and more powerful than he would ever be. No compromise he could make would be enough. His death-self was unfolding in him, and the dark blooming took no effort. It was a relief, a relaxation, a long, slow exhale after decades of holding it in.

He was in ruins, but it was okay, because he was dying.

"Hey," Holden said. His voice was stronger than Miller had expected it might be.

"Yeah?"

"Did you ever watch *Misko and Marisko* when you were a kid?"

Miller frowned. "The kids' show?" he asked.

"The one with the five dinosaurs and the evil guy in the big pink hat," Holden said, then starting humming a bright, boppy tune. Miller closed his eyes and then started singing along. The music had had words once. Now it was only a series of rises and falls, runs up and down a major scale, with every dissonance resolved in the note that followed.

"Guess I must have," Miller said when they reached the end.

"I loved that show. I must have been eight or nine last time I saw it," Holden said. "Funny how that stuff stays with you."

"Yeah," Miller said. He coughed, turned his head, and spat out something red. "How are you holding together?"

"I think I'm okay," Holden said. Then, a moment later, he added, "As long as I don't stand up."

"Nauseated?"

"Yeah, some."

"Me too."

"What is this?" Holden asked. "I mean, what the hell is this all about? Why are they *doing* this?"

It was a fair question. Slaughtering Eros—slaughtering any station in the Belt—was a pretty easy job. Anyone with first-year orbital mechanics skills could find a way to sling a rock big enough and fast enough to crack the station open. With the effort Protogen had put in, they could have killed the air supply or drugged it or whatever the hell they wanted to do. This wasn't a murder. This wasn't even a genocide.

And then there was all the observation equipment. Cameras, communications arrays, air and water sensors. There were only two reasons for that kind of shit. Either the mad bastards at Protogen got off on watching people die, or...

"They don't know," Miller said.

"What?"

He turned to look at Holden. The first Miller, the detective, the optimist, the one who needed to know, was driving now. His death-self didn't fight, because of course it didn't. It didn't fight anything. Miller raised his hand, like he was giving a lecture to a rookie.

"They don't know what it's about, or... you know, at least they don't know what's going to happen. This isn't even built like a torture chamber. It's all being watched, right? Water and air sensors. It's a petri dish. They don't know what that shit that killed Julie does, and this is how they're finding out."

Holden frowned.

"Don't they have laboratories? Places where you could maybe put that crap on some animals or something? Because as experimental design goes, this seems a little messed up."

"Maybe they need a really big sample size," Miller said. "Or maybe it's not about the people. Maybe it's about what happens to the station."

"There's a cheery thought," Holden said.

The Julie Mao in Miller's mind brushed a lock of hair out of her eyes. She was frowning, looking thoughtful, interested, concerned. It all had to make sense. It was like one of those basic orbital mechanics problems where every hitch and veer seemed random until all the variables slipped into place. What had been inexplicable became inevitable. Julie smiled at him. Julie as she had been. As he imagined she had been. The Miller who hadn't resigned himself to death smiled back. And then she was gone, his mind shifting to the noise from the pachinko machines and the low, demonic wailing of the crowds.

Another group—twenty men hunkered low, like linebackers— made a rush toward the mercenaries guarding the opening to the port. The gunmen mowed them down.

"If we had enough people," Holden said after the sound of machine guns fell away, "we could make it. They couldn't kill all of us."

"That's what the patrol goons are for," Miller said. "Make sure no one can organize a big enough push. Keep stirring the pot."

"But if it was a mob, I mean a really big mob, it could..."

"Maybe," Miller agreed. Something in his chest clicked in a way it hadn't a minute before. He took a slow, deep breath, and the click happened again. He could feel it deep in his left lung.

"At least Naomi got away," Holden said.

"That is good."

"She's amazing. She'd never put Amos and Alex in danger if she could help it. I mean, she's serious. Professional. Strong, you know? I mean, she's really, really..."

"Pretty, too," Miller said. "Great hair. Love the eyes."

"No, that wasn't what I meant," Holden said.

"You don't think she's a good-looking woman?"

"She's my XO," Holden said. "She's...you know..."

"Off-limits."

Holden sighed.

"She got away, didn't she?" Holden asked.

"Almost for sure."

They were silent. One of the linebackers coughed, stood up, and limped back into the casino, trailing blood from a hole in his ribs. The bhangra gave way to an afropop medley with a low, sultry voice singing in languages Miller didn't know.

"She'd wait for us," Holden said. "Don't you think she'd wait for us?"

"Almost for sure," Miller's death-self said, not particularly caring if it was a lie. He thought about it for a long moment, then turned to face Holden again. "Hey. Just so you know it? I'm not exactly at my best right now."

"Okay."

"All right."

The glowing orange lockdown lights on the tube station across the level clicked to green. Miller sat forward, interested. His back felt sticky, but it was probably just sweat. Other people had noticed the change too. Like a current in a water tank, the attention of the nearby crowds shifted from the mercenaries blocking the way to the port to the brushed-steel doors of the tube station.

The doors opened, and the first zombies appeared. Men and women, their eyes glassy and their muscles slack, stumbled out through the open doors. Miller had seen a documentary feed about hemorrhagic fevers as part of his training on Ceres Station. Their movements were the same: listless, driven, autonomic. Like rabid dogs whose minds had already been given over to their disease.

"Hey," Miller said, his hand on Holden's shoulder. "Hey, it's happening."

An older man in a pair of emergency services scrubs approached the shambling newcomers. His hands were out before him, as if he could corral them by simple force of will. The first zombie in the pack turned empty eyes toward him and vomited up a spray of very familiar brown goo.

"Look," Holden said.

"I saw."

"No, *look*!"

All down the casino level, tube station lights were going off lockdown. Doors were opening. The people were pulsing toward the open tubes and the implicit, empty promise of escape, and away from the dead men and women walking out from them.

"Vomit zombies," Miller said.

"From the rad shelters," Holden said. "The thing, the organism. It goes faster in radiation, right? That's why what's-her-name was so freaky about the lights and the vac suit."

"Her name's Julie. And yeah. Those incubators were for this. Right here," Miller said, and sighed. He thought about standing up. "Well. We may not die of radiation poisoning after all."

"Why not just pump that shit into the air?" Holden asked.

"Anaerobic, remember?" Miller said. "Too much oxygen kills 'em."

The vomit-covered emergency medicine guy was still trying to treat the shambling zombies like they were patients. Like they were still humans. There were smears of the brown goo on people's clothes, on the walls. The tube doors opened again, and Miller saw half a dozen people dodge into a tube car coated in brown. The mob churned, unsure what to do, the group mind stretched past its breaking point.

A riot cop jumped forward and started spraying down the zombies with gunfire. The entrance and exit wounds spilled out fine loops of black filament, and the zombies went down. Miller chuckled even before he knew what was funny. Holden looked at him.

"They didn't know," Miller said. "The bully boys in riot gear? They aren't gonna get pulled out. Meat for the machine, just like the rest of us."

Holden made a small approving sound. Miller nodded, but something was niggling at the back of his mind. The thugs from Ceres in their stolen armor were being sacrificed. That didn't mean everyone was. He leaned forward.

The archway leading to the port was still manned. Mercenary fighters in formation, guns at the ready. If anything, they looked more disciplined now than they had before. Miller watched as the guy in the back with extra insignia on his armor barked into a mic.

Miller had thought hope was dead. He'd thought all his chances had been played, and then, like a bitch, it all hauled itself up out of the grave.

"Get up," Miller said.

"What?"

"Get up. They're going to pull back."

"Who?"

Miller nodded at the mercenaries.

"They knew," he said. "Look at them. They aren't freaking out. They aren't confused. They were waiting for this."

"And you think that means they'll fall back?"

"They aren't going to be hanging out. Stand up."

Almost as if he'd been giving the order to himself, Miller groaned and creaked to his feet. His knees and spine ached badly. The click in his lung was getting worse. His belly made a soft, complicated noise that would have been concerning under different circumstances. As soon as he started moving, he could feel how far the damage had gone, his skin not yet in pain but in the soft presentiment of it, like the gap between a serious burn and the blisters that followed. If he lived, it was going to hurt.

If he lived, *everything* was going to hurt.

His death-self tugged at him. The sense of release, of relief, of *rest* felt like something precious being lost. Even while the chattering, busy, machinelike mind kept grinding, grinding, grinding forward, the soft, bruised center of Miller's soul urged him to pause, sit back down, let the problems go away.

"What are we looking for?" Holden said. He'd stood up. A blood vessel in the man's left eye had given way, the white of the sclera turning a bright, meaty red.

What are we looking for? the death-self echoed.

"They're going to fall back," Miller said, answering the first question. "We follow. Just outside the range so whoever's going last doesn't feel like he has to shoot us."

"Isn't everyone going to do the same thing? I mean, once they're gone, isn't everyone in this place going to head in for the port?"

"I expect so," Miller said. "So let's try to slip in ahead of the rush. Look. There."

It wasn't much. Just a change in the mercenaries' stance, a shift in their collective center of gravity. Miller coughed. It hurt more than it should have.

What are we looking for? his death-self asked again, its voice more insistent. *An answer? Justice? Another chance for the universe to kick us in the balls? What is through that archway that there isn't a faster, cleaner, less painful version of in the barrel of our gun?*

The mercenary captain took a casual step back and strode down the exterior corridor and out of sight. Where he had been, Julie Mao sat, watching him go. She looked at Miller. She waved him on.

"Not yet," he said.

"When?" Holden said, his voice surprising Miller. Julie in his head flickered out, and he was back in the real world.

"It's coming," Miller said.

He should warn the guy. It was only fair. You got into a bad place, and at the very least, you owed your partner the courtesy of letting him know. Miller cleared his throat. That hurt too.

It's possible I may start hallucinating or become suicidal. You might have to shoot me.

Holden glanced over at him. The pachinko machines lit them blue and green and shrieked in artificial delight.

"What?" Holden said.

"Nothing. Getting my balance," Miller said.

Behind them, a woman shouted. Miller glanced back to see her pushing a vomit zombie away, a slick of brown goo already covering the live woman. At the archway, the mercenaries quietly stepped back and started down the corridor.

"Come on," Miller said.

He and Holden walked toward the archway, Miller pulling his hat on. Loud voices, screams, the low, liquid sound of people being violently ill. The air scrubbers were failing, the air taking on a deep, pungent odor like beef broth and acid. Miller felt like there was a stone in his shoe, but he was almost certain if he looked, there would be only a point of redness where his skin was starting to break down.

No one shot at them. No one told them to stop.

At the archway, Miller led Holden against the wall, then ducked his head around the corner. A quarter second was all it took to know the long, wide corridor was empty. The mercs were done here and leaving Eros to its fate. The window was open. The way was clear.

Last chance, he thought, and he meant both the last chance to live and the last one to die.

"Miller?"

"Yeah," he said. "It looks good. Come on. Before everyone gets the idea."

Chapter Thirty-One: Holden

Something was moving in Holden's gut. He ignored it and kept his eyes on Miller's back. The lanky detective barreled down the corridor toward the port, stopping occasionally at junctions to peek around the corner and look for trouble. Miller had become a machine. All Holden could do was try to keep up.

Always the same distance ahead were the mercenaries who'd been guarding the exit from the casino. When they moved, Miller moved. When they slowed down, he slowed. They were clearing a path to the port, but if they thought that any of the citizens were getting too close, they'd probably open fire. They were definitely shooting anyone they ran into along the way. They'd already shot two people who'd run at them. Both had been vomiting brown goo. *Where the hell did those vomit zombies come from so fast?*

"Where the hell did those vomit zombies come from so fast?" he said to Miller's back.

The detective shrugged with his left hand, his right still clutching his pistol.

"I don't think enough of that crap came out of Julie to infect the whole station," he replied without slowing down. "I'm guessing they were the first batch. The ones they incubated to get enough goo to infect the shelters with."

That made sense. And when the controlled portion of the experiment went to shit, you just turned them loose on the populace. By the time people figured out what was going on, half of them were infected already. Then it was just a matter of time.

They paused briefly at a corridor intersection, watching as the leader of the merc group stopped a hundred meters ahead and talked on his radio for a minute. Holden was gasping and trying to catch his breath when the group started up again, and Miller moved to follow. He reached out and grabbed the detective's belt and let Miller drag him along. Where did the skinny Belter keep this reserve of energy?

The detective stopped. His expression was blank.

"They're arguing," Miller said.

"Huh?"

"The leader of that group and some of the men. Arguing about something," Miller replied.

"So?" Holden asked, then coughed something wet into his hand. He wiped it off on the back of his pants, not looking to see if it was blood. *Please don't let it be blood.*

Miller shrugged with his hand again.

"I don't think everyone's on the same team here," he said.

The merc group turned down another corridor, and Miller followed, yanking Holden along behind him. These were the outer levels, filled with warehouse space and ship repair and resupply depots. They didn't see a lot of foot traffic at the best of times. Now the corridor echoed like a mausoleum with their footsteps. Up ahead, the merc group turned again, and before Miller and Holden could reach the junction, a lone figure wandered into view.

He didn't appear to be armed, so Miller moved toward him

cautiously, impatiently reaching behind himself and pulling Holden's hand off his belt. Once he was free, Miller held up his left hand in an unmistakably cop-like gesture.

"This is a dangerous place to be wandering around, sir," he said.

The man was now less than fifteen meters ahead of them and began moving toward them at a lurch. He was dressed for a party in a cheap tuxedo with a frilly shirt and sparkly red bow tie. He was wearing one shiny black shoe, the other foot covered with only a red sock. Brown vomit trickled from the corners of his mouth and stained the front of his white shirt.

"Shit," Miller said, and brought up his gun.

Holden grabbed his arm and yanked it back down.

"He's innocent in this," Holden said, the sight of the injured and infected man making his eyes burn. "He's innocent."

"He's still coming," Miller said.

"So walk faster," Holden said. "And if you shoot anyone else and I haven't given you permission to, you don't get a ride on my ship. Got me?"

"Trust me," Miller said. "Dying is the best thing that could happen to that guy today. You're not doing him any favors."

"You don't get to decide that," Holden replied, his tone edging into real anger.

Miller started to reply, but Holden held up one hand and cut him off.

"You want on the *Roci*? I'm the boss, then. No questions, no bullshit."

Miller's smirk turned into a smile. "Yes, sir," he said. "Our mercs are getting ahead of us." He pointed down the corridor.

Miller nodded and moved off again at his steady, machinelike pace. Holden didn't turn around, but he could hear the man Miller had almost shot crying in the corridor behind him for a long time. To cover up the sound, which probably existed only in his head once they'd made a couple more turns in the corridor, he began humming the theme to *Misko and Marisko* again.

Mother Elise, who'd been the one to stay home with him when he was very young, had always brought him something to eat while he watched, and then sat by him with her hand on his head, playing with his hair. She'd laughed at the dinosaur antics even harder than he had. One Halloween she'd made him a big pink hat to wear so that he could be the evil Count Mungo. Why had that guy been trying to capture the dinosaurs, anyway? It had never really been clear. Maybe he just liked dinosaurs. One time he'd used a shrink ray and—

Holden slammed into Miller's back. The detective had stopped suddenly and now moved quickly to one side of the corridor, crouching low to keep himself in the shadows. Holden followed suit. About thirty meters ahead, the mercenary group had gotten much bigger and had split into two factions.

"Yep," Miller said. "Whole lot of people having really bad days today."

Holden nodded and wiped something wet off his face. It was blood. He didn't think he'd hit Miller's back hard enough to bloody his nose, and he had a suspicion it wasn't going to stop on its own. Mucous membranes getting fragile. Wasn't that part of radiation burning? He tore strips off his shirt and stuffed them up his nostrils while he watched the scene at the end of the corridor.

There were two clear groups, and they did seem to be engaged in some sort of heated argument. Normally, that would have been fine. Holden didn't care about the social lives of mercenaries. But these mercenaries numbered by this time close to a hundred, were heavily armed, and blocked the corridor that led to his ship. That made their argument worth watching.

"Not everyone from Protogen left, I think," Miller said quietly, pointing at one of the two groups. "Those guys on the right don't look like the home team."

Holden looked at the group and nodded. They were definitely the more professional-looking soldiers. Their armor fit well. The other group looked like it was largely made up of guys dressed in police riot gear, with only a few men in combat armor.

"Want to guess what the argument is about?" Miller asked.

"Hey, can we have a ride too?" Holden said mockingly with a Ceres accent. *"Uh, no, we need you guys to stay here and, uh, keep an eye on things, which we promise will be* totally *safe and* absolutely not *involve you turning into vomit zombies."*

He actually got a chuckle from Miller and then the corridor erupted in a barrage of gunfire. Both sides of the discussion were firing automatic weapons at each other from point-blank range. The noise was deafening. Men screamed and flew apart, spraying the corridor and each other with blood and body parts. Holden dropped flat to the floor but continued watching the firefight.

After the initial barrage, the survivors from both groups began falling back in opposite directions, still firing as they moved. The floor at the corridor junction was littered with bodies. Holden estimated that twenty or more men had died in that first second of the fight. The sounds of gunfire grew more distant as the two groups fired at each other down the corridor.

In the middle of the junction, one of the bodies on the floor suddenly stirred and raised its head. Even before the wounded man could get to his feet, a bullet hole appeared in the middle of his face shield and he dropped back to the floor with limp finality.

"Where's your ship?" Miller asked.

"The lift is at the end of this corridor," Holden replied.

Miller spat what looked like bloody phlegm on the floor.

"And the corridor that crosses it is now a war zone, with armed camps sniping at each other from both sides," he said. "I guess we could try just running through it."

"Is there another option?" Holden asked.

Miller looked at his terminal.

"We're fifty-three minutes past the deadline Naomi set," he said. "How much more time do you want to waste?"

"Look, I was never particularly good at math," Holden said. "But I'd guess there are as many as forty guys in either direction down that other corridor. A corridor which is a good three, maybe three and a half meters wide. Which means that we give eighty guys three meters worth of shots at us. Even dumb luck means we get hit a lot and then die. Let's think of a plan B."

As if to underline his argument, another fusillade broke out in the cross corridor, gouging chunks out of the rubbery wall insulation and chewing up the bodies lying on the floor.

"They're still withdrawing," Miller said. "Those shots came from farther away. I guess we can just wait them out. I mean, if we can."

The rags Holden had stuffed up his nose hadn't stopped the bleeding; they had just dammed it up. He could feel a steady trickle down the back of his throat that made his stomach heave with nausea. Miller was right. They were getting down to the last of their ability to wait anyone out at this point.

"Goddamn, I wish we could call and see if Naomi is even there," Holden said, looking at the flashing *Network Not Available* on his terminal.

"Shhh," Miller whispered, putting one finger on his lips. He pointed back down the corridor in the direction they'd come, and now Holden could hear heavy footsteps approaching.

"Late guests to the party," Miller said, and Holden nodded. The two men swiveled around, pointing their guns down the corridor and waiting.

A group of four men in police riot armor rounded the corner. They didn't have their guns out, and two of them had their helmets off. Apparently they hadn't heard about the new hostilities. Holden waited for Miller to fire and, when he didn't, turned to look at him. Miller was staring back.

"I didn't dress real warm," Miller said, almost apologetically. It took Holden half a second to understand what he meant.

Holden gave him permission by shooting first. He targeted one of the mafia thugs without a helmet and shot him in the face, then continued firing at the group until his gun's slide locked open when the magazine was empty. Miller had begun firing a split second after Holden's first shot and also fired until his gun was empty. When it was over, all four thugs were lying facedown in the corridor. Holden let out a long breath that turned into a sigh, and sat down on the floor.

Miller walked to the fallen men and nudged each one in turn with his foot as he replaced the magazine in his gun. Holden didn't bother reloading his. He was done with gunfights. He put the empty pistol in his pocket and got up to join the cop. He bent down and began unbuckling the least damaged armor he could find. Miller raised an eyebrow but didn't move to help.

"We're making a run for it," Holden said, swallowing back the vomit-and-blood taste in his throat as he pulled the chest and back armor free of the first man. "But maybe if we wear this stuff, it will help."

"Might," Miller said with a nod, then knelt down to help strip a second man.

Holden put on the dead man's armor, working hard to believe that the pink trail down the back was absolutely not part of the man's brain. Undoing the straps was exhausting. His fingers felt numb and awkward. He picked up the thigh armor, then put it down again. He'd rather run fast. Miller had finished buckling his on too and picked up one of the undamaged helmets. Holden found one with just a dent in it and slipped it onto his head. It felt greasy inside, and he was glad he had no sense of smell. He suspected that its previous occupant hadn't bathed often.

Miller fiddled with the side of his helmet until the radio came on. The cop's voice was echoed a split second later over the helmet's tinny speakers as he said, "Hey, we're coming out into the corridor! Don't shoot! We're coming to join up!"

Thumbing off the mic, he turned to Holden and said, "Well, maybe one side won't be shooting at us now."

They moved back down the corridor and stopped ten meters from the intersection. Holden counted down from three and then took off at the best run he could manage. It was dishearteningly slow; his legs felt like they were filled with lead. Like he was running in a pool of water. Like he was in a nightmare. He could hear

Miller just behind him, his shoes slapping on the concrete floor, his breath coming in ragged gasps.

Then he heard only the sound of gunfire. He couldn't tell if Miller's plan had worked. Couldn't tell which direction the gunfire was coming from. It was constant and deafening and started the instant he entered the cross corridor. When he was three meters from the other side, he lowered his head and jumped forward. In Eros' light gravity, he seemed to fly, and he was nearly to the other side when a burst of bullets caught him in the armor over his ribs and slammed him into the corridor wall with a spine-jarring crack. He dragged himself the rest of the way as bullets continued to hit all around his legs, one of them passing through the meaty part of his calf.

Miller tripped over him, flying a few feet farther down the hall and then collapsing in a heap. Holden crawled to his side.

"Still alive?"

Miller nodded. "Got shot. Arm's broke. Keep moving," he gasped out.

Holden climbed to his feet, his left leg feeling like it was on fire as the muscle in his calf clenched around his gaping wound. He pulled Miller up and then leaned on him as they limped toward the elevator. Miller's left arm was dangling boneless at his side, and blood was pouring off his hand.

Holden punched the button to call the lift, and he and Miller leaned on each other while they waited. He hummed the *Misko and Marisko* theme to himself, and after a few seconds, Miller started too.

Holden punched the button for the *Rocinante*'s berth and waited for the elevator to stop at a blank gray airlock door with no ship beyond it. That would be when he finally had permission to lie down on the floor and die. He looked forward to that moment when his exertions could end with a relief that would have surprised him if he'd still been capable of surprise. Miller let go of him and slid down the lift wall, leaving a blood trail on the shiny metal and ending in a pile on the floor. The man's eyes were closed.

He could almost have been sleeping. Holden watched the detective's chest rise and fall in ragged, painful breaths that grew smoother and more shallow.

Holden envied him, but he had to see that closed airlock door before he could lie down. He began to feel faintly angry with the elevator for taking so long.

It stopped, lift doors sliding open with a cheerful ding.

Amos stood in the airlock on the other side, an assault rifle in each hand and two belts of magazines for the rifles slung on his shoulders. He looked Holden up and down once, then glanced over to Miller and back again.

"Jesus, Captain, you look like shit."

Chapter Thirty-Two: Miller

Miller's mind reassembled slowly and with several false starts. In his dreams, he was fitting a puzzle together as the pieces kept changing shape, and each time, just as he was on the verge of slipping the whole mechanism together, the dream began again. The first thing he became aware of was the ache at the small of his back, then the heaviness of his arms and legs, then the nausea. The nearer he came to consciousness, the more he tried to postpone it. Imaginary fingers tried to complete the puzzle, and before he could make it all fit, his eyes opened.

He couldn't move his head. Something was in his neck: a thick bundle of black tubes reaching out of him and up past the limits of his vision. He tried to lift his arms, to push the invading, vampiric thing away, but he couldn't.

It got me, he thought with a thrill of fear. *I'm infected.*

The woman appeared from his left. He was surprised she wasn't

Julie. Deep brown skin, dark eyes with just a hint of an epicanthic fold. She smiled at him. Black hair draped down the side of her face.

Down. There was a *down*. There was gravity. They were under thrust. That seemed very important, but he didn't know why.

"Hey, Detective," Naomi said. "Welcome back."

Where am I? he tried to say. His throat felt solid. Crowded like too many people in a tube station.

"Don't try to get up or talk or anything," she said. "You've been under for about thirty-six hours. Good news is we have a sick bay with a military-grade expert system and supplies for fifteen Martian soldiers. I think we burned half of what we've got on you and the captain."

The captain. Holden. That was right. They'd been in a fight. There had been a corridor and people shooting. And someone had been sick. He remembered a woman, covered in brown vomit, with vacant eyes, but he didn't know whether it was part of a nightmare.

Naomi was still talking. Something about full plasma flushes and cell damage. He tried to lift a hand, to reach out to her, but a strap restrained him. The ache in his back was his kidneys, and he wondered what exactly was getting filtered out of his blood. Miller closed his eyes, asleep before he could decide whether to rest.

No dreams troubled him this time. He roused again when something deep in his throat shifted, pulled at his larynx, and retreated. Without opening his eyes, he rolled to his side, coughed, puked, and rolled back.

When he woke, he was breathing on his own. His throat felt sore and abused, but his hands weren't tied down. Drainage tubes ran out of his belly and side, and there was a catheter the size of a pencil coming out his penis. Nothing particularly hurt, so he had to assume he was on pretty nearly all the narcotics there were. His clothes were gone, his modesty preserved only by a thin paper gown and a cast that held his left arm stony and immovable. Someone had put his hat on the next bed over.

The sick bay, now that he could see it, looked like a ward on a high-production entertainment feed. It wasn't a hospital; it was the matte-black-and-silver idea of what a hospital was supposed to be. The monitors hung suspended in the air on complex armatures, reporting his blood pressure, nucleic acid concentrations, oxygenation, fluid balance. There were two separate countdowns running, one to the next round of autophagics, the other for pain medication. And across the aisle, at another station, Holden's statistics looked more or less the same.

Holden looked like a ghost. His skin was pale and his sclera were red with a hundred little hemorrhages. His face was puffy from steroids.

"Hey," Miller said.

Holden lifted a hand, waving gently.

"We made it," Miller said. His voice sounded like it had been dragged down an alley by its ankles.

"Yeah," Holden said.

"That was ugly."

"Yeah."

Miller nodded. That had taken all the energy he had. He lay back down and fell, if not asleep, at least unconscious. Just before his mind flickered back into forgetfulness, he smiled. He'd made it. He was on Holden's ship. And they were going to find whatever Julie had left behind for them.

Voices woke him.

"Maybe you shouldn't, then."

It was the woman. Naomi. Part of Miller cursed her for disturbing him, but there was a buzz in her voice—not fear or anger, but close enough to be interesting. He didn't move, didn't even swim all the way back to awareness. But he listened.

"I need to," Holden said. He sounded phlegmy, like someone who needed to cough. "What happened on Eros...it's put a lot of things in perspective. I've been holding something back."

"Captain—"

"No, hear me out. When I was in there thinking that all I was going to have left was half an hour of rigged pachinko games and then death...when that happened, I knew what my regrets were. You know? I felt all the things that I wished I'd done and never had the courage for. Now that I know, I can't just ignore it. I can't pretend it isn't there."

"Captain," Naomi said again, and the buzz in her voice was stronger.

Don't say it, you poor bastard, Miller thought.

"I'm in love with you, Naomi," Holden said.

The pause lasted no longer than a heartbeat.

"No, sir," she said. "You aren't."

"I am. I know what you're thinking. I've been through this big traumatic experience and I'm doing the whole thing where I want to affirm life and make connections, and maybe some of that's part of it. But you have to believe that I know what I feel. And when I was down there, I knew that the thing that I wanted the most was to get back to you."

"Captain. How long have we served together?"

"What? I don't know exactly..."

"Ballpark estimate."

"Eight and a half runs makes it almost five years," Holden said. Miller could hear the confusion in his voice.

"All right. And in that time, how many of the crew did you share bunks with?"

"Does it matter?"

"Only a little."

"A few."

"More than a dozen?"

"No," he said, but he didn't sound sure.

"Let's call it ten," Naomi said.

"Okay. But this is different. I'm not talking about having a little shipboard romance to pass the time. Ever since——"

Miller imagined the woman holding up her hand or taking Holden's or maybe just glaring at him. Something to stop the flow of words.

"And do you know when I fell for you, sir?"

Sorrow. That was what the strain in her voice was. Sorrow. Disappointment. Regret.

"When...when you..."

"I can tell you the day," Naomi said. "You were about seven weeks into that first run. I was still smarting that some Earther had come in from out of the ecliptic and taken my XO job. I didn't like you much right at the start. You were too charming, too pretty, and too damn comfortable in my chair. But there was a poker game in the engine room. You and me and those two Luna boys out of engineering and Kamala Trask. You remember Trask?"

"She was the comm tech. The one who was..."

"Built like a refrigerator? Face like a bulldog puppy?"

"I remember her."

"She had the biggest crush on you. Used to cry herself to sleep at night all through that run. She wasn't in that game because she cared about poker. She just wanted to breathe some of your air, and everyone knew it. Even you. And all that night, I watched you and her, and you never once led her along. You never gave her any reason to think she had a chance with you. And you still treated her with respect. That was the first time I thought you might be a decent XO, and it was the first time I wished that I could be the girl in your bunk at shift's end."

"Because of Trask?"

"That and you've got a great ass, sir. My point is we flew together for four years and more. And I would have come along with you any day of that if you'd asked me."

"I didn't know," Holden said. He sounded a little strangled.

"You didn't ask. You always had your sights set someplace else. And, honestly, I think Belter women just put you off. Until the *Cant*...Until it was just the five of us. I've seen you looking at me. I know exactly what those looks mean, because I spent four years on the other side of them. But I only got your attention when I was the only female on board, and that's not good enough for me."

"I don't know—"

"No, sir, you don't. That's my point. I've watched you seduce a lot of women, and I know how you do it. You get fixed on her, you get excited by her. Then you convince yourself that the two of you have some kind of special connection, and by the time you believe it, she usually thinks it's true too. And then you sleep together for a while, and the connection gets a little faded. One or the other of you says something like *professional* or *appropriate boundaries* or starts worrying what the crew will think, and the whole thing slides away. Afterwards they still like you. All of them. You do it all so well they don't even feel like they get to hate you for it."

"That's not true."

"It is. And until you figure out that you don't have to love everyone you bed down with, I'm never going to know whether you love me or just want to bed down. And I won't sleep with you until *you* know which it is. The smart money isn't on love."

"I was just —"

"If you want to sleep with me," Naomi said, "be honest. Respect me enough for that. Okay?"

Miller coughed. He hadn't meant to, hadn't even been aware he was going to. His belly went tight, his throat clamped down, and he coughed wet and deep. Once he started, it was hard to stop. He sat up, eyes watering from the effort. Holden was lying back on his bed. Naomi sat on the next bed over, smiling like there had been nothing to overhear. Holden's monitors showed an elevated heart rate and blood pressure. Miller could only hope the poor bastard hadn't gotten an erection with the catheter still in.

"Hey, Detective," Naomi said. "How're you feeling?"

Miller nodded.

"I've felt worse," he said. Then, a moment later: "No. I haven't. But I'm all right. How bad was it?"

"You're both dead," Naomi said. "Seriously, we had to override the triage filters on both of you more than once. The expert system kept clicking you over into hospice care and shooting you full of morphine."

She said it lightly, but he believed her. He tried to sit up. His body still felt terribly heavy, but he didn't know if it was from weakness or the ship thrust. Holden was quiet, jaw clamped tight. Miller pretended not to notice.

"Long-term estimates?"

"You're both going to need to be checked for new cancers every month for the rest of your lives. The captain has a new implant where his thyroid used to be, since his real one was pretty much cooked down. We had to take out about a foot and a half of your small bowel that wouldn't stop bleeding. You're both going to bruise easy for a while, and if you wanted kids, I hope you have some sperm in a bank someplace, because all your little soldiers have two heads now."

Miller chuckled. His monitors blinked into alarm mode and then back out.

"You sound like you trained as a med tech," he said.

"Nope. Engineer. But I've been reading the printouts every day, so I've got the lingo down. I wish Shed was still here," she said, and sounded sad for the first time.

That was the second time someone had mentioned Shed. There was a story there, but Miller let it drop.

"Hair going to fall out?" he asked.

"Maybe," Naomi said. "The system shot you full of the drugs that are supposed to stop that, but if the follicles die, they die."

"Well. Good thing I've still got my hat. What about Eros?"

Naomi's false light tone failed her.

"It's dead," Holden said from his bed, turning to look at Miller. "I think we were the last ship out. The station isn't answering calls, and all the automatic systems have it in a quarantine lockdown."

"Rescue ships?" Miller asked, and coughed again. His throat was still sore.

"Not going to happen," Naomi said. "There were a million and a half people on station. No one has the resources to put into that kind of rescue op."

"After all," Holden said, "there's a war on."

The ship system dimmed the lights for night. Miller lay on his bed. The expert system had shifted his treatment regimen into a new phase, and for the past three hours, he'd alternated between spiking fevers and teeth-chattering chills. His teeth and the nail beds of his fingers and toes ached. Sleep wasn't an option, so he lay in the gloom and tried to pull himself together.

He wondered what his old partners would have made of his behavior on Eros. Havelock. Muss. He tried to imagine them in his place. He'd killed people, and he'd done it cold. Eros had been a kill box, and when the people in charge of the law wanted you dead, the law didn't apply anymore. And some of the dead assholes had been the ones who'd killed Julie.

So. Revenge killing. Was he really down to revenge killing? That was a sad thought. He tried to imagine Julie sitting beside him the way Naomi had with Holden. It was like she'd been waiting for the invitation. Julie Mao, who he'd never really known. She raised a hand in greeting.

And what about us? he asked her as he looked into her dark, unreal eyes. *Do I love you, or do I just want to love you so bad I can't tell the difference?*

"Hey, Miller," Holden said, and Julie vanished. "You awake?"

"Yeah. Can't sleep."

"Me either."

They were silent for a moment. The expert system hummed. Miller's left arm itched under its cast as the tissue went through another round of forced regrowth.

"You doing okay?" Miller asked.

"Why wouldn't I be?" Holden said sharply.

"You killed that guy," Miller said. "Back on the station. You shot him. I mean, I know you shot at guys before that. Back at the hotel. But right at the end there, you actually hit somebody in the face."

"Yeah. I did."

"You good with that?"

"Sure," Holden said, too quickly.

The air recyclers hummed, and the blood pressure cuff on Miller's good arm squeezed him like a hand. Holden didn't speak, but when Miller squinted, he could see the elevated blood pressure and the uptick in brain activity.

"They always made us take time off," Miller said.

"What?"

"When we shot someone. Whether they died or not, they always made us take a leave of absence. Turn in our weapon. Go talk to the headshrinker."

"Bureaucrats," Holden said.

"They had a point," Miller said. "Shooting someone does something to you. Killing someone...that's even worse. Doesn't matter that they had it coming or you didn't have a choice. Or maybe a little difference. But it doesn't take it away."

"Seems like you got over it, though."

"Maybe," Miller said. "Look. All that I said back there about how you kill someone? About how leaving them alive wasn't doing them any favors? I'm sorry that happened."

"You think you were wrong?"

"I wasn't. But I'm still sorry it happened."

"Okay."

"Jesus. Look, I'm saying it's good that it bothers you. It's good that you can't stop seeing it or hearing it. That part where it haunts you some? That's the way it's supposed to be."

Holden was quiet for a moment. When he spoke again, his voice was gray as stone.

"I've killed people before, you know. But they were blips in a radar track. I—"

"It's not the same, is it?" Miller said.

"No, it isn't," Holden replied. "Does this go away?"

Sometimes, Miller thought.

"No," he said. "Not if you've still got a soul."

"Okay. Thanks."

"One other thing?"

"Yeah?"

"I know it's none of my business, but I really wouldn't let her put you off. So you don't understand sex and love and women. Just means you were born with a cock. And this girl? Naomi? She seems like she's worth putting a little effort into it. You know?"

"Yeah," Holden said. Then: "Can we never talk about that again?"

"Sure."

The ship creaked and gravity shifted a degree to Miller's right. Course correction. Nothing interesting. Miller closed his eyes and tried to will himself to sleep. His mind was full of dead men and Julie and love and sex. There was something Holden had said about the war that was important, but he couldn't make the pieces fit. They kept changing. Miller sighed, shifted his weight so that he blocked one of his drainage tubes and had to shift back to stop the alarm.

When the blood pressure cuff fired off again, it was Julie holding him, pulling herself so close her lips brushed his ear. His eyes opened, his mind seeing both the imaginary girl and the monitors that she would have blocked if she'd really been there.

I love you too, she said, *and I* will *take care of you.*

He smiled at seeing the numbers change as his heart raced.

Chapter Thirty-Three: Holden

For five more days, Holden and Miller lay on their backs in sick bay while the solar system burned down around them. The reports of Eros' death ran from massive ecological collapse brought about by war-related supply shortages, to covert Martian attack, to secret Belt bioweapon laboratory accident. Analysis from the inner planets had it that the OPA and terrorists like them had finally shown how dangerous they could be to innocent civilian populations. The Belt blamed Mars, or the maintenance crews of Eros, or the OPA for not stopping it.

And then a group of Martian frigates blockaded Pallas, a revolt on Ganymede ended in sixteen dead, and the new government of Ceres announced that all ships with Martian registry docked on station were being commandeered. The threats and accusations, all set to the constant human background noise of war drums, moved on. Eros had been a tragedy and a crime, but it was finished, and there were new dangers popping up in every corner of human space.

Holden turned off his newsfeed, fidgeted in his bunk, and tried to wake Miller up by staring at him. It didn't work. The massive radiation exposure had failed to give him superpowers. Miller began to snore.

Holden sat up, testing the gravity. Less than a quarter g. Alex wasn't in a hurry, then. Naomi was giving him and Miller time to heal before they arrived at Julie's magical mystery asteroid.

Shit.

Naomi.

The last few times she'd come into sick bay had been awkward. She never brought the subject of his failed romantic gesture back up, but he could feel a barrier between them now that filled him with regret. And every time she left the room, Miller would look away from him and sigh, which just made it worse.

But he couldn't avoid her forever, no matter how much he felt like an idiot. He swung his feet off the edge of the bed and pressed down on the floor. His legs felt weak but not rubbery. The soles of his feet hurt, but quite a bit less than nearly everything else on his body. He stood up, one hand still on the bed, and tested his balance. He wobbled but remained upright. Two steps reassured him that walking was possible in the light gravity. The IV tugged at his arm. He was down to just one bag of something a faint blue. He had no idea what it was, but after Naomi's description of how close to death he'd come, he figured it must be important. He pulled it off the wall hook and held it in his left hand. The room smelled like antiseptic and diarrhea. He was happy to be leaving.

"Where you going?" Miller asked, his voice groggy.

"Out." Holden had the sudden, visceral memory of being fifteen.

"Okay," Miller said, then rolled onto his side.

The sick bay hatch was four meters from the central ladder, and Holden covered the ground with a slow, careful shuffle, his paper booties making a whispery scuffing sound on the fabric-covered metal floor. The ladder itself defeated him. Even though ops was only one deck up, the three-meter climb might as well have been a thousand. He pressed the button to call the lift, and a few seconds later, the floor hatch slid open and the lift climbed through with an electric whine. Holden tried to hop on but managed only a sort of slow-motion fall that ended with his clutching the ladder and kneeling on the lift platform. He stopped the lift, pulled himself upright, and started it again, then rode it up to the next deck in what he hoped was a less beaten and more captain-like pose.

"Jesus, Captain, you *still* look like shit," Amos said as the lift came to a stop. The mechanic was sprawled across two chairs at the sensor stations and munching on what looked like a strip of leather.

"You keep saying that."

"Keeps bein' true."

"Amos, don't you have work to do?" Naomi said. She was sitting at one of the computer stations, watching something flash by on the screen. She didn't look up when Holden came onto the deck. That was a bad sign.

"Nope. Most boring ship I ever worked, Boss. She don't break, she don't leak, she don't even have an annoying rattle to tighten down," Amos replied as he sucked down the last of his snack and smacked his lips.

"There's always mopping," Naomi said, then tapped out something on the screen in front of her. Amos looked from her to Holden and back again.

"Oh, that reminds me. I better get down to the engine room and look at that...thing I've been meaning to look at," Amos said, and jumped to his feet. " 'Scuse me, Cap."

He squeezed past Holden, hopped on the lift, and rode it sternward. The deck hatch closed behind him.

"Hey," Holden said to Naomi once Amos was gone.

"Hey," she said without turning around. That wasn't good either. When she'd sent Amos away, he'd hoped she wanted to talk. It didn't look like it. Holden sighed and shuffled over to the chair next to her. He collapsed into it, his legs tingling like he'd run a kilometer instead of just walking twenty-odd steps. Naomi had left her hair down, and it hid her face from him. Holden wanted to brush it back but was afraid she'd snap his elbow with Belter kung fu if he tried.

"Look, Naomi," he started, but she ignored him and hit a button on her panel. He stopped when Fred's face appeared on the display in front of her.

"Is that Fred?" he said, because he couldn't think of anything even more idiotic to say.

"You should see this. Got it from Tycho a couple hours ago on the tightbeam after I sent them an update on our status."

Naomi tapped the play button and Fred's face sprang to life.

"Naomi, sounds like you guys have had a tough time of it. The air's full of chatter on the station shutdown, and the supposed nuclear explosion. No one knows what to make of it. Keep us informed. In the meantime, we managed to hack open that data cube you left here. I don't think it'll help much, though. Looks like a bunch of sensor data from the *Donnager,* mostly EM stuff. We've tried looking for hidden messages, but my smartest people can't find anything. I'm passing the data along to you. Let me know if you find anything. Tycho out."

The screen went blank.

"What does the data look like?" Holden asked.

"It's just what the man said," Naomi said. "EM sensor data from the *Donnager* during the pursuit by the six ships, and the battle itself. I've dug through raw stuff, looking for anything hidden inside, but for the life of me, I can't find a thing. I've even had the *Roci* digging through the data for the last couple hours, looking for patterns. She has really good software for that sort of thing. But so far, nothing."

She tapped on the screen again and the raw data began spooling past faster than Holden could follow. In a small window inside the larger screen, the *Rocinante*'s pattern-recognition software worked to find meaning. Holden watched it for a minute, but his eyes quickly unfocused.

"Lieutenant Kelly died for this data," he said. "He left the ship while his mates were still fighting. Marines don't do that unless it matters."

Naomi shrugged and pointed at the screen with resignation.

"That's what was on his cube," she said. "Maybe there's something steganographic, but I don't have another dataset to compare it to."

Holden began tapping on his thigh, his pain and romantic failures momentarily forgotten.

"So let's say that this data is all that it is. There's nothing hidden. What would this information mean to the Martian navy?"

Naomi leaned back in her chair and closed her eyes in thought, one finger twisting and untwisting a curl of hair by her temple.

"It's mostly EM data, so lots of engine-signature stuff. Drive radiation is the best way to keep track of other ships. So that tells you where which ships were during the fight. Tactical data?"

"Maybe," Holden said. "Would that be important enough to send Kelly out with?"

Naomi took a deep breath and let it out slowly.

"I don't think so," she said.

"Me either."

Something tapped at the edge of his conscious mind, asking to be let in.

"What was that thing with Amos all about?" he said.

"Amos?"

"Him showing up at the airlock with two guns when we arrived," he said.

"There was some trouble on our trip back to the ship."

"Trouble for who?" Holden asked. Naomi actually smiled at that.

"Some bad men didn't want us to hack the lockdown on the *Roci*. Amos talked it over with them. You didn't think it was because we were *waiting* for you, did you, sir?"

Was there a smile in her voice? A hint of coyness? Flirtation? He stopped himself from grinning.

"What did the *Roci* say about the data when you ran it?" Holden asked.

"Here," Naomi replied, and hit something on her panel. The screen began displaying long lists of data in text. "Lots of EM and light spectrum stuff, some leakage from damaged—"

Holden yelped. Naomi looked up at him.

"I'm such an idiot," Holden said.

"Granted. Elaborate?"

Holden touched the screen and began scrolling up and down through the data. He tapped one long list of numbers and letters and leaned back with a grin.

"There, that's it," he said.

"That's what?"

"Hull structure isn't the only recognition metric. It's the most accurate, but it's also got the shortest range and"—he gestured around him at the *Rocinante*—"is the easiest to fool. The next best method is drive signature. Can't mask your radiation and heat patterns. And they're easy to spot even from really far away."

Holden turned on the screen next to his chair and pulled up the ship's friend/foe database, then linked it to the data on Naomi's screen.

"That's what this message is, Naomi. It's telling Mars who killed the *Donnager* by showing them what the drive signature was."

"Then why not just say, 'So-and-so killed us,' in a nice easy-to-read text file?" Naomi asked, a skeptical frown on her face.

Holden leaned forward and paused, opened his mouth, then closed it and sat back again with a sigh.

"I don't know."

A hatch banged open with a hydraulic whine; then Naomi looked past Holden to the ladder and said, "Miller's coming up."

Holden turned to watch the detective finish the slow climb up from the sick bay deck. He looked like a plucked chicken, pink-gray skin stippled with gooseflesh. His paper gown went poorly with the hat.

"Uh, there's a lift," Holden said.

"Wish I'd known that," Miller replied, then dragged himself up onto the ops deck with a gasp. "We there yet?"

"Trying to figure out a mystery," Holden said.

"I hate mysteries," Miller said, then hauled himself to his feet and made his way to a chair.

"Then solve this one for us. You find out who murdered someone. You can't arrest them yourself, so you send the information to your partner. But instead of just sending the perp's name, you send your partner all the clues. Why?"

Miller coughed and scratched his chin. His eyes were fixed on something, like he was reading a screen Holden couldn't see.

"Because I don't trust myself. I want my partner to arrive at the same conclusion I did, without my biasing him. I give him the dots, see what it looks like when he connects 'em."

"Especially if guessing wrong has consequences," Naomi said.

"You don't like to screw up a murder charge," Miller said with a nod. "Looks unprofessional."

Holden's panel beeped at him.

"Shit, I know why they were careful," he said after reading his screen. "The *Roci* thinks those were standard light-cruiser engines built by the Bush Shipyards."

"They were Earth ships?" Naomi said. "But they weren't flying any colors, and...Son of a *bitch*!"

It was the first time Holden had ever heard her yell, and he understood. If UNN black ops ships had killed the *Donnager,* then that meant Earth was behind the whole thing. Maybe even killing the *Canterbury* in the first place. It would mean that Martian warships were killing Belters for no reason. Belters like Naomi.

Holden leaned forward and called up the comm display, then tapped out a general broadcast. Miller caught his breath.

"That button you just pressed doesn't do what I think it does, does it?" he said.

"I finished Kelly's mission for him," Holden said.

"I have no idea who the fuck Kelly is," Miller said, "but please tell me that his mission wasn't broadcasting that data to the solar system at large."

"People need to know what's going on," Holden said.

"Yes, they do, but maybe we should actually know what the hell is going on before we tell them," Miller replied, all the weariness gone from his voice. "How gullible *are* you?"

"Hey," Holden said, but Miller got louder.

"You found a Martian battery, right? So you told everyone in the solar system about it and started the single largest war in human history. Only turns out the Martians maybe weren't the ones that left it there. Then, a bunch of mystery ships kill the *Donnager,* which Mars blames on the Belt, only, dammit, the Belt didn't even know it was *capable* of killing a Martian battle cruiser."

Holden opened his mouth, but Miller grabbed a bulb of coffee Amos had left behind on the console and threw it at his head.

"Let me finish! And now you find some data that implicates Earth. First thing you do is blab it to the universe, so that Mars *and* the Belt drag Earth into this thing, making the largest war of all time even bigger. Are you seeing a pattern here?"

"Yes," Naomi said.

"So what do you think's going to happen?" Miller said. "This is how these people work! They made the *Canterbury* look like Mars. It wasn't. They made the *Donnager* look like the Belt. It wasn't. Now it looks like the whole damn thing's Earth? Follow the pattern. It probably isn't! You never, *never* put that kind of accusation out there until you know the score. You look. You listen. You're quiet, fercrissakes, and when you know, *then* you can make your case."

The detective sat back, clearly exhausted. He was sweating. The deck was silent.

"You done?" Holden said.

Miller nodded, breathing heavily. "Think I might have strained something."

"I haven't accused anyone of doing anything," Holden said.

"I'm not building a case. I just put the data out there. Now it's not a secret. They're doing something on Eros. They don't want it interrupted. With Mars and the Belt shooting at each other, everyone with the resources to help is busy elsewhere."

"And you just dragged Earth into it," Miller said.

"Maybe," Holden said. "But the killers *did* use ships that were built, at least in part, at Earth's orbital shipyards. Maybe someone will look into that. And *that's* the point. If everyone knows everything, nothing stays secret."

"Yeah, well," Miller said. Holden ignored him

"Eventually, someone'll figure out the big picture. This kind of thing requires secrecy to function, so exposing all the secrets hurts them in the end. It's the only way this really, permanently stops."

Miller sighed, nodded to himself, took off his hat, and scratched his scalp.

"I was just going to put 'em out an airlock," Miller said.

BA834024112 wasn't much of an asteroid. Barely thirty meters across, it had long ago been surveyed and found completely devoid of useful or valuable minerals. It existed in the registry only to warn ships not to run into it. Julie had left it tethered to wealth measured in the billions when she flew her small shuttle to Eros.

Up close, the ship that had killed the *Scopuli* and stolen its crew looked like a shark. It was long and lean and utterly black, almost impossible to see against the backdrop of space with the naked eye. Its radar-deflecting curves gave it an aerodynamic look almost always lacking in space-going vessels. It made Holden's skin crawl, but it was beautiful.

"Motherfucker," Amos said under his breath as the crew clustered in the cockpit of the *Rocinante* to look at it.

"The *Roci* doesn't even see it, Cap," Alex said. "I'm pourin' ladar into it, and all we see is a slightly warmer spot on the asteroid."

"Like Becca saw just before the *Cant* died," Naomi said.

"Her shuttle's been launched, so I'm guessin' this is the right stealth ship someone left tied to a rock," Alex added. "Case there's more than one."

Holden tapped his fingers on the back of Alex's chair for a moment as he floated over the pilot's head.

"It's probably full of vomit zombies," Holden finally said.

"Want to go see?" said Miller.

"Oh yeah," Holden said.

Chapter Thirty-Four: Miller

The environment suit was better than Miller was used to. He'd only done a couple walks outside during his years on Ceres, and the Star Helix equipment had been old back then: thick corrugated joints, separable air-supply unit, gloves that left his hands thirty degrees colder than the rest of his body. The *Rocinante*'s suits were military and recent, no bulkier than standard riot gear, with integrated life support that could probably keep fingers warm after a hand got shot off. Miller floated, one hand on a strap in the airlock, and flexed his fingers, watching the sharkskin pattern of the knuckle joints.

It didn't feel like enough.

"All right, Alex," Holden said. "We're in place. Have the *Roci* knock for us."

A deep, rumbling vibration shook them. Naomi put a hand against the airlock's curved wall to steady herself. Amos shifted forward to take point, a reactionless automatic rifle in his hands. When he bent his neck, Miller could hear the vertebrae cracking through his radio. It was the only way he could have heard it; they were already in vacuum.

"Okay, Captain," Alex said. "I've got a seal. The standard security override isn't working, so give me a second...to..."

"Problem?" Holden said.

"Got it. I've got it. We have a connection," Alex said. Then, a moment later: "Ah. It doesn't look like there's much to breathe over there."

"Anything?" Holden asked.

"Nope. Hard vacuum," Alex said. "Both her lock doors are open."

"All right, folks," Holden said, "keep an eye on your air supply. Let's go."

Miller took a long breath. The external airlock went from soft red to soft green. Holden slid it open, and Amos launched forward, the captain just behind him. Miller gestured to Naomi with a nod. *Ladies first.*

The connecting gantry was reinforced, ready to deflect enemy lasers or slow down slugs. Amos landed on the other ship as the hatch to the *Rocinante* closed behind them. Miller had a moment's vertigo, the ship before them suddenly clicking from *ahead* to *down* in his perception, as if they were falling into something.

"You all right?" Naomi asked.

Miller nodded, and Amos passed into the other ship's hatch. One by one, they went in.

The ship was dead. The lights coming off their environment suits played over the soft, almost streamlined curves of the bulkheads, the cushioned walls, the gray suit lockers. One locker was bent out of shape, like someone or something had forced its way out from within. Amos pushed off slow. Under normal circumstances, hard vacuum would have been assurance enough that nothing was about to jump out at them. Right now, Miller figured it was only even money.

"Whole place is shut down," Holden said.

"Might be backups in the engine room," Amos said.

"So the ass end of the ship from here," Holden said.

"Pretty much."

"Let's be careful," Holden said.

"I'm heading up to ops," Naomi said. "If there's anything running off battery, I can—"

"No, you aren't," Holden said. "We aren't splitting up the group until we know what we're looking at. Stay together."

Amos moved down, sinking into the darkness. Holden pushed off after him. Miller followed. He couldn't tell from Naomi's body language whether she was annoyed or relieved.

The galley was empty, but signs of struggle showed here and there. A chair with a bent leg. A long, jagged scratch down the wall where something sharp had flaked the paint. Two bullet holes set high along one bulkhead where a shot had gone wide. Miller put a hand out, grabbed one of the tables, and swung slowly.

"Miller?" Holden said. "Are you coming?"

"Look at this," Miller said.

The dark spill was the color of amber, flaky and shining like glass in his flashlight beam. Holden hovered closer.

"Zombie vomit?" Holden said.

"Think so."

"Well. I guess we're on the right ship. For some value of right."

The crew quarters hung silent and empty. They went through each of them, but there were no personal markings—no terminals, no pictures, no clues to the names of the men and women who had lived and breathed and presumably died on the ship. Even the captain's cabin was indicated only by a slightly larger bunk and the face of a locked safe.

There was a massive central compartment as high and wide as the hull of the *Rocinante,* the darkness dominated by twelve huge cylinders encrusted with narrow catwalks and scaffolds. Miller saw Naomi's expression harden.

"What are they?" Miller asked.

"Torpedo tubes," she said.

"*Torpedo* tubes?" he said. "Jesus *Christ,* how many are they packing? A million?"

"Twelve," she said. "Just twelve."

"Capital-ship busters," Amos said. "Built to pretty much kill whatever you're aiming at with the first shot."

"Something like the *Donnager*?" Miller asked.

Holden looked back at him, the glow of his heads-up display lighting his features.

"Or the *Canterbury*," he said.

The four of them passed between the wide black tubes in silence.

In the machine and fabrication shops, the signs of violence were more pronounced. There was blood on the floor and walls, along with wide swaths of the glassy gold resin that had once been vomit. A uniform lay in a ball. The cloth had been wadded and soaked in something before the cold of space had frozen it. Habits formed from years of walking through crime scenes put a dozen small things in place: the pattern of scratches on the floor and lift doors, the spatter of blood and vomit, the footprints. They all told the story.

"They're in engineering," Miller said.

"Who?" Holden said.

"The crew. Whoever was on the ship. All except that one," he said, gesturing at half a footprint that led toward the lift. "You see how her footprints are over the top of everything else. And there, where she stepped in that blood, it was already dry. Flaked instead of smearing."

"How you know it was a girl?" Holden asked.

"Because it was Julie," Miller said.

"Well, whoever's in there, they've been sucking vacuum for a long time," Amos said. "Want to go see?"

No one said yes, but they all floated forward. The hatch stood open. If the darkness beyond it seemed more solid, more ominous, more *personal* than the rest of the dead ship had, it was only Miller's imagination playing tricks. He hesitated, trying to summon up the image of Julie, but she wouldn't come.

Floating into the engineering deck was like swimming into a cave. Miller saw the other flashlights playing over walls and panels, looking for live controls, or else controls that could come alive. He aimed his own beam into the body of the room, the dark swallowing it.

"We got batteries, Cap'n," Amos said. "And...looks like the reactor got shut down. Intentional."

"Think you can get it back up?"

"Want to run some diagnostics," Amos said. "There could be a reason they shut it off, and I don't want to find out the hard way."

"Good point."

"But I can at least get us...some...come *on,* you bastard."

All around the deck, blue-white lights flared up. The sudden brilliance blinded Miller for a half second. His vision returned with a sense of growing confusion. Naomi gasped, and Holden yelped. Something in the back of Miller's own mind started to shriek, and he forced it into silence. It was just a crime scene. They were only bodies.

Except they weren't.

The reactor stood before him, quiescent and dead. All around it, a layer of human flesh. He could pick out arms, hands with fingers splayed so wide they hurt to look at. The long snake of a spine curved, ribs fanning out like the legs of some perverse insect. He tried to make what he was seeing make sense. He'd seen men eviscerated before. He knew that the long, ropy swirl to the left of the thing were intestines. He could see where the small bowel widened to become a colon. The familiar shape of a skull looked out at him.

But then, among the familiar anatomy of death and dismemberment, there were other things: nautilus spirals, wide swaths of soft black filament, a pale expanse of something that might have been skin cut by a dozen gill-like vents, a half-formed limb that looked equally like an insect and a fetus without being either one.

The frozen, dead flesh surrounded the reactor like the skin of an orange. The crew of the stealth ship. Maybe of the *Scopuli* as well.

All but Julie.

"Yeah," Amos said. "This could take a little longer than I was thinking, Cap."

"It's okay," Holden said. His voice on the radio sounded shaky. "You don't have to."

"It's no trouble. As long as none of *that* freaky shit broke the containment, reactor should boot up just fine."

"You don't mind being around...it?" Holden said.

"Honest, Cap'n, I'm not thinking about it. Give me twenty minutes, I'll tell you if we got power or if we have to patch a line over from the *Roci*."

"Okay," Holden said. And then again, his voice more solid: "Okay, but don't touch any of that."

"Wasn't going to," Amos said.

They floated back out through the hatch, Holden and Naomi and Miller coming last.

"Is that..." Naomi said, then coughed and started again. "Is that what's happening on Eros?"

"Probably," Miller said.

"Amos," Holden said. "Do you have enough battery power to light up the computers?"

There was a pause. Miller took a deep breath, the plastic-and-ozone scent of the suit's air system filling his nose.

"I think so," Amos said dubiously. "But if we can get the reactor up first..."

"Bring up the computers."

"You're the captain, Cap'n," Amos said. "Have it to you in five."

In silence, they floated up—back—to the airlock, and past it to the operations deck. Miller hung back, watching the way Holden's trajectory kept him near Naomi and then away from her.

Protective and head-shy both, Miller thought. Bad combination.

Julie was waiting in the airlock. Not at first, of course. Miller slid back into the space, his mind churning through everything he'd seen, just like it was a case. A normal case. His gaze drifted toward the broken locker. There was no suit in it. For a moment, he was back on Eros, in the apartment where Julie had died. There had been an environment suit there. And then Julie was there with him, pushing her way out of the locker.

What were you doing there? he thought.

"No brig," he said.

"What?" Holden said.

"I just noticed," Miller said. "Ship's got no brig. They aren't built to carry prisoners."

Holden made a low agreeing grunt.

"Makes you wonder what they were planning to do with the crew of the *Scopuli*," Naomi said. The tone of her voice meant she didn't wonder at all.

"I don't think they were," Miller said slowly. "This whole thing...they were improvising."

"Improvising?" Naomi said.

"Ship was carrying an infectious something or other without enough containment to contain it. Taking on prisoners without a brig to hold 'em in. They were making this up as they went along."

"Or they had to hurry," Holden said. "Something happened that made them hurry. But what they did on Eros must have taken months to arrange. Maybe years. So maybe something happened at the last minute?"

"Be interesting to know what," Miller said.

Compared to the rest of the ship, the ops deck looked peaceful. Normal. The computers had finished their diagnostics, screens glowing placidly. Naomi went to one, holding the back of the chair with one hand so the gentle touch of her fingers against the screen wouldn't push her backward.

"I'll do what I can here," she said. "You can check the bridge."

There was a pause that carried weight.

"I'll be fine," Naomi said.

"All right. I know you'll...I...C'mon, Miller."

Miller let the captain float ahead into the bridge. The screens there were spooling through diagnostics so standard Miller recognized them. It was a wider space than he'd imagined, with five stations with crash couches customized for other people's bodies. Holden strapped in at one. Miller took a slow turn around the deck. Nothing seemed out of place here—no blood, no broken chairs or torn padding. When it happened, the fight had been down near the reactor. He wasn't sure yet what that meant. He sat at what, under a standard layout, would have been the security station, and opened a private channel to Holden.

"Anything you're looking for in particular?"

"Briefings. Overviews," Holden said shortly. "Whatever's useful. You?"

"See if I can get into the internal monitors."

"Hoping to find...?"

"What Julie found," Miller said.

The security assumed that anyone sitting at the console had access to the low-level feeds. It still took half an hour to parse the command structure and query interface. Once Miller had that down, it wasn't hard. The time stamp on the log listed the feed as the day the *Scopuli* had gone missing. The security camera in the airlock bay showed the crew—Belters, most of them—being escorted in. Their captors were in armor, with faceplates lowered. Miller wondered if they'd meant to keep their identities secret. That would almost have suggested they were planning to keep the crew alive. Or maybe they were just wary of some last-minute resistance. The crew of the *Scopuli* weren't wearing environment suits or armor. A couple of them weren't even wearing uniforms.

But Julie was.

It was strange, watching her move. With a sense of dislocation, Miller realized that he'd never actually seen her in motion. All the pictures he'd had in his file back on Ceres had been stills. Now here she was, floating with her chosen compatriots, her hair back out of her eyes, her jaw clamped. She looked very small surrounded by her crew and the men in armor. The little rich girl who'd turned her back on wealth and status to be with the down-trodden Belt. The girl who'd told her mother to sell the *Razor-back*—the ship she'd loved—rather than give in to emotional blackmail. In motion, she looked a little different from the imaginary version he'd built of her—the way she pulled her shoulders back, the habit of reaching her toes toward the floor even in null g—but the basic image was the same. He felt like he was filling in blanks with the new details rather than reimagining the woman.

The guards said something—the security feed's audio was playing to vacuum—and the *Scopuli* crew looked aghast. Then, hesitantly, the captain started taking his uniform off. They were stripping the prisoners. Miller shook his head.

"Bad plan."

"What?" Holden said.

"Nothing. Sorry."

Julie wasn't moving. One of the guards moved toward her, his legs braced on the wall. Julie, who'd lived through being raped, maybe, or something as bad. Who'd studied jiu jitsu to feel safe afterward. Maybe they thought she was just being modest. Maybe they were afraid she was hiding a weapon under her clothes. Either way, they tried to force the point. One of the guards pushed her, and she latched on to his arm like her life depended on it. Miller winced when he saw the man's elbow bend the wrong way, but he also smiled.

That's my girl, he thought. *Give 'em hell.*

And she did. For almost forty seconds, the airlock bay was a battleground. Even some of the cowed *Scopuli* crew tried to join in. But then Julie didn't see a thick-shouldered man launch from behind her. Miller felt it when the gauntleted hand hammered Julie's temple. She wasn't out, but she was groggy. The men with guns stripped her with a cold efficiency, and when there were no weapons or comm devices, they handed her a jumpsuit and shoved her in a locker. The others, they led down into the ship. Miller matched time stamps and switched feeds.

The prisoners were taken to the galley, then bound to the tables.

One of the guards spent a minute or so talking, but with his face-plate down, the only clues Miller had to the content of the sermon were the reactions of the crew—wide-eyed disbelief, confusion, outrage, and fear. The guard could have been saying anything.

Miller started skipping. A few hours, then a few more. The ship was under thrust, the prisoners actually sitting at the tables instead of floating near them. He flipped to other parts of the ship. Julie's locker was still closed. If he hadn't known better, he'd have assumed she was dead.

He skipped ahead.

One hundred and thirty-two hours later, the crew of the *Scopuli* grew a pair. Miller saw it in their bodies even before the violence started. He'd seen holding cells rise up before, and the prisoners had the same sullen-but-excited look. The feed showed the stretch of wall where he'd seen the bullet holes. They weren't there yet. They would be. A man came into the picture with a tray of food rations.

Here it comes, Miller thought.

The fight was short and brutal. The prisoners didn't stand a chance. Miller watched as they hauled one of them—a sandy-haired man—to the airlock and spaced him. The others were put in heavy restraints. Some wept. Some screamed. Miller skipped ahead.

It had to be in there someplace. The moment when it—whatever it was—got loose. But either it had happened in some unmonitored crew quarters or it had been there from the beginning. Almost exactly one hundred and sixty hours after Julie had gone into the locker, a man in a white jumper, eyes glassy and stance unsure, lurched out of the crew quarters and vomited on one of the guards.

"Fuck!" Amos shouted.

Miller was out of his chair before he knew what had happened. Holden was up too.

"Amos?" Holden said. "Talk to me."

"Hold on," Amos said. "Yeah, it's okay, Cap'n. It's just these fuckers stripped off a bunch of the reactor shielding. We've got her up, but I sucked down a few more rads than I'd have picked."

"Get back to the *Roci*," Holden said. Miller steadied himself against a wall, pushing back down toward the control stations.

"No offense, sir, but it ain't like I'm about to start pissing blood or anything fun like that," Amos said. "I got surprised more than anything. I start feeling itchy, I'll head back over, but I can get some atmosphere for us by working out of the machine shop if you give me a few more minutes."

Miller watched Holden's face as the man struggled. He could make it an order; he could leave it be.

"Okay, Amos. But you start getting light-headed or anything — I mean *anything* — and you get over to the sick bay."

"Aye, aye," Amos said.

"Alex, keep an eye on Amos' biomed feed from over there. Give us a heads-up if you see a problem," Holden said on the general channel.

"Roger," came Alex's lazy drawl.

"You finding anything?" Holden asked Miller on their private channel.

"Nothing unexpected," Miller said. "You?"

"Yeah, actually. Take a look."

Miller pushed himself to the screen Holden had been working. Holden pulled himself back into the station and started pulling up feeds.

"I was thinking that someone had to go last," Holden said. "I mean, there had to be someone who was the least sick when whatever it was got loose. So I went through the directory to see what activity was going on before the system went dead."

"And?"

"There's a whole bunch of activity that looks like it happened a couple days before the system shutdown, and then nothing for two solid days. And then a little spike. A lot of accessed files and system diagnostics. Then someone hacked the override codes to blow atmosphere."

"It was Julie, then."

"That's what I was thinking," Holden said. "But one of the feeds she accessed was . . . Shit, where is it? It was right . . . Oh. Here. Watch this."

The screen blinked, controls dropping to standby, and a high-res emblem, green and gold, came up. The corporate logo of Protogen, with a slogan Miller hadn't seen before. *First. Fastest. Furthest.*

"What's the time stamp on the file?" Miller asked.

"The original was created about two years ago," Holden said. "This copy was burned eight months ago."

The emblem faded, and a pleasant-faced man sitting at a desk took its place. He had dark hair, with just a scattering of gray at the temples, and lips that seemed used to smiling. He nodded at the camera. The smile didn't reach his eyes, which were as empty as a shark's.

Sociopath, Miller thought.

The man's lips began moving soundlessly. Holden said, "Shit," and hit a switch to have the audio transmitted to their suits. He rewound the video feed and started it over.

"Mr. Dresden," the man said. "I would like to thank you and the members of the board for taking the time to review this information. Your support, both financial and otherwise, has been absolutely essential to the incredible discoveries we've seen on this project. While my team has been point man, as it were, Protogen's tireless commitment to the advancement of science has made our work possible.

"Gentlemen, I will be frank. The Phoebe protomolecule has exceeded all our expectations. I believe it represents a genuinely game-changing technological breakthrough. I know that these kinds of corporate presentations are prone to hyperbole. Please understand that I have thought about this carefully and chosen my words: Protogen can become the most important and powerful entity in the history of the human race. But it will require initiative, ambition, and bold action."

"He's talking about killing people," Miller said.

"You've seen this already?" Holden said.

Miller shook his head. The feed changed. The man faded out, and an animation took his place. A graphic representation of the solar system. Orbits marked in wide swaths of color showed the plane of the ecliptic. The virtual camera swirled out from the inner planets, where Mr. Dresden and board members presumably were, and out toward the gas giants.

"For those of you on the board unfamiliar with the project, eight years ago, the first manned landing was made on Phoebe," the sociopath said.

The animation zoomed in toward Saturn, rings and planet flying past in a triumph of graphic design over accuracy.

"A small ice moon, the assumption was that Phoebe would eventually be mined for water, much like the rings themselves. The Martian government commissioned a scientific survey more out of a sense of bureaucratic completeness than from expectation of economic gain. Core samples were taken, and when silicate anomalies raised flags, Protogen was approached as cosponsor of a long-term research facility."

The moon itself—Phoebe—filled the frame, turning slowly to show all sides like a prostitute at a cheap brothel. It was a crater-marked lump, indistinguishable from a thousand other asteroids and planetesimals Miller had seen.

"Given Phoebe's extra-ecliptical orbit," the sociopath went on, "one theory has been that it was a body that originated in the Kuiper belt and had been captured by Saturn when it happened to pass through the solar system. The existence of complex silicon structures within the interior ice, along with suggestions of impact-resistant structures within the architecture of the body itself, have forced us to reevaluate this.

"Using analyses proprietary to Protogen and not yet shared with the Martian team, we have determined beyond any credible doubt that what you are seeing now is not a naturally formed planetesimal, but a weapon. Specifically, a weapon designed to carry its payload through the depths of interplanetary space and deliver it safely onto Earth two and one third billion years ago, when life itself was in its earliest stages. And the payload, gentlemen, is this."

The display clicked to a graphic that Miller couldn't quite parse. It looked like the medical text of a virus, but with wide, looping structures that were at once beautiful and improbable.

"The protomolecule first caught our interest for its ability to maintain its primary structure in a wide variety of conditions through secondary and tertiary changes. It also showed an affinity for carbon and silicon structures. Its activity suggested it was not in itself a living thing, but a set of free-floating instructions designed to adapt to and guide other replicating systems. Animal experiments suggest that its effects are not exclusive to simple replicators, but are, in fact, scalable."

"Animal tests," Miller said. "What, they dumped it on a cat?"

"The initial implication of this," the sociopath went on, "is that a larger biosphere exists, of which our solar system is only a part, and that the protomolecule is an artifact of that environment. That alone, I think you must agree, would revolutionize human understanding of the universe. Let me assure you, it's small beer. If accidents of orbital mechanics had not captured Phoebe, life as we know it would not presently exist. But something else would. The earliest cellular life on Earth would have been hijacked. Reprogrammed along lines contained within the structure of the protomolecule."

The sociopath reappeared. For the first time, smile lines appeared around his eyes, like a parody of themselves. Miller felt a visceral hatred growing in his gut and knew himself well enough to recognize it for what it was. Fear.

"Protogen is in a position to take sole possession of not only the first technology of genuinely extraterrestrial origin, but also a prefabricated mechanism for the manipulation of living systems and the first clues as to the nature of the larger—I will call it *galactic*—biosphere. Directed by human hands, the applications of this are limitless. I believe that the opportunity now facing not only us but life itself is as profound and transformative as anything that has ever happened. And, further, the control of this technology will represent the base of all political and economic power from now on.

"I urge you to consider the technical details I have outlined in the attached. Moving quickly to understand the programming, mechanism, and intent of the protomolecule, as well as its direct application to human beings, will mark the difference between a Protogen-led future and being left behind. I urge immediate and decisive action to take exclusive control of the protomolecule and move forward with large-scale testing.

"Thank you for your time and attention."

The sociopath smiled again, and the corporate logo reappeared. *First. Fastest. Furthest.* Miller's heart was racing.

"Okay. All right," he said. And then: "Fuck *me.*"

"Protogen, protomolecule," Holden said. "They had no idea what it does, but they slapped their label on it like they'd made it. They found an alien weapon, and all they could think to do was *brand* it."

"There's reason to think these boys are pretty impressed with themselves," Miller replied with a nod.

"Now, I'm not a scientist or anything," Holden said, "but it seems to me like taking an *alien supervirus* and dropping it into a space station would be a bad idea."

"It's been two years," Miller said. "They've been doing tests. They've been...I don't know what the hell they've been doing. But Eros is what they decided on. And everyone knows what happened on Eros. The other side did it. No research and recovery ships because they're all fighting each other or guarding something. The war? It's a distraction."

"And Protogen is doing...what?"

"Seeing what their toy does when you take it out for a spin is my guess," Miller said.

They were silent for a long moment. Holden spoke first.

"So you take a company that seems to be lacking an institutional conscience, that has enough government research contracts to almost be a privately run branch of the military. How far will they go for the holy grail?"

"First, fastest, furthest," Miller replied.

"Yeah."

"Guys," Naomi said, "you should come down here. I think I've got something."

Chapter Thirty-Five: Holden

I've found the comm logs," Naomi said as Holden and Miller drifted into the room behind her.

Holden put a hand on her shoulder, pulled it back, and hated that he'd pulled back. A week earlier she'd have been fine with a simple gesture of affection like that, and he wouldn't have been afraid of her reaction. He regretted the new distance between them only slightly less than he would have regretted not saying anything at all. He wanted to tell her that.

Instead, he said, "Find anything good?"

She tapped the screen and pulled up the log.

"They were hard-core about comm discipline," she said, pointing at the long list of dates and times. "Nothing ever went out on radio, everything was tightbeam. And everything was double-speak, lots of obvious code phrases."

Miller's mouth moved inside his helmet. Holden tapped on his face shield. Miller rolled his eyes in disgust and then chinned the comm link to the general channel.

"Sorry. Don't spend a lot of time in suits," he said. "What've we got that's good?"

"Not much. But the last communication was in plain English," she said, then tapped the last line on the list.

THOTH STATION

CREW DEGENERATING. PROJECTING 100% CASUALTIES. MATERIALS SECURED. STABILIZING COURSE AND SPEED. VECTOR DATA TO FOLLOW. EXTREME CONTAMINATION HAZARD FOR ENTRY TEAMS.

CPT. HIGGINS

Holden read it several times, imagining Captain Higgins watching the infection spread through his crew, helpless to stop it. His people vomiting all over in a vacuum-sealed metal box, even one molecule of the substance on your skin a virtual death sentence. Black filament-covered tendrils erupting from their eyes and mouths. And then that... soup that covered the reactor. He let himself shudder, grateful that Miller wouldn't see it through the atmosphere suit.

"So this Higgins fella realizes his crew is turning into vomit zombies and sends a last message to his bosses, right?" Miller said, breaking into Holden's reverie. "What's this stuff about vector data?"

"He knew they'd all be dead, so he was letting his people know how to catch the ship," Holden replied.

"But they didn't, because it's here, because Julie took control and flew it somewhere else," Miller said. "Which means they're looking for it, right?"

Holden ignored that and put his hand back on Naomi's shoulder with what he hoped was companionable casualness.

"We have tightbeam messages and the vector info," he said. "Are they all going to the same place?"

"Sort of," she said, nodding with her right hand. "Not the same place, but all to what appear to be points in the Belt. But based on the changes in direction and the times they were sent, to one point in the Belt that is moving around, and not in a stable orbit either."

"A ship, then?"

Naomi gave another nod.

"Probably," she said. "I've been playing with the locations, and I can't find anything in the registry that looks likely. No stations or inhabited rocks. A ship would make sense. But—"

Holden waited for Naomi to finish, but Miller leaned forward impatiently.

"But what?" he said.

"But how did they know where it would be?" she replied. "I have no incoming comms in the log. If a ship was moving around randomly in the Belt, how'd they know where to send these messages?"

Holden squeezed her shoulder, lightly enough that she probably didn't even feel it in the heavy environment suit, then pushed off and allowed himself to drift toward the ceiling.

"So it's not random," he said. "They had some sort of map of where this thing would be at the time they sent the laser comms. Could be one of their stealth ships."

Naomi turned around in her chair to look up at him.

"Could be a station," she said.

"It's the lab," Miller broke in. "They're running an experiment on Eros, they need the white coats nearby."

"Naomi," Holden said. " 'Materials secured.' There's a safe in the captain's quarters that's still locked down. Think you can get it open?"

Naomi gave a one-handed shrug.

"I don't know," she said. "Maybe. Amos could probably blast it open with some of the explosives we found in that big box of weapons."

Holden laughed.

"Well," he said. "Since it's probably full of little vials of nasty alien viruses, I'm going to nix the blasting option."

Naomi shut down the comm log and pulled up a general ship's systems menu.

"I can look around and see if the computer has access to the safe," she said. "Try to open it that way. It might take some time."

"Do what you can," Holden said. "We'll get out of your hair."

Holden pushed himself off the ceiling and over to the ops compartment hatch, then pulled himself through, into the corridor beyond. A few moments later, Miller followed. The detective planted his feet on the deck with magnetic boots, then stared at Holden, waiting.

Holden floated down to the deck next to him.

"What do you think?" Holden asked. "Protogen being the whole thing? Or is this another one where it looks like them, so it isn't?"

Miller was silent for the space of two long breaths.

"This one smells like the real thing," Miller said. He sounded almost grudging.

Amos pulled himself up the crew ladder from below, dragging a large metal case behind him.

"Hey, Cap'n," he said. "I found a whole case of fuel pellets for the reactor in the machine shop. We'll probably want to take these with us."

"Good work," Holden said, holding up one hand to let Miller know to wait. "Go ahead and take those across. Also, I need you to work up a plan for scuttling this ship."

"Wait, what?" Amos said. "This thing is worth a *jillion* bucks, Captain. Stealth missile ship? The OPA would sell their grandmothers for this thing. And six of those tubes still have fish in them. Capital-ship busters. You could slag a small moon with those. Forget their grannies, the OPA would pimp their daughters for that gear. Why the fuck would we blow it up?"

Holden stared at him in disbelief.

"Did you forget what's in the engine room?" he asked.

"Hell, Cap," Amos snorted. "That shit is all frozen. Couple hours with a torch and I can chop it up and chuck it out the airlock. Good to go."

The mental image of Amos hacking the melted bodies of the ship's former crew apart with a plasma torch and then cheerfully hurling the chunks out an airlock tipped Holden over the edge into full-fledged nausea. The big mechanic's ability just to ignore anything that he didn't want to notice probably came in handy while he was crawling around in tight and greasy engine compartments. His ability to shrug off the horrible mutilation of several dozen people threatened to change Holden's disgust into anger.

"Forgetting the mess," he said, "and the very real possibility of infection by what *made* that mess, there is also the fact that someone is desperately searching for this very expensive and very stealthy ship, and so far *Alex can't find the ship that's looking.*"

He stopped talking and nodded at Amos while the mechanic mulled that over. He could see Amos' broad face working as he put it together in his head. *Found a stealth ship. Other people looking for stealth ship. We can't see the other people looking for it.*

Shit.

Amos' face went pale.

"Right," he said. "I'll set the reactor up to slag her." He looked down at the time on his suit's forearm display. "Shit, we've been here too long. Better get the lead out."

"Better had," Miller agreed.

Naomi was good. *Very* good. Holden had discovered this when he'd signed on with the *Canterbury,* and over the course of years, he'd added it to his list of facts, along with *space is cold* and *the direction of gravity is down.* When something stopped working on the water hauler, he'd tell Naomi to fix it, and then never think of it again. Sometimes she'd claim not to be able to fix something, but it was always a negotiating tactic. A short conversation would lead to a request for spare parts or an additional crewman hired on at the next port, and that would be that. There was no problem that involved electronics or spaceship parts she couldn't solve.

"I can't open the safe," she said.

She floated next to the safe in the captain's quarters, one foot resting lightly on his bunk to stabilize herself as she gestured. Holden stood on the floor with his boot mags on. Miller was in the hatchway to the corridor.

"What would you need?" Holden asked.

"If you won't let me blast it or cut it, I can't open it."

Holden shook his head, but Naomi either didn't see it or ignored him.

"The safe is designed to open when a very specific pattern of magnetic fields is played across that metal plate on the front," she said. "Someone has a key designed to do that, but that key isn't on this ship."

"It's at that station," Miller said. "He wouldn't send it there if they couldn't open it."

Holden stared at the wall safe for a moment, his fingers tapping on the bulkhead beside it.

"What're the chances cutting it sets off a booby trap?" he said.

"Fucking excellent, Cap," Amos said. He was listening in from the torpedo bay as he hacked the small fusion reactor that powered one of the six remaining torpedoes to go critical. Working on the ship's main reactor was too dangerous with the shielding stripped off.

"Naomi, I really want that safe and the research notes and samples it contains," Holden said.

"You don't know that's what's in there," Miller said, then laughed. "No, of course that's what's in there. But it won't help us if we get blown up or, worse, if some piece of goo-coated shrapnel makes a hole in our nice suits."

"I'm taking it," Holden replied, then pulled a piece of chalk from his suit's pocket and drew a line around the safe on the bulkhead. "Naomi, cut a small hole in the bulkhead and see if there's anything that would stop us from just cutting the whole damned thing out and taking it with us."

"We'd have to take out half the wall."

"Okay."

Naomi frowned, then shrugged, then smiled and nodded with one hand.

"All right, then," she said. "Thinking of taking it to Fred's people?"

Miller laughed again, a dry humorless rasp that made Holden uneasy. The detective had been watching the video of Julie Mao's fight with her captors over and over again while they'd waited on Naomi and Amos to finish their work. It gave Holden the disquieting feeling that Miller was storing the footage in his head. Fuel for something he planned to do later.

"Mars would give you your lives back in exchange for this," Miller said. "I hear Mars is nice if you're rich."

"Fuck rich," Amos said with a grunt as he worked on something below. "They'd build statues of us."

"We have an agreement with Fred to let him outbid any other contracts we take," Holden said. "Of course, this isn't really a contract per se..."

Naomi smiled and winked at Holden.

"So what is it, sir?" she said, her voice faintly mocking. "OPA heroes? Martian billionaires? Start your own biotech firm? What are we doing here?"

Holden pushed away from the safe and kicked out toward the airlock and the cutting torch that waited there with their other tools.

"I don't know yet," he said. "But it sure feels nice to have choices again."

Amos pushed the button again. No new stars flared in the dark. The radiation and infrared sensors remained quiet.

"There's supposed to be an explosion, right?" Holden asked.

"Fuck, yes," Amos said, then pushed the button on the black box in his hand a third time. "This isn't an exact science or anything. Those missile drives are as simple as it gets. Just a reactor with one wall missing. Can't exactly predict…"

"It isn't rocket science," Holden said with a laugh.

"What?" Amos asked, ready to be angry if he was being mocked.

"You know, 'it isn't rocket science,'" Holden said. "Like 'it isn't hard.' You're a rocket scientist, Amos. For real. You work on fusion reactors and starship drives for a living. Couple hundred years ago, people would have been lining up to give you their children for what you know."

"What the fu—" Amos started, but stopped when a new sun flared outside the cockpit window, then faded quickly. "See? Fucking told you it would work."

"Never doubted it," Holden said, then slapped Amos on one meaty shoulder and headed aft down the crew ladder.

"What the fuck was that about?" Amos asked no one in particular as Holden drifted away.

He headed through the ops deck. Naomi's chair was empty. He'd ordered her to get some sleep. Strapped down to loops inset in the deck was the stealth ship's safe. It looked bigger cut out of the wall. Black and imposingly solid. The kind of container in which one kept the end of the solar system.

Holden floated over to it and quietly said, "Open sesame."

The safe ignored him, but the deck hatch opened and Miller pulled himself up into the compartment. His environment suit had been traded in for a stale-smelling blue jumpsuit and his ever-present hat. There was something about the look on his face that made Holden uncomfortable. Even more so than the detective usually made him.

"Hey," Holden said.

Miller just nodded and pulled himself over to one of the workstations, then buckled in to one of the chairs.

"We decided on a destination yet?" he asked.

"No. I'm having Alex run the numbers on a couple of possibilities, but I haven't made up my mind."

"Been watching the news at all?" the detective asked.

Holden shook his head, then moved over to a chair on the other side of the compartment. Something in Miller's face was chilling his blood.

"No," he said. "What happened?"

"You don't hedge, Holden. I admire that about you, I guess."

"Just tell me," Holden said.

"No, I mean it. A lot of people claim to believe in things. 'Family is most important,' but they'll screw a fifty-dollar hooker on payday. 'Country first,' but they cheat on their taxes. Not you, though. You say everyone should know everything, and by God, you put your money where your mouth is."

Miller waited for him to say something, but Holden didn't know what. This speech had the feel of something the detective had prepared ahead of time. Might as well let him finish it.

"So Mars finds out that maybe Earth's been building ships on the side, ones with no flag on them. Some of them might have killed a Martian flagship. I bet Mars calls up to check. I mean, it's the Earth-Mars Coalition Navy, one big happy hegemony. Been policing the solar system together for almost a hundred years. Commanding officers are practically sleeping together. So it must be a mistake, right?"

"Okay," Holden said, waiting.

"So Mars calls," Miller said. "I mean, I don't know for sure, but I bet that's how it starts. A call from some bigwig on Mars to some bigwig on Earth."

"Seems reasonable," Holden said.

"What d'you think Earth says back?"

"I don't know."

Miller reached over and flipped on one of the screens, then pulled up a file with his name on it, date stamped from less than an hour before. A recording of video from a Martian news source, showing the night sky through a Martian dome. Streaks and flashes fill the sky. The ticker across the bottom of the feed says that Earth ships in orbit around Mars suddenly and without warning fired on their Martian counterparts. The streaks in the sky are missiles. The flashes are ships dying.

And then a massive white flare turns the Martian night into day for a few seconds, and the crawl says that the Deimos deep radar station has been destroyed.

Holden sat and watched the video display the end of the solar system in vivid color and with expert commentary. He kept waiting for the streaks of light to begin descending on the planet itself, for the domes to fly apart in nuclear fire, but it seemed someone had kept some measure of restraint, and the battle remained in the sky.

It couldn't stay that way forever.

"You're telling me that I did this," Holden said. "That if I hadn't broadcast that data, those ships would still be alive. Those people."

"That, yeah. And that if the bad guys wanted to keep people from watching Eros, it just worked."

Chapter Thirty-Six: Miller

The war stories flowed in. Miller watched the feeds five at a time, subscreens crowding the face of his terminal. Mars was shocked, amazed, reeling. The war between Mars and the Belt—the biggest, most dangerous conflict in the history of mankind—was suddenly a sideshow. The reactions of the talking heads of Earth security forces ran the gamut from calm, rational discussion of preemptive defense to foaming-at-the-mouth denunciations of Mars as a pack of baby-raping animals. The attack on Deimos had turned the moon into a slowly spreading ring of gravel in the moon's old orbit, a smudge on the Martian sky, and with that, the game had changed again.

Miller watched for ten hours as the attack became the blockade. The Martian navy, spread throughout the system, was turning home under heavy burn. The OPA feeds were calling it a victory, and maybe someone thought that was true. The pictures came through from the ships, from the sensor arrays. Dead warships, their sides ripped open by high-energy explosions, spinning out into their irregular orbital graves. Medical bays like the *Roci*'s filled with boys and girls half his age bleeding, burning, dying. Each cycle, new footage came in, new details of death and carnage. And each time some new clip appeared, he sat forward, hand on his mouth, waiting for the word to come. The one event that would signal the end of it all.

But it hadn't come yet, and every hour that didn't bring it gave another sliver of hope that maybe, *maybe* it wasn't going to happen.

"Hey," Amos said. "You slept at all?"

Miller looked up, his neck stiff. Red creases of his pillow still on his cheek and forehead, the mechanic stood in the open doorway of Miller's cabin.

"What?" Miller said. Then: "Yeah, no. I've been...watching."

"Anyone drop a rock?"

"Not yet. It's all still orbital or higher."

"What kind of half-assed apocalypse are they running down there?" Amos said.

"Give 'em a break. It's their first."

The mechanic shook his broad head, but Miller could see the relief under the feigned disgust. As long as the domes were still standing on Mars, as long as the critical biosphere of Earth wasn't in direct threat, humanity wasn't dead. Miller had to wonder what they were hoping for out in the Belt, whether they'd managed to talk themselves into believing that the rough ecological pockets of the asteroids would sustain life indefinitely.

"You want a beer?" Amos asked.

"You're having beer for breakfast?"

"Figure it's dinner for you," Amos said.

The man was right. Miller needed sleep. He hadn't managed more than a catnap since they'd scuttled the stealth ship, and that had been plagued by strange dreams. He yawned at the thought of yawning, but the tension in his gut said he was more likely to spend the day watching newsfeeds than resting.

"It's probably breakfast again," Miller said.

"Want some beer for breakfast?" Amos asked.

"Sure."

Walking through the *Rocinante* felt surreal. The quiet hum of the air recyclers, the softness of the air. The journey out to Julie's ship was a haze of pain medication and sickness. The time on Eros before that was a nightmare that wouldn't fade. To walk through the spare, functional corridors, thrust gravity holding him gently to the floor, with very little chance of anyone trying to kill him felt suspicious. When he imagined Julie walking with him, it wasn't so bad.

As he ate, his terminal chimed, the automatic reminder for another blood flush. He stood, adjusted his hat, and headed off to let the needles and pressure injectors do their worst. The captain was already there and hooked into a station when Miller arrived.

Holden looked like he'd slept, but not well. There weren't the bruise-dark marks under his eyes that Miller had, but his shoulders were tense, his brow on the edge of furrowed. Miller wondered whether he'd been a little too hard on the guy. *I told you so* could be an important message, but the burden of innocent death, of the chaos of a failing civilization might also be too much for one man to carry.

Or maybe he was still mooning over Naomi.

Holden raised the hand that wasn't encased in medical equipment.

"Morning," Miller said.

"Hey."

"Decided where we're going yet?"

"Not yet."

"Getting harder and harder to get to Mars," Miller said, easing himself into the familiar embrace of the medical station. "If that's what you're aiming for, you'd better do it soon."

"While there's still a Mars, you mean?"

"For instance," Miller agreed.

The needles snaked out on gently articulated armatures. Miller looked at the ceiling, trying not to tense up as the lines forced their way into his veins. There was a moment's stinging, then a low, dull ache, and then numbness. The display above him announced the state of his body to doctors who were watching young soldiers die miles above Olympus Mons.

"Do you think they'd stop?" Holden asked. "I mean, Earth has got to be doing this because Protogen owns some generals or senators or something, right? It's all because they want to be the only ones who have this thing. If Mars has it too, Protogen doesn't have a reason to fight."

Miller blinked. Before he could pick his answer—*They'd try to annihilate Mars completely*, or *It's gone too far for that*, or *Exactly how naive are you, Captain?*—Holden went on.

"Screw it. We've got the datafiles. I'm going to broadcast them."

Miller's reply was as easy as reflex.

"No, you aren't."

Holden propped himself up, storm clouds in his expression.

"I appreciate that you might have a reasonable difference of opinion," he said, "but this is still my ship. You're a passenger."

"True," Miller said. "But you have a hard time shooting people, and you are going to have to shoot me before you send that thing out."

"I'm *what*?"

The new blood flowed into Miller's system like a tickle of ice water crawling toward his heart. The medical monitors shifted to a new pattern, counting up the anomalous cells as they hit its filters.

"You are going to have to shoot me," Miller said, slowly this time. "Twice now you've had the choice of whether or not to break the solar system, and both times you've screwed it up. I don't want to see you strike out."

"I think you may have an exaggerated idea of how much influence the second-in-command of a long-distance water hauler actually has. Yes, there's a war. And yes, I was there when it started up. But the Belt has hated the inner planets since a long time before the *Cant* was attacked."

"You've got the inner planets divided up too," Miller said.

Holden tilted his head.

"Earth has always hated Mars," Holden said like he was reporting that water was wet. "When I was in the navy, we ran projections for this. Battle plans if Earth and Mars ever really got into it. Earth loses. Unless they hit first, hit hard, and don't let up, Earth just plain loses."

Maybe it was distance. Maybe it was a failure of imagination. Miller had never seen the inner planets as divided.

"Seriously?" he asked.

"They're the colony, but they have all the best toys and everyone knows it," Holden said. "Everything that's happening out there right now has been building up for a hundred years. If it hadn't been there to start with, this couldn't have happened."

"That's your defense? 'Not my powder keg; I just brought the match'?"

"I'm not making a defense," Holden said. His blood pressure and heart rate were spiking.

"We've been through this," Miller said. "So let me just ask, why is it you think this time will be different?"

The needles in Miller's arm seemed to heat up almost to the point of being painful. He wondered if that was normal, if every blood flush he had was going to feel the same way.

"This time *is* different," Holden said. "All the crap that's going on out there is what happens when you have imperfect information. Mars and the Belt wouldn't have been going after each other in the first place if they'd known what we know now. Earth and Mars wouldn't be shooting each other if everyone knew the fight was being engineered. The problem isn't that people know too much, it's that they don't know enough."

Something hissed and Miller felt a wave of chemical relaxation swim through him. He resented it, but there was no calling the drugs back.

"You can't just throw information at people," Miller said. "You have to know what it *means*. What it's going to *do*. There was a case back on Ceres. Little girl got killed. For the first eighteen hours, we were all sure Daddy did it. He was a felon. A drunk. He was the last one who saw her breathing. All the classic signs. Hour nineteen, we get a tip. Turned out Daddy owed a lot of money to one of the local syndicates. All of a sudden, things are more complicated. We have more suspects. Do you think if I'd been broadcasting everything I knew, Daddy would still have been alive when the tip came? Or would someone have put it all together and done the obvious thing?"

Miller's medical station chimed. Another new cancer. He ignored it. Holden's cycle was just finishing, the redness of his cheeks speaking as much to the fresh, healthy blood in his body as to his emotional state.

"That's the same ethos they have," Holden said.

"Who?"

"Protogen. You may be on different sides, but you're playing the same game. If everyone said what they knew, none of this would have happened. If the first lab tech on Phoebe who saw something weird had gotten on his system and said, 'Hey, everyone! Look, this is weird,' none of this would have happened."

"Yeah," Miller said, "because telling everyone there's an alien virus that wants to kill them all is a great way to maintain calm and order."

"Miller," Holden said. "I don't mean to panic you, but there's an alien virus. And it wants to kill everyone."

Miller shook his head and smiled like Holden had said something funny. "So look, maybe I can't point a gun at you and make you do the right thing. But lemme ask you something. Okay?"

"Fine," Holden said. Miller leaned back. The drugs were making his eyelids heavy.

"What happens?" Miller said.

There was a long pause. Another chime from the medical system. Another rush of cold through Miller's abused veins.

"What happens?" Holden repeated. It occurred to Miller he could have been more specific. He forced his eyes open again.

"You broadcast everything we've got. What happens?"

"The war stops. People go after Protogen."

"There's some holes in that, but let it go. What happens after that?"

Holden was quiet for a few heartbeats.

"People start going after the Phoebe bug," he said.

"They start experimenting. They start fighting for it. If that little bastard's as valuable as Protogen thinks, you can't stop the war. All you can do now is change it."

Holden frowned, angry lines at the corners of his mouth and eyes. Miller watched a little piece of the man's idealism die and was sorry that it gave him joy.

"So what happens if we get to Mars?" Miller went on, his voice low. "We trade out the protomolecule for more money than any of us have ever seen. Or maybe they just shoot you. Mars just wins against Earth. And the Belt. Or you go to the OPA, who are the best hope the Belt has of independence, and they're a bunch of crazy zealots, half of 'em thinking we can actually sustain out there without Earth. And trust me, they'll probably shoot you too. Or you just tell everyone everything and pretend that however it comes down, you kept your hands clean."

"There's a right thing to do," Holden said.

"You don't have a right thing, friend," Miller said. "You've got a whole plateful of maybe a little less wrong."

Holden's blood flush finished. The captain pulled the needles out of his arm and let the thin metallic tentacles retract. As he rolled down his sleeve, the frown softened.

"People have a right to know what's going on," Holden said. "Your argument boils down to you not thinking people are smart enough to figure out the right way to use it."

"Has anyone used anything you've broadcast as something besides an excuse to shoot someone they already didn't like? Giving them a new reason won't stop them killing each other," Miller said. "You started these wars, Captain. Doesn't mean you can stop them. But you have to try."

"And how am I supposed to do that?" Holden said. The distress in his voice could have been anger. It could have been prayer.

Something in Miller's belly shifted, some inflamed organ calming enough to slip back into place. He hadn't been aware he'd felt wrong until he suddenly felt right again.

"You ask yourself *what happens*," Miller said. "Ask yourself what Naomi'd do."

Holden barked out a laugh. "Is that how you make your decisions?"

Miller let his eyes close. Juliette Mao was there, sitting on the couch at her old apartment on Ceres. Fighting the crew of the stealth ship to a standstill. Burst open by the alien virus on the floor of her shower stall.

"Something like it," Miller said.

The report from Ceres, a break from the usual competing press releases, came that night. The governing council of the OPA announced that a ring of Martian spies had been rooted out. The video feed showed the bodies floating out an industrial airlock in what looked like the old docks in sector six. At a distance, the victims seemed almost peaceful. The feed cut to the head of security. Captain Shaddid looked older. Harder.

"We regret the necessity of this action," she said to everyone everywhere. "But in the cause of freedom, there can be no compromise."

That's what it's come to, Miller thought, rubbing a hand across his chin. *Pogroms after all. Cut off just a hundred more heads, just a thousand more heads, just ten thousand more heads, and then we'll be free.*

A soft alert sounded, and a moment later, gravity shifted a few degrees to Miller's left. Course change. Holden had made a decision.

He found the captain sitting alone and staring at a monitor in ops. The glow lit his face from below, casting shadows up into his eyes. The captain looked older too.

"You make the broadcast?" Miller asked.

"Nope. We're just one ship. We tell everyone what this thing is and that we've got it, we'll be dead before Protogen."

"Probably true," Miller said, sitting at an empty station with a grunt. The gimbaled seat shifted silently. "We're going someplace."

"I don't trust them with it," Holden said. "I don't trust any of them with that safe."

"Probably smart."

"I'm going to Tycho Station. There's someone there I...trust."

"Trust?"

"Don't actively distrust."

"Naomi think it's the right thing?"

"I don't know. I didn't ask her. But I think so."

"Close enough," Miller said.

Holden looked up from the monitor for the first time.

"You know the right thing?" Holden said.

"Yeah."

"What is it?"

"Throw that safe into a long collision course with the sun and find a way to make sure no one ever, ever goes to Eros or Phoebe again," Miller said. "Pretend none of this ever happened."

"So why aren't we doing that?"

Miller nodded slowly. "How do you throw away the holy grail?"

Chapter Thirty-Seven: Holden

Alex had the *Rocinante* running at three-quarters of a g for two hours while the crew prepared and ate dinner. He would run it back up to three when the break was over, but in the meantime, Holden enjoyed standing on his own two legs at something not too far off from Earth gravity. It was a little heavy for Naomi and Miller, but neither of them complained. They both understood the need for haste.

Once the gravity had dropped from the crush of high acceleration, the whole crew quietly gathered in the galley and started making dinner. Naomi blended together fake eggs and fake cheese. Amos cooked tomato paste and the last of their fresh mushrooms into a red sauce that actually smelled like the real thing. Alex, who had the duty watch, had forwarded ship ops down to a panel in the galley and sat at a table next to it, spreading the fake cheese paste and red sauce onto flat noodles in hopes that the end result would approximate lasagna. Holden had oven duty and had spent the lasagna prep time baking frozen lumps of dough into bread. The smell in the galley was not entirely unlike actual food.

Miller had followed the crew into the galley but seemed uncomfortable asking for something to do. Instead, he set the table and then sat down at it and watched. He wasn't exactly avoiding Holden's eyes, but he wasn't going out of his way to catch his attention. By unspoken mutual agreement, no one had any of the news channels on. Holden was sure everyone would rush back to check the current state of the war as soon as dinner was over, but for now they all worked in companionable silence.

When the prep was done, Holden switched off bread duty and on to moving lasagna-filled cookware into and out of the oven. Naomi sat down next to Alex and began a quiet conversation with him about something she'd seen on the ops screen. Holden split his time between watching her and watching the lasagna. She laughed at something Alex said and unconsciously twisted one finger into her hair. Holden felt his belly tighten a notch.

Out of the corner of his eye, he thought he saw Miller staring at him. When he looked, the detective had turned away, a hint of a smile on his face. Naomi laughed again. She had one hand on Alex's arm, and the pilot was blushing and talking as fast as his silly Martian drawl would let him. They looked like friends. That both made Holden happy and filled him with jealousy. He wondered if Naomi would ever be his friend again.

She caught him looking and gave him a conspiratorial wink that probably would have made a lot of sense if he'd been able to hear what Alex was saying. He smiled and winked back, grateful just to be included in the moment. A sizzling sound from inside the oven called his attention back. The lasagna was beginning to bubble and run over the sides of the dishes.

He pulled on his oven mitts and opened the door.

"Soup's on," he said, pulling the first of the dishes and putting it on the table.

"That's mighty ugly-looking soup," Amos said.

"Uh, yeah," Holden said. "It's just something Mother Tamara used to say when she'd finished cooking. Not sure where it comes from."

"One of your *three* mothers did the cooking? How traditional," Naomi said with a smirk.

"Well, she split it pretty evenly with Caesar, one of my fathers."

Naomi smiled at him, a genuine smile now.

"It sounds really nice," she said. "Big family like that."

"Yeah, it really was," he replied, a vision in his head of nuclear fire tearing apart the Montana farmhouse he'd grown up in, his family blowing into ash. If it happened, he was sure Miller would be there to let him know it was his fault. He wasn't sure he'd be able to argue anymore.

As they ate, Holden felt a slow release of tension in the room. Amos belched loudly, then reacted to the chorus of protests by doing it again even more loudly. Alex retold the joke that had made Naomi laugh. Even Miller got into the mood and told a long and increasingly improbable story about hunting down a black market cheese operation that ended in a gunfight with nine naked Australians in an illegal brothel. By the finish of the story, Naomi was laughing so hard she'd drooled on her shirt, and Amos kept repeating "No fucking way!" like a mantra.

The story was amusing enough, and the detective's dry delivery suited it well, but Holden only half listened. He watched his crew, saw the tension falling from their faces and shoulders. He and Amos were both from Earth, though if he had to guess, he'd say Amos had forgotten about his home world the first time he'd shipped out. Alex was from Mars and clearly still loved it. One bad mistake on either side and both planets might be radioactive rubble by the end of dinner. But right now they were just friends having a meal together. It was right. It was what Holden had to keep fighting for.

"I actually remember that cheese shortage," Naomi said once Miller had stopped talking. "Belt-wide. That was your fault?"

"Yeah, well, if they'd only been sneaking cheese past the government auditors, we wouldn't have had a problem," Miller said. "But they had this habit of shooting the other cheese smugglers. Makes the cops notice. Bad business."

"Over fucking *cheese*?" Amos said, tossing his fork onto his plate with a clack. "Are you serious? I mean, drugs or gambling or something. But cheese?"

"Gambling's legal, most places," Miller said. "And a chemistry class dropout can cook up just about any drug you like in his bathroom. No way to control supply."

"Real cheese comes from Earth, or Mars," Naomi added. "And after they tack on shipping costs and the Coalition's fifty percent in taxes, it costs more than fuel pellets."

"We wound up with one hundred and thirty kilos of Vermont Cheddar in the evidence lockup," Miller said. "Street value that would have probably bought someone their own ship. It had disappeared by the end of the day. We wrote it up as lost to spoilage. No one said a word, as long as everyone went home with a brick."

The detective leaned back in his chair with a distant look on his face.

"My God, that was good cheese," he said with a smile.

"Yeah, well, this fake stuff does taste like shit," Amos said, then added in a hurry, "No offense, Boss, you did a real good job whipping it up. But that's still weird to me, fighting over cheese."

"It's why they killed Eros," Naomi said.

Miller nodded but said nothing.

"How do you figure that?" Amos said.

"How long have you been flying?" Naomi asked.

"I dunno," Amos replied, his lips compressing as he did the mental math. "Twenty-five years, maybe?"

"Fly with a lot of Belters, right?"

"Yeah," Amos said. "Can't get better shipmates than Belters. 'Cept me, of course."

"You've flown with us for twenty-five years, you like us, you've learned the patois. I bet you can order a beer and a hooker on any station in the Belt. Heck, if you were a little taller and a lot skinnier, you could pass for one of us by now."

Amos smiled, taking it as a compliment.

"But you still don't get us," Naomi said. "Not really. No one who grew up with free air ever will. And that's why they can kill a million and a half of us to figure out what their bug really does."

"Hey now," Alex interjected. "You serious 'bout that? You think the inners and outers see themselves as that different?"

"Of course they do," Miller said. "We're too tall, too skinny, our heads look too big, and our joints too knobby."

Holden noticed Naomi glancing across the table at him, a speculative look on her face. *I like your head,* Holden thought at her, but the radiation hadn't given him telepathy either, because her expression didn't change.

"We've practically got our own language now," Miller said. "Ever see an Earther try to get directions in the deep dig?"

"'Tu run spin, pow, Schlauch tu way acima and ido,'" Naomi said with a heavy Belter accent.

"Go spinward to the tube station, which will take you back to the docks," Amos said. "The fuck's so hard about that?"

"I had a partner wouldn't have known that after two years on Ceres," Miller said. "And Havelock wasn't stupid. He just wasn't...*from* there."

Holden listened to them talk and pushed cold pasta around on his plate with a chunk of bread.

"Okay, we get it," he said. "You're weird. But to kill a million and a half people over some skeletal differences and slang..."

"People have been getting tossed into ovens for less than that ever since they invented ovens," Miller said. "If it makes you feel better, most of us think you're squat and microcephalic."

Alex shook his head.

"Don't make a lick of sense to me, turnin' that bug loose, even if you hated every single human on Eros personally. Who knows what that thing'll do?"

Naomi walked to the galley sink and washed her hands, the running water drawing everyone's attention.

"I've been thinking about that," she said, then turned around, wiping her hands on a towel. "The point of it, I mean."

Miller started to speak, but Holden hushed him with a quick gesture and waited for Naomi to continue.

"So," she said. "I've been thinking of it as a computing problem. If the virus or nanomachine or protomolecule or whatever was designed, it has a purpose, right?"

"Definitely," Holden said.

"And it seems like it's trying to do something—something complex. It doesn't make sense to go to all that trouble just to kill people. Those changes it makes look intentional, just...not complete, to me."

"I can see that," Holden said. Alex and Amos nodded along with him but stayed quiet.

"So maybe the issue is that the protomolecule isn't smart enough yet. You can compress a lot of data down pretty small, but unless it's a quantum computer, processing takes space. The easiest way to get that processing in tiny machines is through distribution. Maybe the protomolecule isn't finishing its job because it just isn't smart enough to. Yet."

"Not enough of them," Alex said.

"Right," Naomi said, dropping the towel into a bin under the sink. "So you give them a lot of biomass to work with, and see what it is they are ultimately made to do."

"According to that guy in the video, they were made to hijack life on Earth and wipe us out," Miller said.

"And that," Holden said, "is why Eros is perfect. Lots of biomass in a vacuum-sealed test tube. And if it gets out of hand, there's already a war going on. A lot of ships and missiles can be used for nuking Eros into glass if the threat seems real. Nothing to make us forget our differences like a new player butting in."

"Wow," Amos said. "That is really, really fucked up."

"Okay. But even though that's probably what's happened," Holden said, "I still can't believe that there are enough evil people all in one place to do it. This isn't a one-man operation. This is the work of dozens, maybe hundreds, of very smart people. Does Protogen just go around recruiting every potential Stalin and Jack the Ripper it runs across?"

"I'll make sure to ask Mr. Dresden," Miller said, an unreadable expression on his face, "when we finally meet."

Tycho's habitat rings spun serenely around the bloated zero-g factory globe in the center. The massive construction waldoes that sprouted from the top were maneuvering an enormous piece of hull plating onto the side of the *Nauvoo.* Looking at the station on the ops screens while Alex finished up docking procedures, Holden felt something like relief. So far, Tycho was the one place no one had tried to shoot them, or blow them up, or vomit goo on them, and that practically made it home.

Holden looked at the research safe clamped securely to the deck and hoped that he hadn't just killed everyone on the station by bringing it there.

As if on cue, Miller pulled himself through the deck hatch and drifted over to the safe. He gave Holden a meaningful look.

"Don't say it. I'm already thinking it," Holden said.

Miller shrugged and drifted over to the ops station.

"Big," he said, nodding at the *Nauvoo,* on Holden's screen.

"Generation ship," Holden said. "Something like that will give us the stars."

"Or a lonely death on a long trip to nowhere," Miller replied.

"You know," Holden said, "some species' version of the great galactic adventure is shooting virus-filled bullets at their neighbors. I think ours is pretty damn noble in comparison."

Miller seemed to consider that, nodded, and watched Tycho Station swell on the monitor as Alex brought them closer. The detective kept one hand on the console, making the micro adjustments necessary to remain still even as the pilot's maneuvers threw unexpected bursts of gravity at them from every direction. Holden was strapped into his chair. Even concentrating, he couldn't handle zero g and intermittent thrust half that well. His brain just couldn't be trained out of the twenty-odd years he'd spent with gravity as a constant.

Naomi was right. It would be so easy to see Belters as alien. Hell, if you gave them time to develop some really efficient implantable oxygen storage and recycling and kept trimming the environment suits down to the minimum necessary for heat, you might wind up with Belters who spent more time outside their ships and stations than in.

Maybe that was why they were taxed to subsistence level. The bird was out of the cage, but you couldn't let it stretch its wings too far or it might forget it belonged to you.

"You trust this Fred?" Miller asked.

"Sort of," Holden said. "He treated us well last time, when everyone else wanted us dead or locked up."

Miller grunted, as if that proved nothing.

"He's OPA, right?"

"Yeah," Holden said. "But I think maybe the real OPA. Not the cowboys who want to shoot it out with the inners. And not those nuts on the radio calling for war. Fred's a politician."

"What about the ones keeping Ceres in line?"

"I don't know," Holden said. "I don't know about them. But Fred's the best shot we have. Least wrong."

"Fair enough," Miller said. "We won't find a political solution to Protogen, you know."

"Yeah," Holden said, then began unbuckling his harness as the *Roci* slid into its berth with a series of metallic bangs. "But Fred isn't *just* a politician."

Fred sat behind his large wooden desk, reading the notes Holden had written about Eros, the search for Julie, and the discovery of the stealth ship. Miller sat across from him, watching Fred like an entomologist might watch a new species of bug, guessing if it was likely to sting. Holden was a little farther away on Fred's right, trying not to keep looking at the clock on his hand terminal. On the huge screen behind the desk, the *Nauvoo* drifted by like the metal bones of some dead and decaying leviathan. Holden could see the tiny spots of brilliant blue light where workers used welding torches on the hull and frame. To occupy himself, he started counting them.

He'd reached forty-three when a small shuttle appeared in his field of view, a load of steel beams clutched in a pair of heavy manipulator arms, and flew toward the half-built generation ship. The shuttle shrank to a point no larger than the tip of a pen before it stopped. The *Nauvoo* suddenly shifted in Holden's mind from a large ship relatively nearby, to a gigantic ship farther away. It gave him a short rush of vertigo.

His hand terminal beeped at almost the same instant that Miller's did. He didn't even look at it; he just tapped the face to shut it up. He knew this routine by now. He pulled out a small bottle, took out two blue pills, and swallowed them dry. He could hear Miller pouring pills out of his bottle as well. The ship's expert medical system dispensed them for him every week with a warning that failing to take them on schedule would lead to horrific death. He took them. He would for the rest of his life. Missing a few would just mean that wasn't very long.

Fred finished reading and threw his hand terminal down on the desk, then rubbed his eyes with the heels of his hands for several seconds. To Holden, he looked older than the last time they'd seen each other.

"I have to tell you, Jim, I have no idea what to make of this," he finally said.

Miller looked at Holden and mouthed, *Jim*, at him with a question on his face. Holden ignored him.

"Did you read Naomi's addition at the end?" Holden asked.

"The bit with the networked nanobugs for increased processing power?"

"Yeah, that bit," Holden said. "It makes sense, Fred."

Fred laughed without humor, then stabbed one finger at his terminal.

"That," he said. "That only makes sense to a psychopath. No one sane could do that. No matter what they thought they might get out of it."

Miller cleared his throat.

"You have something to add, Mr. Muller?" Fred asked.

"Miller," the detective replied. "Yes. First—and all respect here—don't kid yourself. Genocide's old-school. Second, the facts aren't in question. Protogen infected Eros Station with a lethal alien disease, and they're recording the results. Why doesn't matter. We need to stop them."

"And," Holden said, "we think we can track down where their observation station is."

Fred leaned back in his chair, the fake leather and metal frame creaking under his weight even in the one-third g.

"Stop them how?" he asked. Fred knew. He just wanted to hear them say it out loud. Miller played along.

"I'd say we fly to their station and shoot them."

"Who is 'we'?" Fred asked.

"There are a lot of OPA hotheads looking to shoot it out with Earth and Mars," Holden said. "We give them some real bad guys to shoot at instead."

Fred nodded in a way that didn't mean he agreed to anything.

"And your sample? The captain's safe?" Fred said.

"That's mine," Holden said. "No negotiation on that."

Fred laughed again, though there was some humor in it this time. Miller blinked in surprise and then stifled a grin.

"Why would I agree to that?" Fred asked.

Holden lifted his chin and smiled.

"What if I told you that I've hidden the safe on a planetesimal booby-trapped with enough plutonium to break anyone who touches it into their component atoms even if they could find it?" he said.

Fred stared at him for a moment, then said, "But you didn't."

"Well, no," Holden said. "But I could tell you I did."

"You are too honest," Fred said.

"And you can't trust anyone with something this big. You already know what I'm going to do with it. That's why, until we can agree on something better, you're leaving it with me."

Fred nodded.

"Yes," he said, "I guess I am."

Chapter Thirty-Eight: Miller

The observation deck looked out over the *Nauvoo* as the behemoth slowly came together. Miller sat on the edge of a soft couch, his fingers laced over his knee, his gaze on the immense vista of the construction. After his time on Holden's ship and, before that, in Eros, with its old-style closed architecture, a view so wide seemed artificial. The deck itself was wider than the *Rocinante* and decorated with soft ferns and sculpted ivies. The air recyclers were eerily quiet, and even though the spin gravity was nearly the same as Ceres', the Coriolis felt subtly wrong.

He'd lived in the Belt his whole life, and he'd never been anywhere that was designed so carefully for the tasteful display of wealth and power. It was pleasant as long as he didn't think about it too much.

He wasn't the only one drawn to the open spaces of Tycho. A few dozen station workers sat in groups or walked through together. An hour before, Amos and Alex had gone by, deep in their own conversation, so he wasn't entirely surprised when, standing up and walking back toward the docks, he saw Naomi sitting by herself with a bowl of food cooling on a tray at her side. Her gaze was fixed on her hand terminal.

"Hey," he said.

Naomi looked up, recognized him, and smiled distractedly.

"Hey," she said.

Miller nodded toward the hand terminal and shrugged a question.

"Comm data from that ship," she said. It was always *that ship,* Miller noticed. The same way people would call a particularly godawful crime scene *that place.* "It's all tightbeam, so I thought it wouldn't be so hard to triangulate. But..."

"Not so much?"

Naomi lifted her eyebrows and sighed.

"I've been plotting orbits," she said. "But nothing's fitting. There could be relay drones, though. Moving targets the ship system was calibrated for that would send the message on to the actual station. Or another drone, and then the station, or who knows?"

"Any data coming off Eros?"

"I assume so," Naomi said, "but I don't know that it would be any easier to make sense of than this."

"Can't your OPA friends do something?" Miller asked. "They've got more processing power than one of these handhelds. Probably have a better activity map of the Belt too."

"Probably," she said.

He couldn't tell if she didn't trust this Fred that Holden had given them over to, or just needed to feel like the investigation was still hers. He considered telling her to back off it for a while, to let the others carry it, but he didn't see he had the moral authority to make that one stick.

"What?" Naomi said, an uncertain smile on her lips.

Miller blinked.

"You were laughing a little," Naomi said. "I don't think I've ever seen you laugh before. I mean, not when something was funny."

"I was just thinking about something a partner of mine told me about letting cases go when you got pulled from them."

"What did he say?"

"That it's like taking half a shit," Miller said.

"Had a way with words, that one."

"He was all right for an Earther," Miller said, and something tickled at the back of his mind. Then, a moment later: "Ah, Jesus. I may have something."

Havelock met him in an encrypted drop site that lived on a server cluster on Ganymede. The latency kept them from anything like real-time conversation. It was more like dropping notes, but it did the trick. The waiting made Miller anxious. He sat with his terminal set to refresh every three seconds.

"Would you like anything else?" the woman asked. "Another bourbon?"

"That'd be great," Miller said, and checked to see if Havelock had replied yet. He hadn't.

Like the observation deck, the bar looked out on the *Nauvoo*, though from a slightly different angle. The great ship looked foreshortened, and arcs of energy lit it where a layer of ceramic was annealing. A bunch of religious zealots were going to load themselves into that massive ship, that small self-sustaining world, and launch themselves into the darkness between the stars. Generations would live and die in it, and if they were mind-bendingly lucky enough to find a planet worth living on the end of the journey, the people who came out of it would never have known Earth or Mars or the Belt. They'd be aliens already. And if whatever had made the protomolecule was out there to greet them, then what?

Would they all die like Julie had?

There was life out there. They had proof of it now. And the proof came in the shape of a weapon, so what did that tell him?

Except that maybe the Mormons deserved a little warning about what they were signing their great-grandkids up for.

He laughed to himself when he realized that was exactly what Holden would say.

The bourbon arrived at the same moment his hand terminal chimed. The video file had a layered encryption that took almost a minute to unpack. That alone was a good sign.

The file opened, and Havelock grinned out from the screen. He was in better shape than he'd been on Ceres, and it showed in the shape of his jaw. His skin was darker, but Miller didn't know if it was purely cosmetic or if his old partner had been basking in false sunlight for the joy of it. It didn't matter. It made the Earther look rich and fit.

"Hey, buddy," Havelock said. "Good to hear from you. After what happened with Shaddid and the OPA, I was afraid we were going to be on different sides now. I'm glad you got out of there before the shit hit the fan.

"Yeah, I'm still with Protogen, and I've got to tell you, these guys are kind of scary. I mean, I've worked contract security before, and I'm pretty clear when someone's hard-core. These guys aren't cops. They're troops. You know what I mean?

"Officially, I don't know dick about a Belt station, but you know how it is. I'm from Earth. There are a lot of these guys who gave me shit about Ceres. Working with the vacuum-heads. That kind of thing. But the way things are here, it's better to be on the good side of the bad guys. It's just that kind of job."

There was an apology in his expression. Miller understood. Working in some corporations was like going to prison. You adopted the views of the people around you. A Belter might get hired on, but he'd never belong. Like Ceres, just pointed the other way. If Havelock had made friends with a set of inner planet mercs who spent their off nights curb-stomping Belters outside bars, then he had.

But making friends didn't mean he was one of them.

"So. Off the record, yeah, there's a black ops station in the Belt.

I hadn't heard it called Thoth, but it could be. Some sort of very scary deep research and development lab. Heavy science crew, but not a huge place. I think *discreet* would be the word. Lots of automated defenses, but not a big ground crew.

"I don't need to tell you that leaking the coordinates would get my ass killed out here. So wipe the file when you're done, and let's not talk again for a long, long time."

The datafile was small. Three lines of plaintext orbital notation. Miller put it into his hand terminal and killed the file off the Ganymede server. The bourbon still sat beside his hand, and he drank it off neat. The warmth in his chest might have been the alcohol or it might have been victory.

He turned on the hand terminal's camera.

"Thanks. I owe you one. Here's part of the payment. What happened on Eros? Protogen was part of it, and it's big. If you get the chance to drop your contract with them, do it. And if they try to rotate you out to that black ops station, don't go."

Miller frowned. The sad truth was that Havelock was probably the last real partner he'd had. The only one who'd looked on him as an equal. As the kind of detective Miller had imagined himself to be.

"Take care of yourself, partner," he said, then ended the file, encrypted it, shipped it out. He had the bone-deep feeling he wasn't ever going to talk to Havelock again.

He put through a connection request to Holden. The screen filled with the captain's open, charming, vaguely naive face.

"Miller," Holden said. "Everything okay?"

"Yeah. Great. But I need to talk to your Fred guy. Can you arrange that?"

Holden frowned and nodded at the same time.

"Sure. What's going on?"

"I know where Thoth Station is," Miller said.

"You know what?"

Miller nodded.

"Where the hell did you get that?"

Miller grinned. "If I gave you that information and it got out, a good man would get killed," he said. "You see how that works?"

It struck Miller as he, Holden, and Naomi waited for Fred that he knew an awful lot of inner planet types fighting against the inner planets. Or at least not for them. Fred, supposedly a high-ranking OPA member. Havelock. Three-quarters of the crew of the *Rocinante*. Juliette Mao.

It wasn't what he would have expected. But maybe that was shortsighted. He was seeing the thing the way Shaddid and Protogen did. There were two sides fighting—that was true enough—but they weren't the inner planets versus the Belters. They were the people who thought it was a good idea to kill people who looked or acted differently against the people who didn't.

Or maybe that was a crap analysis too. Because given the chance to put the scientist from the Protogen pitch, the board of directors, and whoever this Dresden piece of shit was into an airlock, Miller knew he'd agonize about it for maybe half a second after he blew them all into vacuum. Didn't put him on the side of angels.

"Mr. Miller. What can I do for you?"

Fred. The Earther OPA. He wore a blue button-down shirt and a nice pair of slacks. He could have been an architect or a mid-level administrator for any number of good, respectable corporations. Miller tried to imagine him coordinating a battle.

"You can convince me that you've really got what it takes to kill the Protogen station," Miller said. "Then I'll tell you where it is."

Fred's eyebrows rose a millimeter.

"Come into my office," Fred said.

Miller went. Holden and Naomi followed. When the doors closed behind them, Fred was the first to speak.

"I'm not sure exactly what you want from me. I'm not in the habit of making my battle plans public knowledge."

"We're talking about storming a station," Miller said. "Something with damn good defenses and maybe more ships like the one that killed the *Canterbury*. No disrespect intended, but that's a pretty tall order for a bunch of amateurs like the OPA."

"Ah, Miller?" Holden said. Miller held up a hand, cutting him off.

"I can give you the directions to Thoth Station," Miller said. "But if I do that and it turns out you haven't got the punch to see this through, then a lot of people die and nothing gets resolved. I'm not up for that."

Fred cocked his head, like a dog hearing an unfamiliar sound. Naomi and Holden shared a glance that Miller couldn't parse.

"This is a war," Miller said, warming to the subject. "I've worked with the OPA before, and frankly you folks are a lot better at little guerrilla bullshit than at coordinating anything real. Half of the people who claim to speak for you are crackpots who happened to have a radio nearby. I see you've got a lot of money. I see you've got a nice office. What I don't see—what I need to see—is that you've got what it takes to bring these bastards down. Taking out a station isn't a game. I don't care how many simulations you've run. This is real now. If I'm going to help you, I need to know you can handle it."

There was a long silence.

"Miller?" Naomi said. "You know who Fred is, right?"

"The Tycho mouthpiece for the OPA," Miller said. "That doesn't draw a whole lot of water with me."

"He's Fred *Johnson*," Holden said.

Fred's eyebrows rose another millimeter. Miller frowned and crossed his arms.

"Colonel Frederick Lucius Johnson," Naomi said, clarifying.

Miller blinked. "The Butcher of Anderson Station?" he said.

"The same," Fred said. "I have been talking with the central council of the OPA. I have a cargo ship with more than enough troops to secure the station. Air support is a state-of-the-art Martian torpedo bomber."

"The *Roci*?" Miller said.

"The *Rocinante*," Fred agreed. "And while you may not believe it, I actually know what I'm doing."

Miller looked at his feet, then up toward Holden.

"*That* Fred Johnson?" he said.

"I thought you knew," Holden said.

"Well. Don't I feel like the flaming idiot," Miller said.

"It'll pass," Fred said. "Was there anything else you wanted to demand?"

"No," Miller said. And then: "Yes. I want to be part of the ground assault. When we take that station crew, I want to be there."

"Are you sure?" Fred said. " 'Taking out a station isn't a game.' What makes you think *you* have what it takes?"

Miller shrugged.

"One thing it takes is the coordinates," Miller said. "I have got those."

Fred laughed. "Mr. Miller. If you'd like to go down to this station and have whatever's waiting for us down there try to kill you along with the rest of us, I won't stand in your way."

"Thanks," Miller said. He pulled up his hand terminal and sent the plaintext coordinates to Fred. "There you go. My source is solid, but he's not working from firsthand data. We should confirm before we commit."

"I'm not an amateur," Colonel Fred Johnson said, looking at the file. Miller nodded, adjusted his hat, and walked out. Naomi and Holden flanked him. When they reached the wide, clean public hallway, Miller looked to his right, catching Holden's eyes.

"Really, I thought you knew," Holden said.

Eight days later, the message came. The cargo ship *Guy Molinari* had arrived, full up with OPA soldiers. Havelock's coordinates had been verified. Something was sure as hell out there, and it appeared to be collecting the tightbeamed data from Eros. If Miller wanted to be part of this, the time had come to move out.

He sat in his quarters in the *Rocinante* for what was likely the last time. He realized with a little twinge, equal parts surprise and sorrow, that he was going to miss the place. Holden, for all his faults and Miller's complaints, was a decent guy. In over his head and only half aware of the fact, but Miller could think of more than one person who fit that bill. He was going to miss Alex's odd, affected drawl and Amos' casual obscenity. He was going to wonder if and how Naomi ever worked things out with her captain.

Leaving was a reminder of things he'd already known: that he didn't know what would come next, that he didn't have much money, and that while he was sure he could get back from Thoth Station, where and how he went from there was going to be improvisation. Maybe there would be another ship he could sign on with. Maybe he'd have to take a contract and save up some money to cover his new medical expenses.

He checked the magazine in his gun. Packed his spare clothes into the small, battered pack he'd taken on the transport from Ceres. Everything he owned still fit in it.

He turned off the lights and made his way down the short corridor toward the ladder-lift. Holden was in the galley, twitching nervously. The dread of the coming battle was already showing in the corners of the man's eyes.

"Well," Miller said. "Here we go, eh?"

"Yep," Holden said.

"It's been a hell of a ride," Miller said. "Can't say it's all been pleasant, but..."

"Yeah."

"Tell the others I said goodbye," Miller said.

"Will do," Holden said. Then, as Miller moved past him toward the lift: "So assuming we all actually live through this, where should we meet up?"

Miller turned.

"I don't understand," he said.

"Yeah, I know. Look, I trust Fred or I wouldn't have come here. I think he's honorable, and he'll do the right thing by us. That doesn't mean I trust the whole OPA. After we get this thing done,

I want the whole crew together. Just in case we need to get out in a hurry."

Something painful happened under Miller's sternum. Not a sharp pain, just a sudden ache. His throat felt thick. He coughed to clear it.

"As soon as we get the place secure, I'll get in touch," Miller said.

"Okay, but don't take too long. If Thoth Station has a whorehouse left standing, I'm going to need help prying Amos out of it."

Miller opened his mouth, closed it, and tried again.

"Aye, aye, Captain," he said, forcing a lightness into his voice.

"Be careful," Holden said.

Miller left, pausing in the passageway between ship and station until he was sure he'd stopped weeping, and then making his way to the cargo ship and the assault.

Chapter Thirty-Nine: Holden

The *Rocinante* hurtled through space like a dead thing, tumbling in all three axes. With the reactor shut down and all the cabin air vented, it radiated neither heat nor electromagnetic noise. If it weren't for its speeding toward Thoth Station significantly faster than a rifle shot, the ship would be indistinguishable from the rocks in the Belt. Nearly half a million kilometers behind it, the *Guy Molinari* screamed the *Roci*'s innocence to anyone who would listen, and fired its engines in a long slow deceleration.

With the radio off, Holden couldn't hear what they were saying, but he'd helped write the warning, so it echoed in his head anyway. *Warning! Accidental detonation on the cargo ship* Guy Molinari *has broken large cargo container free. Warning to all ships in its path: Container is traveling at high speed and without independent control. Warning!*

There had been some discussion about not broadcasting at all.

Because Thoth was a black station, they'd be using only passive sensors. Scanning every direction with radar or ladar would light them up like a Christmas tree. It was possible that with its reactor off, the *Rocinante* could sneak up on the station without being noticed. But Fred had decided that if they were somehow spotted, it would be suspicious enough to probably warrant an immediate counterattack. So instead of playing it quiet, they'd decided to play it loud and count on confusion to help them.

With luck the Thoth Station security systems would scan them and see that they were in fact a big chunk of metal flying on an unchanging vector and lacking apparent life support, and ignore them just long enough to let them get close. From far away, the stations' defense systems might be too much for the *Roci*. But up close, the maneuverable little ship could dart around the station and cut it to pieces. All their cover story needed to do was buy them time while the station's security team tried to figure out what was going on.

Fred, and by extension everyone in the assault, was betting that the station wouldn't fire until they were absolutely certain they were under attack. Protogen had gone to a lot of trouble to hide their research lab in the Belt. As soon as they launched their first missile, their anonymity was lost forever. With the war going on, monitors would pick up the fusion torch trails and wonder what was up. Firing a weapon would be Thoth Station's last resort.

In theory.

Sitting alone inside the tiny bubble of air contained in his helmet, Holden knew that if they were wrong, he'd never even realize it. The *Roci* was flying blind. All radio contact was down. Alex had a mechanical timepiece with a glow-in-the-dark face, and a to-the-second schedule memorized. They couldn't beat Thoth at high-tech, so they were flying as low-tech as you could get. If they'd missed their guess and the station fired on them, the *Roci* would be vaporized without warning. Holden had once dated a Buddhist who said that death was merely a different state of being, and people only feared the unknown that lay behind that transition. Death without warning was preferable, as it removed all fear.

He felt he now had the counterargument.

To keep his mind busy, he ran through the plan again. When they were practically close enough to spit on Thoth Station, Alex would fire up the reactor and do a braking maneuver at nearly ten g's. The *Guy Molinari* would begin spraying radio static and laser clutter at the station to confuse its targeting package for the few moments the *Roci* would need to come around on an attack vector. The *Roci* would engage the station's defenses, disabling anything that could hurt the *Molinari*, while the cargo ship moved in to breach the station's hull and drop off her assault troops.

There were any number of things wrong with this plan.

If the station decided to fire early, just in case, the *Roci* could die before the fight even started. If the station's targeting system could cut the *Molinari*'s static and laser clutter, they might begin firing while the *Roci* was still getting into position. And even if all that worked perfectly, there was still the assault team, cutting their way into the station and fighting corridor to corridor to the nerve center to take control. Even the inner planets' best marines were terrified of breaching actions, and for good reason. Moving through unfamiliar metal hallways without cover while the enemy ambushed you at every intersection was a good way to get a lot of people killed. In training simulations back in the Earth navy, Holden had never seen the marines do better than 60 percent casualties. And these weren't inner planet marines with years of training and state-of-the-art equipment. They were OPA cowboys with whatever gear they could scrape together at the last minute.

But even that wasn't what really worried Holden.

What really worried him was the large, slightly-warmer-than-space area just a few dozen meters above Thoth Station. The *Molinari* had spotted it and warned them before cutting them loose. Having seen the stealth ships before, no one on the *Roci* doubted that this was another one.

Fighting the station would be bad enough, even up close, where most of the station's advantages were lost. But Holden didn't look forward to dodging torpedo fire from a missile frigate at the same time. Alex had assured him that if they could get in close enough to the station, they could keep the frigate from firing at them for fear of damaging Thoth, and that the *Roci*'s greater maneuverability would make it more than a match for the larger and more heavily armed ship. The stealth frigates were a strategic weapon, he'd said, not a tactical one. Holden hadn't said, *Then why do they have one here?*

Holden moved to glance down at his wrist, then snorted with frustration in the pitch black of the ops deck. His suit was powered down, chronometers and lights both. The only system on in his suit was air circulation, and that was strictly mechanical. If something got fouled up with it, no little warning lights would come on; he'd just choke and die.

He glanced around the dark room and said, "Come on, how much longer?"

As if in answer, lights began flickering on through the cabin. There was a burst of static in his helmet; then Alex's drawling voice said, "Internal comms online."

Holden began flipping switches to bring the rest of the systems back up.

"Reactor," he said.

"Two minutes," Amos replied from the engine room.

"Main computer."

"Thirty seconds to reboot," Naomi said, and waved at him from across the ops deck. The lights had come up enough for them to see each other.

"Weps?"

Alex laughed with something like genuine glee over the comm.

"Weapons are coming online," he said. "As soon as Naomi gives me back the targeting comp, we'll be cocked, locked, and ready to rock."

Hearing everyone check in after the long and silent darkness of their approach reassured him. Being able to look across the room and see Naomi working at her tasks eased a dread he hadn't even realized he'd been feeling.

"Targeting should be up now," Naomi said.

"Roger that," Alex replied. "Scopes are up. Radar, up. Ladar, up— Shit, Naomi, you seeing this?"

"I see it," Naomi said. "Captain, getting engine signatures from the stealth ship. They're powering up too."

"We expected that," Holden said. "Everyone stay on task."

"One minute," Amos said.

Holden turned on his console and pulled up his tactical display. In the scope, Thoth Station turned in a lazy circle while the slightly warm spot above it got hot enough to resolve a rough hull outline.

"Alex, that doesn't look like the last frigate," Holden said. "Does the *Roci* recognize it yet?"

"Not yet, Cap, but she's workin' on it."

"Thirty seconds," Amos said.

"Getting ladar searches from the station," Naomi said. "Broadcasting chatter."

Holden watched on his screen as Naomi tried to match the wavelength the station was using to target them, and began spraying the station with their own laser comm array to confuse the returns.

"Fifteen seconds," Amos said.

"Okay, buckle up, kids," Alex said. "Here comes the juice."

Even before Alex had finished saying it, Holden felt a dozen pinpricks as his chair pumped him full of drugs to keep him alive during the coming deceleration. His skin went tight and hot, and his balls crawled up into his belly. Alex seemed to be speaking in slow motion.

"Five…four…three…two…"

He never said *one*. Instead, a thousand kilos sat on Holden's chest and rumbled like a laughing giant as the *Roci*'s engine slammed on the brakes at ten g's. Holden thought he could actually feel his lungs scraping the inside of his rib cage as his chest did its best to collapse. But the chair pulled him into a soft gel-filled embrace, and the drugs kept his heart beating and his brain processing. He didn't black out. If the high-g maneuvering killed him, he'd be wide awake and lucid for the entire thing.

His helmet filled with the sound of gurgling and labored breathing, only some of which was his own. Amos managed part of a curse before his jaw was clamped shut. Holden couldn't hear the *Roci* shuddering with the strain of her course change, but he could feel it through the seat. She was tough. Tougher than any of them. They'd be long dead before the ship pulled enough g's to hurt itself.

When relief came, it came so suddenly that Holden almost vomited. The drugs in his system stopped that too. He took a deep breath and the cartilage of his sternum clicked painfully back into place.

"Check in," he muttered. His jaw hurt.

"Comm array targeted," Alex replied immediately. Thoth Station's comm and targeting array was the first item on their target priority list.

"All green," Amos said from below.

"Sir," Naomi said, a warning in her voice.

"Shit, I see it," Alex said.

Holden told his console to mirror Naomi's so he could see what she was looking at. On her screen, the *Roci* had figured out why it couldn't identify the stealth ship.

There were two ships, not one large and ungainly missile frigate that they could dance around and cut to pieces at close range. No, that would have been too easy. These were two much smaller ships parked close together to trick enemy sensors. And now they were both firing their engines and splitting up.

Okay, Holden thought. *New plan.*

"Alex, get their attention," he said. "Can't let them go after the *Molinari*."

"Roger," Alex replied. "One away."

Holden felt the *Roci* shudder as Alex fired a torpedo at one of the two ships. The smaller ships were rapidly changing speed and vector, and the torpedo had been fired hastily and from a bad angle. It wouldn't score a hit, but the *Roci* would be on everyone's scope as a threat now. So that was good.

Both of the smaller ships darted away in opposite directions at full burn, spraying chaff and laser chatter behind them as they went. The torpedo wobbled in its trajectory and then limped away in a random direction.

"Naomi, Alex, any idea what we're facing here?" Holden asked.

"*Roci* still doesn't recognize them, sir," Naomi said.

"New hull design," Alex said over her. "But they're flyin' like fast interceptors. Guessin' a torpedo or two on the belly, and a keel-mounted rail gun."

Faster and more maneuverable than the *Roci*, but they'd be able to fire in only one direction.

"Alex, come around to—" Holden's order was cut short when the *Rocinante* shuddered and jumped sideways, hurling him into the side of his restraints with rib-bruising force.

"We're hit!" Amos and Alex yelled at the same time.

"Station shot us with some sort of heavy gauss cannon," Naomi said.

"Damage," Holden said.

"Went clean through us, Cap," Amos said. "Galley and the machine shop. Got yellows on the board, but nothing that'll kill us."

Nothing that'll kill us sounded good, but Holden felt a pang for his coffeemaker.

"Alex," Holden said. "Forget the little ships, kill that comm array."

"Roger," Alex replied, and the *Roci* lurched sideways as Alex changed course to begin his torpedo run on the station.

"Naomi, as soon as the first one of those fighters comes around on his attack run, give him the comm laser in the face, full strength, and start dropping chaff."

"Yes, sir," she replied. Maybe the laser would be enough to screw up his targeting system for a few seconds.

"Station's openin' up with the PDCs," Alex said. "This'll get a mite bumpy."

Holden switched from mirroring Naomi's screen to watching Alex's. His panel filled with thousands of rapidly moving balls of light and Thoth Station rotating in the background. The *Roci*'s threat computer was outlining the incoming point defense cannon fire with bright light on Alex's HUD. It was moving impossibly fast, but at least with the system doing a bright overlay on each round, the pilot could see where the fire was coming from and which direction it was traveling. Alex reacted to this threat information with consummate skill, maneuvering away from the PDCs' direction of fire in quick, almost random movements that forced the automated targeting of the point defense cannons to adjust constantly.

To Holden, it looked like a game. Incredibly fast blobs of light flew up from the space station in chains, like long and thin pearl necklaces. The ship moved restlessly, finding the gaps between the threads and dodging away to a new gap before the strands could react and touch her. But Holden knew that each blob of light represented a chunk of Teflon-coated tungsten steel with a depleted uranium heart, going thousands of meters per second. If Alex lost the game, they'd know it when the *Rocinante* was cut to pieces.

Holden almost jumped out of his skin when Amos spoke. "Shit, Cap, got a leak somewhere. Three port maneuvering thrusters are losing water pressure. Going to patch it."

"Copy, Amos. Go fast," Holden said.

"You hang on down there, Amos," Naomi said.

Amos just snorted.

On his console, Holden watched as Thoth Station grew larger on the scope. Somewhere behind them, the two fighters were probably coming about. The thought made the back of Holden's head itch, but he tried to keep focus. The *Roci* didn't have enough torpedoes for Alex to fire shot after shot at the station from far off and hope one made it through the point defense fire. Alex had to bring them in so close that the cannons couldn't shoot the torpedo down.

A blue highlight appeared on the HUD surrounding a portion of the station's central hub. The highlighted portion expanded into a smaller subscreen. Holden could make out the dishes and antennas that made up the comm and targeting array.

"One away," Alex said, and the *Roci* vibrated as her second torpedo was fired.

Holden shook violently in his restraints and then slapped back into his chair as Alex took the *Roci* through a series of sudden maneuvers and then slammed down the throttle to evade the last of the PDC fire. Holden watched his screen as the red dot of their missile streaked toward the station and struck the comm array. A flash blanked out his screen for a second and then faded. Almost immediately the PDC fire stopped.

"Good sh—" Holden was cut off by Naomi yelling, "Bogey one has fired! Two fast movers!"

Holden flipped back to her screen and saw the threat system tracking both fighters and two smaller and much faster objects moving toward the *Roci* on an intercept course.

"Alex!" Holden said.

"Got it, Chief. Going defensive."

Holden slammed back into his chair again as Alex poured on the speed. The steady rumble of the engine seemed to stutter, and Holden realized he was feeling the constant fire of their own PDCs as they tried to shoot down the pursuing missiles.

"Well, fuck," Amos said almost conversationally.

"Where are you?" Holden asked, then flipped his screen to Amos' suit camera. The mechanic was in a dimly illuminated crawl space filled with conduit and piping. That meant he was between the inner and outer hulls. In front of him, a section of damaged pipe looked like snapped bones. A cutting torch floated nearby. The ship bounced violently, banging the mechanic around in the tight space. Alex whooped over the comm.

"Missiles did not impact!" he said.

"Tell Alex to stop jerking her around," Amos said. "Makes it hard to hang on to my tools."

"Amos, get back to your crash couch!" Naomi said.

"Sorry, Boss," Amos replied with a grunt as he yanked one end of the broken pipe free. "If I don't fix this and we lose pressure, Alex won't be able to turn to starboard anymore. Bet that'll fuck us up good."

"Keep working, Amos," Holden said over Naomi's protests. "But hang on. This is going to get worse."

Amos said, "Roger that."

Holden switched back to Alex's HUD display.

"Holden," Naomi said. There was fear in her voice. "Amos is going to get—"

"He's doing his job. Do yours. Alex, we have to take these two out before the *Molinari* gets here. Get me an intercept on one of them and let's kick its ass."

"Roger that, Cap," Alex said. "Going after bogey two. Could use some help with bogey one."

"Bogey one is Naomi's priority," Holden said. "Do what you can to keep it off of our backside while we kill his friend."

"Roger," Naomi said in a tight voice.

Holden switched back to Amos' helmet camera, but the mechanic seemed to be doing fine. He was cutting the damaged pipe free with his torch, and a length of replacement pipe floated nearby.

"Strap that pipe down, Amos," Holden said.

"All respect, Captain," Amos said, "but safety standards can kiss my ass. I'm getting this done fast and getting outta here."

Holden hesitated. If Alex had to make a course correction, the floating pipe could turn into a projectile massive enough to kill Amos or break the *Roci*. *It's Amos,* he told himself. *He knows what he's doing.*

Holden flipped to Naomi's screen as she poured everything the comm system had at the small interceptor, trying to blind it with light and radio static. Then he went back to his tactical display.

The *Roci* and bogey two flew toward each other at suicidal speeds. As soon as they passed the point where incoming torpedo fire couldn't be avoided, bogey two launched both his missiles. Alex flagged the two fast movers for the PDCs and kept up his intercept course but didn't launch missiles.

"Alex, why aren't we shooting?" Holden said.

"Gonna shoot his torpedoes down, then get in close and let the PDCs chew him up," the pilot replied.

"Why?"

"We've only got so many torpedoes and no resupply. No call to waste 'em on these munchkins."

The incoming torpedoes arced forward on Holden's display, and he felt the *Roci*'s PDCs firing to shoot them down.

"Alex," he said. "We didn't pay for this ship. Feel free to use it up. If I get killed so you can save ammo, I am going to put a reprimand in your permanent file."

"Well, you put it that way..." Alex said. Then: "One away."

The red dot of their torpedo streaked off toward bogey two. The incoming missiles got closer and closer, and then one disappeared from the display.

Alex said, "Shit," in a flat voice, and then the *Rocinante* slammed sideways hard enough that Holden broke his nose on the inside of his helmet. Yellow emergency lights began rotating on all the bulkheads, though with the ship evacuated of air, Holden mercifully couldn't hear the Klaxons that were trying to sound throughout it. His tactical display flickered, went out, and then came back after a second. When it came back up, all three torpedoes, as well as bogey two, were gone. Bogey one continued to bear down on them from astern.

"Damage!" Holden yelled, hoping the comm was still up.

"Major damage to the outer hull," Naomi replied. "Four maneuvering thrusters gone. One PDC nonresponsive. We've also lost O2 storage, and the crew airlock looks like it's slag."

"Why are we alive?" Holden asked while he flipped through the damage report and then over to Amos' suit camera.

"The fish didn't hit us," Alex said. "The PDC got it, but it was close. Warhead detonated and sprayed us down pretty good."

It didn't look like Amos was moving. Holden yelled, "Amos! Report!"

"Yeah, yeah, still here, Captain. Just hanging on in case we get knocked around like that again. I think I busted a rib on one of the hull braces, but I'm strapped down. Good fucking thing I didn't waste time with that pipe, though."

Holden didn't take time to answer. He flipped back to his tactical display and watched the rapidly approaching bogey one. It had already fired its torpedoes, but at close range it could still cut them apart with its cannon.

"Alex, can you get us turned around and get a firing solution on that fighter?" he said.

"Working on it. Don't have much maneuverability," Alex replied, and the *Roci* began rotating with a series of lurches.

Holden switched to a telescope and zoomed in on the approaching fighter. Up close, the muzzle of its cannon looked as big around as a corridor on Ceres, and it appeared to be aimed directly at him.

"Alex," he said.

"Working on it, Chief, but the *Roci*'s hurtin'."

The enemy ship's cannon flared open, preparing to fire.

"Alex, kill it. Kill it *kill it kill it*."

"One away," the pilot said, and the *Rocinante* shuddered.

Holden's console threw him out of the scope view and back to the tactical view automatically. The *Roci*'s torpedo flew toward the fighter at almost the same instant that the fighter opened up with its cannon. The display showed the incoming rounds as small red dots moving too fast to follow.

"Incom—" he shouted, and the *Rocinante* came apart around him.

Holden came to.

The inside of the ship was filled with flying debris and bits of superheated metal shavings that looked like slow-motion showers of sparks. With no air, they bounced off walls and then floated, slowly cooling, like lazy fireflies. He had a vague memory of one corner of a wall-mounted monitor detaching and bouncing off three bulkheads in the world's most elaborate billiards shot, then hitting him right below the sternum. He looked down, and the little chunk of monitor was floating a few centimeters in front of him, but there was no hole in his suit. His guts hurt.

The ops console chair next to Naomi had a hole in it; green gel slowly leaked into small balls that floated away in the zero g. Holden looked at the hole in the chair, and the matching hole in the bulkhead across the room, and realized that the round must have passed within centimeters of Naomi's leg. A shudder swept through him, leaving him nauseated in its wake.

"What the fuck was that?" Amos asked quietly. "And how about we don't do it anymore?"

"Alex?" Holden said.

"Still here, Cap," the pilot replied, his voice eerily calm.

"My panel's dead," Holden said. "Did we kill that son of a bitch?"

"Yeah, Cap, he's dead. About half a dozen of his rounds actually hit the *Roci*. Looks like they went through us from bow to stern. That anti-spalling webbing on the bulkheads really keeps the shrapnel down, doesn't it?"

Alex's voice had started shaking. He meant *We should all be dead.*

"Open a channel to Fred, Naomi," Holden said.

She didn't move.

"Naomi?"

"Right. Fred," she said, then tapped on her screen.

Holden's helmet was filled with static for a second, then with Fred's voice.

"*Guy Molinari* here. Glad you guys are still alive."

"Roger that. Begin your run. Let us know when we can limp over to one of the station's docks."

"Roger," Fred replied. "We'll find you a nice place to land. Fred out."

Holden pulled the quick release on his chair's restraints and floated toward the ceiling, his body limp.

Okay, Miller. Your turn.

Chapter Forty: Miller

Oi, Pampaw," the kid in the crash couch to Miller's right said. "Popped seal, you and bang, hey?"

The kid's combat armor was gray-green, articulated pressure seals at the joints and stripes across the front plates where a knife or flechette round had scraped the finish. Behind the face mask, the kid could have been fifteen. His hand gestures spoke of a childhood spent in vacuum suits, and his speech was pure Belt creole.

"Yeah," Miller said, raising his arm. "Saw some action recently. I'll be fine."

"Fine's fine as fine," the kid said. "But you hold to the foca, and neto can pass the air out to you, hey?"

No one on Mars or Earth would have the first clue what you're saying, Miller thought. *Shit, half the people on Ceres would be embarrassed by an accent that thick. No wonder they don't mind killing you.*

"Sounds good to me," Miller said. "You go first, and I'll try to keep anyone from shooting you in the back."

The kid grinned. Miller had seen thousands like him. Boys in the throes of adolescence, working through the normal teenage drive to take risks and impress girls, but at the same time they lived in the Belt, where one bad call meant dead. He'd seen thousands. He'd arrested hundreds. He'd watched a few dozen picked up in hazmat bags.

He leaned forward to look down the long rows of close-packed gimbaled crash couches that lined the gut of the *Guy Molinari*. Miller's rough estimate put the count at between ninety and a hundred of them. So by dinner, chances were good he'd have seen a couple dozen more die.

"What's your name, kid?"

"Diogo."

"Miller," he said, and gave the kid his hand to shake. The high-quality Martian battle armor Miller had taken from the *Rocinante* let his fingers flex a lot more than the kid's.

The truth was Miller was in no shape for the assault. He was still getting occasional waves of inexplicable nausea, and his arm ached whenever the medication level in his blood started thinning out. But he knew his way around a gun, and he probably knew more about corridor-to-corridor fighting than nine-tenths of the OPA rock jumpers and ore hogs like Diogo who were about to go in. It would have to be good enough.

The ship's address system clicked once.

"This is Fred. We've had word from air support, and we're green for breach in ten minutes. Final checks start now, people."

Miller sat back in his couch. The clicking and chattering of a hundred suits of armor, a hundred sidearms, a hundred assault weapons filled the air. He'd been over his own enough times now; he didn't feel the urge to do it again.

In a few minutes, the burn would come. The cocktail of high-g drugs was kept on the ragged edge, since they'd be going straight from the couches into a firefight. No point having your assault force more doped than necessary.

Julie sat on the wall beside him, her hair swirling around her like she was underwater. He imagined the dappled light flashing across her face. Portrait of the young pinnace racer as a mermaid. She smiled at the idea, and Miller smiled back. She would have been here, he knew. Along with Diogo and Fred and all the other OPA militia, patriots of the vacuum, she'd have been in a crash couch, wearing borrowed armor, heading into the station to get herself killed for the greater good. Miller knew he wouldn't have. Not before her. So in a sense, he'd taken her place. He'd become her.

They made it, Julie said, or maybe only thought. If the ground attack was going forward, it meant the *Rocinante* had survived — at least long enough to knock out the defenses. Miller nodded, acknowledging her and letting himself feel a moment's pleasure at the idea, and then thrust gravity pushed him into his couch so hard that his consciousness flickered, and the hold around him dimmed. He felt it when the braking burn came, all the crash couches spinning to face the new up. Needles dug into Miller's flesh. Something deep and loud happened, the *Guy Molinari* ringing like a gigantic bell. The breaching charge. The world pulled hard to the left, the couch swinging for the last time as the assault ship matched the station's spin.

Someone was shouting at him. "Go go go!" Miller lifted his assault rifle, tapped the sidearm strapped to his thigh, and joined the press of bodies making for the exit. He missed his hat.

The service corridor they'd cut into was narrow and dim. The schematics the Tycho engineers had worked up suggested they wouldn't see any real resistance until they got into the manned parts of the station. That had been a bad guess. Miller staggered in with the other OPA soldiers in time to see an automatic defense laser cut the first rank in half.

"Team three! Gas it!" Fred snapped in all their ears, and half a dozen blooms of thick white anti-laser smoke burst into the close air. The next time a defense laser fired, the walls flashed with mad iridescence, and the smoke of burning plastic filled the air, but no one died. Miller pressed forward and up a red metal ramp. A welding charge flared, and a service door swung open.

The corridors of Thoth Station were wide and roomy, with long swaths of ivy grown in carefully tended spirals, niches every few feet with tastefully lit bonsai. Soft light the pure white of sunlight made the place feel like a spa or a rich man's private residence. The floors were carpet.

The HUD in his armor flickered, marking the path the assault was meant to take. Miller's heart stepped up to a fast, constant flutter, but his mind seemed to grow perfectly still. At the first intersection, a riot barrier was manned by a dozen men in Protogen security uniforms. The OPA troops hung back, using the curve of the ceiling as cover. What suppressing fire there was came in kneecap low.

The grenades were perfectly round, not even a hole where the pin had been pulled. They didn't roll as well on the soft industrial carpet as they would have on stone or tiling, so one of the three went off before it reached the barrier. The concussion was like being hit in the ears with a hammer; the narrow, sealed corridors channeled the blast back at them almost as much as at the enemy. But the riot barrier shattered, and the Protogen security men fell back.

As they all rushed forward, Miller heard his new, temporary compatriots whooping with the first taste of victory. The sound was muffled, as if they were a long way away. Maybe his earpieces hadn't dampened the blast as much as they were supposed to. Making the rest of the assault with blown eardrums wouldn't be easy.

But then Fred came on, and his voice was clear enough.

"Do not advance! Hold back!"

It was almost enough. The OPA ground force hesitated, Fred's orders pulling at them like a leash. These weren't troops. They weren't even cops. They were a Belter irregular militia; discipline and respect for authority weren't natural to them. They slowed. They got careful. So rounding the corner, they didn't walk into the trap.

The next corridor was long and straight, leading—the HUD suggested—to a service ramp up toward the control center. It looked empty, but a third of the way to the curve horizon, the carpeting started to fly apart in ragged tufts. One of the boys beside Miller grunted and went down.

"They are using low-shrapnel rounds and bouncing them off the curve," Fred said into all their ears at once. "Bank-shot ricochet. Stay low, and do exactly as I say."

The calm in the Earther's voice had more effect than his shouting had. Miller thought he might have been imagining it, but there also seemed to be a deeper tone. A certainty. The Butcher of Anderson Station doing what he did best, leading his troops against the tactics and strategies he'd helped create back when he'd been the enemy.

Slowly, the OPA forces moved forward, up one level, and then the next, then the next. The air grew hazy with smoke and ablated paneling. The wide corridors opened into broad plazas and squares, as airy as prison yards, with the Protogen forces in the guard towers. The side corridors were locked down, local security trying to channel them into situations where they could be caught in crossfire.

It didn't work. The OPA forced open the doors, taking cover in display-rich rooms, something between lecture halls and manufacturing complexes. Twice, unarmored civilians, still at their work despite the ongoing assault, attacked them when they entered. The OPA boys mowed them down. Part of Miller's mind—the part that was still a cop and not a soldier—twitched at that. They were civilians. Killing them was, at the very least, bad form. But then Julie whispered in the back of his mind, *No one here is innocent,* and he had to agree.

The operations center was a third of the way up the station's slight gravity well, defended better than anything they had seen so far. Miller and five others, directed by the all-knowing voice of Fred, took cover in a narrow service corridor, keeping a steady suppressing fire up the main corridor toward ops, and making sure no Protogen counterattack would go unanswered. Miller checked his assault weapon and was surprised to see how much ammunition was left.

"Oi, Pampaw," the kid next to him said, and Miller smiled, recognizing Diogo's voice behind the face mask. "Day's the day, passa?"

"I've seen worse," Miller agreed, then paused. He tried to scratch his injured elbow, but the armor plates kept anything satisfying from happening.

"Beccas tu?" Diogo asked.

"No, I'm fine. It's just...this place. I don't get it. It looks like a spa, and it's built like a prison."

The boy's hands shifted in query. Miller shook his fist in response, thinking through the ideas as he spoke.

"It's all long sight lines and locked-down side passages," Miller said. "If I was going to build a place like this, I'd—"

The air sang, and Diogo went down, his head snapping back as he fell. Miller yelped and wheeled. Behind them in the side corridor, two figures in Protogen security uniform dove for cover. Something hissed through the air by Miller's left ear. Something else bounced off the breastplate of his fancy Martian armor like a hammer blow. He didn't think about raising his assault weapon; it was just there, coughing out return fire like an extension of his will. The other three OPA soldiers turned to help.

"Get back," Miller barked. "Keep your fucking eyes on the main corridor! I'm *on* this."

Stupid, Miller told himself, *stupid to let them get behind us. Stupid to stop and talk in the middle of a firefight.* He should have known better, and now, because he'd lost focus, the boy was...

Laughing?

Diogo sat up, lifted his own assault weapon, and peppered the side corridor with rounds. He got unsteadily to his feet, then whooped like a child who'd just gotten off a thrill ride. A wide streak of white goo stretched from his collarbone up across the right side of his face mask. Behind it, Diogo was grinning. Miller shook his head.

"What the hell are they using crowd suppression rounds for?" he said to himself as much as the boy. "They think this is a riot?"

"Forward teams," Fred said in Miller's ear, "get ready. We're moving in five. Four. Three. Two. Go!"

We don't know what we're getting into here, Miller thought as he joined the sprint down the corridor, pressing toward the assault's final target. A wide ramp led up to a set of blast doors done in wood-grain veneer. Something detonated behind them, but Miller kept his head low and didn't look back. The press of bodies jostling in their ragtag armor grew thicker, and Miller stumbled on something soft. A body in Protogen uniform.

"Give us some room!" a woman at the front shouted. Miller pushed toward her, cutting through the crowd of OPA soldiers with his shoulder and elbow. The woman shouted again as he reached her.

"What's the problem?" Miller shouted.

"I can't cut through this bitch with all these dick-lickers pushing me," she said, lifting a cutting torch already glowing white at the edge. Miller nodded and slid his assault rifle into the sling on his back. He grabbed two of the nearest shoulders, shook the men until they noticed him, and then locked his elbows with theirs.

"Just need to give the techs some room," Miller said, and together they waded into their own men, pushing them back. *How many battles, all through history, fell apart at moments like this?* he wondered. *The victory all but delivered until allied forces started tripping over each other.* The welder popped to life behind him, the heat pressing at his back like a hand even in armor.

At the edge of the crowd, automatic weapons gurgled and choked.

"How's it going back there?" Miller shouted over his shoulder.

The woman didn't answer. Hours seemed to pass, though it couldn't have been more than five minutes. The haze of hot metal and aerosolized plastic filled the air.

The welding torch turned off with a pop. Over his shoulder, Miller saw the bulkhead sag and shift. The tech placed a card-thin jack into the gap between plates, activated it, and stood back. The station around them groaned as a new set of pressures and strains reshaped the metal. The bulkhead opened.

"Come on," Miller shouted, then tucked his head and moved through the new passageway, up a carpeted ramp, and into the ops center. A dozen men and women looked up from their stations, eyes wide with fear.

"You're under arrest!" Miller shouted as the OPA soldiers boiled in around him. "Well, no you're not, but…shit. Put your hands up and back away from the controls!"

One of the men—tall as a Belter, but built solid as a man in full gravity—sighed. He wore a good suit, linen and raw silk, without the lines and folds that spoke of computer tailoring.

"Do what they say," the linen suit said. He sounded peeved, but not frightened.

Miller's eyes narrowed.

"Mr. Dresden?"

The suit raised a carefully shaped eyebrow, paused, and nodded.

"Been looking for you," Miller said.

Fred walked into the ops center like he belonged there. With a tighter set of the shoulders and a degree's shift of the spine, the master engineer of Tycho Station was gone, and the general was in his place. He looked over the ops center, sucking in every detail with a flicker of his eyes, then nodded at one of the senior OPA techs.

"All locked down, sir," the tech said. "The station's yours."

Miller had almost never been present to witness another man's moment of absolution. It was such a rare thing, and so utterly private that it approached the spiritual. Decades ago, this man—younger, fitter, not as much gray in his hair—had taken a space station, wading up to his knees in the gore and death of Belters, and Miller saw the barely perceptible relaxation in his jaw, the opening of his chest that meant that burden had lifted. Maybe it wasn't gone, but it was near enough. It was more than most people managed in a lifetime.

He wondered what it would feel like if he ever got the chance.

"Miller?" Fred said. "I hear you've got someone we'd like to talk to."

Dresden unfolded from his chair, ignoring the sidearms and assault weapons as if such things didn't apply to him.

"Colonel Johnson," Dresden said. "I should have expected that a man of your caliber would be behind all this. My name is Dresden."

He handed Fred a matte black business card. Fred took it as if by reflex but didn't look at it.

"You're the one responsible for this?"

Dresden gave him a chilly smile and looked around before he answered.

"I'd say you're responsible for at least part of it," Dresden said. "You've just killed quite a few people who were simply doing their jobs. But maybe we can dispense with the moral finger-pointing and get down to what actually matters?"

Fred's smile reached all the way to his eyes.

"And what exactly would that be?"

"Negotiating terms," Dresden replied. "You are a man of experience. You understand that your victory here puts you in an untenable position. Protogen is one of the most powerful corporations on Earth. The OPA has attacked it, and the longer you try to hold it, the worse the reprisals will be."

"Is that so?"

"Of course it is," Dresden said, waving Fred's tone away with a dismissing hand. Miller shook his head. The man genuinely didn't understand what was going on. "You've taken your hostages. Well, here we are. We can wait until Earth sends a few dozen battleships and negotiate while you look down the barrels, or we can end this now."

"You're asking me…how much money I want to take my people and just leave," Fred said.

"If money's what you want," Dresden said with a shrug. "Weapons. Ordinance. Medical supplies. Whatever it is you need to prosecute your little war and get this over with quickly."

"I know what you did on Eros," Fred said quietly.

Dresden chuckled. The sound made Miller's flesh crawl.

"Mr. Johnson," Dresden said. "*Nobody* knows what we did on Eros. And every minute I have to spend playing games with you is one I can't use more productively elsewhere. I will swear this: You are in the best bargaining position right now that you will ever have. There is no incentive for you to draw this out."

"And you're offering?"

Dresden spread his hands. "Anything you like and amnesty besides. As long as it gets you out of here and lets us return to our work. We both win."

Fred laughed. It was mirthless.

"Let me get this straight," he said. "You'll give me all the kingdoms of the Earth if I just bow down and do one act of worship for you?"

Dresden cocked his head. "I don't know the reference."

Chapter Forty-One: Holden

The *Rocinante* docked with Thoth Station on the last gasps from her maneuvering thrusters. Holden felt the station's docking clamps grab the hull with a thud, and then gravity returned at a low one-third g. The close detonation of a plasma warhead had torn off the outer door of the crew airlock and flooded the chamber with superheated gas, effectively welding it shut. That meant they'd be using the cargo airlock at the stern of the ship and space-walking over to the station.

That was fine; they were still in their suits. The *Roci* had more holes now than the air cycling system could keep up with, and their shipboard O2 supply had been vented into space by the same explosion that killed the airlock.

Alex dropped from the cockpit, face hidden by his helmet, his belly unmistakable even in his atmosphere suit. Naomi finished locking her station and powering down the ship, then joined Alex, and the three of them climbed down the crew ladder to the ship's aft. Amos was waiting there, buckling an EVA pack onto his suit and charging it with compressed nitrogen from a storage tank. The mechanic had assured Holden that the EVA maneuvering pack had enough thrust to overcome the station's spin and get them back up to an airlock.

No one spoke. Holden had expected banter. He'd expected to want to banter. But the damaged *Roci* seemed to call for silence. Maybe awe.

Holden leaned against the cargo bay bulkhead and closed his eyes. The only sounds he could hear were the steady hiss of his air supply and the faint static of the comm. He could smell nothing through his broken and blood-clogged nose, and his mouth was filled with a coppery taste. But even so, he couldn't keep a smile off his face.

They'd won. They'd flown right up to Protogen, taken every-thing the evil bastards could throw at them, and bloodied *their* noses. Even now OPA soldiers were storming their station, shoot-ing the people who'd helped kill Eros.

Holden decided that he was okay with not feeling any remorse for them. The moral complexity of the situation had grown past his ability to process it, so he just relaxed in the warm glow of vic-tory instead.

The comm chirped and Amos said, "Ready to move."

Holden nodded, remembered he was still in his atmosphere suit, and said, "Okay. Hook on, everyone."

He, Alex, and Naomi pulled tethers from their suits and clamped them to Amos' broad waist. Amos cycled the cargo air-lock and flew out the door on puffs of gas. They were immediately hurled away from the ship by station spin, but Amos quickly got them under control and flew back up toward Thoth's emergency airlock.

As Amos flew them past the *Roci*, Holden studied the outside of the ship and tried to catalog repair requirements. There were a dozen holes in both her bow and aft that corresponded to holes all along the inside of the ship. The gauss cannon rounds the interceptor had fired probably hadn't even slowed appreciably on their path through the *Roci*. The crew was just lucky none of them had found the reactor and punched a hole in it.

There was also a huge dent in the false superstructure that made the ship look like a compressed gas freighter. Holden knew it would match an equally ugly wound in the armored outer hull. The damage hadn't extended to the inner hull, or the ship would have cracked in two.

With the damage to the airlock, and the total loss of their oxygen storage tanks and recycling systems, there would be millions of dollars in damage and weeks in dry dock, assuming they could make it to a dry dock somewhere.

Maybe the *Molinari* could give them a tow.

Amos flashed the EVA pack's yellow warning lights three times, and the station's emergency airlock door cycled open. He flew them inside, where four Belters in combat armor waited.

As soon as the airlock finished cycling, Holden pulled his helmet off and touched his nose. It felt twice its normal size and throbbed with every heartbeat.

Naomi reached out and held his face still, her thumbs on either side of his nose, her touch surprisingly gentle. She turned his head from side to side, examining the injury, then let go.

"It'll be crooked without some cosmetic surgery," she said. "But you were too pretty before anyway. It'll give your face character."

Holden felt a slow grin coming on, but before he could reply, one of the OPA troops started talking.

"Watched the fight, hermano. You guys really kicked some ass."

"Thanks," said Alex. "How's it goin' in here?"

The soldier with the most stars on his OPA insignia said, "Less resistance than expected, but the Protogen security's been fighting for every foot of real estate. Even some of the eggheads have been coming at us. We've had to shoot a few."

He pointed at the inner airlock door.

"Fred's heading up to ops. Wants you people up there, pronto."

"Lead the way," Holden replied, his nose turning it into *lee da way.*

"How's that leg, Cap?" Amos asked as they walked along the station corridor. Holden realized he'd forgotten about the limp his gunshot to the calf had left him.

"Doesn't hurt, but the muscle doesn't flex as much," he replied. "Yours?"

Amos grinned and glanced down at the leg that still limped from the fracture he'd suffered on the *Donnager* months earlier.

"No biggie," he said. "The ones that don't kill you don't count."

Holden started to reply, then stopped when the group rounded a corner into a slaughterhouse. They were clearly coming up behind the assault team, because now the corridor floor was littered with bodies, the walls with bullet holes and scorch marks. To his relief, Holden saw a lot more bodies in Protogen security armor than in OPA gear. But there were enough dead Belters on the floor to make his stomach twist. When he passed a dead man in a lab coat, he had to stop himself from spitting on the floor. The security guys had maybe made a bad decision in going to work for the wrong team, but the scientists on this station had killed a million and a half people just to see what would happen. They couldn't be dead enough for Holden's comfort.

Something tugged at him, and he paused. Lying next to the dead scientist was what looked like a kitchen knife.

"Huh," Holden said. "He didn't come at you guys with that, did he?"

"Yeah, crazy, no?" said one of their escorts. "I heard of bringing a knife to a gunfight, but..."

"Ops is up ahead," said the ranking trooper. "General's waiting."

Holden entered the station's ops center and saw Fred, Miller, a bunch of OPA troops, and one stranger in an expensive-looking suit. A line of technicians and operations staff in Protogen uniform had their wrists cuffed and were being led away. The room was covered deck to ceiling in screens and monitors, most of which were spooling text data too fast to read.

"Let me get this straight," Fred was saying. "You'll give me all the kingdoms of the Earth if I just bow down and do one act of worship for you?"

"I don't know the reference," the stranger said.

Whatever else they were about to say stopped when Miller noticed Holden and tapped Fred on the shoulder. Holden could swear that the detective gave him a warm smile, though on his dour face it was hard to tell.

"Jim," Fred said, then gestured for him to come closer. He was reading a matte black business card. "Meet Antony Dresden, executive VP of bio research for Protogen, and the architect of the Eros project."

The asshole in the suit actually reached out like he was going to shake hands. Holden ignored him.

"Fred," he said. "Casualties?"

"Shockingly low."

"Half their security had non-lethals," Miller said. "Riot control. Sticky rounds. Like that."

Holden nodded and then shook his head and frowned.

"I saw a lot of Protogen security bodies out there in the corridor. Why have so many guys and then give them weapons that can't repel boarders?"

"Good question," Miller agreed.

Dresden chuckled.

"This is what I mean, Mr. Johnson," Dresden said. He turned to Holden. "Jim? Well then, Jim. The fact that you don't understand this station's security needs tells me that you have no idea what you've become involved with. And I think you know that as well as I do. As I was saying to Fred here—"

"Antony, you need to shut the fuck up," Holden said, surprised by the sudden flush of anger. Dresden looked disappointed.

The bastard had no right to be comfortable. Condescending. Holden wanted the man terrified, begging for his life, not sneering behind his cultured accent.

"Amos, if he talks to me again without being told to, break his jaw."

"My pleasure, Captain," Amos said, and took half a step forward.

Dresden smirked at the ham-fisted threat but kept his mouth shut.

"What do we know?" Holden asked, aiming the question at Fred.

"We know the Eros data is coming here, and we know this piece of shit is in charge. We'll know more once we've taken the place apart."

Holden turned to look at Dresden again, taking in the blue blood European good looks, the gym-sculpted physique, the expensive haircut. Even now, surrounded by men with guns, Dresden managed to look like he was in charge. Holden could imagine him glancing down at his watch and wondering how much more of his expensive time this boarding party was going to take.

Holden said, "I need to ask him something."

Fred nodded. "You earned it."

"Why?" Holden asked. "I want to know why."

Dresden's smile was almost pitying, and he stuck his hands into his pockets as casually as a man talking sports at a dockside bar.

"'Why' is a very big question," Dresden said. "Because God wanted it that way? Or perhaps you want to narrow it for me."

"Why Eros?"

"Well, Jim—"

"You can call me Captain Holden. I'm the guy that found your lost ship, so I've seen the video from Phoebe. I know what the protomolecule is."

"Really!" Dresden said, his smile becoming half a degree more genuine. "I have you to thank for turning the viral agent over to us on Eros. Losing the *Anubis* was going to put our timeline back months. Finding the infected body already there on the station was a godsend."

I knew it. I fucking knew it, Holden thought. Out loud, he said, "Why?"

"You know what the agent is," Dresden said, at a loss for the first time since Holden had come into the room. "I don't know what more I can tell you. This is the most important thing to ever happen to the human race. It's simultaneously proof that we are not alone in the universe, and our ticket out of the limitations that bind us to our little bubbles of rock and air."

"You aren't answering me," Holden said, hating the way his broken nose made his voice slightly comical when he wanted to be threatening. "I want to know *why* you killed a million and a half people."

Fred cleared his throat, but he didn't interrupt. Dresden looked from Holden to the colonel and back again.

"I *am* answering, Captain. A million and a half people is small potatoes. What we're working with here is bigger than that," Dresden said, then moved over to a chair and sat down, pulling up his pants leg as he crossed his knees, so as not to stretch the fabric. "Are you familiar with Genghis Khan?"

"What?" Holden and Fred said at almost the same instant. Miller only stared at Dresden with a blank expression, tapping the barrel of his pistol against his own armored thigh.

"Genghis Khan. There are some historians who claim that Genghis Khan killed or displaced one quarter of the total human population of Earth during his conquest," Dresden said. "He did that in pursuit of an empire that would begin falling apart as soon as he died. In today's scale, that would mean killing nearly ten billion people in order to affect a generation. A generation and a half. Eros isn't even a rounding error by comparison."

"You really don't care," Fred said, his voice quiet.

"And unlike Khan, we aren't doing it to build a brief empire. I know what you think. That we're trying to aggrandize ourselves. Grab power."

"You don't want to?" Holden said.

"Of course we do." Dresden's voice was cutting. "But you're thinking too small. Building humanity's greatest empire is like building the world's largest anthill. Insignificant. There is a civilization out there that built the protomolecule and hurled it at us over two billion years ago. They were *already* gods at that point. What have they become since then? With another two billion years to advance?"

With a growing dread, Holden listened to Dresden speak. This speech had the air of something spoken before. Perhaps many times. And it had worked. It had convinced powerful people. It was why Protogen had stealth ships from the Earth shipyards and seemingly limitless behind-the-scenes support.

"We have a terrifying amount of catching up to do, gentlemen," Dresden was saying. "But fortunately we have the tool of our enemy to use in doing it."

"Catching up?" a soldier to Holden's left said. Dresden nodded at the man and smiled.

"The protomolecule can alter the host organism at the molecular level; it can create genetic change on the fly. Not just DNA, but any stable replicator. But it is only a machine. It doesn't think. It follows instructions. If we learn how to alter that programming, then *we* become the architects of that change."

Holden interrupted. "If it was supposed to wipe out life on Earth and replace it with whatever the protomolecule's creators wanted, why turn it loose?"

"Excellent question," Dresden said, holding up one finger like a college professor about to deliver a lecture. "The protomolecule doesn't come with a user's manual. In fact, we've never before been able to actually watch it carry out its program. The molecule requires significant mass before it develops enough processing power to fulfill its directives. Whatever they are."

Dresden pointed at the screens covered with data around them.

"We are going to watch it at work. See what it intends to do.

How it goes about doing it. And, hopefully, learn how to change that program in the process."

"You could do that with a vat of bacteria," Holden said.

"I'm not interested in remaking bacteria," Dresden said.

"You're fucking insane," Amos said, and took another step toward Dresden. Holden put a hand on the big mechanic's shoulder.

"So," Holden said. "You figure out how the bug works, and then what?"

"Then *everything*. Belters who can work outside a ship without wearing a suit. Humans capable of sleeping for hundreds of years at a time flying colony ships to the stars. No longer being bound to the millions of years of evolution inside one atmosphere of pressure at one g, slaves to oxygen and water. We decide what we want to be, and we reprogram ourselves to be that. That's what the protomolecule gives us."

Dresden had stood back up as he'd delivered this speech, his face shining with the zeal of a prophet.

"What we are doing is the best and only hope of humanity's survival. When we go out there, we will be facing *gods*."

"And if we don't go out?" Fred asked. He sounded thoughtful.

"They've already fired a doomsday weapon at us once," Dresden said.

The room was silent for a moment. Holden felt his certainty slip. He hated everything about Dresden's argument, but he couldn't quite see his way past it. He knew in his bones that something about it was dead wrong, but he couldn't find the words.

Naomi's voice startled him.

"Did it convince them?" she asked.

"Excuse me?" Dresden said.

"The scientists. The technicians. Everyone you needed to make it happen. They actually had to do this. They had to watch the video of people dying all over Eros. They had to design those radioactive murder chambers. So unless you managed to round up every serial killer in the solar system and send them through a postgraduate program, how did you do this?"

"We modified our science team to remove ethical restraints."

Half a dozen clues clicked into place in Holden's head.

"Sociopaths," he said. "You turned them into sociopaths."

"High-functioning sociopaths," Dresden said with a nod. He seemed pleased to explain it. "And extremely curious ones. As long as we kept them supplied with interesting problems to solve and unlimited resources, they remained quite content."

"And a big security team armed with riot control rounds for when they aren't," Fred said.

"Yes, there are occasional issues," Dresden said. He looked around, the slightest frown creasing his forehead. "I know. You think it's monstrous, but I am saving the human *race*. I am giving humanity the *stars*. You disapprove? Fine. Let me ask you this. Can you save Eros? Right now."

"No," Fred said, "but we can—"

"Waste the data," Dresden said. "You can make certain that every man, woman, and child who died on Eros died for nothing."

The room was silent. Fred was frowning, his arms crossed. Holden understood the struggle going on in the man's mind. Everything Dresden said was repulsive and eerie and rang too much of the truth.

"Or," Dresden said, "we can negotiate a price, you can go on your way, and I can—"

"Okay. That's enough," Miller said, speaking for the first time since Dresden had begun his pitch. Holden glanced over at the detective. His flat expression had gone stony. He wasn't tapping the barrel of his pistol against his leg.

Oh, shit.

Chapter Forty-Two: Miller

Dresden didn't see it coming. Even as Miller raised the pistol, the man's eyes didn't register a threat. All he saw was Miller with an object in his hand that happened to be a gun. A dog would have known to be scared, but not Dresden.

"Miller!" Holden shouted from a great distance. "Don't!"

Pulling the trigger was simple. A soft click, the bounce of metal against his glove-cushioned palm, and then again two more times. Dresden's head snapped back, blooming red. Blood spattered a wide screen, obscuring the data stream. Miller stepped close, fired two more rounds into Dresden's chest, considered for a moment, then holstered the pistol.

The room was silent. The OPA soldiers were all looking at each other or at Miller, surprised, even after the press of the assault, by the sudden violence. Naomi and Amos were looking at Holden, and the captain was staring at the corpse. Holden's injured face was set as a mask; fury, outrage, maybe even despair. Miller understood that. Doing the obvious thing still wasn't natural for Holden. There had been a time when it hadn't come so easily for Miller either.

Only Fred didn't flinch or look nervous. The colonel didn't smile or frown, and he didn't look away.

"What the fuck was that?" Holden said through his blood-plugged nose. "You shot him in cold blood!"

"Yeah," Miller said.

Holden shook his head. "What about a trial? What about justice? You just decide, and that's the way it goes?"

"I'm a cop," Miller said, surprised by the apology in his voice.

"Are you even human anymore?"

"All right, gentlemen!" Fred said, his voice booming out in the quiet. "Show's over. Let's get back to work. I want the decryption team in here. We've got prisoners to evacuate and a station to strip down."

Holden looked from Fred to Miller to the still-dying Dresden. His jaw was set with rage.

"Hey, Miller," Holden said.

"Yeah?" Miller said softly. He knew what was coming.

"Find your own ride home," the captain of the *Rocinante* said, then spun and stalked out of the room, his crew following. Miller watched them walk away. Regret tapped gently at his heart, but there was nothing to be done about it. The broken bulkhead seemed to swallow them. Miller turned to Fred.

"Hitch a lift?"

"You're wearing our colors," Fred said. "We'll get you as far as Tycho."

"I appreciate that," Miller said. Then, a moment later: "You know it had to be done."

Fred didn't reply. There wasn't anything to say.

Thoth Station was injured, but not dead. Not yet. Word of the sociopathic crew spread fast, and the OPA forces took the warning to heart. The occupation and control phase of the attack lasted forty hours instead of the twenty that it would have taken with normal prisoners. With humans. Miller did what he could with prisoner control.

The OPA kids were well intentioned, but most of them had never worked with captive populations before. They didn't know how to cuff someone at the wrist and elbow so that the perp couldn't get his hands out in front to strangle them. They didn't know how to restrain someone with a length of cord around the neck so that the prisoner couldn't choke himself to death, by accident or intentionally. Half of them didn't even know how to pat someone down. Miller knew all of it like a game he'd played since childhood. In five hours, he found twenty hidden blades on the science crew alone. He hardly had to think about it.

A second wave of transport ships arrived: personnel haulers that looked ready to spill their air out into the vacuum if you spat on them, salvage trawlers already dismantling the shielding and superstructure of the station, supply ships boxing and packing the precious equipment and looting the pharmacies and food banks. By the time news of the assault reached Earth, the station would be stripped to a skeleton and its people hidden away in unlicensed prison cells throughout the Belt.

Protogen would know sooner, of course. They had outposts much closer than the inner planets. There was a calculus of response time and possible gain. The mathematics of piracy and war. Miller knew it, but he didn't let it worry him. Those were decisions for Fred and his attachés to make. Miller had taken more than enough initiative for one day.

Posthuman.

It was a word that came up in the media every five or six years, and it meant different things every time. Neural regrowth hormone? Posthuman. Sex robots with inbuilt pseudo intelligence? Posthuman. Self-optimizing network routing? Posthuman. It was a word from advertising copy, breathless and empty, and all he'd ever thought it really meant was that the people using it had a limited imagination about what exactly humans were capable of.

Now, as he escorted a dozen captives in Protogen uniforms to a docked transport heading God-knew-where, the word was taking on new meaning.

Are you even human anymore?

All *posthuman* meant, literally speaking, was what you were when you weren't human anymore. Protomolecule aside, Protogen aside, Dresden and his Mengele-as-Genghis-Khan self-righteous fantasies aside, Miller thought that maybe he'd been ahead of the curve all along. Maybe he'd been posthuman for years.

The min-max point came forty hours later, and it was time to go. The OPA had skeletonized the station, and it was time to get out before anyone came along with vengeance in mind. Miller sat in a crash couch, his blood dancing with spent amphetamines and his mind slipping into and out of exhaustion psychosis. The thrust gravity was like a pillow over his face. He was vaguely aware that he was weeping. It didn't mean anything.

In Miller's haze, Dresden was talking again, pouring out promises and lies, half-truths and visions. Miller could see the words themselves like a dark smoke, coalescing into the spilling black filament of the protomolecule. The threads of it were reaching toward Holden, Amos, Naomi. He tried to find his gun, to stop it, to do the obvious thing. His despairing shout woke him, and he remembered he'd already won.

Julie sat beside him, her hand cool against his forehead. Her smile was gentle, understanding. Forgiving.

Sleep, she said, and his mind fell into the deep black.

"Oi, Pampaw," Diogo said. "Acima and out, sabez?"

It was Miller's tenth morning back on Tycho, his seventh hot-bunking in Diogo's closet-sized apartment. He could tell from the buzz in the boy's voice it would have to be one of the last. Fish and company start to smell after three days. He rolled off the thin bed, ran fingers through his hair, and nodded. Diogo stripped down and crawled into the bed without speaking. He stank of liquor and cheap tub-grown marijuana.

Miller's terminal told him that the second shift had ended two hours before, the third shift halfway into its morning. He gathered his things in his suitcase, turned off the lights on Diogo's already snoring form, and trundled out to the public showers to spend a few of his remaining credits trying to look less homeless.

The pleasant surprise of his return to Tycho Station was the boost of money in his account. The OPA, meaning Fred Johnson, had paid him for his time on Thoth. He hadn't asked for it, and there was part of him that wanted to turn the payment down. If there had been an alternative, he might have. Since there wasn't, he tried to stretch the funds out as far as they would go and appreciate the irony. He and Captain Shaddid were on the same payroll after all.

For the first few days after his return to Tycho, Miller had expected to see the attack on Thoth in the newsfeeds. EARTH CORPORATION LOSES RESEARCH STATION TO CRAZED BELTERS, or some such. He should have been finding a job or a place to sleep that wasn't charity. He meant to. But the hours seemed to dissolve as he sat in the bar or the lounges, watching the screens for just a few more minutes.

The Martian navy had suffered a series of harassing attacks by Belters. A half ton of super-accelerated gravel had forced two of their battleships to change course. A slowdown in water harvesting on Saturn's rings was either an illegal work stoppage, and therefore treasonous, or the natural response to increased security needs. Two Earth-owned mining operations had been attacked by either Mars or the OPA. Four hundred people were dead. Earth's blockade of Mars was entering its third month. A coalition of scientists and terraforming specialists were screaming that the cascading processes were in danger, and that while the war would be over in a year or two, the loss of supplies would set the terraforming effort back generations. Everyone blamed everyone else for Eros. Thoth Station didn't exist.

It would, though.

With most of the Martian navy still in the outer planets, Earth's siege was a brittle thing. Time was getting short. Either the Martians would go home and try facing down the somewhat older, somewhat slower, but more numerous ships of Earth, or they'd go straight for the planet itself. Earth was still the source of a thousand things that couldn't be grown elsewhere, but if someone got happy or cocksure or desperate, it wouldn't take much to start dropping rocks down the gravity wells.

All of it as a distraction.

There was an old joke. Miller didn't remember where he'd heard it. Girl's at her own father's funeral, meets this really cute guy. They talk, hit it off, but he leaves before she can get his number. Girl doesn't know how to track the guy down.

So a week later, she kills her mom.

Big laugh.

It was the logic of Protogen, of Dresden, of Thoth. *Here is the problem,* they said to themselves, *and there is the solution.* That it was drowned in innocent blood was as trivial as the font the reports were printed in. They had disconnected themselves from humanity. Shut off the cell clusters in their brains that made life besides their own sacred. Or valuable. Or worth saving. All it had cost them was every human connection.

Funny how familiar that sounded.

The guy who walked into the bar and nodded to Miller was one of Diogo's friends. Twenty years old or maybe a little south of that. A veteran of Thoth Station, just like Miller. He didn't remember the kid's name, but he'd seen him around often enough to know that the way he held himself was different than usual. Tight-wound. Miller tapped the mute on his terminal's newsfeed and made his way over.

"Hey," he said, and the kid looked up sharply. The face was tense, but a softer, intentional ease tried to mask it. It was just

Diogo's old grandpa. The one, everyone on Thoth knew, who'd killed the biggest dick in the universe. It won Miller some points, so the kid smiled and nodded to the stool beside him.

"All pretty fucked up, isn't it?" Miller said.

"You don't know the half," the kid said. He had a clipped accent. Belter by his height, but educated. Technician, probably. The kid tabbed in a drink order, and the bar offered up a glass of clear fluid so volatile Miller could watch it evaporate. The kid drank it down with a gulp.

"Doesn't work," Miller said.

The kid looked over. Miller shrugged.

"They say drinking helps, but it doesn't," Miller said.

"No?"

"Nope. Sex sometimes, if you've got a girl who'll talk to you after. Or target practice. Working out, sometimes. Liquor doesn't make you feel better. Just makes you not so worried about feeling bad."

The kid laughed and shook his head. He was on the edge of talking, so Miller sat back and let the quiet do his work for him. He figured the kid had killed someone, probably on Thoth, and it was sneaking up on him. But instead of telling the story, the kid took Miller's terminal, keyed in a few local codes, and handed it back. A huge menu of feeds appeared — video, audio, air pressure and content, radiological. It took Miller half a second to understand what he was seeing. They'd cracked the encryption on the Eros feeds.

He was looking at the protomolecule in action. He was seeing Juliette Andromeda Mao's corpse writ large. For a moment, his imagined Julie flickered beside him.

"If you ever wonder if you did the right thing shooting that guy," the kid said, "look at that."

Miller opened a feed. A long corridor, wide enough for twenty people to walk abreast. The flooring was wet and undulating like the surface of a canal. Something small rolled awkwardly through the mush. When Miller zoomed in, it was a human torso — rib cage, spine, trailing lengths of what used to be intestines and were now the long black threads of the protomolecule—pushing itself along on the stump of an arm. There was no head. The feed output bar showed there was sound, and Miller undid the mute. The high, mindless piping reminded him of mentally ill children singing to themselves.

"It's all like that," the kid said. "Whole station's crawling with...shit like that."

"What's it doing?"

"Building something," the kid said, and shuddered. "I thought you should see it."

"Yeah?" Miller said, his gaze nailed to the screen. "What did I ever do to you?"

The kid laughed.

"Everyone thinks you're a hero for killing that guy," the kid said. "Everyone thinks we should push every last prisoner we took off that station out an airlock."

Probably should, Miller thought, *if we can't make them human again.* He switched the feed. The casino level where he and Holden had been, or else a section very like it. A webwork of something like bones linked ceiling and roof. Black sluglike things a yard long slithered up and between them. The sound was a hushing, like the recordings he'd heard of surf against a beach. He switched again. The port, with bulkheads closed and encrusted with huge nautilus spirals that seemed to shift while he watched them.

"Everyone thinks you're a fucking hero," the kid said, and this time, it bit a little. Miller shook his head.

"Nah," he said. "Just a guy who used to be a cop."

Why should going into a firefight, charging into an enemy station filled with people and automatic systems built to kill you, seem less frightening than talking to people who you shipped with for weeks?

And still.

It was third shift, and the bar at the observation platform was set to imitate night. The air was scented with something smoky that wasn't smoke. A piano and bass dueled lazily with each other while a man's voice lamented in Arabic. Dim lights glowed at the bases of the tables, casting soft shadows up across faces and bodies, emphasizing the customers' legs and bellies and breasts. The shipyards beyond the windows were busy as always. If he went close, he could pick out the *Rocinante,* still recovering from its wounds. Not dead, and being made stronger.

Amos and Naomi were at a table in a corner. No sign of Alex. No sign of Holden. That made it easier. Not easy, but closer. He made his way toward them. Naomi saw him first, and Miller read the discomfort in her expression, covered over as quickly as it appeared. Amos turned to see what she'd been reacting to, and the corners of his mouth and eyes didn't shift into a frown or a smile. Miller scratched his arm even though it didn't itch.

"Hey," he said. "Buy you folks a round?"

The silence lasted a beat longer than it should have, and then Naomi forced a smile.

"Sure. Just one. We've got…that thing. For the captain."

"Oh yeah," Amos said, lying even more awkwardly than Naomi had, making his awareness of the fact part of the message. "The thing. That's important."

Miller sat, lifted a hand for the waiter to see, and, when the man nodded, leaned forward with his elbows on the table. It was the seated version of a fighter's crouch, bent forward with his arms protecting the soft places in his neck and belly. It was the way a man stood when he expected injury.

The waiter came, and then beers all around. Miller paid for them with the OPA's money and took a sip.

"How's the ship?" he asked at last.

"Coming together," Naomi said. "They really banged the hell out of her."

"She'll still fly," Amos said. "She's one tough bitch."

"That's good. When—" Miller said, then tripped on his words and had to start again. "When are you folks shipping out?"

"Whenever the captain says," Amos said with a shrug. "We're airtight now, so could go tomorrow, if he's got someplace he wants to be."

"And if Fred lets us," Naomi said, and then grimaced like she wished she'd kept silent.

"That an issue?" Miller asked. "Is the OPA leaning on Holden?"

"It's just something I was thinking about," Naomi said. "It's nothing. Look, thanks for the drink, Miller. But I really think we'd better be going."

Miller took a long breath and let it out slow.

"Yeah," he said. "Okay."

"You head out," Amos said to Naomi. "I'll catch up."

Naomi shot a confused look at the big man, but Amos only gave back a smile. It could have meant anything.

"Okay," Naomi said. "But don't be long, okay? The thing."

"For the captain," Amos said. "No worries."

Naomi rose and walked away. Her effort not to look back over her shoulder was visible. Miller looked at Amos. The lights gave the mechanic a slightly demonic appearance.

"Naomi's a good person," Amos said. "I like her, you know? Like my kid sister, only smart and I'd do her if she let me. You know?"

"Yeah," Miller said. "I like her too."

"She's not like us," Amos said, and the warmth and humor were gone.

"That's why I like her," Miller said. It was the right thing to say. Amos nodded.

"So here's the thing. As far as the captain goes, you're dipped in shit right now."

The scrim of bubbles where his beer touched the glass glowed white in the dim light. Miller gave the glass a quarter turn, watching them closely.

"Because I killed someone who needed it?" Miller asked. The bitterness in his voice wasn't surprising, but it was deeper than he'd intended. Amos didn't hear it or else didn't care.

"Because you've got a habit of that," Amos said. "Cap'n's not like that. Killing people without talking it over first makes him jumpy. You did a lot of it on Eros, but...you know."

"Yeah," Miller said.

"Thoth Station wasn't Eros. Next place we go won't be Eros either. Holden doesn't want you around."

"And the rest of you?" Miller asked.

"We don't want you around either," Amos said. His voice wasn't hard or gentle. He was talking about the gauge of a machine part. He was talking about anything. The words hit Miller in the belly, just where he'd expected it. He couldn't have blocked them.

"Here's the thing," Amos went on. "You and me, we're a lot the same. Been around. I know what I am, and my moral compass? I'll tell you, it's fucked. A few things fell different when I was a kid. I could have been those ass-bandits on Thoth. I know that. Captain couldn't have been. It's not in him. He's as close to righteous as anyone out here gets. And when he says you're out, that's just the way it is, because the way I figure it, he's probably right. Sure as hell has a better chance than I do."

"Okay," Miller said.

"Yeah," Amos said. He finished his beer. Then he finished Naomi's. And then he walked away, leaving Miller to himself and his empty gut. Outside, the *Nauvoo* fanned a glittering array of sensors, testing something or else just preening. Miller waited.

Beside him, Julie Mao leaned on the table, just where Amos had been.

So, she said. *Looks like it's just you and me now.*

"Looks like," he said.

Chapter Forty-Three: Holden

A Tycho worker in blue coveralls and a welding mask sealed up the hole in one of the galley bulkheads. Holden watched with his hand shielding his eyes from the harsh blue glare of the torch. When the plate steel was secured in place, the welder flipped her mask up to check the bead. She had blue eyes and a small mouth in a heart-shaped pixie face and a mop of red hair pulled into a bun. Her name was Sam, and she was the team leader on the *Rocinante* repair project. Amos had been chasing her for two weeks now with no success. Holden was glad, because the pixie had turned out to be one of the best mechanics he'd ever met, and he'd hate for her to focus on anything other than his ship.

"It's perfect," he said to her as she ran one gloved hand over the cooling metal.

"It's okay," she said with a shrug. "We'll grind this down smooth enough, paint it nice, then you'll never even know your ship had a boo-boo." She had a surprisingly deep voice that contrasted with her looks and her habit of using mockingly childlike phrases. Holden guessed that her appearance combined with her chosen profession had led to a lot of people underestimating her in the past. He didn't want to make that mistake.

"You've done amazing work, Sam," he said. He guessed Sam was short for something, but he'd never asked and she'd never volunteered. "I keep telling Fred how happy we are to have you in charge of this job."

"Maybe I'll get a gold star in my next report card," she said while she put her torch away and stood up. Holden tried to think of something to say to that and failed.

"Sorry," she said, turning to face him. "I appreciate your praise to the boss. And to be honest, it's been a lot of fun working on your little girl. She's quite a ship. The beating she took would have blown anything we own into scrap."

"It was a close thing, even for us," Holden replied.

Sam nodded, then began putting the rest of her gear away. As she worked, Naomi climbed down the crew ladder from the upper decks, her gray coveralls hung with electrician's tools.

"How are things up there?" Holden asked.

"Ninety percent," Naomi said as she crossed the galley to the refrigerator and took out a bottle of juice. "Give or take." She took out a second bottle and tossed it to Sam, who caught it one-handed.

"Naomi," Sam said, raising the bottle in mock toast before downing half of it in one swallow.

"Sammy," Naomi said in return with a grin.

The two of them had hit it off right away, and now Naomi was spending a lot of her off time with Sam and her Tycho crowd. Holden hated to admit it, but he missed being the only social circle Naomi had. When he did admit it to himself, like now, it made him feel like a creep.

"Golgo comp in rec, tonight?" Sam said after she'd gulped down the last of her drink.

"Think those C7 chumps are tired of getting their asses handed to them?" Naomi said in return. To Holden, it sounded like they were speaking in code.

"We can throw the first one," Sam said. "Get 'em hooked tight before we drop the hammer and wipe their roll."

"Sounds good to me," Naomi said, then tossed her empty bottle into the recycling bin and started back up the ladder. "See you at eight, then." She tossed a little wave at Holden. "Later, Captain."

Holden said, "How much longer, do you think?" to Sam's back as she finished with her tools.

Sam shrugged. "Couple days, maybe, to get her to perfect. She could probably fly now, if you're not worried about nonessentials and cosmetics."

"Thanks, again," Holden said, holding out his hand to Sam as she turned around. She shook it once, her palm heavily calloused and her grip firm. "And I hope you mop the floor with those chumps from C7."

She gave him a predatory grin.

"It's not even in doubt."

Through Fred Johnson, the OPA had provided the crew with living quarters on the station during the renovation of the *Roci,* and over the past few weeks, Holden's cabin had almost come to feel like home. Tycho had money, and they seemed to spend a lot of it on their employees. Holden had three rooms to himself, including a bath and a kitchen nook off the public space. On most stations, you'd have to be the governor to have that kind of luxury. Holden had the impression it was fairly standard for management on Tycho.

He tossed his grimy jumpsuit into the laundry bin and started a pot of coffee before jumping into his private shower. A shower every night after work: another almost unthinkable luxury. It would be easy to get distracted. To start thinking of this period of ship repair and quiet home life as normalcy, not interlude. Holden couldn't let that happen.

Earth's assault on Mars filled the newsfeeds. The domes of Mars still stood, but two showers of meteors had pocked the wide slopes of Olympus Mons. Earth claimed that it was debris from Deimos, Mars that it was an intentional threat and provocation. Martian ships from the gas giants were burning hard for the inner planets. Every day, every hour brought the moment closer when Earth would have to commit to annihilating Mars or backing away. The OPA's rhetoric seemed built to ensure that whoever won would kill them next. Holden had just helped Fred with what Earth would see as the largest act of piracy in the history of the Belt.

And a million and a half people were dying right now on Eros. Holden thought of the video feed he'd seen of what was happening to the people on the station, and shuddered even in the heat of the shower.

Oh, and aliens. Aliens that had tried to take over the Earth two billion years ago, and failed because Saturn got in the way. *Can't forget the aliens.* His brain still hadn't figured out a way to process that, so it kept trying to pretend it didn't exist.

Holden grabbed a towel and turned on the wall screen in his living room while he dried off. The air was filled with the competing scents of coffee, humidity from the shower, and the faintly grassy and floral scent Tycho pumped into all the residences. Holden tried the news, but it was speculation about the war without any new information. He changed to a competition show with incomprehensible rules and psychotically giddy contestants. He flipped through a few feeds that he could tell were comedies, because the actors paused and nodded where they expected the laughs to be.

When his jaw started aching, he realized he was gritting his teeth. He turned off the screen and threw the remote onto his bed in the next room. He wrapped the towel around his waist, then poured a mug of coffee and collapsed onto the couch just in time for his door to chime.

"What?" he yelled at the top of his lungs. No one replied. Good insulation on Tycho. He went to the door, arranging his towel for maximum modesty along the way, and yanked it open.

It was Miller. He was dressed in a rumpled gray suit he'd probably brought from Ceres, and was fumbling around with that stupid hat.

"Holden, hey—" he started, but Holden cut him off.

"What the hell do you want?" Holden said. "And are you *really* standing outside my door with your hat in your hands?"

Miller smiled, then put the hat back on his head. "You know, I always wondered what that meant."

"Now you know," Holden replied.

"You got a minute?" Miller said.

Holden waited a moment, staring up at the lanky detective. He quickly gave up. He probably outweighed Miller by twenty kilos, but it was impossible to be intimidating when the person you were staring down was a foot taller than you.

"Okay, come in," he said, then headed for his bedroom. "Let me get dressed. There's coffee."

Holden didn't wait for a reply; he just closed the bedroom door and sat on the bed. He and Miller hadn't exchanged more than a dozen words since returning to Tycho. He knew they couldn't leave it at that, as much as he might like to. He owed Miller at least the conversation where he told him to get lost.

He put on a pair of warm cotton pants and a pullover, ran one hand through his damp hair, and went back out to the living room. Miller was sitting on his couch holding a steaming mug.

"Good coffee," the detective said.

"So, let's hear it," Holden replied, sitting in a chair across from him.

Miller took a sip of his coffee and said, "Well—"

"I mean, this is the conversation where you tell me how you were right to shoot an unarmed man in the face, and how I'm just too naive to see it. Right?"

"Actually—"

"I fucking told you," Holden said, surprised to feel the heat rise in his cheeks. "No more of that judge, jury, and executioner shit or you could find your own ride, and you did it anyway."

"Yes."

The simple affirmative took Holden off guard.

"Why?"

Miller took another sip of his coffee, then set the mug down. He reached up and took off his hat, tossed it onto the couch next to him, then leaned back.

"He was going to get away with it."

"Excuse me?" Holden replied. "Did you miss the part where he confessed to everything?"

"That wasn't a confession. That was a boast. He was untouchable, and he knew it. Too much money. Too much power."

"That's bullshit. No one gets to kill a million and a half people and get away with it."

"People get away with things all the time. Guilty as hell, but something gets in the way. Evidence. Politics. I had a partner for a while, name of Muss. When Earth pulled out of Ceres—"

"Stop," Holden said. "I don't care. I don't want to hear any more of your stories about how being a cop makes you wiser and deeper and able to face the truth about humanity. As far as I can tell, all it did was break you. Okay?"

"Yeah, okay."

"Dresden and his Protogen buddies thought they could choose who lives and who dies. That sound familiar? And don't tell me it's different this time, because everyone says that, every time. And it's not."

"Wasn't revenge," Miller said, a little too hotly.

"Oh really? This wasn't about the girl in the hotel? Julie Mao?"

"Catching him was. Killing him…"

Miller sighed and nodded to himself, then got up and opened the door. He stopped in the doorway and turned around, real pain on his face.

"He was talking us into it," Miller said. "All that about getting the stars and protecting ourselves from whatever shot that thing at Earth? I was starting to think maybe he should get away with it. Maybe things were just too big for right and wrong. I'm not saying he convinced me. But he made me think maybe, you know? Just maybe."

"And for that, you shot him."

"I did."

Holden sighed, then leaned against the wall next to the open door, his arms crossed.

"Amos calls you righteous," Miller said. "You know that?"

"Amos thinks he's a bad guy because he's done some things he's ashamed of," Holden said. "He doesn't always trust himself, but the fact that he cares tells me he *isn't* a bad guy."

"Yeah—" Miller started, but Holden cut him off.

"He looks at his soul, sees the stains, and wants to be clean," he said. "But you? You just shrug."

"Dresden was—"

"This isn't about Dresden. It's about you," Holden said. "I can't trust you around the people I care about."

Holden stared at Miller, waiting for him to reply, but the cop just nodded sadly, then put his hat on and walked away down the gently curving corridor. He didn't turn around.

Holden went back inside and tried to relax, but he felt jumpy and nervous. He would never have gotten off Eros without Miller's help. There was no question about it: Tossing him out on his ear felt wrong. Incomplete.

The truth was Miller made his scalp crawl every time they were in the same room. The cop was like an unpredictable dog that might lick your hand or take a bite out of your leg.

Holden thought about calling Fred and warning him. He called Naomi instead.

"Hey," she answered on the second chime. Holden could hear a bar's frantic, alcohol-fueled merriment in the background.

"Naomi," he said, then paused, trying to think of some excuse to have called. When he couldn't think of one, he said, "Miller was just here."

"Yeah, he cornered Amos and me a while back. What did he want?"

"I don't know," Holden said with a sigh. "Say goodbye, maybe."

"What are you doing?" Naomi asked. "Want to meet up?"

"Yes. Yes I do."

Holden didn't recognize the bar at first, but after ordering a scotch from a professionally friendly waiter, he realized it was the same place he'd watched Naomi sing karaoke to a Belter punk song what seemed like centuries before. She wandered in and plopped down across from him in the booth just as his drink showed up. The waiter gave her a questioning smile.

"Gah, no," she said quickly, waving her hands at him. "I've had plenty tonight. Just some water, thanks."

As the waiter bustled away, Holden said, "How did your, uh… What exactly is Golgo, anyway? And how did it go?"

"Game they play here," Naomi said, then took a glass of water from their returning waiter and drank half of it in one gulp. "Like a cross between darts and soccer. Never seen it before, but I seem to be good at it. We won."

"Great," Holden said. "Thanks for coming. I know it's late, but this Miller thing freaked me out a bit."

"He wants you to absolve him, I think."

"Because I'm 'righteous,'" Holden said with a sarcastic laugh.

"You are," Naomi said with no irony. "I mean, it's a loaded term, but you're as close to it as anyone I've ever known."

"I've fucked everything up," Holden blurted out before he could stop himself. "Everyone who's tried to help us, or that we've tried to help, has died spectacularly. This whole fucking war. And Captain McDowell and Becca and Ade. And Shed—" He had to stop and swallow a sudden lump in his throat.

Naomi just nodded, then reached across the table and took his hand in hers.

"I need a win, Naomi," he continued. "I need to do something that makes a difference. Fate or Karma or God or whatever dropped me in the middle of this thing, and I need to know I'm making a difference."

Naomi smiled at him and squeezed his hand.

"You're cute when you're being noble," she said. "But you need to stare off into the distance more."

"You're making fun of me."

"Yeah," she said. "I am. Want to come home with me?"

"I—" Holden started, then stopped and stared at her, looking for the joke. Naomi was still smiling at him, nothing in her eyes but warmth and a touch of mischief. While he watched, one curly lock of hair fell over her eye, and she pushed it up without looking away from him. "Wait, what? I thought you'd—"

"I said don't tell me you love me to get me into bed," she said. "But I also said I'd have gone to your cabin anytime you asked over the last four years. I didn't think I was being subtle, and I'm sort of tired of waiting."

Holden leaned back in the booth and tried to remember to breathe. Naomi's grin changed to pure mischief now, and one eyebrow went up.

"You okay, sailor?" she asked.

"I thought you were avoiding me," he said once he was capable of speech. "Is this your way of giving me a win?"

"Don't be insulting," she said, though there was no hint of anger in her voice. "But I've waited weeks for you to get your nerve up, and the ship's almost done. That means you'll probably volunteer us for something really stupid and this time our luck will run out."

"Well—" he said.

"If that happens without us at least giving this a try *once*, I will be very unhappy about it."

"Naomi, I—"

"It's simple, Jim," she said, reaching out for his hand and pulling him back toward her. She leaned across the table between them until their faces were almost touching. "It's a yes or no question."

"*Yes.*"

Chapter Forty-Four: Miller

Miller sat by himself, staring out the wide observation windows without seeing the view. The fungal-culture whiskey on the low black table beside him remained at the same level in the glass as when he'd bought it. It wasn't really a drink. It was permission to sit. There had always been a handful of drifters, even on Ceres. Men and women whose luck had run out. No place to go, no one to ask favors of. No connection to the vast net of humanity. He'd always felt a kind of sympathy for them, his spiritual kindred.

Now he was part of that disconnected tribe in earnest.

Something bright happened on the skin of the great generation ship—a welding array firing off some intricate network of subtle connection, maybe. Past the *Nauvoo*, nestled in the constant hive-like activity of Tycho Station, was a half-degree arc of the *Rocinante*, like a home he'd once had. He knew the story of Moses seeing a promised land he would never enter. Miller wondered how the old prophet would have felt if he'd been ushered in for a moment—a day, a week, a year—and then dropped back out in the desert. Kinder never to leave the wastelands. Safer.

Beside him, Juliette Mao watched him from the corner of his mind carved out for her.

I was supposed to save you, he thought. *I was supposed to find you. Find the truth.*

And didn't you?

He smiled at her, and she smiled back, as world-weary and tired as he was. Because of course he had. He'd found her, he'd found who killed her, and Holden was right. He'd taken revenge. All that he'd promised himself, he'd done. Only it hadn't saved him.

"Can I get you anything?"

For half a second, Miller thought Julie had said it. The serving girl had opened her mouth to ask him again before he shook his head. She couldn't. And even if she had been able to, he couldn't afford it.

You knew it couldn't last, Julie said. *Holden. His crew. You knew you didn't really belong there. You belong with me.*

A sudden shot of adrenaline revved his tired heart. He looked around for her, but Julie was gone. His own privately generated fight-or-flight reaction didn't have room for daydream hallucinations. And still. *You belong with me.*

He wondered how many people he'd known who had taken that path. Cops had a tradition of eating their guns that went back to long before humanity had lifted itself up the gravity well. Here he was, without a home, without a friend, with more blood on his hands from the past month than from his whole career before it. The in-house shrink on Ceres called it suicidal ideation in his yearly presentation to the security teams. Something to watch out for, like genital lice or high cholesterol. Not a big deal if you were careful.

So he'd be careful. For a while. See where it went.

He stood, hesitated for three heartbeats, then scooped up his bourbon and drank it in a gulp. Liquid courage, they called it, and it seemed to do the trick. He pulled up his terminal, put in a connect request, and tried to compose himself. He wasn't there yet. And if he was going to live, he needed a job.

"Sabez nichts, Pampaw," Diogo said. The kid was wearing a meshwork shirt and pants cut in a fashion as youthful as it was ugly, and in his previous life, Miller would probably have written him off as too young to know anything useful. Now Miller waited. If anything could wring a prospect out of Diogo, it would be the promise of Miller getting a hole of his own. The silence dragged. Miller forced himself not to speak for fear of begging.

"Well…" Diogo said warily. "Well. There's one hombre might could. Just arm and eye."

"Security guard work's fine with me," Miller said. "Anything that pays the bills."

"Il conversa á do. Hear what's said."

"I appreciate anything you can do," Miller replied, then gestured at the bed. "You mind if I…?"

"Mi cama es su cama," Diogo said. Miller lay down.

Diogo stepped into the small shower, and the sound of water against flesh drowned out the air cycler. Even on board ship, Miller hadn't lived in physical circumstances this intimate with anyone since his marriage. Still, he wouldn't have gone as far as to call Diogo a friend.

Opportunity was thinner on Tycho than he'd hoped, and he didn't have much by way of references. The few people who knew him weren't likely to speak on his behalf. But surely there'd be something. All he needed was a way to remake himself, to start over and be someone different from who he'd been.

Assuming, of course, that Earth or Mars—whichever one came out on top of the war—didn't then wipe the OPA and all the stations loyal to it out of the sky. And that the protomolecule didn't escape Eros and slaughter a planet. Or a station. Or him. He had a moment's chill, recalling that there was still a sample of the thing on board the *Roci*. If something happened with it, Holden and Naomi, Alex and Amos might all join Julie long before Miller did.

He told himself that wasn't his problem anymore. Still, he hoped they'd be all right. He wanted them to be well, even if he wasn't.

"Oi, Pampaw," Diogo said as the door to the public hall slid open. "You hear that Eros started talking?"

Miller lifted himself to one elbow.

"Sí," Diogo said. "Whatever that shit is, it started broadcasting. There's even words and shit. I've got a feed. You want a listen?"

No, Miller thought. *No, I have seen those corridors. What's happened to those people almost happened to me. I don't want anything to do with that abomination.*

"Sure," he said.

Diogo scooped up his own hand terminal and keyed in something. Miller's terminal chimed that it had received the new feed route.

"Chicá perdída in ops been mixing a bunch of it to bhangra," Diogo said, making a shifting dance move with his hips. "Hardcore, eh?"

Diogo and the other OPA irregulars had breached a high-value research station, faced down one of the most powerful and evil corporations in a history of power and evil. And now they were making music from the screams of the dying. Of the dead. They were dancing to it in the low-rent clubs. *What it must be like*, Miller thought, *to be young and soulless.*

But no. That wasn't fair. Diogo was a good kid. He was just naive. The universe would take care of that, given a little time.

"Hard-core," Miller said. Diogo grinned.

The feed sat in queue, waiting. Miller turned out the lights, letting the little bed bear him up against the press of spin. He didn't want to hear. He didn't want to know. He had to.

At first, the sound was nothing—electric squeals and a wildly fluting static. Then, maybe somewhere deep in the back of it, music. A chorus of violas churning away together in a long, distant crescendo. And then, as clear as if someone were speaking into a microphone, a voice.

"Rabbits and hamsters. Ecologically unstabilizing and round and blue as moonbeams. August."

It almost certainly wasn't a real person. The computer systems on Eros could generate any number of perfectly convincing dialects and voices. Men's, women's, children's. And how many millions of hours of data could there be on the computers and storage dumps all through the station?

Another electronic flutter, like finches looped back against themselves. A new voice—feminine and soft this time—with a throbbing pulse behind it.

"Patient complains of rapid heartbeat and night sweats. Symptom onset reported as three months previous, but with a history..."

The voice faded, and the throbbing rose. Like an old man with Swiss cheese holes in his brain, the complex system that had been Eros was dying, changing, losing its mind. And because Protogen had wired it all for sound, Miller could listen to the station fail.

"I didn't tell him, I didn't tell him, I didn't tell him. The sunrise. I've never seen the sunrise."

Miller closed his eyes and slid down toward sleep, serenaded by Eros. As consciousness faded, he imagined a body in the bed beside him, warm and alive and breathing slowly in time with the rise and fall of the static.

The manager was a thin man, weedy, with hair combed high above his brow like a wave that never crashed. The office hunched close around them, humming at odd moments when the infrastructure—water, air, energy—of Tycho impinged on it. A business built between ducts, improvisational and cheap. The lowest of the low.

"I'm sorry," the manager said. Miller felt his gut tighten and sink. Of all the humiliations the universe had in store for him, this one he hadn't foreseen. It made him angry.

"You think I can't handle it?" he asked, keeping his voice soft.

"It's not that," the weedy man said. "It's…Look, between us, we're looking for a thumb, you know? Someone's idiot kid brother could guard this warehouse. You've got all this experience. What do we need with riot control protocols? Or investigative procedure? I mean, come on. This gig doesn't even come with a gun."

"I don't care," Miller said. "I need something."

The weedy man sighed and gave the exaggerated shrug of a Belter.

"You need something else," he said.

Miller tried not to laugh, afraid it would sound like despair. He stared at the cheap plastic wall behind the manager until the guy started to get uncomfortable. It was a trap. He was too experienced to start over. He knew too much, so there was no going back and doing fresh beginnings.

"All right," he said at last, and the manager across the desk from him let out a breath, then had the good grace to look embarrassed.

"Can I just ask," the weedy man said. "Why did you leave your old job?"

"Ceres changed hands," Miller said, putting on his hat. "I wasn't on the new team. That was all."

"Ceres?"

The manager looked confused, which in turn confused Miller. He glanced down at his own hand terminal. There was his work history, just the way he'd presented it. The manager couldn't have missed it.

"That's where I was," Miller said.

"For the police thing. But I meant the last job. I mean, I've been around, I understand not putting OPA work on your resume, but you have to figure we all know that you were part of the thing… you know, with the station. And all."

"You think I was working for the OPA," Miller said.

The weedy man blinked.

"You were," he said.

Which, after all, was true.

Nothing had changed in Fred Johnson's office, and everything had. The furnishings, the smell of the air, the sense of its existing somewhere between a boardroom and a command and control center. The generation ship outside the window might have been half a percent closer to completion, but that wasn't it. The stakes of the game had shifted, and what had been a war was something else now. Something bigger. It shone in Fred's eyes and tightened his shoulders.

"We could use a man with your skills," Fred agreed. "It's always the small-scale things that trip you up. How to frisk someone. That kind of thing. Tycho security can handle themselves, but once we're off our station and shooting our way into someone else's, not as much."

"Is that something you're looking to do more of?" Miller said, trying to make it a casual joke. Fred didn't answer. For a moment, Julie stood at the general's side. Miller saw the pair of them reflected in the screens, the man pensive, the ghost amused. Maybe Miller had gotten it wrong from the start, and the divide between the Belt and the inner planets was something besides politics and resource management. He knew as well as anyone that the Belt offered a harder, more dangerous life than Mars or Earth provided. And yet it called these people—the best people—out of humanity's gravity wells to cast themselves into the darkness.

The impulse to explore, to stretch, to leave home. To go as far as possible out into the universe. And now that Protogen and Eros offered the chance to become gods, to re-create humanity into beings that could go beyond merely human hopes and dreams, it occurred to Miller how hard it would be for men like Fred to turn that temptation away.

"You killed Dresden," Fred said. "That's a problem."

"It needed to happen."

"I'm not sure it did," Fred replied, but his voice was careful. Testing. Miller smiled, a little sadly.

"That's why it needed to happen," he said.

The small, coughing laugh told Miller that Fred understood him. When the general turned back to consider him again, his gaze was steady.

"When it comes to the negotiating table, someone's going to have to answer for it. You killed a defenseless man."

"I did," Miller said.

"When the time comes, I will hand-feed you to the wolves as the first chip I offer. I won't protect you."

"Wouldn't ask you to protect me," Miller said.

"Even if it meant being a Belter ex-cop in an Earth-side prison?"

It was a euphemism, and they both knew it. *You belong with me,* Julie said. And so what did it matter, really, how he got there?

"I've got no regrets," he said, and half a breath later was shocked to discover it was almost true. "If there's a judge out there who wants to ask me about something, I'll answer. I'm looking for a job here, not protection."

Fred sat in his chair, eyes narrow and thoughtful. Miller leaned forward in his seat.

"You've got me in a hard position," Fred said. "You're saying all the right things. But I have a hard time trusting that you'd follow through. Keeping you on the books would be risky. It could undermine my position in the peace negotiations."

"It's a risk," Miller said. "But I've been on Eros and Thoth Station. I flew on the *Rocinante* with Holden and his crew. When it comes to analysis of the protomolecule and how we got into this mess, there isn't anyone in a better position to give you information. You can argue I knew too much. That I was too valuable to let go."

"Or too dangerous."

"Sure. Or that."

They were silent for a moment. On the *Nauvoo*, a bank of lights glittered in a gold-and-green test pattern and then went dark.

"Security consultant," Fred said. "Independent. I won't give you a rank."

I'm too dirty for the OPA, Miller thought with a glow of amusement.

"If it comes with my own bunk, I'll take it," he said. It was only until the war was over. After that, he was meat for the machine. That was fine. Fred leaned back. His chair hissed softly into its new configuration.

"All right," Fred said. "Here's your first job. Give me your analysis. What's my biggest problem?"

"Containment," Miller said.

"You think I can't keep the information about Thoth Station and the protomolecule quiet?"

"Of course you can't," Miller said. "For one thing, too many people already know. For another thing, one of them's Holden, and if he hasn't already broadcast the whole thing on every empty frequency, he will soon. And besides that, you can't make a peace deal without explaining what the hell's going on. Sooner or later, it has to come out."

"And what do you advise?"

For a moment, Miller was back in the darkness, listening to the gibbers of the dying station. The voices of the dead calling to him from across the vacuum.

"Defend Eros," he said. "All sides are going to want samples of the protomolecule. Locking down access is going to be the only way you get yourself a seat at that table."

Fred chuckled.

"Nice thought," he said. "But how do you propose we defend something the size of Eros Station if Earth and Mars bring their navies to bear?"

It was a good point. Miller felt a tug of sorrow. Even though Julie Mao—his Julie—was dead and gone, it felt like disloyalty to say it.

"Then you have to get rid of it," he said.

"And how would I do that?" Fred said. "Even if we studded the thing with nukes, how would we be sure that no little scrap of the thing would make its way to a colony or down a well? Blowing that thing up would be like blowing dandelion fluff into the breeze."

Miller had never seen a dandelion, but he saw the problem. Even the smallest portion of the goo filling Eros might be enough to start the whole evil experiment over again. And the goo thrived on radiation; simply cooking the station might hurry the thing along its occult path rather than end it. To be sure that the proto-molecule on Eros never spread, they'd need to break everything on the station down to its constituent atoms...

"Oh," Miller said.

"Oh?"

"Yeah. You're not going to like this."

"Try me."

"Okay. You asked. You drive Eros into the sun."

"Into the sun," Fred said. "Do you have any idea how much mass we're talking about here?"

Miller nodded to the wide, clear expanse of window, to the construction yards beyond it. To the *Nauvoo*.

"Big engines on that thing," Miller said. "Get some fast ships out to the station, make sure no one can get in before you get there. Run the *Nauvoo* into Eros Station. Knock it sunward."

Fred's gaze turned inward as he planned, calculated.

"Got to make sure no one gets into it until it hits corona. That'll be hard, but Earth and Mars are both just as interested in keeping the other guy from having it as in getting it themselves."

I'm sorry I couldn't do better, Julie, he thought. *But it'll be a hell of a funeral.*

Fred's breath grew slow and deep, his gaze flickering as if he were reading something in the air that only he could see. Miller didn't interrupt, even when the silence got heavy. It was almost a minute later that Fred let out a short, percussive breath.

"The Mormons are going to be pissed," he said.

Chapter Forty-Five: Holden

Naomi talked in her sleep. It was one of a dozen things Holden hadn't known about her before tonight. Even though they'd slept in crash couches a few feet apart on many occasions, he'd never heard it. Now, with her face against his bare chest, he could feel her lips move and the soft, punctuated exhalations of her words. He couldn't hear what she was saying.

She also had a scar on her back, just above her left buttock. It was three inches long and had the uneven edges and rippling that came from a tear rather than a slice. Naomi would never get herself knifed in a bar fight, so it had to have come on the job. Maybe she had been climbing through tight spaces in the engine room when the ship maneuvered unexpectedly. A competent plastic surgeon could have made it invisible in one visit. That she hadn't bothered and clearly didn't care was another thing he had learned about her tonight.

She stopped murmuring and smacked her lips a few times, then said, "Thirsty."

Holden slid out from under her and headed for the kitchen, knowing that this was the obsequiousness that always accompanied a new lover. For the next couple of weeks, he wouldn't be able to stop himself from fulfilling every whim Naomi might have. It was a behavior some men carried at the genetic level, their DNA wanting to make sure that first time wasn't just a fluke.

Her room was laid out differently than his, and the unfamiliarity made him clumsy in the dark. He fumbled around for a few minutes in her small kitchen nook, looking for a glass. By the time he found it, filled it, and headed back into the bedroom, Naomi was sitting up in bed. The sheet lay pooled on her lap. The sight of her half nude in the dimly lit room gave him an embarrassingly sudden erection.

Naomi panned her gaze up his body, pausing at his midsection, then at the water glass, and said, "Is that for me?"

Holden didn't know which thing she was asking about, so he just said, "Yes."

"You asleep?"

Naomi's face was on his belly, her breathing slow and deep, but to his surprise she said, "No."

"Can we talk?"

Naomi rolled off him and pulled herself up until her face lay next to his on the pillow. Her hair fell across her eyes, and Holden reached out and brushed it away in a move that felt so intimate and proprietary that he had to swallow a lump in his throat.

"Are you about to get serious on me?" she asked, her eyes half lidded.

"Yeah, I am," he said, and kissed her forehead.

"My last lover was over a year ago," she said. "I'm a serial monogamist, so as far as I'm concerned, this is an exclusive-rights deal until one of us decides it isn't. As long as I get advance warning that you've decided to end the deal, there won't be any hard feelings. I'm open to the idea of it being more than just sex, but in my experience that will happen on its own if it's going to. I have eggs in storage on Europa and Luna, if that matters to you."

She rolled up onto her elbow, her face hovering over his.

"Did I cover all the bases?" she asked.

"No," he said. "But I agree to the conditions."

She flopped onto her back, letting out a long contented sigh.

"Good."

Holden wanted to hold her, but he felt too hot and sticky with sweat, so he just reached down and held her hand instead. He wanted to tell her that this meant something, that it was already more than sex for him, but all the words he tried out in his head came off sounding phony or maudlin.

"Thank you," he said instead, but she was already snoring quietly.

They had sex again in the morning. After a long night with too little sleep, it wound up being far more effort than release for Holden, but there was a pleasure in that too, as if less than mind-blowing sex somehow meant something different and funnier and gentler than what they'd already done together. Afterward, Holden went to the kitchen and made coffee, then brought it back to bed on a tray. They drank it without talking, some of the shyness they'd avoided the night before coming now in the artificial morning of the room's LEDs.

Naomi put her empty coffee cup down and touched the badly healed lump in his recently broken nose.

"Is it hideous?" Holden asked.

"No," she said. "You were too perfect before. It makes you seem more substantial."

Holden laughed. "That sounds like a word you use to describe a fat man or a history professor."

Naomi smiled and touched his chest lightly with her fingertips. It wasn't an attempt to arouse, just the exploration that came when satiation had removed sex from the equation. Holden tried to remember the last time the cold sanity following sex had been this comfortable, but maybe that had been never. He was making plans to spend the remainder of the day in Naomi's bed, running through a mental list of restaurants on the station that delivered, when his terminal began buzzing on the nightstand.

"God dammit," he said.

"You don't have to answer," Naomi replied, and moved her explorations to his belly.

"You've been paying attention the last couple months, right?" Holden said. "Unless it's a wrong number, then it's probably some end-of-the-solar-system-type shit and we have five minutes to evacuate the station."

Naomi kissed his ribs, which simultaneously tickled him and caused him to question his assumptions about his own refractory period.

"That's not funny," she said.

Holden sighed and picked up the terminal off the table. Fred's name flashed as it buzzed again.

"It's Fred," he said.

Naomi stopped kissing him and sat up.

"Yeah, then it's probably not good news."

Holden tapped on the screen to accept the call and said, "Fred."

"Jim. Come see me as soon as you get a chance. It's important."

"Okay," Holden replied. "Be there in half an hour."

He ended the call and tossed his hand terminal across the room onto the pile of clothes he'd left at the foot of the bed.

"Going to shower, then go see what Fred wants," he said, pulling off the sheet and getting up.

"Should I come, too?" Naomi asked.

"Are you kidding? I'm never letting you out of my sight again."

"Don't get creepy on me," Naomi replied, but she was smiling when she said it.

The first unpleasant surprise was Miller sitting in Fred's office when they arrived. Holden nodded at the man once, then said to Fred, "We're here. What's up?"

Fred gestured for them to sit, and when they had, he said, "We've been discussing what to do about Eros."

Holden shrugged. "Okay. What about it?"

"Miller thinks that someone will try to land there and recover some samples of the protomolecule."

"I have no trouble believing that someone will be that stupid," Holden said with a nod.

Fred stood up and tapped something on his desk. The screens that normally showed a view of the *Nauvoo* construction outside suddenly switched to a 2-D map of the solar system, tiny lights of different colors marking fleet positions. An angry swarm of green dots surrounded Mars. Holden assumed that meant the greens were Earth ships. There were a lot of red and yellow dots in the Belt and outer planets. Red was probably Mars, then.

"Nice map," Holden said. "Accurate?"

"Reasonably," Fred said. With a few quick taps on his desk, he zoomed in on one portion of the Belt. A potato-shaped lump labeled EROS filled the middle of the screen. Two tiny green dots inched toward it from several meters away.

"That is the Earth science vessel *Charles Lyell* moving toward Eros at full burn. She's accompanied by what we think is a Phantom-class escort ship."

"The *Roci*'s Earth navy cousin," Holden said.

"Well, the Phantom class is an older model, and largely relegated to rear-echelon assignments, but still more than a match for anything the OPA can quickly field," Fred replied.

"Exactly the sort of ship that would be escorting science ships around, though," Holden said. "How'd they get out there so quick? And why just the two of them?"

Fred backed the map up until it was a distant view of the entire solar system again.

"Dumb luck. The *Lyell* was returning to Earth from doing

non-Belt asteroid mapping when it diverted course toward Eros. It was close; no one else was. Earth must have seen a chance to grab a sample while everyone else was figuring out what to do."

Holden looked over at Naomi, but her face was unreadable. Miller was staring at him like an entomologist trying to figure out exactly where the pin went.

"So they know, then?" Holden said. "About Protogen and Eros?"

"We assume so," Fred said.

"You want us to chase them away? I mean, I think we can, but that will only work until Earth can reroute a few more ships to back them up. We won't be able to buy much time."

Fred smiled.

"We won't need much," he said. "We have a plan."

Holden nodded, waiting to hear it, but Fred sat down and leaned back in his chair. Miller stood up and changed the view on the screen to a close-up of the surface of Eros.

Now we get to find out why Fred is keeping this jackal around, Holden thought, but said nothing.

Miller pointed at the picture of Eros.

"Eros is an old station. Lots of redundancy. Lot of holes in her skin, mostly small maintenance airlocks," the former detective said. "The big docks are in five main clusters around the station. We're looking at sending six supply freighters to Eros, along with the *Rocinante.* The *Roci* keeps the science vessel from landing, and the freighters secure themselves to the station, one at each docking cluster."

"You're sending people in?" Holden said.

"Not in," Miller replied. "Just on. Surface work. Anyway, the sixth freighter evacuates the crews once the others are docked. Each abandoned freighter will have a couple dozen high-yield fusion warheads wired to the ship's proximity detectors. Anything tries to land at the docks, and there's a few-hundred-megaton fusion explosion. It should be enough to take out the approaching ship, but even if it doesn't, the docks will be too slagged to land at."

Naomi cleared her throat. "Uh, the UN and Mars both have bomb squads. They'll figure out how to get past your booby traps."

"Given enough time," Fred agreed.

Miller continued as though he hadn't been interrupted.

"The bombs are just a second line of deterrence. *Rocinante* first, bombs second. We're trying to buy Fred's people enough time to prep the *Nauvoo*."

"The *Nauvoo?*" Holden said, and half a breath later, Naomi whistled low. Miller nodded to her almost as if he were accepting applause.

"The *Nauvoo*'s launching in a long parabolic course, building up speed. It'll hit Eros at a velocity and angle calculated to knock Eros toward the sun. Set off the bombs too. Between the impact energy and the fusion warheads, we figure the surface of Eros'll be hot and radioactive enough to cook anything that tries to land until it's too damn late," Miller finished, then sat back down. He looked up as if he was waiting for reactions.

"This was your idea?" Holden asked Miller.

"*Nauvoo* part was. But we didn't know about the *Lyell* when we first talked about it. The booby trap thing's kind of improvised. I think it'll work, though. Buy us enough time."

"I agree," Holden said. "We need to keep Eros out of anyone's hands, and I can't think of a better way to do it. We're in. We'll shoo the science ship away while you do your work."

Fred leaned forward in his chair with a creak and said, "I knew you'd be on board. Miller was more skeptical."

"Throwing a million people into the sun seemed like something you might balk at," the detective said with a humorless grin.

"There's nothing human left on that station. What's your part in all of this? You armchair quarterbacking now?"

It came out nastier than he'd intended, but Miller didn't appear offended.

"I'll be coordinating security."

"Security? Why will they need security?"

Miller smiled. All his smiles looked like he was hearing a good joke at a funeral.

"In case something crawls out of an airlock, tries to thumb a ride," he said.

Holden frowned. "I don't like to think those things can get around in vacuum. I don't like that idea at all."

"Once we bring the surface temp of Eros up to a nice balmy ten thousand degrees, I'm thinking it won't matter much," Miller replied. "Until then, best be safe."

Holden found himself wishing he shared the detective's confidence.

"What are the odds the impact and detonations just break Eros into a million pieces and scatter them all over the solar system?" Naomi asked.

"Fred's got some of his best engineers calculating everything to the last decimal to make sure that doesn't happen," Miller replied. "Tycho helped build Eros in the first place. They've got the blueprints."

"So," said Fred. "Let's deal with the last bit of business."

Holden waited.

"You still have the protomolecule," Fred said.

Holden nodded again. "And?"

"And," replied Fred. "And the last time we sent you out, your ship was almost wrecked. Once Eros has been nuked, it will be the only confirmed sample around, outside of what might still be on Phoebe. I can't find any reason to let you keep it. I want it to remain here on Tycho when you go."

Holden stood up, shaking his head.

"I like you, Fred, but I'm not handing that stuff over to anyone who might see it as a bargaining chip."

"I don't think you have a lot of—" Fred started, but Holden held up a finger and cut him off. While Fred stared at him in surprise, he grabbed his terminal and opened the crew channel.

"Alex, Amos, either of you on the ship?"

"I'm here," Amos said a second later. "Finishing up some—"

"Lock it down," Holden said over him. "Right now. Seal it up. If I don't call you in an hour, or if anyone other than me tries to board, leave the dock and fly away from Tycho at best possible speed. Direction is your choice. Shoot your way free if you have to. Read me?"

"Loud and clear, Cap," Amos said. If Holden had asked him to get a cup of coffee, Amos would have sounded exactly the same.

Fred was still staring at him incredulously.

"Don't force this issue, Fred," Holden said.

"If you think you can threaten me, you're mistaken," Fred said, his voice flat and frightening.

Miller laughed.

"Something funny?" Fred said.

"That wasn't a threat," Miller replied.

"No? What would you call it?"

"An accurate report of the world," Miller said. He stretched slowly as he talked. "If it was Alex on board, he might think the captain was trying to intimidate someone, maybe back down at the last minute. Amos, though? Amos will absolutely shoot his way free, even if it means he goes down with the ship."

Fred scowled, and Miller shook his head.

"It's not a bluff," Miller said. "Don't call it."

Fred's eyes narrowed, and Holden wondered if he'd finally gone too far with the man. He certainly wouldn't be the first person Fred Johnson had ordered shot. And he had Miller standing right next to him. The unbalanced detective would probably shoot him at the first hint someone thought it was a good idea. It shook Holden's confidence in Fred that Miller was even here.

Which made it a little more surprising when Miller saved him.

"Look," the detective said. "Fact is, Holden is the best person to carry that shit around until you decide what to do with it."

"Talk me into it," Fred said, his voice still tight with anger.

"Once Eros goes up, he and the *Roci* are going to have their asses hanging in the breeze. Someone might be angry enough to nuke him just on general principles."

"And how does that make the sample safer with him?" Fred asked, but Holden had understood Miller's point.

"They might be less inclined to blow me up if I let them know that I've got the sample and all the Protogen notes," he said.

"Won't make the sample safer," Miller said. "But it makes the mission more likely to work. And that's the point, right? Also, he's an idealist," Miller continued. "Offer Holden his weight in gold and he'll just be offended you tried to bribe him."

Naomi laughed. Miller glanced at her, a small shared smile at the corner of his mouth, then turned back to Fred.

"Are you saying he can be trusted and I can't?" Fred said.

"I was thinking more about the crew," Miller said. "Holden's got a small bunch, and they do what he says. They think he's righteous, so they are too."

"My people follow me," Fred said.

Miller's grin was weary and unassailable.

"There's a lot of people in the OPA," he said.

"The stakes are too high," Fred said.

"You're kind of in the wrong career for safe," Miller said. "I'm not saying it's a great plan. Just you won't get a better one."

Fred's slitted eyes glittered with equal parts frustration and rage. His jaw worked silently for a moment before he spoke.

"Captain Holden? I'm disappointed with your lack of trust after all I've done for you and yours."

"If the human race still exists a month from now, I'll apologize," Holden said.

"Get your crew out to Eros before I change my mind."

Holden rose, nodded to Fred, and left. Naomi walked at his side.

"Wow, that was close," she said under her breath.

Once they'd left the office, Holden said, "I think Fred was half a second from ordering Miller to shoot me."

"Miller's on our side. Haven't you figured that out yet?"

Chapter Forty-Six: Miller

Miller had known when he'd taken Holden's side against his new boss that there were going to be consequences. His position with Fred and the OPA was tenuous to start with, and pointing out that Holden and his crew were not only more dedicated but also more trustworthy than Fred's people wasn't the thing you did when you were kissing up. That it was the truth only made it worse.

He'd expected some kind of payback. He would have been naive not to.

"*Rise up, O men of God, in one united throng,*" the resisters sang. "*Bring in the days of bro-ther-hood, and end the night of wrong...*"

Miller took off his hat and ran fingers through his thinning hair. It wasn't going to be a good day.

The interior of the *Nauvoo* showed more patchwork and process than its hull suggested. Two kilometers long, its designers had built it as more than a huge ship. The great levels stacked one atop the other; alloy girders worked organically with what would have been pastoral meadows. The structure echoed the greatest cathedrals of Earth and Mars, rising up through empty air and giving both thrust-gravity stability and glory to God. It was still metal bones and woven agricultural substrate, but Miller could see where it was all heading.

A generation ship was a statement of overarching ambition and utter faith. The Mormons had known that. They'd embraced it. They'd constructed a ship that was prayer and piety and celebration all at the same time. The *Nauvoo* would be the greatest temple mankind had ever built. It would shepherd its crew through the uncrossable gulfs of interstellar space, humanity's best hope of reaching the stars.

Or it would have been, if not for him.

"You want us to gas them, Pampaw?" Diogo asked.

Miller considered the resisters. At a guess, there might have been two hundred of them strung in linked chains across the access paths and engineering ducts. Transport lifts and industrial waldoes stood idle, their displays dark, their batteries shorted.

"Yeah, probably should," Miller sighed.

The security team—his security team—numbered fewer than three dozen. Men and women more unified by the OPA-issued armbands than by their training, experience, loyalties, or politics. If the Mormons had chosen violence, it would have been a bloodbath. If they'd put on environment suits, the protest would have lasted hours. Days, possibly. Instead, Diogo gave the signal, and three minutes later, four small comets arced out into the null-g space, wavering on their tails of NNLP-alpha and tetrahydrocannabinol.

It was the kindest, gentlest riot control device in the arsenal. Any of the protesters with compromised lungs could still be in trouble, but within half an hour, all of them would be relaxed into near stupor and high as a kite. NNLPa and THC wasn't a combination Miller had ever used on Ceres. If they'd tried to stock it, it would have been stolen for office parties. He tried to take some comfort in the thought. As if it would make up for the lifetimes of dreams and labor he was taking away.

Beside him, Diogo laughed.

It took them three hours to make the primary sweep of the ship, and another five to hunt down all the stowaways huddled in ducts and secure rooms, waiting to make their presence known at the last minute and sabotage the mission. As those were hauled weeping off the ship, Miller wondered whether he'd just saved their lives. If all he'd done with his life was keep Fred Johnson from deciding whether to let a handful of innocent people die with the *Nauvoo,* or risk keeping Eros around for the inner planets, that wasn't so bad.

As soon as Miller gave the word, the OPA tech team moved into action, reengaging the waldoes and transports, fixing the hundred small acts of sabotage that would have kept the *Nauvoo*'s engines from firing, clearing out equipment they wanted to save. Miller watched industrial lifts big enough to house a family of five shift crate after crate, moving out things that had only recently been moved in. The docks were as busy as Ceres at mid-shift. Miller half expected to see his old cohorts wandering among the stevedores and lift tubes, keeping what passed for the peace.

In the quiet moments, he set his hand terminal to the Eros feed. Back when he'd been a kid, there had been a performance artist making the rounds — Jila Sorormaya, her name was. As he recalled, she'd intentionally corrupted data-storage devices and then put the data stream through her music kit. She'd gotten into trouble when some of the proprietary code of the storage device software got incorporated into her music and posted. Miller hadn't been a sophisticate. He'd figured another nutcase artist had to get a real job, and the universe could only be a better place.

Listening to the Eros feed — Radio Free Eros, he called it — he thought maybe he'd been a little rough on old Jila. The squeaks and cross-chatter, the flow of empty noise punctuated by voices, were eerie and compelling. Just like the broken data stream, it was the music of corruption.

…asciugare il pus e che possano sentirsi meglio…

…ja minä nousivat kuolleista ja halventaa kohtalo pakottaa minut ja siskoni…

…do what you have to…

He'd listened to the feed for hours, picking out voices. Once, the whole thing had fluttered, cutting in and out like a piece of equipment on the edge of failure. Only after it had resumed did Miller wonder if the stutters of quiet had been Morse code. He leaned against the bulkhead, the overwhelming mass of the *Nauvoo* towering above him. The ship only half born and already marked for sacrifice. Julie sat beside him, looking up. Her hair floated around her face; her eyes never stopped smiling. Whatever trick of the imagination had kept his own internal Juliette Andromeda Mao from coming back to him as her corpse, he thanked it.

It would have been something, wouldn't it? she said. *Flying through vacuum without a suit. Sleeping for a hundred years and waking up in the light of a different sun.*

"I didn't shoot that fucker fast enough," Miller said aloud.

He could have given us the stars.

A new voice broke in. A human voice shaking with rage.

"Antichrist!"

Miller blinked, returning to reality, and thumbed off the Eros feed. A prisoner transport wound its lazy way through the dock, a dozen Mormon technicians bound to its restraint poles. One was a young man with a pocked face and hatred in his eyes. He was staring at Miller.

"You're the Antichrist, you vile excuse for a human! God knows you! He'll *remember* you!"

Miller tipped his hat as the prisoners ambled by.

"Stars are better off without us," he said, but too softly for anyone but Julie to hear.

A dozen tugs flew before the *Nauvoo*, the web of nanotubule tethers invisible at this distance. All Miller saw was the great behemoth, as much a part of Tycho Station as the bulkheads and air, shift in its bed, shrug, and begin to move. The tugs' drive flares lit the interior space of the station, flickering in their perfectly choreographed duties like Christmas lights, and a nearly subliminal shudder passed through the deep steel bones of Tycho. In eight hours, the *Nauvoo* would be far enough out that the great engines could be brought online without endangering the station with their exhaust plume. It might be more than two weeks after that before it reached Eros.

Miller would beat it there by eighty hours.

"Oi, Pampaw," Diogo said. "Done-done?"

"Yeah," Miller said with a sigh. "I'm ready. Let's get everyone together."

The boy grinned. In the hours since the commandeering of the *Nauvoo*, Diogo had added bright red plastic decorations to three of his front teeth. It was apparently deeply meaningful in the youth culture of Tycho Station, and signified prowess, possibly sexual. Miller felt a moment's relief that he wasn't hot-bunking at the boy's place anymore.

Now that he was running security ops for the OPA, the irregular nature of the group was clearer to him than ever. There had been a time when he'd thought the OPA might be something that could take on Earth or Mars when it came to a real war. Certainly, they had more money and resources than he'd thought. They had Fred Johnson. They had Ceres now, for as long as they could hold it. They'd taken on Thoth Station and won.

And yet the same kids he'd gone on the assault with had been working crowd control at the *Nauvoo*, and more than half of them would be on the demolitions ship when it left for Eros. It was the thing that Havelock would never understand. For that matter, it was the thing Holden would never understand. Maybe no one who had lived with the certainty and support of a natural atmosphere would ever completely accept the power and fragility of a society based in doing what needed doing, in becoming fast and flexible, the way the OPA had. In becoming articulated.

If Fred couldn't build himself a peace treaty, the OPA would never win against the discipline and unity of an inner planet navy. But they would also never lose. War without end.

Well, what was history if not that?

And how would having the stars change anything?

As he walked to his apartment, he opened a channel request on his hand terminal. Fred Johnson appeared, looking tired but alert.

"Miller," he said.

"We're getting ready to ship out if the ordinance is ready."

"It's loading now," Fred replied. "Enough fissionable material to keep the surface of Eros unapproachable for years. Be careful with it. If one of your boys goes down for a smoke in the wrong place, we aren't going to be able to replace the mines. Not in time."

Not *you'll all be dead*. The weapons were precious, not the people.

"Yeah, I'll watch it," Miller said.

"The *Rocinante*'s already on its way."

That wasn't something Miller needed to know, so there was some other reason Fred had mentioned it. His carefully neutral tone made it something like an accusation. The only controlled sample of protomolecule had left Fred's sphere of influence.

"We'll get out there to meet her in plenty of time to keep anybody off of Eros," Miller said. "Shouldn't be a problem."

On the tiny screen, it was hard to tell how genuine Fred's smile was.

"I hope your friends are really up for this," he said.

Miller felt something odd. A little hollowness just below his breastbone.

"They aren't my friends," he said, keeping his tone of voice light.

"No?"

"I don't exactly have friends. It's more I've got a lot of people I used to work with," he said.

"You put a lot of faith in Holden," Fred said, making it almost a question. A challenge, at least. Miller smiled, knowing that Fred would be just as unsure if his was genuine.

"Not faith. Judgment," he said.

Fred coughed out a laugh.

"And that's why you don't have friends, friend."

"Part of it," Miller said.

There was nothing more to say. Miller dropped the connection. He was almost at his hole, anyway.

It was nothing much. An anonymous cube on the station with even less personality to it than his place back on Ceres. He sat on his bunk, checked his terminal for the status of the demolitions ship. He knew that he should just go up to the docks. Diogo and the others were assembling, and while it wasn't likely that the drug haze of the pre-mission parties would allow them all to arrive on time, it was at least possible. He didn't even have that excuse.

Julie sat in the space behind his eyes. Her legs were folded under her. She was beautiful. She'd been like Fred and Holden and Havelock. Someone born in a gravity well who came to the Belt by choice. She'd died for her choice. She'd come looking for help and killed Eros by doing it. If she'd stayed there, on that ghost ship...

She tilted her head, her hair swinging against the spin gravity. There was a question in her eyes. She was right, of course. It would have slowed things down, maybe. It wouldn't have stopped them. Protogen and Dresden would have found her eventually. Would have found it. Or gone back and dug up a fresh sample. Nothing would have stopped them.

And he knew—knew the way he knew he was himself—that Julie wasn't like the others. That she'd understood the Belt and Belters, and the need to push on. If not for the stars, at least close to them. The luxury available to her was something Miller had never experienced, and never would. But she'd turned away. She'd come out here, and stayed even when they were going to sell her racing pinnace. Her childhood. Her pride.

That was why he loved her.

When Miller reached the dock, it was clear something had happened. It was in the way the dockworkers held themselves and the looks half amusement and half pleasure, on their faces. Miller signed in and crawled through the awkward Ojino-Gouch-style airlock, seventy years out of date and hardly larger than a torpedo tube, into the cramped crew area of the *Talbot Leeds*. The ship looked like it had been welded together from two smaller ships, without particular concern for design. The acceleration couches were stacked three deep. The air smelled of old sweat and hot metal. Someone had been smoking marijuana recently enough that the filters hadn't cleared it out yet. Diogo was there along with a half dozen others. They all wore different uniforms, but they also all had the OPA armband.

"Oi, Pampaw! Kept top bunk á dir."

"Thanks," Miller said. "I appreciate that."

Thirteen days. He was going to spend thirteen days sharing this tiny space with the demolitions crew. Thirteen days pressed into these couches, with megatons of fission mines in the ship's hold. And yet the others were all smiling. Miller hauled himself up to the acceleration couch Diogo had saved for him, and pointed to the others with his chin.

"Someone have a birthday?"

Diogo gave an elaborate shrug.

"Why's everyone in such a good fucking mood?" Miller said, more sharply than he'd intended. Diogo took no offense. He smiled his great red-and-white teeth.

"Audi-nichts?"

"No, I haven't heard, or I wouldn't be asking," Miller said.

"Mars did the right thing," Diogo said. "Got the feed off Eros, put two and two, and—"

The boy slammed a fist into his open palm. Miller tried to parse what he was saying. They'd attacked Eros? They'd taken on Protogen?

Ah. Protogen. Protogen and Mars. Miller nodded. "The Phoebe science station," he said. "Mars quarantined it."

"Fuck that, Pampaw. *Autoclaved* it, them. Moon is gone. Dropped enough nukes on it to split it subatomic."

They better have, Miller thought. It wasn't a big moon. If Mars had really destroyed it and there was any protomolecule left on a hunk of ejecta...

"Tu sabez?" Diogo said. "They're on our side now. They get it. Mars-OPA alliance."

"You don't really think that," Miller said.

"Nah," Diogo said, just as pleased with himself in admitting that the hope was fragile at best and probably false. "But don't hurt to dream, que no?"

"You don't think?" Miller said, and lay back.

The acceleration gel was too stiff to conform to his body at the dock's one-third g, but it wasn't uncomfortable. He checked the news on his hand terminal, and indeed someone in the Martian navy had made a judgment call. It was a lot of ordinance to use, especially in the middle of a shooting war, but they'd expended it. Saturn had one fewer moon, one more tiny, unformed, filamentous ring — if there was even enough matter left from the detonations to form that. It looked to Miller's unpracticed eye as if the explosions had been designed to drop debris into the protective and crushing gravity of the gas giant.

It was foolish to think it meant the Martian government wouldn't want samples of the protomolecule. It was naive to pretend that any organization of that size and complexity was univocal about anything, much less something as dangerous and transforming as this.

But still.

Perhaps it was enough just knowing that someone on the other side of the political and military divide had seen the same evidence they had seen and drawn the same conclusions. Maybe it left room for hope. He switched his hand terminal back to the Eros feed. A strong throbbing sound danced below a cascade of noise. Voices rose and fell and rose again. Data streams spewed into one another, and the pattern-recognition servers burned every spare cycle making something from the resultant mess. Julie took his hand, the dream so convincing he could almost pretend he felt it.

You belong with me, she said.

As soon as it's over, he thought. It was true he kept pushing back the end point of the case. First find Julie, then avenge her, and now destroy the project that had claimed her life. But after that was accomplished, he could let go.

He just had this one last thing he needed to do.

Twenty minutes later, the Klaxon sounded. Thirty minutes later, the engines kicked on, pressing him into the acceleration gel at a joint-crushing high-g burn for thirteen days, with one-g breaks for biological function every four hours. And when they were done, the half-trained jack-of-all-trades crew would be handling nuclear mines capable of annihilating them if they screwed it up.

But at least Julie would be there. Not really, but still.

It didn't hurt to dream.

Chapter Forty-Seven: Holden

Even the wet cellulose taste of reconstituted artificial scrambled eggs was not enough to ruin Holden's warm, self-satisfied glow. He shoveled the faux eggs into his mouth, trying not to grin. Sitting at his left around the galley table, Amos ate with lip-smacking enthusiasm. To Holden's right, Alex pushed the limp eggs around on his plate with a piece of equally fake toast. Across the table, Naomi sipped a cup of tea and looked at him from under her hair. He stifled the urge to wink at her.

They'd talked about how to break the news to the crew but hadn't come to any consensus. Holden hated to hide anything. Keeping it secret made it seem dirty or shameful. His parents had raised him to believe that sex was something you did in private not because it was embarrassing, but because it was intimate. With five fathers and three mothers, the sleeping arrangements were always complex at his house, but the discussions about who was bedding with whom were never hidden from him. It left him with a strong aversion to hiding his own activities.

Naomi, on the other hand, thought they shouldn't do anything to upset the fragile equilibrium they'd found, and Holden trusted her instincts. She had an insight into group dynamics that he often lacked. So, for now, he was following her lead.

Besides, it would have felt like boasting, and that would have been rude.

Keeping his voice neutral and professional, he said, "Naomi, can you pass the pepper?"

Amos' head snapped up, and he dropped his fork on the table with a loud clatter.

"Holy shit, you guys are doing it!"

"Um," Holden said. "What?"

"Something's been screwy ever since we got back on the *Roci,* but I couldn't figure. But that's *it*! You guys are finally playing hide the weasel."

Holden blinked twice at the big mechanic, unsure of what to say. He glanced at Naomi for support, but her head was down, and her hair completely covered her face. Her shoulders were shaking in silent laughter.

"Jesus, Cap," Amos said, a grin on his wide face. "It fucking took you long enough. If she'd been throwing herself at me like that, I'd have been neck deep in that shit."

"Uh," Alex said, looking shocked enough that it was clear he hadn't shared Amos' insights. "Wow."

Naomi stopped laughing and wiped tears away from the corners of her eyes.

"Busted," she said.

"Look. Guys, it's important that you know this doesn't affect our—" Holden said, but Amos cut him off with a snort.

"Hey, Alex," Amos said.

"Yo," Alex replied.

"XO boning the captain going to make you a really shitty pilot?"

"Don't believe it will," Alex said with a grin, exaggerating his drawl.

"And, oddly enough, I don't feel the need to be a lousy mechanic."

Holden tried again. "I think it's important that—"

"Cap'n?" Amos continued, ignoring him. "Consider that no one gives a fuck, it won't stop us from doing our jobs, and just enjoy it, since we'll probably all be dead in a few days anyway."

Naomi started laughing again.

"Fine," she said. "I mean, everyone knows I'm only doing it to get a promotion. Oh, wait, right. Already the second-in-command. Hey, can I be captain now?"

"No," Holden said, laughing. "It's a shit job. I'd never ask you to do it."

Naomi grinned and shrugged. *See? I'm not always right.* Holden glanced at Alex, who was looking at him with genuine affection, clearly happy about the idea of him and Naomi together. Everything seemed right.

Eros spun like a potato-shaped top, its thick skin of rock hiding the horrors inside. Alex brought them in close to do a thorough scan of the station. The asteroid swelled on Holden's screen until it looked close enough to touch. At the other ops station, Naomi swept the surface with ladar, looking for anything that might pose a danger to the Tycho freighter crews, still a few days behind. On Holden's tactical display, the UNN science ship continued to flare in a braking maneuver toward Eros, its escort right beside it.

"Still not talking, huh?" Holden asked.

Naomi shook her head, then tapped on her screen and sent the comm's monitoring information to his workstation.

"Nope," she said. "But they see us. They've been bouncing radar off of us for a couple hours now."

Holden tapped his fingers on the arm of his chair and thought about the choices. It was possible that the hull modifications Tycho had made to the *Roci* were fooling the Earth corvette's recognition software. They might just ignore the *Roci,* thinking she was a Belter gas runner that happened to be hanging around. But the *Roci* was running without a transponder, which made her illegal no matter what hull configuration she was showing. That the corvette wasn't trying to warn off a ship that was running dark made him nervous. The Belt and the inner planets were in a shooting war. A Belter ship with no identification was hanging around Eros while two Earth ships flew toward it. No way any captain with half a brain would just ignore them.

The corvette's silence meant something else.

"Naomi, I have a feeling that corvette is going to try and blow us up," Holden said with a sigh.

"It's what I'd do," she replied.

Holden tapped one last complicated rhythm on his chair, then put his headset on.

"All right, I guess I make the first overture, then," he said.

Not wishing to make their conversation public, Holden targeted the Earther corvette with the *Rocinante*'s laser array and signaled a generic linkup request. After a few seconds, the *link established* light went green, and his earplugs began to hiss with faint background static. Holden waited, but the UN ship offered no greeting. They wanted him to speak first.

He flicked off his mic, switching to the shipwide comm.

"Alex, get us moving. One g for now. If I can't bluff this guy, it'll be a shooting match. Be ready to open her up."

"Roger," drawled Alex. "Goin' on the juice, just in case."

Holden glanced over at Naomi's station, but she'd already switched to her tactical screen and had the *Roci* plotting firing solutions and jamming tactics on the two approaching ships. Naomi had been in only one battle, but she was reacting now like a seasoned veteran. He smiled at her back, then turned around before she had time to realize he was staring.

"Amos?" he said.

"Locked down and shipshape down here, Cap. The *Roci*'s pawing at the turf. Let's go kick some ass."

Let's hope we don't have to, Holden thought.

He turned his mic back on.

"This is Captain James Holden of the *Rocinante,* calling the captain of the approaching United Nations Navy corvette, call sign unknown. Please respond."

There was a static-filled pause, followed by "*Rocinante.* Leave our flight path immediately. If you do not begin moving away from Eros at best possible speed, you will be fired upon."

The voice was young. An aging corvette with the tedious task of following an asteroid-mapping ship around wouldn't be a much sought after command. The captain was probably a lieutenant without patrons or prospects. He'd be inexperienced, but he might see a confrontation as an opportunity to prove himself to his superiors. And that made the next few moments treacherous to navigate.

"Sorry," said Holden. "Still don't know your call sign, or your name. But I can't do what you want. In fact, I can't let anyone land on Eros. I'm going to need you to stop approaching the station."

"*Rocinante,* I don't think you—"

Holden took control of the *Roci*'s targeting system and began painting the approaching corvette with its targeting laser.

"Let me explain what's happening here," he said. "Right now, you're looking at your sensors, and you're seeing what looks like a thrown-together gas freighter that's giving your ship-recognition software fits. And all of a sudden, meaning *right now,* it's painting you with a state-of-the-art target-acquisition system."

"We don't—"

"Don't lie. I know that's what's happening. So here's the deal. Despite how it looks, my ship is newer, faster, tougher, and better armed than yours. The only way for me to really prove that is to open fire, and I'm hoping not to do that."

"Are you threatening me, *Rocinante*?" the young voice on Holden's headset said, its tone hitting just the right notes of arrogance and disbelief.

"You? No," said Holden. "I'm threatening the big, fat, slow-moving, and unarmed ship you're supposed to be protecting. You keep flying toward Eros, and I will unload everything I've got at it. I guarantee we will blow that flying science lab out of the sky. Now, it's possible you might get us while we do it, but by then your mission is screwed anyway, right?"

The line went silent again, only the hiss of background radiation letting him know his headset hadn't died.

When his answer came, it came on the shipwide comms.

Alex said, "They're stoppin', Captain. They just started hard brakin'. Tracking says they'll be relative stopped about two million klicks out. Want me to keep flyin' toward 'em?"

"No, bring us back to our stationary position over Eros," Holden replied.

"Roger that."

"Naomi," Holden said, spinning his chair around to face her. "Are they doing anything else?"

"Not that I can see through the clutter of their exhaust. But they could be tightbeaming messages the other direction and we'd never know," she said.

Holden flipped the shipwide comm off. He scratched his head for a minute, then unbuckled his restraints.

"Well, we stopped them for now. I'm going to hit the head and then grab a drink. Want anything?"

"He's not wrong, you know," Naomi said later that night.

Holden was floating in zero g on the ops deck, his station a few feet away. He'd turned down the deck lights, and the cabin was as dim as a moonlit night. Alex and Amos were sleeping two decks below. They might as well have been a million light-years away. Naomi was floating near her own station, two meters away, her hair unbound and drifting around her like a black cloud. The panel behind her lit her face in profile: the long forehead, flat nose, large lips. He could tell that her eyes were closed. He felt like they were the only two people in the universe.

"Who's not wrong?" he said, just to be saying something.

"Miller," she replied as though it were obvious.

"I have no idea what you're talking about."

Naomi laughed, then swatted with one hand to rotate her body and face him in the air. Her eyes were open now, though with the panel lights behind her, they were visible only as black pools in her face.

"I've been thinking about Miller," she said. "I treated him badly on Tycho. Ignored him because you were angry. I owed him better than that."

"Why?"

"He saved your life on Eros."

Holden snorted, but she kept going anyway.

"When you were in the navy," she finally said, "what were you supposed to do when someone went crazy on the ship? Started doing things that endangered everyone?"

Thinking they were talking about Miller, Holden said, "You restrain him and remove him as a danger to the ship and crew. But Fred didn't—"

Naomi cut him off.

"What if it's wartime?" she said. "The middle of a battle?"

"If he can't be easily restrained, the chief of the watch has an obligation to protect the ship and crew by whatever means necessary."

"Even shooting him?"

"If that's the only way to do it," Holden replied. "Sure. But it would only be in the most pressing circumstances."

Naomi nodded with her hand, sending her body slowly twisting the other way. She stopped her motion with one unconscious gesture. Holden was pretty good in zero g, but he'd never be that good.

"The Belt is a network," Naomi said. "It's like one big distributed ship. We have nodes that make air, or water, or power, or structural materials. Those nodes may be separated by millions of kilometers of space, but that doesn't make them any less interconnected."

"I see where this is going," Holden said with a sigh. "Dresden was a madman on the ship, Miller shot him to protect the rest of us. He gave me that speech back on Tycho. Didn't buy it then either."

"Why?"

"Because," Holden said. "Dresden wasn't an immediate threat. He was just an evil little man in an expensive suit. He didn't have a gun in his hand, or his finger on a bomb trigger. And I will never trust a man who believes he has the right to unilaterally execute people."

Holden put his foot against the bulkhead and tapped off just hard enough to float a few feet closer to Naomi, close enough to see her eyes, read her reaction to him.

"If that science ship starts flying toward Eros again, I will throw every torpedo we have at it, and tell myself I was protecting the rest of the solar system from what's on Eros. But I won't just start shooting at it now, on the idea that it *might* decide to head to Eros again, because that's murder. What Miller did was murder."

Naomi smiled at him, then grabbed his flight suit and pulled him close enough for a kiss.

"You might be the best person I know. But you're totally uncompromising on what you think is right, and that's what you hate about Miller."

"I do?"

"Yes," she said. "He's totally uncompromising too, but he has different ideas on how things work. You hate that. To Miller, Dresden was an active threat to the ship. Every second he stayed alive endangered everyone else around him. To Miller, it was self-defense."

"But he's wrong. The man was helpless."

"The man talked the UN Navy into giving his company state-of-the-art ships," she said. "He talked his company into murdering a million and a half people. Everything Miller said about why the protomolecule is better off with us was just as true about Dresden. How long is he in an OPA lockup before he finds the jailer who can be bought?"

"He was a prisoner," Holden said, feeling the argument slipping away from him.

"He was a monster with power, access, and allies who would have paid any price to keep his science project going," Naomi said. "And I'm telling you as a Belter, Miller wasn't wrong."

Holden didn't answer; he just continued to float next to Naomi, keeping himself in her orbit. Was he angrier about the killing of Dresden or about Miller's making a decision that disagreed with him?

And Miller had known. When Holden had told him to find his own ride back to Tycho, he'd seen it in the detective's sad basset hound face. Miller had known it was coming, and had made no attempt to fight or argue. That meant that Miller had made his choice fully cognizant of the cost and ready to pay it. That meant something. Holden wasn't sure exactly what, but something.

A red telltale began flashing on the wall, and Naomi's panel woke up and began throwing data onto the screen. She pulled herself down to it using the back of her chair, then tapped out several quick commands.

"Shit," she said.

"What is it?"

"The corvette or science ship must have called for help," Naomi said, pointing at her screen. "We've got ships on their way from all over the system."

"How many are coming?" Holden asked, trying to get a better look at her screen.

Naomi made a small sound in the back of her throat, halfway between a chuckle and a cough.

"At a guess? All of them."

Chapter Forty-Eight: Miller

You are, and you aren't," the Eros feed said through a semi-random drumming of static. "You are, and you aren't. You are, and you aren't."

The little ship shuddered and bumped. From a crash couch, one of the OPA techs called out a string of obscenities remarkable more for inventiveness than actual rancor. Miller closed his eyes, trying to keep the micro-g adjustments of their nonstandard docking from nauseating him. After days of joint-aching acceleration and an equally bruising braking routine, the small shifts and movements felt arbitrary and strange.

"You are, are, are, are, *are, are, are . . .*"

He'd spent some time listening to the newsfeeds. Three days after they'd left Tycho, the news of Protogen's involvement with Eros broke. Amazingly, Holden hadn't been the one to do it. Since then, the corporation had gone from total denial, to blaming a rogue subcontractor, to claiming immunity under an Earth defense secrets statute. It didn't sound good for them. Earth's blockade of Mars was still in place, but attention had shifted to the power struggle within Earth, and the Martian navy had slowed its burn, giving the Earth forces a little more breathing room before any permanent decisions had to be made. It looked like they'd postponed Armageddon for a few weeks, anyway. Miller found he could take a certain joy in that. It also left him tired.

More often, he listened to the voice of Eros. Sometimes he watched the video feeds too, but usually, he just listened. Over the hours and days, he began to hear, if not patterns, at least common structures. Some of the voices spooling out of the dying station were consistent—broadcasters and entertainers who were over-represented in the audio files archives, he guessed. There seemed to be some specific tendencies in, for want of a better term, the music of it too. Hours of random, fluting static and snatched bits of phrases would give way, and Eros would latch on to some word or phrase, fixating on it with greater and greater intensity until it broke apart and the randomness poured back in.

"... are, are, are, ARE, ARE, ARE..."

Aren't, Miller thought, and the ship suddenly shoved itself up, leaving Miller's stomach about half a foot from where it had been. A series of loud clanks followed, and then the brief wail of a Klaxon.

"Dieu! Dieu!" someone shouted. "Bombs son vamen roja! Going to fry it! Fry us toda!"

There was the usual polite chuckle that the same joke had occasioned over the course of the trip, and the boy who'd made it—a pimply Belter no more than fifteen years old—grinned with pleasure at his own wit. If he didn't stop that shit, someone was going to beat him with a crowbar before they got back to Tycho. But Miller figured that someone wasn't him.

A massive jolt forward pushed him hard into the couch, and then gravity was back, the familiar 0.3 g. Maybe a little more. Except that with the airlocks pointing toward ship's down, the pilot had to grapple the spinning skin of Eros' belly first. The spin gravity made what had been the ceiling the new floor; the lowest rank of couches was now the top; and while they rigged the fusion bombs to the docks, they were all going to have to climb up onto a cold, dark rock that was trying to fling them off into the vacuum.

Such were the joys of sabotage.

Miller suited up. After the military-grade suits of the *Rocinante,* the OPA's motley assortment of equipment felt like third-hand clothes. His suit smelled of someone else's body, and the Mylar faceplate had a deformation where it had cracked and been repaired. He didn't like thinking about what had happened to the poor bastard who'd been wearing it. The magnetic boots had a thick layer of corroded plastic and old mud between the plates and a triggering mechanism so old that Miller could feel it click on and off even before he moved his foot. He had the image of the suit locking on to Eros and never letting go.

The thought made him smile. *You belong with me,* his own private Julie had said. It was true, and now that he was here, he felt perfectly certain that he wasn't going to leave. He'd been a cop for too long, and the idea of trying to reconnect to humanity again filled him with the presentiment of exhaustion. He was here to do the last part of his job. And then he was done.

"Oi! Pampaw!"

"I'm coming," Miller said. "Hold your damn horses. It's not like the station's going anyplace."

"A rainbow is a circle you can't see. Can't see. Can't see," Eros said in a child's singsong voice. Miller turned down the volume of his feed.

The rocky surface of the station had no particular purchase for the suits and control waldoes. Two other ships had made polar landings where there was no spin gravity to fight against, but the Coriolis would leave everyone with a subliminal nausea. Miller's team had to keep to the exposed metal plates of the dock, clinging like flies looking down into the starlit abyss.

Engineering the placement of the fusion bombs wasn't trivial work. If the bombs didn't pump enough energy into the station, the surface might cool enough to give someone another chance to put a science team on it before the penumbra of the sun swallowed it and whatever parts of the *Nauvoo* were still clinging to it. Even with the best minds of Tycho, there was still the chance that the detonations wouldn't sync up. If the pressure waves traveling through the rock amplified in ways they hadn't anticipated, the station could crack open like an egg, spreading the protomolecule through the wide, empty track of the solar system like scattering a handful of dust. But the difference between success and disaster might be literally a question of meters.

Miller crawled up the airlock and out to the station surface. The first wave of technicians were setting up resonance seismographs, the glow of the work lights and readouts the brightest thing in the universe. Miller set his boots on a wide swath of a ceramic steel alloy and let the spin stretch the kinks out of his back. After days in the acceleration couch, the freedom felt euphoric. One of the techs raised her hands, the physical Belter idiom that called for attention. Miller upped the suit volume.

"...insectes rampant sur ma peau..."

With a stab of impatience, he switched from the Eros feed to the team channel.

"Got to move," a woman's voice said. "Too much splashback here. We have to get to the other side of the docks."

"These go on for almost two kilometers," Miller said.

"Is," she agreed. "We can unmoor and move the ship under power or we can tow it. We've got enough lead line."

"Which one's fastest? We don't have a lot of spare time here."

"Towing."

"Tow it, then," Miller said.

Slowly, the ship rose, twenty small, crawling transport drones clinging to leads like they were hauling a great metallic zeppelin. The ship was going to stay with him, here on the station, strapped to the rock like a sacrifice to the gods. Miller walked with the crew as they crossed the wide, closed bay doors. The only sounds were the tapping of his soles as the electromagnets jolted onto the surface and then a tick when they let go again. The only smells were of his own body and the fresh plastic of the air recycler. The metal under his feet shone like someone had cleaned it. Any dust or pebbles had been hurled away long ago.

They worked fast to place the ship, arm the bombs, and fit the security codes, everyone tacitly aware of the great missile that had been the *Nauvoo* speeding toward them.

If another ship came down and tried to disarm the trap, the ship would send synchronizing signals to all the other OPA bomb ships studding the moon's surface. Three seconds later, the surface of Eros would be scrubbed clean. The spare air and supplies were loaded off the ship, bundled together and ready for reclamation. No reason to waste the resources.

Nothing horrific crawled out of an airlock and tried to attack the crew, which made Miller's presence during the mission entirely superfluous. Or maybe not. Maybe it was just a ride.

When everything was done that could be, Miller sent the all clear, relayed through the now-dead ship's system. The return transport appeared slowly, a dot of light that grew gradually brighter and then spread, the null-g boarding web strung out like scaffolding. At the new ship's word, Miller's team turned off their boots and fired simple maneuvering thrusters either from their suits or, if the suits were too old, from shared ablative evacuation shells. Miller watched them drop away.

"Call va and roll, Pampaw," Diogo said from someplace. Miller wasn't sure which of them he was at this distance. "This tube don't sit."

"I'm not coming," Miller said.

"Sa que?"

"I decided. I'm staying here."

There was a moment of silence. Miller had been waiting for this. He had the security codes. If he needed to crawl back into the shell of their old ship and lock the door behind him, he could. But he didn't want to. He'd prepared his arguments: He would only be going back to Tycho as a political pawn for Fred Johnson's negotiations; he was tired and old in a way that years didn't describe; he'd already died on Eros once, and he wanted to be here to finish it. He'd earned that much. Diogo and the others owed it to him.

He waited for the boy to react, to try to talk him out of it.

"All correct, then," Diogo said. "Buona morte."

"Buona morte," Miller said, and shut off his radio. The universe was silent. The stars below him shifted slowly but perceptibly as the station he hung from spun. One of those lights was the *Rocinante*. Two others were the ships Holden had been sent out to stall. Miller couldn't pick them out. Julie floated beside him, her dark hair floating in the vacuum, the stars shining through her. She looked peaceful.

If you had it to do again, she said. *If you could do it all over from the beginning?*

"I wouldn't," he said.

He watched the OPA transport ship start up its engines, glowing gold and white, and pull away until it was a star again. A small one. And then lost. Miller turned and considered the dark, empty moonscape and the permanent night.

He just needed to be with her for another few hours, and they would both be safe. They would *all* be safe. It was enough. Miller found himself smiling and weeping, the tears tracking up from his eyes and into his hair.

It's going to be fine, Julie said.

"I know," Miller said.

He stood silently for almost an hour, then turned and made his slow, precarious way back to the sacrificed ship, down the airlock, and into the dim belly. There was enough residual atmosphere that he didn't need to sleep in his suit. He stripped naked, chose an acceleration couch, and curled up on the hard blue gel. Not twenty meters away, five fusion devices powerful enough to outshine the sun waited for a signal. Above him, everything that had once been human in Eros Station changed and re-formed, pouring from one shape to another like Hieronymus Bosch made real. And still almost a day away, the *Nauvoo,* the hammer of God, hurtled toward him.

Miller set his suit to play some old pop tunes he'd enjoyed when he was young and let himself be sung to sleep. When he dreamed, he dreamed he'd found a tunnel at the back of his old hole on Ceres that meant he would at last, at *last,* be free.

His last breakfast was a hard kibble bar and a handful of chocolate scrounged from a forgotten survival pack. He ate it with tepid recycled water that tasted of iron and rot. The signals from Eros were almost drowned by the oscillating frequencies blasting out from the station above him, but Miller made out enough to know where things stood.

Holden had won, much as Miller had expected him to. The OPA was responding to a thousand angry accusations from Earth and Mars and, in the true and permanent style, factions within the OPA itself. It was too late. The *Nauvoo* was due in hours now. The end was coming.

Miller put on his suit for the last time, turned out the lights, and crawled back up the airlock. For a long moment, the exterior release didn't respond, the safety lights glowing red, and he had a stab of fear that he would spend his last moments there, trapped in a tube like a torpedo ready to fire. But he cycled the lock's power, and it opened.

The Eros feed was wordless now, with only a soft murmuring like water over stone. Miller walked out across the wide mouth of the docking bays. The sky above him turned, and the *Nauvoo* rose from the horizon like the sun. His splayed hand held at full arm's length wasn't big enough to cover the glow of its engines. He hung by his boots, watching the ship approach. The phantom Julie watched with him.

If he'd done the math right, the *Nauvoo*'s impact site would be at the center of Eros' major axis. Miller would be able to see it when it happened, and the giddy excitement in his chest reminded him of being young. It would be a show. Oh, it would be something to see. He considered recording it. His suit would be able to make a simple visual file and stream the data out in real time. But no. This was his moment. His and Julie's. The rest of humanity could guess what it had been like if they cared.

The massive glow of the *Nauvoo* filled a quarter of the sky now, and the full circle of it was free of the horizon. The Eros feed's soft murmur shifted to something more clearly synthetic: a rising, spiraling sound that reminded him for no particular reason of the green sweeping radar screens of ancient films. There were voices at the back of it, but he couldn't make out the words or even the language.

The great torch of the *Nauvoo* was a full half of the sky, the stars around it blotted out by the light of full burn. Miller's suit chirped a radiation warning and he shut it off.

A manned *Nauvoo* would never have sustained a burn like that; even in the best couch, the thrust gravity would have pulped bones. He tried to guess how fast the ship would be going when it hit.

Fast enough. That was all that mattered. Fast enough.

There, in the center of the fiery bloom, Miller saw a dark spot, no more than the dot of a pencil's tip. The ship itself. He took a deep breath. When he closed his eyes, the light pressed red through his lids. When he opened them again, the *Nauvoo* had length. Shape. It was a needle, an arrow, a missile. A fist rising from the depths. For the first time in memory, Miller felt awe.

Eros shouted.

"DON'T YOU *FUCKING* TOUCH ME!"

Slowly, the bloom of engine fire changed from a circle to an oval to a great feathery plume, the *Nauvoo* itself showing silver in rough profile. Miller gaped.

The *Nauvoo* had missed. It had turned. It was right now, right *now,* speeding past Eros and not into it. But he hadn't seen any kind of maneuvering rockets fire. And how would you turn something that big, moving that quickly, so abruptly that it would veer off between one breath and the next without also tearing the ship apart? The acceleration g alone...

Miller looked at the stars as if there was some answer written in them. And to his surprise, there was. The sweep of the Milky Way, the infinite scattering of stars were still there. But the angles had changed. The rotation of Eros had shifted. Its relation to the plane of the ecliptic.

For the *Nauvoo* to change course at the last minute without falling apart would have been impossible. And so it hadn't happened. Eros was roughly six hundred cubic kilometers. Before Protogen, it had housed the second-largest active port in the Belt.

And without so much as overcoming the grip of Miller's magnetic boots, Eros Station had dodged.

Chapter Forty-Nine: Holden

H oly shit," said Amos in a flat voice.

"Jim," Naomi said to Holden's back, but he waved her off and opened a channel to Alex in the cockpit.

"Alex, did we just see what my sensors say we saw?"

"Yeah, Cap," the pilot replied. "Radar and scopes are both sayin' Eros jumped two hundred klicks spinward in a little less than a minute."

"Holy shit," Amos repeated in exactly the same emotionless tone. The metallic bang of deck hatches opening and closing echoed through the ship, signaling Amos' approach up the crew ladder.

Holden shook off the flush of irritation he felt at Amos' leaving his post. He'd deal with that later. He needed to be sure that the *Rocinante* and her crew hadn't just experienced a group hallucination.

"Naomi, give me comms," he said.

Naomi turned around in her chair to face him, her face ashen.

"How can you be so calm?" she asked.

"Panic won't help. We need to know what's going on before we can plan intelligently. Please transfer the comms to me."

"Holy shit," Amos said as he climbed into the ops deck. The deck hatch shut with a punctuating bang.

"I don't remember ordering you to leave your post, sailor," Holden said.

"Plan intelligently," Naomi said like they were words in a foreign language that she almost understood. "Plan intelligently."

Amos threw himself at a chair hard enough that the cushioning gel grabbed him and kept him from bouncing off.

"Eros is really fucking big," Amos said.

"Plan intelligently," Naomi repeated, speaking to herself now.

"I mean, *really* fucking big," Amos said. "Do you know how much energy it took to spin that rock up? I mean, it took *years* to do that shit."

Holden put his headset on to drown Amos and Naomi out, and called up Alex again.

"Alex, is Eros still changing velocity?"

"No, Cap. Just sitting there like a rock."

"Okay," Holden said. "Amos and Naomi are vapor locked. How are you doing?"

"Not taking my hands off the stick while that bastard is anywhere in my space, that's for damn sure."

Thank God for military training, Holden thought.

"Good, keep us at a constant distance of five thousand klicks until I say otherwise. Let me know if it moves again, even an inch."

"Roger that, Cap," said Alex.

Holden took off his headset and turned to face the rest of the crew. Amos was looking at the ceiling, ticking points off with his fingers, his eyes unfocused.

"—don't really remember the mass of Eros off the top of my head..." he was saying to no one in particular.

"About seven thousand trillion kilos," Naomi replied. "Give or take. And the heat signature's up about two degrees."

"*Jesus,*" the mechanic said. "I can't do that math in my head. That much mass coming up two degrees like that?"

"A lot," Holden said. "So let's move on—"

"About ten exajoules," Naomi said. "That's just off the top of my head, but I'm not off by an order of magnitude or anything."

Amos whistled.

"Ten exajoules is like, what, a two-gigaton fusion bomb?"

"It's about a hundred kilos converted directly to energy," Naomi said. Her voice began to steady. "Which, of course, we couldn't do. But at least whatever they did wasn't magic."

Holden's mind grabbed on to her words with an almost physical sensation. Naomi was, in fact, about the smartest person he knew. She had just spoken directly to the half-articulated fear he'd been harboring since Eros had jumped sideways: that this was magic, that the protomolecule didn't have to obey the laws of physics. Because if that was true, humans didn't stand a chance.

"Explain," he said.

"Well," she replied, tapping on her keypad. "Heating Eros up didn't move it. So I assume that means it was waste heat from whatever it was they actually did."

"And that means?"

"That entropy still exists. That they can't convert mass to energy with perfect efficiency. That their machines or processes or whatever they use to move seven thousand trillion kilos of rock wastes some energy. About a two-gigaton bomb's worth of it."

"Ah."

"You couldn't move Eros two hundred kilometers with a two-gigaton bomb," Amos said with a snort.

"No, you couldn't," Naomi replied. "This is just the leftovers. Heat by-product. Their efficiency is still off the charts, but it isn't perfect. Which means the laws of physics still hold. Which means it isn't magic."

"Might as well be," Amos said.

Naomi looked at Holden.

"So, we—" he started when Alex interrupted over the shipwide comm.

"Cap, Eros is movin' again."

"Follow it, get me a course and speed as soon as you can," Holden said, turning back to his console. "Amos, get back down to engineering. If you leave it again without a direct order, I'll have the XO beat you to death with a pipe wrench."

The only reply was the hiss of the deck hatch opening and the bang as it closed behind the descending mechanic.

"Alex," Holden said, staring at the data stream the *Rocinante* was feeding him about Eros. "Tell me something."

"Sunward is all we know for sure," Alex replied, his voice still calm and professional. When Holden had been in the military, he'd been officer track right from the start. He'd never been to military pilot school, but he knew that years of training had compartmentalized Alex's brain into two halves: piloting problems and, secondarily, everything else. Matching Eros and getting a course for it was the former. Extra-solar space aliens trying to destroy humanity wasn't a piloting issue and could be safely ignored until he left the cockpit. He might have a nervous breakdown afterward, but until then, Alex would keep doing his job.

"Drop back to fifty thousand klicks and maintain a constant distance," Holden told him.

"Huh," said Alex. "Maintainin' a constant distance might be tough, Cap. Eros just disappeared off the radar."

Holden felt his throat go tight.

"Say again?"

"Eros just disappeared off the radar," Alex was saying, but Holden was already punching up the sensor suite to check for himself. His telescopes showed the rock still moving on its new course toward the sun. Thermal imaging showed it as slightly warmer than space. The weird feed of voices and madness that had been leaking out of the station was still detectable, if faint. But radar said there was nothing there.

Magic, a small voice at the back of his mind said again.

No, not magic. Humans had stealth ships too. It was just a matter of absorbing the radar's energy rather than reflecting it. But suddenly, keeping the asteroid in visual range became all the more important. Eros had shown that it could move fast and maneuver wildly, and it was now invisible to radar. It was entirely possible that a mountain-sized rock could disappear completely.

Gravity began to pile up as the *Roci* chased Eros toward the sun.

"Naomi?"

She looked up at him. The fear was still in her eyes, but she was holding it together. For now.

"Jim?"

"The comm? Could you…?"

The chagrin on her face was the most reassuring thing he'd seen in hours. She shifted control to his station, and he opened a connection request.

"UNN corvette, this is the *Rocinante,* please respond."

"Go ahead, *Rocinante,*" the other ship said after half a minute of static.

"Calling to confirm our sensor data," Holden said, then transmitted the data regarding Eros' movement. "You guys seeing the same thing?"

Another delay, this one longer.

"Roger that, *Rocinante.*"

"I know we were just about to shoot each other and all, but I think we're a little past that now," Holden said. "Anyway, we're chasing the rock. If we lose sight of it, we might never find it again. Want to come with? Might be nice to have some backup if it decides to shoot at us or something."

Another delay, this one almost two minutes long; then a different voice came on the line. Older, female, and totally lacking the arrogance and anger of the young male voice he'd been dealing with so far.

"*Rocinante,* this is Captain McBride of the UNN Escort Vessel

Ravi." *Ah,* thought Holden. *I've been talking to the first officer all along. The captain finally took the horn. That might be a good sign.* "I've sent word to fleet command, but it's a twenty-three minute lag right now, and that rock's putting on speed. You have a plan?"

"Not really, *Ravi.* Just follow and gather intel until we find an opportunity to do something that makes a difference. But if you came along, maybe none of your people will shoot at us accidentally while we figure it out."

There was a long pause. Holden knew that the captain of the *Ravi* was weighing the chance that he was telling the truth against the threat he'd made against their science vessel. What if he was in on whatever was happening? He'd be wondering the same thing in their position.

"Look," he said. "I've told you my name. James Holden. I served as a lieutenant in the UNN. My records should be on file. It'll show a dishonorable discharge, but they'll also show that my family lives in Montana. I don't want that rock to hit Earth any more than you do."

The silence on the other end continued for another few minutes.

"Captain," she said, "I believe my superiors would want me to keep an eye on you. We'll be coming along for the ride while the brains figure this out."

Holden let out a long, noisy exhale.

"Thanks for that, McBride. Keep trying to get your people on the line. I'm going to make a few calls myself. Two corvettes are not going to fix this problem."

"Roger that," the *Ravi* replied, then killed the connection.

"I've opened a connection with Tycho," Naomi said.

Holden leaned back in his chair, the mounting gravity of their acceleration pressing against him. A watery lump was gathering low in his gut, the loose knot telling him that he had no idea what he was doing, that all the best plans had failed, and that the end was near. The brief hope he'd felt was already starting to slip away.

How can you be so calm?

I think I'm watching the end of the human race, Holden

thought. *I'm calling Fred so that it isn't my fault when no one has an idea how to stop it. Of course I'm not calm.*

I'm just spreading the guilt.

"How fast?" Fred Johnson asked incredulously.

"Four g's now and climbing," Holden replied, his voice thick as his throat compressed. "Oh, and it's invisible to radar now."

"*Four g.* Do you know how heavy Eros is?"

"There's, uh, been some discussion," Holden said, only the acceleration keeping his impatience from showing in his voice. "The question is, now what? The *Nauvoo* missed. Our plans are shot to shit."

There was another perceptible increase in pressure as Alex sped the ship up to keep up with Eros. A little while longer and speech wouldn't be possible.

"It's definitely headed for Earth?" Fred asked.

"Alex and Naomi are ninety percent or so. Hard to be totally accurate when we can only use visual data. But I trust them. I'd go to where there are thirty billion new hosts too."

Thirty billion new hosts. Eight of whom were his parents. He imagined Father Tom as a bundle of tubes oozing brown goo. Mother Elise as a rib cage dragging itself across the floor with one skeletal arm. And with that much biomass, what could it do then? Move Earth? Turn out the sun?

"Have to warn them," Holden said, trying not to strangle on his own tongue as he spoke.

"You don't think they know?"

"They see a threat. They may not see the end of all native life in the solar system," Holden said. "You wanted a reason to sit at the table? How about this one: Come together or die."

Fred was quiet for a moment. Background radiation spoke to Holden in mystic whispers full of dire portents while he waited. *Newcomer,* it said. *Hang around for fourteen billion years or so. See what I've seen. Then all this nonsense won't seem so important.*

"I'll see what I can do," Fred said, interrupting the universe's lecture on transience. "In the meantime, what are you going to do?"

Get outrun by a rock and then watch the cradle of humanity die.

"I'm open to suggestions," Holden said.

"Maybe you could detonate some of the surface nukes the demo team put down. Deflect Eros' course. Buy us time."

"They're on proximity fuses. Can't set them off," Holden said, the last word turning into a yelp as his chair stabbed him in a dozen different places and injected him full of fire. Alex had hit them with the juice, which meant Eros was still speeding up, and he was worried they'd all black out. How fast was it going to go? Even on the juice they couldn't sustain prolonged acceleration past seven or eight g without serious risk. If Eros kept this rate of increase up, it would outrun them.

"You can remote detonate," Fred said. "Miller will have the codes. Have the demo team calculate which ones to set off for maximum effect."

"Roger that," Holden said. "I'll give Miller a call."

"I'll work on the inners," Fred said, using the Belter slang without a hint of self-consciousness. "See what I can do."

Holden broke the connection, then linked up to Miller's ship.

"Yo," said whoever was manning the radio there.

"This is Holden, on the *Rocinante.* Give me Miller."

"Uh…" said the voice. "Okay."

There was a click, then static, then Miller saying hello with a faint echo. Still wearing his helmet, then.

"Miller, this is Holden. We need to talk about what just happened."

"Eros moved."

Miller sounded strange, his voice distant, as though he was only barely paying attention to the conversation. Holden felt a flush of irritation but tamped it back down. He needed Miller right now, whether he wanted to or not.

"Look," he said. "I've talked to Fred and he wants us to coordinate with your demo guys. You've got remote codes. If we set off all of them on one side, we can deflect its course. Get your techs on the line, and we'll work it out."

"Huh, yeah, that sounds like a good idea. I'll send the codes along," said Miller, his voice no longer distant, but holding back a laugh. Like a man about to tell the punch line of a really good joke. "But I can't really help you with the techs."

"Shit, Miller, you pissed those people off, too?"

Miller did laugh now, a free, soft sound that someone who wasn't piling on g could afford. If there was a punch line, Holden had missed it.

"Yeah," Miller said. "Probably. But that's not why I can't get them for you. I'm not on the ship with them."

"What?"

"I'm still on Eros."

Chapter Fifty: Miller

What do you mean you're on Eros?" Holden said.

"Pretty much that," Miller said, covering his growing sense of shame with a casual tone of voice. "Hanging upside down outside the tertiary docks, where we moored one of the ships. Feel like a freaking bat."

"But—"

"Funny thing, too. I didn't feel it when the thing moved. You'd think accelerating like that, it would have thrown me off or squashed me flat, one or the other. But there was nothing."

"Okay, hold on. We're coming to get you."

"Holden," Miller said. "Just stop it, all right?"

The silence didn't last more than a dozen seconds, but it carried a wealth of meaning. *It's not safe to bring the* Rocinante *to Eros*, and *I came here to die*, and *Don't make this harder than it is*.

"Yeah, I just…" Holden said. And then: "Okay. Let me…let

me coordinate with the technicians. I'll…Jesus. I'll let you know what they say."

"One thing, though," Miller said. "You're talking about deflecting this sonofabitch? Just keep in mind it's not a rock anymore. It's a ship."

"Right," Holden said. And a moment later: "Okay."

The connection dropped with a tick. Miller checked his oxygen supply. Three hours in-suit, but he could head back to his little ship and refill it well before that. So Eros was moving, was it? He still didn't feel it, but watching the curved surface of the asteroid, he could see micro-asteroids, all coming from the same direction, bouncing off. If the station kept accelerating, they'd start coming more often, more powerfully. He'd need to stay in the ship.

He turned his hand terminal back to the Eros feed. The station beneath him was chirping and muttering, long slow vowel sounds radiating out from it like recorded whale song. After the angry words and static, the voice of Eros sounded peaceful. He wondered what kind of music Diogo's friends would be making out of this. Slow dancing didn't seem like their style. An annoying itch settled in the small of his back, and he shifted in his suit, trying to rub it away. Almost without his noticing it, he grinned. And then laughed. A wave of euphoria passed into him.

There was alien life in the universe, and he was riding on it like a tick on a dog. Eros Station had moved of its own free will and by mechanisms he couldn't begin to imagine. He didn't know how many years it had been since he'd been overwhelmed by awe. He'd forgotten the feeling. He raised his arms to his sides, reaching out as if he could embrace the endless dark vacuum below him.

Then, with a sigh, he turned back toward the ship.

Back in the protective shell, he took off the vac suit and hooked the air supply to the recyclers to charge up. With only one person to care for, even low-level life support would have it ready to go within the hour. The ship batteries were still almost fully charged. His hand terminal chimed twice, reminding him that it was once again time for the anti-cancer meds. The ones he'd earned the last time he'd been on Eros. The ones he'd be on for the rest of his life. Good joke.

The fusion bombs were in the ship's cargo hold: gray square boxes about half again as long as they were tall, like bricks in a mortar of pink adhesive foam. It took Miller twenty minutes of searching through storage lockers to find a can of solvent that still had charge in it. The thin spray from it smelled like ozone and oil, and the stiff pink foam melted under it. Miller squatted beside the bombs and ate a ration bar that tasted convincingly like apples. Julie sat beside him, her head resting weightlessly on his shoulder.

There had been a few times that Miller had flirted with faith. Most had been when he was young and trying out everything. Then when he was older, wiser, more worn, and in the crushing pain of the divorce. He understood the longing for a greater being, a huge and compassionate intelligence that could see everything from a perspective that dissolved the pettiness and evil and made everything all right. He still felt that longing. He just couldn't convince himself it was true.

And still, maybe there was something like a plan. Maybe the universe had put him in the right place at the right time to do the thing that no one else would do. Maybe all the pain and suffering he'd been through, all the disappointments and soul-crushing years wallowing through the worst that humanity had to offer up, had been meant to bring him here, to this moment, when he was ready to die if it bought humanity a little time.

It would be pretty to think so, Julie said in his mind.

"It would," he agreed with a sigh. At the sound of his voice, the vision of her vanished, just another daydream.

The bombs were heavier than he'd remembered. Under a full g, he wouldn't have been able to move them. At only one-third, it was a struggle, but possible. An agonizing centimeter at a time, he dragged one of them onto a handcart and hauled it to the airlock. Eros, above him, sang to itself.

He had to rest before he tackled the hard work. The airlock was thin enough that only the bomb or he could fit through at a time.

He climbed on top of it to get out the outer airlock door, then had to lift the bomb out with straps he rigged from cargo netting. And once out, it had to be tethered to the ship with magnetic clamps to keep Eros' spin from slinging it out into the void. After he'd pulled it out and strapped it to the cart, he stopped to rest for half an hour.

There were more impacts now, a rough sign that Eros was indeed accelerating. Each one a rifle shot, capable of bouncing clean through him or the ship behind him if bad luck sent it in the right direction. But the odds were low of one of the occasional rocks lining up a killing shot with his tiny antlike figure crawling across the surface. Once Eros cleared the Belt, they'd stop, anyway. Was Eros leaving the Belt? He realized he had no idea where Eros was going. He'd assumed it was Earth. Holden would know by now, probably.

His shoulders ached a little from his efforts, but not badly. He worried that he'd overloaded the cart. Its wheels were stronger than his mag boots, but they could still be overcome. The asteroid above him lurched once, a new and unsettling motion that didn't repeat. His hand terminal cut off the Eros feed, alerting him that he had an incoming connection. He looked at it, shrugged, and let the call come through.

"Naomi," he said before she could speak. "How've you been doing?"

"Hey," she said.

The silence between them stretched.

"You talked to Holden, then?"

"I did," she said. "He's still talking about ways to get you off that thing."

"He's a good guy," Miller said. "Talk him out of it for me, okay?"

The silence hung long enough that Miller started to get uncomfortable.

"What are you doing there?" she asked. As if there were an answer for that. As if all his life could be summarized in answer to one simple question. He danced around what she meant and replied only to what she'd said.

"Well, I've got a nuclear bomb strapped to a cargo wagon. I'm hauling it over to the access hatch and taking it into the station."

"Miller—"

"The thing is, we were treating this like a rock. Now everyone knows that's a little simplistic, but it's going to take people time to adjust. Navies are still going to be thinking of this thing like a billiard ball when it's really a rat."

He was talking too fast. The words spilling out of him in a rush. If he didn't give her room, she wouldn't talk. He wouldn't have to hear what she had to say. He wouldn't have to keep her from talking him down.

"It's going to have structure. Engines or control centers. Something. If I truck this thing inside, get it close to whatever coordinates the thing, I can break it. Turn it back into a billiard ball. Even if it's just for a little while, that gives the rest of you a chance."

"I figured," she said. "It makes sense. It's the right thing to do."

Miller chuckled. A particularly solid impact tocked against the ship beneath him, the vibration of it jarring his bones. Gas started venting out of the new hole. The station was moving faster.

"Yeah," he said. "Well."

"I was talking to Amos," she said. "You need a dead man's switch. So that if something happens, the bomb still goes off. If you have the access codes...?"

"I do."

"Good. I've got a routine you can put on your hand terminal. You'll need to keep your finger on the select button. If you go away for five seconds, it sends the go signal. If you want, I can upload it to you."

"So I have to wander around the station with my finger mashed on a button?"

Naomi's tone made it an apology. "They might take you out

with a head shot. Or wrestle you down. The longer the gap, the more chance for the protomolecule to disable the bomb before it goes off. If you need more, I can reprogram it."

Miller looked at the bomb resting on its cart just outside the ship's airlock. Its readouts all glowed green and gold. His sigh briefly fogged the inside of his helmet.

"Yeah, no. Five is good. Upload the routine. Am I going to need to tweak it, or is there a simple place I can put the arm-and-fire string?"

"There's a setup section," Naomi said. "It prompts you."

The hand terminal chirped, announcing the new file. Miller accepted it, ran it. It was easy as keying in a door code. Somehow he felt that arming fusion bombs to detonate around him should have been more difficult.

"Got it," he said. "We're good to go. I mean, I still have to move this bastard, but other than that. How fast am I accelerating on this thing, anyway?"

"Eventually it will be faster than the *Roci* can go. Four g and ramping up with no sign of easing off the throttle."

"Can't feel it at all," he said.

"I'm sorry about before," Naomi said.

"It was a bad situation. We did what we had to do. Same as always."

"Same as always," she echoed.

They didn't speak for a few seconds.

"Thanks for the trigger," Miller said. "Tell Amos I appreciate it."

He cut the connection before she could answer. Long goodbyes weren't anyone's strong suit. The bomb rested in the handcart, magnetic clamps in place and a wide woven-steel belt around the whole mess. He moved slowly across the metallic surface of the port docks. If the cart lost its grip on Eros, he wouldn't be strong enough to hold it back. Of course, if one of the increasingly frequent strikes hit him, it would be a lot like getting shot, so waiting around wasn't a good solve either. He put both dangers out of his mind and did the work. For ten nervous minutes, his suit smelled of overheating plastic. All the diagnostics showed within the error bars, and by the time the recyclers cleared it, his air supply still looked good. Another little mystery he wasn't going to solve.

The abyss above him shone with unflickering stars. One of the dots of light was Earth. He didn't know which one.

The service hatch had been tucked in a natural outcropping of stone, the raw-ferrous cart track like a ribbon of silver in the darkness. Grunting, Miller hauled the cart and the bomb and his own exhausted body up around the curve, and spin gravity once again pressed down on his feet instead of stretching his knees and spine. Light-headed, he keyed in the codes until the hatch opened.

Eros lay before him, darker than the empty sky.

He ran the hand terminal connection through the suit, calling Holden for what he expected was the last time.

"Miller," Holden said almost immediately.

"I'm heading in now," he said.

"Wait. Look, there's a way we might be able to get an automated cart. If the *Roci*—"

"Yeah, but you know how it is. I'm already here. And we don't know how fast this sonofabitch can go. We've got a problem we need to fix. This is how we do it."

Holden's hope had been weak, anyway. Pro forma. A gesture and, Miller thought, maybe even heartfelt. Trying to save everyone, right to the last.

"I understand," Holden finally said.

"Okay. So once I've broken whatever the hell I find in there...?"

"We're working on ways to annihilate the station."

"Good. I'd hate to go through the trouble for nothing."

"Is there...Is there anything you want me to do? After?"

"Nah," Miller said, and then Julie was at his side, her hair floating around her like they were underwater. She glowed in more starlight than was actually there. "Wait. Yes. A couple things. Julie's parents. They run Mao-Kwikowski Mercantile. They knew the war was going to start before it did. They've got to have links to Protogen. Make sure they don't get away with it. And if you see them, tell them I'm sorry I didn't find her in time."

"Right," Holden said.

Miller squatted in the darkness. Was there anything else? Shouldn't there be more? A message to Havelock, maybe? Or Muss. Or Diogo and his OPA friends? But then there would have to be something to say.

"Okay," Miller said. "That's it, then. It was good working with you."

"I'm sorry it came down this way," Holden said. It wasn't an apology for what he'd done or said, for what he'd chosen and refused.

"Yeah," Miller said. "But what can you do, right?"

It was as close to goodbye as either of them could get. Miller shut the connection, brought up the script Naomi had sent him, and enabled it. While he was at it, he turned the Eros feed back on.

A soft hushing sound, like fingernails scratching down an endless sheet of paper. He turned on the cart's lights, the dark entrance of Eros brightening to industrial gray, shadows scattering to the corners. His imagined Julie stood in the glare like it was a spotlight, the glow illuminating her and all the structures behind her at the same time, the remnant of a long dream, almost over.

He took off the brakes, pushed, and went inside Eros for the last time.

Chapter Fifty-One: Holden

Holden knew that humans could tolerate extremely high g-forces over short durations. With proper safety systems, professional daredevils had sustained impacts in excess of twenty-five g's and survived. The human body deformed naturally, absorbed energy in soft tissues, and diffused impacts across larger areas.

He also knew that the problem with extended exposure to high g was that the constant pressure on the circulatory system would begin exposing weaknesses. Have a weak spot in an artery that could turn into an aneurysm in forty years? A few hours at seven g might just pop it open now. Capillaries in the eyes started to leak. The eye itself deformed, sometimes causing permanent damage. And then there were the hollow spaces, like the lungs and digestive tract. You piled on enough gravity, and they collapsed.

And while combat ships might maneuver at very high g for

short durations, every moment spent under thrust multiplied the danger.

Eros didn't need to shoot anything at them. It could just keep speeding up until their bodies exploded under the pressure. His console was showing five g, but even as he watched, it shifted to six. They couldn't keep this up. Eros was going to get away. There was nothing he could do about it.

But he still didn't order Alex to stop accelerating.

As if Naomi were reading his mind, WE CAN'T KEEP THIS UP popped up on his console, her user ID in front of the text.

FRED'S WORKING ON IT. THEY MIGHT NEED US TO BE WITHIN RANGE OF EROS WHEN THEY COME UP WITH A PLAN, he replied. Even moving his fingers the millimeters necessary to use the controls built into his chair for exactly this reason was painfully difficult.

WITHIN RANGE FOR WHAT? Naomi typed.

Holden didn't answer. He had no idea. His blood was burning with drugs to keep him awake and alert even while his body was being crushed. The drugs had the contradictory effect of making his brain run at double speed while not allowing him to actually think. But Fred would come up with something. Lots of smart people were thinking about it.

And Miller.

Miller was lugging a fusion bomb through Eros right now. When your enemy had the tech advantage, you came at him as low-tech as you could get. Maybe one sad detective pulling a nuclear weapon on a wagon would slip through their defenses. Naomi had said they weren't magic. Maybe Miller could make it and give them the opening they needed.

Either way, Holden had to be there, even if it was just to see.

FRED, Naomi typed to him.

Holden opened the connection. Fred looked to him like a man suppressing a grin.

"Holden," he said. "How are you guys holding up?"

SIX G'S. SPIT IT OUT.

"Right. So it turns out that the UN cops have been ripping Protogen's network apart, looking for clues as to what the hell's been going on. Guess who showed up as public enemy number one for the Protogen bigwigs? Yours truly. Suddenly all is forgiven, and Earth welcomes me back into her warm embrace. The enemy of my enemy thinks I am a righteous bastard."

GOODY. MY SPLEEN IS COLLAPSING. HURRY UP.

"The idea of Eros crashing into Earth is bad enough. Extinction-level event, even if it's just a rock. But the UN people have been watching the Eros feeds, and it's scaring the shit out of them."

AND.

"Earth is preparing to launch her entire ground-based nuclear arsenal. *Thousands* of nukes. They're going to vaporize that rock. The navy will intercept what's left after the initial attack and sterilize that entire area of space with constant nuclear bombardment. I know it's a risk, but it's what we have."

Holden resisted the urge to shake his head. He didn't want to wind up with one cheek stuck to the chair permanently.

EROS DODGED THE *NAUVOO*. IT'S GOING SIX G'S RIGHT NOW, AND ACCORDING TO NAOMI, MILLER FEELS NO ACCELERATION. WHATEVER IT'S DOING, IT DOESN'T HAVE THE SAME INERTIAL LIMITATIONS WE HAVE. WHAT'S TO STOP IT FROM JUST DODGING AGAIN? AT THESE SPEEDS, THE MISSILES WILL NEVER BE ABLE TO TURN AROUND AND CATCH IT. AND WHAT THE HELL ARE YOU TARGETING ON? EROS DOESN'T REFLECT RADAR ANYMORE.

"That's where you come in. We need you to try bouncing a laser off of it. We can use the *Rocinante*'s targeting system to guide the missiles in."

I HATE TO BREAK IT TO YOU, BUT WE'LL BE OUT OF THIS GAME LONG BEFORE THOSE MISSILES SHOW. WE CAN'T KEEP UP. WE CAN'T GUIDE THE MISSILES IN FOR YOU. AND ONCE WE LOSE VISUAL, NO ONE WILL BE ABLE TO TRACK WHERE EROS IS.

"You might have to put it on autopilot," Fred said.

Meaning *You might all have to die in the seats you're in right now.*

I'VE ALWAYS WANTED TO DIE A MARTYR AND ALL, BUT WHAT MAKES YOU THINK THE ROCI CAN BEAT THIS THING ON ITS OWN? I'M NOT KILLING MY CREW BECAUSE YOU CAN'T COME UP WITH A GOOD PLAN.

Fred leaned toward the screen, his eyes narrowing. For the first time, Fred's mask slipped and Holden saw the fear and helplessness behind it.

"Look, I know what I'm asking, but you know the stakes. This is what we have. I didn't call you to hear how it won't work. Either help or give up. Right now devil's advocate is just another name for asshole."

I'm crushing myself to death, probably doing permanent damage, just because I wouldn't *give up, you bastard. So sorry I didn't sign my crew up to die the minute you said to do it.*

Having to type everything out had the advantage of restraining emotional outbursts. Instead of ripping into Fred for questioning his commitment, Holden just typed LET ME THINK ABOUT IT and cut the connection.

The optical tracking system watching Eros flashed a warning to him that the asteroid was increasing speed again. The giant sitting on his chest added a few pounds as Alex pushed the *Rocinante* to keep up. A flashing red indicator informed Holden that because of the duration they'd spent at the current acceleration, he could expect as much as 12 percent of the crew to stroke out. It would go up. Enough time, and it would reach 100 percent. He tried to remember the *Roci*'s maximum theoretical acceleration. Alex had already flown it at twelve g briefly when they'd left the *Donnager*. The actual limit was one of those trivial numbers, a way to brag about something your ship would never really do. Fifteen g, was it? Twenty?

Miller hadn't felt any acceleration at all. How fast could you go if you didn't even *feel* it?

Almost without realizing he was going to do it, Holden activated the master engine cutoff switch. Within seconds he was in free fall, wracked with coughs as his organs tried to find their original resting places inside his body. When Holden had recovered enough to take one really deep breath, his first in hours, Alex came on the comm.

"Cap, did you kill the engines?" the pilot said.

"Yeah, that was me. We're done. Eros is getting away no matter what we do. We were just prolonging the inevitable, and risking some crew deaths in the process."

Naomi turned her chair and gave him a sad little smile. She was sporting a black eye from the acceleration.

"We did our best," she said.

Holden shoved out of his chair hard enough that he bruised his forearms on the ceiling, then shoved off hard again and pinned his back to a bulkhead by grabbing on to a fire extinguisher mount. Naomi was watching him from across the deck, her mouth a comical O of surprise. He knew he probably looked ridiculous, like a petulant child throwing a tantrum, but he couldn't stop himself. He broke free of his grip on the fire extinguisher and floated into the middle of the deck. He hadn't known he'd been pounding on the bulkhead with his other fist. Now that he did, his hand hurt.

"God dammit," he said. "Just God dammit."

"We—" Naomi started, but he cut her off.

"We did our best? What the hell does that matter?" Holden felt a red haze in his mind, and not all of it was from the drugs. "I did my best to help the *Canterbury,* too. I tried to do the right thing when I let us be taken by the *Donnager.* Did my good intentions mean jack shit?"

Naomi's expression went flat. Now her eyelids dropped, and she stared at him from narrow slits. Her lips pressed together until they were almost white. *They wanted me to kill you,* Holden thought. *They wanted me to kill my crew just in case Eros can't break fifteen g, and I couldn't do it.* The guilt and rage and sorrow played against each other, turning into something thin and unfamiliar. He couldn't put a name to the feeling.

"You're the last person I'd expect to hear self-pity from," she said, her voice tight. "Where's the captain who's always asking, 'What can we do right now to make things better?'"

Holden gestured around himself helplessly. "Show me which button to push to stop everyone on Earth from being killed, I'll push it."

Just as long as it doesn't kill you.

Naomi unbuckled her harness and floated toward the crew ladder.

"I'm going below to check on Amos," she said, then opened the deck hatch. She paused. "I'm your operations officer, Holden. Monitoring communication lines is part of the job. I know what Fred wanted."

Holden blinked, and Naomi pulled herself out of sight. The hatch slammed behind her with a bang that couldn't have been any harder than normal but felt like it was anyway.

Holden called up to the cockpit and told Alex to take a break and get some coffee. The pilot stopped on his way through the deck, looking like he wanted to talk, but Holden just waved him on. Alex shrugged and left.

The watery feeling in his gut had taken root and bloomed into a full-fledged, limb-shaking panic. Some vicious, vindictive, self-flagellating part of his mind insisted on running nonstop movies of Eros hurtling toward Earth. It would come screaming down out of the sky like every religion's vision of apocalypse made real, fire and earthquakes and pestilential rain sweeping the land. But each time Eros hit the Earth in his mind, it was the explosion of the *Canterbury* he saw. A shockingly sudden white light, and then nothing but the sound of ice pebbles rattling across his hull like gentle hail.

Mars would survive, for a while. Pockets of the Belt would hold out even longer, probably. They had a culture of making do, surviving on scraps, living on the bleeding edge of their resources. But in the end, without Earth, everything would eventually die. Humans had been out of the gravity well a long time. Long enough to have developed the technology to cut that umbilical cord, but they'd just never bothered to do it. Stagnant. Humanity, for all its desire to fling itself into every livable pocket it could reach, had become stagnant. Satisfied to fly around in ships built half a century before, using technology that hadn't changed in longer than that.

Earth had been so focused on her own problems that she'd ignored her far-flung children, except when asking for her share of their labors. Mars had bent her entire population to the task of remaking the planet, changing its red face to green. Trying to make a new Earth to end their reliance on the old. And the Belt had become the slums of the solar system. Everyone too busy trying to survive to spend any time creating something new.

We found the protomolecule at exactly the right time for it to do the most damage to us, Holden thought.

It had looked like a shortcut. A way to avoid having to do any of the work, to just jump straight to godhood. And it had been so long since anything was a real threat to humanity outside of itself that no one was even smart enough to be scared. Dresden had said it himself: The things that had made the protomolecule, loaded it into Phoebe, and shot it at the Earth were already godlike back when humanity's ancestors thought photosynthesis and the flagellum were cutting-edge. But he'd taken their ancient engine of destruction and turned the key anyway, because when you got right down to it, humans were still just curious monkeys. They still had to poke everything they found with a stick to see what it did.

The red haze in Holden's vision had taken on a strange strobing pattern. It took him a moment to realize that a red telltale on his panel was flashing, letting him know that the *Ravi* was calling. He kicked off a nearby crash couch, floated back to his station, and opened the link.

"*Rocinante* here, *Ravi,* go ahead."

"Holden, why are we stopped?" McBride asked.

"Because we weren't going to keep up anyway, and the danger of crew casualties was getting too high," he replied. It sounded weak even to him. Cowardly. McBride didn't seem to notice.

"Roger. I'm going to get new orders. Will let you know if anything changes."

Holden killed the connection and stared blankly at the console. The visual tracking system was doing its very best to keep Eros in sight. The *Roci* was a good ship. State of the art. And since Alex had tagged the asteroid as a threat, the computer would do everything in its power to keep track of it. But Eros was a fast-moving, low-albedo object that didn't reflect radar. It could move unpredictably and at high speed. It was just a matter of time before they lost track of it, especially if it wanted to be lost track of.

Next to the tracking information on his console, a small data window opened to inform him that the *Ravi* had turned on its transponder. It was standard practice even for military ships to keep them on when there was no apparent threat or need for stealth. The radio man on the little UNN corvette must have flipped it back on out of habit.

And now the *Roci* registered it as a known vessel and threw it onto the threat display with a gently pulsing green dot and a name tag. Holden looked at it blankly for a long moment. He felt his eyes go wide.

"*Shit,*" Holden said, then opened the shipwide comm. "Naomi, I need you in ops."

"I think I'd rather stay down here for a bit," she replied.

Holden hit the battle station's alert button on his console. The deck lights shifted to red and a Klaxon sounded three times.

"XO Nagata to ops," he said. Let her chew him out later. He'd have it coming. But right now he didn't have any time to waste.

Naomi was on the ops deck in less than a minute. Holden had already buckled back into his crash couch and was pulling up the comm logs. Naomi pushed over to her chair and belted in as well. She gave him an inquiring look—*Are we going to die after all?*—but said nothing. If he said so, she would. He felt a spike of equal parts admiration for and impatience with her. He found what he was looking for in the logs before speaking.

"Okay," he said. "We've had radio contact with Miller after Eros dropped off of radar. Is that right?"

"Yes, that's right," she said. "But his suit isn't powerful enough to transmit through the shell of Eros out to much distance, so one of the moored ships is boosting the signal for him."

"Which means that whatever Eros is doing to kill the radar isn't killing all radio transmissions from outside."

"That seems right," Naomi said, a growing curiosity in her voice.

"And you still have the control codes for the five OPA freighters on the surface, right?"

"Yes, sir." And then a moment later: "Oh, *shit*."

"Okay," Holden said, turning in his chair to face Naomi with a grin. "Why do the *Roci* and every other naval ship in the system have a switch to turn off their transponders?"

"So the enemy can't get a missile lock on the transponder signal and blow them up," she said, sharing his grin now.

Holden spun his chair back around and began opening a comm channel to Tycho Station.

"XO, would you be so kind as to use the control codes Miller gave you to turn those five OPA freighters back on and fire up their transponders? Unless our visitor on Eros can outrun radio waves, I think we've gotten around the acceleration problem."

"Aye, aye, Captain," Naomi replied. Even looking the other way, Holden could hear the smile in her voice, and it melted the last of the ice in his gut. They had a plan. They were going to make a difference.

"Call coming in from the *Ravi*," Naomi said. "You want it before I turn the transponders on?"

"Hell yes."

The line clicked.

"Captain Holden. We've got our new orders. Seems we're going to be chasing that thing a little further."

McBride sounded almost like someone who hadn't just been sent to her death. Stoic.

"You might want to hold off on that for a couple minutes," Holden said. "We have an alternative."

As Naomi activated the transponders on the five OPA freighters

Miller had left moored to the surface of Eros, Holden laid out the plan to McBride and then, on a separate line, Fred. By the time Fred had gotten back to him with an enthusiastic approval of the plan from both him and the UN Naval command, the five freighters were pinging away, telling the solar system where they were. An hour after that, the largest swarm of interplanetary nuclear weapons in the history of humanity had been fired and were winging their way toward Eros.

We're going to win, Holden thought as he watched the missiles take flight like a swarm of angry red dots on his threat display. *We're going to beat this thing*. And what was more, his crew was going to see the end of it. No one else had to die.

Except…

"Miller's calling," Naomi said. "Probably noticed we turned his ships back on."

Holden had a wrenching feeling in his stomach. Miller would be there, on Eros, when those missiles arrived. Not everyone would get to celebrate the coming victory.

"Hey. Miller. How you doing?" he said, not quite able to keep the funereal tone out of his voice.

Miller's voice was choppy, and half drowned by static, but not so garbled that Holden couldn't hear the tone in it and know that he was about to take a piss all over their parade.

"Holden," Miller said. "We have a problem."

Chapter Fifty-Two: Miller

One. Two. Three.

Miller pushed down on the hand terminal, resetting the trigger again. The double doors in front of him had once been one of thousands of quietly automated mechanisms. They had run reliably in their subtle magnetic tracks, maybe for years. Now something black with the texture of tree bark grew like creepers around their sides, deforming the metal. Past them lay the port corridors, the warehouses, the casino. Everything that had been Eros Station and was now the vanguard of an invading alien intelligence. But to reach it, Miller had to pry open a stuck door. In less than five seconds. While wearing an environment suit.

He put the hand terminal down again and reached quickly for the thin crack where the two doors met. One. Two. The door shifted a centimeter, flakes of black matter sifting down. Three.

Four.

He grabbed the hand terminal again, resetting the trigger.

This shit just wasn't going to work.

Miller sat on the ground beside the cart. The Eros feed whispered and muttered, apparently unaware of the tiny invader scratching at the station's skin. Miller took a long, deep breath. Door didn't move. He had to get past it.

Naomi wasn't going to like this.

With his one free hand, Miller loosened the woven metal strap around the bomb until it could rock back and forth a little. Carefully, slowly, he lifted the corner of it. Then, watching the status readouts, he wedged the hand terminal under it, the metal corner digging hard into the touch screen over the enter button. The trigger stayed green. If the station shook or shifted, he'd still have five seconds to get to it.

Good enough.

Braced with both hands, Miller tugged at the doors. More of the black crust fell away as he levered the doors open far enough to see through. The corridor beyond was nearly round; the dark growth had filled in the corners until the passage looked like a huge desiccated blood vessel. The only lights were his suit's headlights and a million tiny luminescent dots that swirled in the air like blue fireflies. When the Eros feed pulsed, growing momentarily louder, the fireflies dimmed and then returned. The environment suit reported breathable air with higher than expected concentrations of argon, ozone, and benzene.

One of the luminescent dots floated past him, swirling on currents he couldn't feel. Miller ignored it, pushing at the doors, widening the gap centimeter by centimeter. He could put in an arm to feel the crust. It seemed solid enough to support the cart. That was a godsend. If it had been thigh-high alien mud, he would have had to find some other way to carry the bomb. It was going to be bad enough hauling the cart up to the rounded surface.

No rest for the wicked, Julie Mao said in his mind. *No peace for the good.*

He went back to work.

By the time he'd shoved the doors wide enough to get through, he was sweating. His arms and back ached. The dark crust had started growing down the corridor, tendrils shooting out toward the airlock, keeping to the edges, where walls met floor or ceiling. The blue glow had colonized the air. Eros was heading out the corridor as quickly as he was heading in. Faster, maybe.

Miller hauled the cart up with both hands, watching the hand terminal closely. The bomb rocked, but not so much it lost its grip on the trigger. Once he was safely in the corridor, he took the terminal back.

One. Two.

The heavy bomb casing had carved a little divot in the touch pad, but it still worked. Miller took the cart handle and leaned forward, the uneven, organic surface beneath him translated into the rough tug and flutter of the cart's vibration.

He'd died here once. He'd been poisoned. Shot. These halls, or ones much like them, had been his battleground. His and Holden's. They were unrecognizable now.

He passed through a wide, nearly empty space. The crust had thinned here, the metal walls of the warehouse showing through in places. One LED still glowed in the ceiling, the cool white light spilling onto the darkness.

The path led him to the casino level, the architecture of commerce still bringing visitors to the same spot. The alien bark was nearly gone, but the space had been transformed. Pachinko machines stood in their rows, half melted or exploded or, like a few, still glittering and asking for the financial information that would unlock the gaudy lights and festive, celebratory sound effects. The card tables were still visible under mushroom caps of clear glutinous gel. Lining the walls and cathedral-high ceilings, black ribs rippled with hairlike threads that glowed at the tips without offering any illumination.

Something screamed, the sound muffled by Miller's suit. The broadcast feed of the station sounded louder and richer now that he was under its skin. He had the sudden, transporting memory of being a child and watching a video feed of a boy who'd been swallowed by a monstrous whale.

Something gray and the size of Miller's two fists together flew by almost too fast to see. It hadn't been a bird. Something scuttled behind an overturned vending machine. He realized what was missing. There had been a million and a half people on Eros, and a large percentage of them had been here, on the casino level, when their own personal apocalypse came. But there were no bodies. Or, no. That wasn't true. The black crust, the millions of dark rills above him with their soft, oceanic glow. Those were the corpses of Eros, re-created. Human flesh, remade. A suit alarm told him he was starting to hyperventilate. Darkness started to creep in at the edge of his vision.

Miller sank to his knees.

Don't pass out, you son of a bitch, he told himself. *Don't pass out, or if you do, at least land so your weight's on the damned trigger.*

Julie put her hand on his. He could almost feel it, and it steadied him. She was right. They were only bodies. Just dead people. Victims. Just another slab of recycled meat, same as every unlicensed whore he'd seen stabbed to death in the cheap hotels on Ceres. Same as all the suicides who'd thrown themselves out of airlocks. Okay, the protomolecule had mutilated the flesh in weird ways. Didn't change what it was. Didn't change what he was.

"When you're a cop," he told Julie, repeating something he'd told every rookie he'd been partnered with in his career, "you don't have the luxury of feeling things. You have to do the job."

So do the job, she said gently.

He nodded. He stood. *Do the job.*

As if in response, the sound in his suit changed, the Eros feed fluting up through a hundred different frequencies before exploding in a harsh flood of what he thought was Hindi. Human voices. *Till human voices wake us,* he thought, without quite being able to recall where the phrase came from.

Somewhere in the station, there was going to be...something.

A control mechanism or a power supply or whatever the proto-molecule was using instead of an engine. He didn't know what it would look like or how it would be defended. He didn't have any idea how it worked, apart from the assumption that if he blew it up, it wouldn't keep going very well.

So we go back, he told Julie. *We go back to what we do know.*

The thing that was growing inside Eros, using the stone skin of the asteroid as its own unarticulated exoskeleton, hadn't cut off the ports. It hadn't moved the interior walls or re-created the chambers and passages of the casino level. So the station's layout should be pretty near what it had always been. Okay.

Whatever it used to drive the station through space, it was using a shitload of energy. Okay.

So find the hot spot. With his free hand, he checked the environment suit. Ambient temperature was twenty-seven degrees: hot but far from unbearable. He walked briskly back toward the port corridor. The temperature dropped by less than a hundredth of a degree, but it did drop. All right, then. He could go to each of the corridors, find which one was hottest, and follow it. When he found a place in the station that was, say, three or four degrees hotter than the rest, that would be the place. He'd roll the cart up beside it, let up his thumb, and count to five.

No problem.

When he got back to the cart, something golden with the soft look of heather was growing around the wheels. Miller scraped it off as best he could, but one of the wheels had still developed a squeak. Nothing to be done about that.

With one hand hauling the cart and the other mashing down on his hand terminal's dead-man's-switch, Miller headed up, deeper into the station.

"She's mine," mindless Eros said. It had been stuck on the phrase for the better part of an hour. "She's *mine.* She's…*mine.*"

"Fine," Miller muttered. "You can have her."

His shoulder ached. The squeak in the cart's wheel had grown worse, the whine of it cutting through the souls-of-the-damned madness of the Eros feed. His thumb was starting to tingle from the constant, relentless pressure of not annihilating himself quite yet. With each level he rose, the spin gravity grew lighter and the Coriolis a little more noticeable. It wasn't quite the same as on Ceres, but it was close and felt like coming home. He found himself looking forward to when the job was done. He imagined himself back in his hole, a six-pack of beer, some music on the speakers that had an actual composer instead of the wild, empty-minded glossolalia of the dead station. Maybe some light jazz.

Who ever thought the idea of light jazz would be appealing?

"Catch me if you can, cocksuckers," Eros said. "I am gone and gone and gone. Gone and gone and gone."

The inner levels of the station were both more familiar and stranger. Away from the mass grave of the casino level, more of Eros' old life showed through. Tube stops still glowed, announcing line errors and counseling patience. Air recyclers hummed. The floors were relatively clean and clear. The sense of near normalcy made the changes stand out eerily. Dark fronds coated the walls with swirling nautilus patterns. Flakes of the stuff drifted down from above, whirling in the spin gravity like soot. Eros still had spin gravity but didn't have gravity from the massive acceleration it was under. Miller chose not to try to figure that out.

A flock of softball-sized spiderlike things crawled through the corridor, leaving a slick sheen of glowing slime behind them. It wasn't until he paused to knock one off the cart that he recognized them as severed hands, the trailing wrist bones charred black and remade. Part of his mind was screaming, but it was a distant one and easy to ignore.

He had to respect the protomolecule. For something that had been expecting prokaryotic anaerobes, it was doing a bang-up job of making do. He paused to check his suit's sensor array. The temperature had risen half a degree since he'd left the casino and a tenth of a degree since he'd entered this particular main hall. The background radiation was also climbing, his poor abused flesh sucking in more rads. The concentration of benzene was going down, and his suit was picking up more exotic aromatic molecules—tetracene, anthracene, naphthalene—with behavior sufficiently strange to confuse the sensors. So it was the right direction. He leaned forward, the cart resisting his pull like a bored kid. As he recalled, the structural layout was roughly like Ceres', and he knew Ceres like he knew his name. One more level up—maybe two—there would be a confluence of services from the lower, high-g levels and the supply and energy systems that did better at lower gravity. It seemed as likely a place to grow a command and control center as any. As good a location for a brain.

"Gone and gone and gone," Eros said. "And gone."

It was funny, he thought, how the ruins of the past shaped everything that came after. It seemed to work on all levels; one of the truths of the universe. Back in the ancient days, when humanity still lived entirely down a well, the paths laid down by Roman legions had become asphalt and later ferroconcrete without ever changing a curve or a turn. On Ceres, Eros, Tycho, the bore of the standard corridor had been determined by mining tools built to accommodate the trucks and lifts of Earth, which had in turn been designed to go down tracks wide enough for a mule cart's axle.

And now the alien—the thing from out in the vast dark—was growing along the corridors, ducts, tube routes, and water pipes laid out by a handful of ambitious primates. He wondered what it would have been like if the protomolecule hadn't been captured by Saturn, had actually found its way into the soup of primordial Earth. No fusion reactors, no navigation drives, no complex flesh to appropriate. What would it have done differently if it hadn't had to build around some other evolution's design choices?

Miller, Julie said. *Keep moving.*

He blinked. He was standing in the empty passageway at the base of an access ramp. He didn't know how long he'd been lost in his own mind.

Years, maybe.

He blew out a long breath and started up the ramp. The corridors above him were reading as considerably hotter than ambient. Almost three degrees. He was getting close. There was no light, though. He took his tingling, half-numbed thumb off the select button, turned on the hand terminal's little utility LED, and got back to the dead man's switch just before the count of four.

"Gone and gone and...and...and and and *and*."

The Eros feed squealed, a chorus of voices chattering in Russian and Hindi clamoring over the old singular voice and being drowned out in turn by a deep creaking howl. Whale song, maybe. Miller's suit mentioned politely that he had half an hour of oxygen left. He shut the alarm down.

The transfer station was overgrown. Pale fronds swarmed along the corridors and twisted into ropes. Recognizable insects—flies, cockroaches, water spiders—crawled along the thick white cables in purposeful waves. Tendrils of something that looked like articulated bile swept back and forth, leaving a film of scurrying larvae. They were as much victim of the protomolecule as the human population. Poor bastards.

"You can't take the razor back," Eros said, and its voice sounded almost triumphant. "You can't take the razor back. She is gone and gone and gone."

The temperature was climbing faster now. It took him a few minutes to decide that spinward might be slightly warmer. He hauled the cart. He could feel the squeaking, a tiny, rattling tremor in the bones of his hand. Between the mass of the bomb and the failing wheel bearings, his shoulders were starting to really ache. Good thing he wasn't going to have to haul this damn thing back down.

Julie was waiting for him in the darkness; the thin beam from his hand terminal cut through her. Her hair floated, spin gravity having, after all, no effect on phantoms of the mind. Her expression was grave.

How does it know? she asked.

Miller paused. Every now and then, all through his career, some daydreamed witness would say something, use some phrase, laugh at the wrong thing, and he'd know that the back of his mind had a new angle on the case.

This was that moment.

"You can't take the razor back," Eros crowed.

The comet that took the protomolecule into the solar system in the first place was a dead drop, not a ship, Julie said, her dark lips never moving. *It was just ballistic. Any ice bullet with the proto-molecule in deep freeze. It was aimed at Earth, but it missed and got grabbed by Saturn instead. The payload didn't steer it. Didn't drive it. Didn't navigate.*

"It didn't need to," Miller said.

It's navigating now. It's going to Earth. How does it know to go to Earth? Where did that information come from? It's talking. Where did that grammar come from?

Who is the voice of Eros?

Miller closed his eyes. His suit mentioned that he only had twenty minutes of air.

"You can't take the *Razorback*! She is gone and gone and gone!"

"Oh fuck," Miller said. "Oh *Jesus.*"

He let go of the cart, turning back toward the ramp and the light and the wide station corridors. Everything was shaking, the station itself trembling like someone on the edge of hypothermia. Only of course it wasn't. The only one shaking was him. It was all in the voice of Eros. It had been there all the time. He should have known.

Maybe he had.

The protomolecule didn't know English or Hindi or Russian or any of the languages it had been spouting. All of that had been in the minds and softwares of Eros' dead, coded in the neurons and grammar programs that the protomolecule had eaten. Eaten, but not destroyed. It had kept the information and languages and complex cognitive structures, building itself on them like asphalt over the roads the legions built.

The dead of Eros weren't dead. Juliette Andromeda Mao was alive.

He was grinning so hard his cheeks ached. With one gloved hand, he tried the connection. The signal was too weak. He couldn't get through. He told his uplink on the surface ship to crank up the power, got a connection.

Holden's voice came over the link.

"Hey. Miller. How you doing?"

The words were soft, apologetic. A hospice worker being gentle to the dying. An incandescent spark of annoyance lit his mind, but he kept his voice steady.

"Holden," he said. "We have a problem."

Chapter Fifty-Three: Holden

Actually, we've sort of figured out how to solve the problem," Holden replied.

"I don't think so. I'm linking you to my suit's med data," Miller said.

A few seconds later, four columns of numbers popped up in a small window on Holden's console. It all looked fairly normal, though there were subtleties that only a med-tech, like Shed, would be able to interpret correctly.

"Okay," Holden said. "That's great. You're getting a little irradiated, but other than that—"

Miller cut him off.

"Am I suffering from hypoxia?" he said.

The data from his suit showed 87 mmHg, comfortably above baseline.

"No," Holden said.

"Anything that would make a guy hallucinate or get demented? Alcohol, opiates. Something like that?"

"Not that I can see," Holden said, growing impatient. "What's this about? Are you seeing things?"

"Just the usual," Miller replied. "I wanted to get that shit out the way, because I know what you're going to say next."

He stopped talking, and the radio hissed and popped in Holden's ear. When Miller spoke again after several seconds of silence, his voice had taken on a different tone. It wasn't quite pleading, but close enough to make Holden shift uncomfortably in his seat.

"She's alive."

There was only one *she* in Miller's universe. Julie Mao. "Uh, okay. Not sure how to respond to that."

"You'll have to take my word that I'm not having a nervous breakdown or psychotic episode or anything like that. But Julie's in here. She's driving Eros."

Holden looked at the suit's medical data again, but it kept reporting normal readings, all the numbers except for radiation comfortably in the green. His blood chemistry didn't even look like he was particularly stressed for a guy carrying a fusion bomb to his own funeral.

"Miller, Julie's dead. We both saw the body. We saw what the protomolecule…did to it."

"We saw her body, sure. We just assumed she was dead because of the damage—"

"She didn't have a *heartbeat*," Holden said. "No brain activity, no metabolism. That's pretty much the definition of *dead*."

"How do we know what dead looks like to the protomolecule?"

"We—" Holden started, then stopped. "We don't, I guess. But no heartbeat, that's a pretty good start."

Miller laughed.

"We've both seen the feeds, Holden. Those rib cages equipped with one arm that drag themselves around, think they have a heartbeat? This shit hasn't been playing by our rules since day one, you expect it to start now?"

Holden smiled to himself. Miller was right.

"Okay, so what makes you think Julie isn't just a rib cage and a mass of tentacles?"

"She might be, but it's not her body I'm talking about," Miller said. "*She's* in here. Her mind. It's like she's flying her old racing pinnace. The *Razorback*. She's been babbling about it on the radio for hours now, and I just didn't put it together. But now that I have, it's pretty goddamn clear."

"Why is she headed toward Earth?"

"I don't know," Miller said. He sounded excited, interested. More alive than Holden had ever heard him. "Maybe the protomolecule wants to get there and it's messing with her. Julie wasn't the first person to get infected, but she's the first one that survived long enough to get somewhere. Maybe she's the seed crystal and everything that the protomolecule's doing is built on her. I don't know that, but I can find out. I just need to find her. Talk to her."

"You need to get that bomb to wherever the controls are and set it off."

"I can't do that," Miller said. Because of course he couldn't.

It doesn't matter, Holden thought. *In a little less than thirty hours, you're both radioactive dust.*

"All right. Can you find your girl in less than" — Holden had the *Roci* do a revised time of impact for the incoming missiles — "twenty-seven hours?"

"Why? What happens in twenty-seven hours?"

"Earth fired her entire interplanetary nuclear arsenal at Eros a few hours ago. We just turned the transponders on in the five freighters you parked on the surface. The missiles are targeting them. The *Roci* is guessing twenty-seven hours to impact based on the current acceleration curve. The Martian and UN navies are on their way to sterilize the area after detonation. Make sure nothing survives or slips the net."

"Jesus."

"Yeah," Holden said with a sigh. "I'm sorry I didn't tell you sooner. I've had a lot going on, and it sort of slipped my mind."

There was another long silence on the line.

"You can stop them," Miller said. "Shut down the transponders."

Holden spun his chair around to face Naomi. Her face had the same *what did he just say?* look that he knew was on his own. She pulled the suit's medical data over to her console, then called up the *Roci*'s medical expert system and began running a full medical diagnostic. The implication was clear. She thought something was wrong with Miller that wasn't immediately apparent from the data they were getting. If the protomolecule had infected him, used him as a last-ditch misdirection…

"Not a chance, Miller. This is our last shot. If we blow this one, Eros can orbit the Earth, spraying brown goo all over it. No way we take that risk."

"Look," Miller said, his tone alternating between the earlier pleading and a growing frustration. "*Julie is in here.* If I can find her, a way to talk to her, I can stop this without the nukes."

"What, ask the protomolecule to pretty please not infect the Earth, when that was what it was designed to do? Appeal to its better nature?"

Miller paused for a moment before speaking again.

"Look, Holden, I think I know what's going on here. This thing was intended to infect single-celled organisms. The most basic forms of life, right?"

Holden shrugged, then remembered there was no video feed and said, "Okay."

"That didn't work, but it's a smart bastard. Adaptive. It got into a human host, a complex multicelled organism. Aerobic. Huge brain. Nothing like what it was built for. It's been improvising ever since. That mess on the stealth ship? That was its first try. We saw what it was doing with Julie in that Eros bathroom. It was learning how to work with us."

"Where are you going with this?" Holden said. There was no time pressure yet, with the missiles still more than a day away, but he couldn't quite keep the impatience out of his voice.

"All I'm saying is Eros now isn't what the protomolecule's

designers planned on. It's their original plan laid over the top of billions of years of our evolution. And when you improvise, you use what you've got. You use what works. Julie's the template. Her brain, her emotions are all over this thing. She sees this run to Earth as a race, and she's crowing about winning. Laughing at you because you can't keep up."

"Wait," Holden said.

"She's not attacking Earth, she's going home. For all we know, she's not heading for Earth at all. Luna, maybe. She grew up there. The protomolecule piggybacked on her structure, her brain. And so she infected it as much as it infected her. If I can make her understand what's really going on, then maybe I can negotiate with her."

"How do you know that?"

"Call it a hunch," Miller said. "I'm good with hunches."

Holden whistled, the entire situation doing a flip-flop in his head. The new perspective was dizzying.

"But the protomolecule still wants to obey its program," Holden said. "And we have no idea what that is."

"I can damn sure tell you it isn't wiping humans out. The things that shot Phoebe at us two billion years ago didn't know what the hell humans were. Whatever it wants to do needed biomass, and it's got that now."

Holden couldn't stop himself from snorting at that.

"So, what? They don't mean us any harm? Seriously? You think if we explain that we'd rather not have it land on Earth, then it will just agree and go somewhere else?"

"Not it," Miller said. "Her."

Naomi looked up at Holden, shaking her head. She wasn't seeing anything organic wrong with Miller either.

"I've been working this case for, shit, almost a year," Miller said. "I've climbed into her life, read her mail, met her friends. I know her. She's about as independent as a person can be, and she loves us."

"Us?" Holden asked.

"People. She loves humans. She gave up being the little rich girl and joined the OPA. She backed the Belt because it was the right thing to do. No way she kills us if she knows that's what's happening. I just need to find a way to explain. I can do this. Give me a chance."

Holden ran a hand through his hair, grimacing at the accumulating grease. A day or two at high g was not conducive to regular showering.

"Can't do it," Holden said. "Stakes are too high. We're going ahead with the plan. I'm sorry."

"She'll beat you," Miller said.

"What?"

"Okay, maybe she won't. You've got a shitload of firepower. But the protomolecule's figured out how to get around inertia. And Julie? She's a fighter, Holden. If you take her on, my money's on her."

Holden had seen the video of Julie fighting off her attackers on board the stealth ship. She'd been methodical and ruthless in her own defense. She'd fought without giving quarter. He'd seen the wildness in her eyes when she felt trapped and threatened. Only her attackers' combat armor had kept her from doing a lot more damage before they took her down.

Holden felt the hair on the back of his neck stand up at the idea of Eros actually fighting. So far it had been content to run from their clumsy attacks. What happened when it went to *war*?

"You could find her," Holden said, "and use the bomb."

"If I can't get through to her," Miller said, "that's my deal. I'll find her. I'll talk to her. If I can't get through, I'll take her out, and you can turn Eros into a cinder. I'm fine with that. But you have to give me time to try it my way first."

Holden looked at Naomi looking back at him. Her face was pale. He wanted to see the answer in her expression, to know what he should do based on what she thought. He didn't. It was his call.

"Do you need more than twenty-seven hours?" Holden finally asked.

He heard Miller exhale loudly. There was gratitude in his voice that was, in its own way, worse than the pleading had been.

"I don't know. There are a couple thousand kilometers of tunnels down here, and none of the transit systems work. I have to walk everywhere pulling this damn wagon. Not to mention the fact that I don't really know what I'm even looking for. But give me a little time, I'll figure it."

"And you know that if this doesn't work, you'll have to kill her. Yourself and Julie?"

"I know."

Holden had the *Roci* calculate how long it would take Eros to reach the Earth at the current rate of acceleration. The missiles from Earth were covering the distance a lot faster than Eros was. The IPBMs were just overpowered Epstein drives with nuclear bombs riding up front. Their acceleration limits were the functional limits of the Epstein drive itself. If the missiles didn't arrive, it would still take nearly a week for Eros to get to Earth, even if it kept a constant rate of acceleration.

There was some flexibility in there.

"Hold on, let me work something out here," Holden said to Miller, then muted the connection. "Naomi, the missiles are flying in a straight line toward Eros, and the *Roci* thinks they'll intercept it in about twenty-seven hours, give or take. How much time do we buy if we turn that straight line into a curve? How much of a curve can we do and still give the missiles a chance to catch Eros before it gets too close?"

Naomi tipped her head to one side, looking at him suspiciously through narrowed eyes.

"What are you about to do?" she said.

"Maybe give Miller a chance to head off the first interspecies war."

"You trust *Miller*?" she said with surprising vehemence. "You think he's insane. You threw him off the ship because you thought he was a psychopath and a killer, and now you're going to let him speak for humanity to an alien God-thing that wants to rip us to shreds?"

Holden had to suppress a smile. Telling an angry woman how

attractive her anger made her would make it stop being cute very quickly. And besides that, he needed it to make sense to her. That was how he'd know if he was right.

"You told me once that Miller was right, even when I thought he was wrong."

"I didn't make it a blanket statement," Naomi said, spacing her words out like she was speaking to an idiot child. "I said he was right to shoot Dresden. That doesn't mean Miller's *stable*. He's in the process of committing suicide, Jim. He's fixated on this dead girl. I can't even begin to imagine what might be going through his head right now."

"Agreed. But he's there, on the scene, and he's got a keen eye for observation and just plain figuring shit out. This guy tracked us to Eros based on the ship name we picked. That's pretty damned impressive. He'd never even met me, and he knew me well enough from researching me to know I'd like naming my ship after Don Quixote's horse."

Naomi laughed. "Really? Is that where that comes from?"

"So when he says that he knows Julie, I believe him."

Naomi started to say something, then paused.

"You think she'll beat the nukes?" Naomi said, more softly.

"He thinks she can. And he thinks he can talk her into not killing us all. I have to give him that chance. I owe it to him."

"Even if it means killing Earth?"

"No," Holden said. "Not that much."

Naomi paused again. Her anger faded.

"So delay the impact, not abort," Naomi said.

"Buy him some time. How much can we get?"

Naomi frowned, looking at the readouts. He could almost see the options clicking through her mind. She smiled, her fierceness gone now, replaced by the mischievous look she got when she knew she was being really clever.

"As much as you want."

"You want to do what?" Fred asked.

"Pull the nukes off course for a while to buy Miller some time, but not so much that we can't still use them to destroy Eros if we need to," Holden said.

"It's simple," Naomi added. "I'm sending you detailed instructions."

"Give me the overview," Fred said.

"Earth has targeted their missiles on the five freighter transponders on Eros," Naomi said, pulling her plan up as an overlay on the comm video. "You have ships and stations all over the Belt. You use the transponder reconfiguring program you gave us way back when, and you keep shifting those transponder codes to ships or stations along these vectors to pull the missiles into a long arc that eventually wraps back around to Eros."

Fred shook his head.

"Won't work. The minute UNN Command sees we're doing it, they'll just tell the missiles to stop following those particular codes, and they'll try to figure out some other way to target Eros," he said. "And they'll also be really pissed at us."

"Yeah, they're going to be pissed all right," Holden said. "But they're not going to get their missiles back. Just before you start leading the missiles off course, we're going to launch a massive hacking attempt from multiple locations on the missiles."

"So they'll assume an enemy is trying to trick them, and shut down mid-flight reprogramming," Fred said.

"Yep," Holden replied. "We'll tell them we're going to trick them so they stop listening, and once they're not listening, we'll trick them."

Fred shook his head again, this time giving Holden the vaguely frightened look of a man who wanted to back slowly out of the room.

"There is no way in hell I am going along with this," he said. "Miller isn't going to work some magical deal with the aliens. We're going to wind up nuking Eros no matter what. Why delay the inevitable?"

"Because," Holden said. "I'm starting to think it might be less dangerous this way. If we use the missiles without taking out Eros' command center…brain…whatever, we don't know if it'll work, but I'm pretty sure our chances go down. Miller's the only one who can do that. And these are his terms."

Fred said something obscene.

"If Miller doesn't manage to talk to it, he'll take it out. I do trust him for that," Holden said. "Come on, Fred, you know these missile designs as well as I do. Better. They put enough fuel pellets in those drives to fly around the solar system twice. We aren't losing anything by giving Miller a little more time."

Fred shook his head a third time. Holden saw his face go hard. He wasn't going to buy it. Before he could say no, Holden said, "Remember that box with the protomolecule samples, and all the lab notes? Want to know what my price is for it?"

"You," Fred said slowly, drawing it out, "are out of your God damn mind."

"Want to buy it or what?" Holden replied. "You want the magic ticket to a seat at the table? You know my price now. Give Miller his chance, and the sample's yours."

"I'd be curious to know how you talked them into it," Miller said. "I was thinking I was probably screwed."

"Doesn't matter," Holden said. "We bought you your time. Go find the girl and save humanity. We'll be waiting to hear back." *And ready to nuke you into dust if we don't* remained unsaid. There was no need.

"I've been thinking about where to go, if I can talk to her," Miller said. He had the already lost hopefulness of a man with a lottery ticket. "I mean, she's got to park this thing somewhere."

If we live. If I can save her. If the miracle is true.

Holden shrugged, even though no one could see it.

"Give her Venus," he said. "It's an awful place."

Chapter Fifty-Four: Miller

I don't and I don't," the voice of Eros muttered. Juliette Mao, talking in her sleep. "I don't and I don't and I don't…"

"Come on," Miller said. "Come *on*, you sonofabitch. *Be* here."

The medical bays were lush and overgrown, black spirals with filaments of bronze and steel climbing the walls, encrusting the examination tables, feeding on the supplies of narcotics, steroids, and antibiotics spilling out of the broken supply cabinets. Miller dug through the clutter with one hand, his suit alarm chiming. His air had the sour taste that came from being through the recyclers too many times. His thumb, still mashed on the dead man's switch, tingled when it wasn't shooting with pain.

He brushed the almost fungal growth off a storage box that wasn't broken yet, found the latch. Four medical gas cylinders: two red, one green, one blue. He looked at the seal. The protomolecule hadn't gotten them yet. Red for anesthetic. Blue nitrogen.

He picked up the green. The sterile shield on the delivery nipple was in place. He took a deep sighing breath of dying air. Another few hours. He put down his hand terminal (*one…two…*), popped the seal (*three…*), fed the nipple into his suit's intake (*four…*), and put a finger on the hand terminal. He stood, feeling the cool of the oxygen tank in his hand while his suit revised his life span. Ten minutes, an hour, four hours. The medical cylinder's pressure hit equality with the suit's, and he popped it off. Four more hours. He'd won himself four more hours.

It was the third time he'd managed an emergency resupply since he'd talked to Holden. The first had been at a fire-suppression station, the second at a backup recycling unit. If he went back down to the port, there would probably be some uncompromised oxygen in some of the supply closets and docked ships. If he went all the way back to the surface, the OPA ships would have plenty.

But there wasn't time for that. He wasn't looking for air; he was looking for Juliette. He let himself stretch. The kinks in his neck and back were threatening to turn into cramps. The CO_2 levels in the suit were still on the high side of acceptable, even with the new oxygen coming into the mix. The suit needed maintenance and a new filter. It'd have to wait. Behind him, the bomb in its cart kept its own counsel.

He had to find her. Somewhere in the maze of corridors and rooms, the dead city, Juliette Mao was driving them back to Earth. He'd tracked four hot spots. Three had been decent candidates for his original plan of vast nuclear immolation: hubs of wire and black alien filament tangling into huge organic-looking nodes. The fourth had been a cheap lab reactor churning on its way to meltdown. It had taken him fifteen minutes to get the emergency shutdown going, and he probably shouldn't have wasted the time. But wherever he went, no Julie. Even the Julie of his imagination was gone, as if the ghost had no place now that he knew the real woman was still alive. He missed having her around, even if she'd only been a vision.

A wave went through the medical bays, all the alien growth rising and falling like iron filings with a magnet passed beneath them. Miller's heart sped up, adrenaline leaking into his blood, but it didn't happen again.

He had to find her. He had to find her soon. He could feel exhaustion grinding at him, little teeth chewing at the back of his mind. He already wasn't thinking as clearly as he should. Back on Ceres, he'd have gone back to his hole, slept for a day, and come back to the problem whole. Not an option here.

Full circle. He'd come full circle. Once, in a different life, he'd taken on the task of finding her; then, when he'd failed, there'd been taking vengeance. And now he had the chance to find her again, to save her. And if he couldn't, he was still pulling a cheap, squeaky-wheeled wagon behind him that would do for revenge.

Miller shook his head. He was having too many moments like this, getting lost in his own thoughts. He took a fresh grip on the cart full of fusion bomb, leaned forward, and headed out. The station around him creaked the way he imagined an old sailing ship might have, timbers bent by waves of salt water and the great tidal tug-of-war between earth and moon. Here, it was stone, and Miller couldn't guess what forces were acting on it. Hopefully nothing that would interfere with the signal between his hand terminal and his cargo. He didn't want to be reduced to his component atoms unintentionally.

It was getting more and more clear that he couldn't cover the whole station. He'd known that from the start. If Julie had gotten herself someplace obscure—hidden in some niche or hole like a dying cat—he wouldn't find her. He'd become a gambler, betting against all hope on drawing the inside straight. The voice of Eros shifted, different voices now, singing something in Hindi. A child's round, Eros harmonizing with itself in a growing richness of voices. Now that he knew to listen for it, he heard Julie's voice threading its way among the others. Maybe it had always been there. His frustration verged on physical pain. She was so close, but he couldn't quite reach her.

He pulled himself back into the main corridor complex. The

hospital bays had been a good place to look for her too. Plausible. Fruitless. He'd looked at the two mercantile bio-labs. Nothing. He'd tried the morgue, the police holding tanks. He'd even gone through the evidence room, bin after plastic bin of contraband drugs and confiscated weapons scattered on the floor like oak leaves in one of the grand parks. It had all meant something once. Each one had been part of a small human drama, waiting to be brought out into the light, part of a trial or at least a hearing. Some small practice for judgment day, postponed now forever. All points were moot.

Something silver flew above him, faster than a bird, and then another, and then a flock, streaming by overhead. Light glittered off the living metal, bright as fish scales. Miller watched the alien molecule improvising in the space above him.

You can't stop here, Holden said. *You have to stop running and get on the right road.*

Miller looked over his shoulder. The captain stood, real and not, where his inner Julie would have been.

Well, that's interesting, Miller thought.

"I know," he said. "It's just...I don't know where she went. And...well, look around. Big place, you know?"

You can stop her or I will, his imaginary Holden said.

"If I just knew where she went," Miller said.

She didn't, Holden said. *She never went.*

Miller turned to look at him. The swarm of silver roiled overhead, chittering like insects or a badly tuned drive. The captain looked tired. Miller's imagination had put a surprising swath of blood at the corner of the man's mouth. And then it wasn't Holden anymore; it was Havelock. The other Earther. His old partner. And then it was Muss, her eyes as dead as his own.

Julie didn't go anyplace. Miller had seen her in the hotel room, back when he still hadn't believed that anything but a bad smell could rise from the grave. Back before. She'd been taken away in a body bag. And then taken somewhere else. The Protogen scientists had recovered her, harvested the protomolecule, and spread

Julie's remade flesh through the station like bees pollinating a field of wildflowers. They'd given her the station, but before they'd done it, they'd put her someplace they thought they would be safe.

Safe room. Until they were ready to distribute the thing, they'd want to contain it. To pretend it could be contained. It wasn't likely they'd have gone to the trouble of cleaning up after they'd gotten what they needed. It wasn't as if anyone else was going to be around to use the space, so chances were good she was still there. That narrowed things.

There would be isolation wards in the hospital, but Protogen wouldn't have been likely to use facilities where non-Protogen doctors and nurses might wonder what was happening. Unnecessary risk.

All right.

They could have set up in one of the manufacturing plants down by the port. There were plenty of places there that required all-waldo work. But again, it would have been at the risk of being discovered or questioned before the trap was ready to spring.

It's a drug house, Muss said in his mind. *You want privacy, you want control. Extracting the bug from the dead girl and extracting the good shit from the poppy seeds might have different chemistry, but it's still crime.*

"Good point," Miller said. "And near the casino level...No, that's not right. The casino was the second stage. The first was the radiation scare. They put a bunch of people in the radiation shelters and cooked them to get the protomolecule good and happy, then *they* infected the casino level."

So where would you put a drug kitchen that was close to the rad shelters? Muss asked.

The roiling silver stream overhead veered left and then right, pouring through the air. Tiny curls of metal began to rain down, drawing thin trails of smoke behind them as they did.

"If I had the access? The backup environment controls. It's an emergency facility. No foot traffic unless someone's running inventory. It's got all the equipment for isolation built in already. Wouldn't be hard."

And since Protogen ran Eros security even before they put the disposable thugs in place, they'd be able to arrange it, Muss said, and she smiled joylessly. *See? I knew you could think that through.*

For less than a second, Muss was gone and Julie Mao—his Julie—was in her place. She was smiling and beautiful. Radiant. Her hair floated around her as if she were swimming in zero g. And then she was gone. His suit alarm warned him about an increasingly corrosive environment.

"Hang tight," he said to the burning air. "I'll be right there."

It was just less than thirty-three hours from the moment he'd realized that Juliette Andromeda Mao wasn't dead to the one when he cycled down the emergency seals and pulled his cart into Eros' backup environmental control facility. The clean, simple lines and error-reducing design of the place still showed under the outgrowth of the protomolecule. Barely. Knots of dark filament and nautilus spirals softened the corners of wall and floor and ceiling. Loops hung from the ceiling like Spanish moss. The familiar LED lights still shone under the soft growth, but more illumination came from the swarm of faint blue dots glowing in the air. His first step onto the floor sank him into a thick carpet up the ankle; the bomb cart would have to stay outside. His suit reported a wild mix of exotic gases and aromatic molecules, but all he smelled was himself.

All the interior rooms had been remade. Transformed. He walked through the wastewater treatment control areas like a scuba diver in a grotto. The blue lights swirled around him as he passed, a few dozen adhering to his suit and glittering there. He almost didn't brush them off the helmet's faceplate, thinking they would smear like dead fireflies, but they only swirled back up into the air. The air recycling monitors still danced and glowed, the thousand alarms and incident reports silhouetting the latticework of protomolecule that covered the screens. Water was flowing somewhere close by.

She was in a hazmat analysis node, lying on a bed of the dark thread that spilled out from her spine until it was indistinguishable from a massive fairy-tale cushion of her own flowing hair. Tiny points of blue light glittered on her face, her arms, her breasts. The bone spurs that had been pressing out of her skin had grown into sweeping, almost architectural connections with the lushness around her. Her legs were gone, lost in the tangle of dark alien webs; she reminded Miller of a mermaid who had traded her fins for a space station. Her eyes were closed, but he could see them shifting and dancing under the lids. And she was breathing.

Miller stood beside her. She didn't have quite the same face as his imagined Julie. The real woman was wider through the jaw, and her nose wasn't as straight as he remembered it. He didn't notice that he was weeping until he tried to wipe the tears away, batting his helmet with a gloved hand. He had to make do with blinking hard until his sight cleared.

All this time. All this way. And here was what he'd come for.

"Julie," he said, putting his free hand on her shoulder. "Hey. Julie. Wake up. I need you to wake up now."

He had his suit's medical supplies. If he needed to, he could dose her with adrenaline or amphetamines. Instead, he rocked her gently, like he had Candace on a sleepy Sunday morning, back when she'd still been his wife, back in some distant, near-forgotten lifetime. Julie frowned, opened her mouth, closed it.

"Julie. You need to wake up now."

She moaned and lifted an ineffectual arm to push him away.

"Come back to me," he said. "You need to come back now."

Her eyes opened. They weren't human anymore—the sclera etched with swirls of red and black, the iris the same luminous blue as the fireflies. Not human, but still Julie. Her lips moved soundlessly. And then:

"Where am I?"

"Eros Station," Miller said. "The place isn't what it used to be. Not even *where* it used to be, but…"

He pressed the bed of filament with his hand, judging it, and then rested his hip at her side like he was sitting on her bed. His body felt achingly tired and also lighter than it should. Not like low gravity. The unreal buoyancy had nothing to do with the weary flesh.

Julie tried to talk again, struggled, stopped, tried again.

"Who are you?"

"Yeah, we haven't officially met, have we? My name's Miller. I used to be a detective for Star Helix Security back on Ceres. Your parents contracted with us, only it was really more a friends-in-high-places thing. I was supposed to track you down, grab you, ship you back down the well."

"Kidnap job?" she said. Her voice was stronger. Her gaze seemed more focused.

"Pretty standard," Miller said, then sighed. "I kind of cocked it up, though."

Her eyes fluttered closed, but she kept talking.

"Something happened to me."

"Yeah. It did."

"I'm scared."

"No, no, no. Don't be scared. It's all right. In an ass-backward kind of way, but it's all right. Look, right now the whole station is heading back for Earth. Really fast."

"I dreamed I was racing. I was going home."

"Yeah, we need to stop that."

Her eyes opened again. She looked lost, anguished, alone. A tear streaked down from the corner of her eye, glowing blue.

"Give me your hand," Miller said. "No, really, I need you to hold something for me."

She lifted her hand slowly, seaweed in a soft current. He took his hand terminal, settled it in her palm, pressed her thumb to the dead man's switch.

"Just hold that there. Don't let it up."

"What is it?" she asked.

"Long story, just don't let up."

His suit alarms shrieked at him when he undid his helmet seals. He turned them off. The air was strange: acetate and cumin and a deep, powerful musk that made him think of hibernating animals. Julie watched him as he stripped off his gloves. Right then, the protomolecule was latching on to him, burrowing into his skin and eyes, getting ready to do to him what it had done to everyone on Eros. He didn't care. He took the hand terminal back and then laced his fingers through hers.

"You're driving this bus, Julie," he said. "Do you know that? I mean, can you tell?"

Her fingers were cool in his, but not cold.

"I can feel...something," she said. "I'm hungry? Not hungry, but...I want something. I want to go back to Earth."

"We can't do that. I need you to change course," Miller replied. What had Holden said? *Give her Venus.* "Head for Venus instead."

"That's not what it wants," she said.

"It's what we've got on offer," Miller said. Then, a moment later: "We can't go home. We need to go to Venus."

She was quiet for a long moment.

"You're a fighter, Julie. You've never let anyone call your shots for you. Don't start now. If we go to Earth—"

"It'll eat them too. The same way it ate me."

"Yeah."

She looked up at him.

"Yeah," he said again. "Like that."

"What happens on Venus?"

"We die maybe. I don't know. But we don't take a lot of people with us, and we make sure no one gets a hold of this crap," he said, gesturing at the grotto around them. "And if we don't die, then... well, that'll be interesting."

"I don't think I can."

"You can. The thing that's doing all this? You're smarter than it is. You're in control. Take us to Venus."

The fireflies swirled around them, the blue light pulsing slightly: bright and dim, bright and dim. Miller saw it in her face when she made the decision. All around them, the lights went bright, the grotto flooding in soft blue, and then dimmed back to where they had been before. Miller felt something catch at the back of his neck like the first warning of a sore throat. He wondered if he'd have time to deactivate the bomb. And then he looked at Julie. Juliette Andromeda Mao. OPA pilot. Heir to the Mao-Kwikowski corporate throne. The seed crystal of a future beyond anything he'd ever dreamed. He'd have plenty of time.

"I'm afraid," she said.

"Don't be," he said.

"I don't know what's going to happen," she said.

"No one ever does. And, look, you don't have to do this alone," he said.

"I can feel something in the back of my mind. It wants something I don't understand. It's so *big*."

Reflexively, he kissed the back of her hand. There was an ache starting deep in his belly. A sense of illness. A moment's nausea. The first pangs of his transformation into Eros.

"Don't worry," he said. "We're gonna be fine."

Chapter Fifty-Five: Holden

Holden dreamed.

He'd been a lucid dreamer most of his life, so when he found himself sitting in his parents' kitchen in the old house in Montana, talking to Naomi, he knew. He couldn't quite understand what she was saying, but she kept pushing her hair out of her eyes as she munched cookies and drank tea. And while he found that he wasn't ever able to pick a cookie up and take a bite out of it, he could smell them, and the memory of Mother Elise's chocolate chip oatmeal cookies was a very good one.

It was a good dream.

The kitchen strobed red once, and something changed. Holden felt the wrongness of it, felt the dream slipping from warm memory into nightmare. He tried to say something to Naomi but couldn't form the words. The room strobed red again, but she didn't seem to notice. He got up and went to the kitchen window and looked out. When the room strobed a third time, he saw what was causing it. Meteors were falling out of the sky, leaving behind them fiery trails the color of blood. He somehow knew they were chunks of Eros as it crashed through the atmosphere. Miller had failed. The nuclear attack had failed.

Julie had come home.

He turned around to tell Naomi to run, but black tendrils had burst through the floor and wrapped her up, pierced her body in multiple places. They poured from her mouth and eyes.

Holden tried to run to her, to help her, but he couldn't move, and when he looked down, he saw that the tendrils had come up and grabbed him too. One wrapped around his waist and held him. Another pressed into his mouth.

He woke with a yell in a dark room that was strobing with red light. Something was holding him around the waist. In a panic he began clawing at it, threatening to tear a fingernail loose on his left hand, before his rational mind reminded him where he was. On the ops deck, in his chair, belted down in zero g.

He popped his finger into his mouth, trying to soothe the abused fingertip he'd damaged on one of the chair buckles, and took a few deep breaths through his nose. The deck was empty. Naomi was asleep down in her cabin. Alex and Amos were off duty and presumably sleeping too. They'd spent almost two days without rest during the high-g chase of Eros. Holden had ordered everyone to get some shut-eye and had volunteered to take first watch.

And then had promptly fallen asleep. Not good.

The room flashed red again. Holden shook his head to clear the last of the sleep away, and refocused his attention on his console. A red warning light pulsed, and he tapped the screen to open up the menu. It was his threat panel. Someone was hitting them with a targeting laser.

He opened up the threat display and turned on the active sensors. The only ship within millions of kilometers was the *Ravi*, and it was the ship that was targeting them. According to the automatic logs, it had just started a few seconds earlier.

He reached out to activate the comm and call the *Ravi* as his incoming-message light flickered on. He opened the connection, and a second later, McBride's voice said, "*Rocinante,* cease maneuvering, open your outer airlock door, and prepare to be boarded."

Holden frowned at his console. Was that a weird joke?

"McBride, this is Holden. Uh, what?"

Her reply was in a clipped tone that was not encouraging.

"Holden, open your outer airlock and prepare for boarding. If I see a single defensive system wake up, I will fire on your ship. Is that understood?"

"No," he said, not quite able to keep the annoyance out of his voice. "It's not understood. And I'm not going to let you board me. What the hell is going on?"

"I've been ordered by UNN Command to take control of your vessel. You're charged with interfering with UNN military operations, unlawfully commandeering UNN military assets, and a list of other crimes I'm not going to bother reading right now. If you do not surrender immediately, we will be forced to fire on you."

"Oh," said Holden. The UNN had discovered that their missiles were changing course, had attempted to reprogram them, and had discovered that the missiles weren't listening.

They were upset.

"McBride," Holden said after a moment. "Boarding us won't do any good. We can't give you those missiles back. And it's unnecessary, anyway. They're just taking a little detour."

McBride's laugh sounded more like the sharp bark of an angry dog just before it bit.

"Detour?" she said. "You handed three thousand five hundred and seventy-three high-yield thermonuclear interplanetary ballistic missiles over to a traitor and accused war criminal!"

It took Holden a minute.

"You mean *Fred*? I think traitor is a bit harsh—"

McBride cut in.

"Deactivate the false transponders leading our missiles away from Eros, and reactivate the transponders on the surface, or we will fire on your ship. You have ten minutes to comply."

The connection dropped with a click. Holden looked at the console with something between disbelief and outrage, then shrugged and hit the battle stations alarm. Deck lights came on all over the ship in an angry red. The warning Klaxon sounded three times. In less than two minutes, Alex rushed up the ladder to the cockpit, and half a minute behind him, Naomi threw herself into her ops station.

Alex spoke first.

"The *Ravi* is four hundred kilometers away," he said. "Ladar says her tube is open, and she's got us locked."

Clearly enunciating his words, Holden said, "Do not—I repeat, do not—open our tubes or attempt to get a target lock on the *Ravi* at this time. Just keep a close eye on her, and prepare to go defensive if she looks like she's firing. Let's not do anything to provoke her."

"Shall I begin jamming?" Naomi said from behind him.

"No, that would look aggressive. But prep a countermeasures package and have your finger on the ready button," Holden said. "Amos, you in engineering?"

"Roger that, Cap. Ready to go down here."

"Bring the reactor up to one hundred percent and pull control of the point defense cannons to your console down there. If they shoot at us at this range, Alex won't have time to fly and shoot back. You see a red dot on the threat console, you open up with the PDCs immediately. Copy?"

"Roger that," Amos said.

Holden blew a long breath through his teeth, then opened the channel to the *Ravi* again.

"McBride, this is Holden. We are not surrendering, we are not going to let you board us, and we aren't going to comply with your demands. Where do we go from here?"

"Holden," McBride said. "Your reactor is coming up. Are you getting ready to fight with us?"

"No, just getting ready to try and survive. Why, are we fighting?"

Another short harsh laugh.

"Holden," McBride said. "Why do I get the feeling you aren't taking this seriously?"

"Oh, I absolutely am," Holden replied. "I don't want you to kill me, and believe it or not, I have no desire to kill you. The nukes are on a little detour, but this isn't something we need to go down in flames over. I can't give you what you want, and I'm not interested in spending the next thirty years in a military prison. You gain nothing by shooting us, and I will fight back if it comes to that."

McBride cut the channel.

"Captain," Alex said. "The *Ravi* is startin' to maneuver. She's spraying clutter. I think she's gettin' ready to make an attack run."

Shit. Holden had been so sure he could talk her out of it.

"Okay, go defensive. Naomi, start your countermeasures. Amos? Got your finger on that button?"

"Ready," Amos replied.

"Don't hit it until you see a missile launch. Don't want to force their hand."

Sudden crushing g's hit Holden, stuffing him into his chair. Alex had started maneuvering.

"At this distance, maybe I can out-turn her. Keep her from bein' able to take a shot," the pilot said.

"Do it, and open the tubes."

"Roger," Alex said, his professional pilot's calm not quite able to keep the excitement about a possible battle out of his voice.

"I've broken the targeting lock," Naomi said. "Their laser array is not nearly as good as the *Roci*'s. I'm just drowning it in clutter."

"Hooray for bloated Martian defense budgets," Holden replied.

The ship jerked suddenly through a series of wild maneuvers.

"Damn," Alex said, his voice strained by the g-force of the sharp turns. "The *Ravi* just opened up on us with her PDCs."

Holden checked his threat display and saw the long glowing pearl strands of incoming rounds displayed there. The shots were falling well behind them. The *Roci* reported the distance between the ships as 370 kilometers—pretty long range for computer targeting systems to hit a wildly maneuvering ship with a ballistic shot from another wildly maneuvering ship.

"Return fire?" Amos yelled into the comm.

"No!" Holden yelled back. "If she wanted us dead, she'd be throwing torpedoes. Don't give her a reason to want us dead."

"Cap, we're out-turnin' her," Alex said. "The *Roci*'s just too fast. We'll have a firing solution in less than a minute."

"Roger," Holden said.

"Do I take the shot?" Alex asked, his silly Martian cowboy accent fading as his tension rose.

"No."

"Their targeting laser just shut off," Naomi said.

"Which means they've given up trying to cut our jamming," Holden replied, "and have just switched their missiles over to radar tracking."

"Not as accurate," Naomi said hopefully.

"A corvette like that carries at least a dozen fish. They only need to hit us with one to make us dead. And at this range..."

A gentle sound came from his threat console, letting him know that the *Roci* had calculated a firing solution to the *Ravi*.

"I've got tone!" Alex yelled. "Fire?"

"No!" Holden said. He knew that inside the *Ravi*, they were getting the loud warning buzz of an enemy lock. *Stop*, Holden willed them. *Please don't make me kill you.*

"Uh," Alex said in a low voice. "Huh."

Behind Holden, at almost the same moment, Naomi said, "Jim?"

Before he could ask, Alex came back on the general comm.

"Hey, Captain, Eros just came back."

"What?" Holden said, a brief image of the asteroid sneaking up like a cartoon villain on the two circling warships popping into his head.

"Yeah," Alex said. "Eros. It just popped back up on radar.

Whatever it was doing to block our sensors, it just stopped doing it."

"What's it doing?" Holden said. "Get me a course."

Naomi pulled the tracking information to her console and began working on it, but Alex was done a few seconds sooner.

"Yeah," he said. "Good guess. It's changing course. Still heading sunward, but deflecting away from the Earth vector it was on."

"If it keeps this course and speed," Naomi chimed in, "I'd say it was heading toward Venus."

"Wow," said Holden. "That was a joke."

"Good joke," Naomi said.

"Well, someone tell McBride she doesn't need to shoot us now."

"Hey," Alex said, his voice thoughtful. "If we made those nukes stop listening, that means we can't shut 'em down, right? Wonder where Fred's going to drop those."

"Hell if I know," Amos said. "Just disarmed Earth, though. That's gotta be fucking embarrassing."

"Unintended consequences," Naomi sighed. "Always with the unintended consequences."

Eros crashing into Venus was the most widely broadcast and recorded event in history. By the time the asteroid reached the sun's second planet, several hundred ships had taken up orbits there. Military vessels tried to keep the civilian ships away, but it was no use. They were just outnumbered. The video of Eros' descent was captured by military gun cameras, civilian ship telescopes, and the observatories on two planets and five moons.

Holden wished he could have been there to see it up close, but Eros had picked up speed after it had turned, almost as though the asteroid were impatient for the journey to end now that the destination was in sight. He and the crew sat in the galley of the *Rocinante* and watched it on the broadcast newsfeeds. Amos had dug up yet another bottle of faux tequila from somewhere and was liberally splashing it into coffee cups. Alex had them flying toward Tycho at a gentle one-third g. No need to hurry now.

It was all over but the fireworks.

Holden reached out, took Naomi's hand, and held it tightly as the asteroid entered Venus orbit and then seemed to stop. He felt like he could feel the entire human race holding their breath. No one knew what Eros—no, what *Julie*—would do now. No one had spoken to Miller after the last time Holden had, and he wasn't answering his hand terminal. No one knew for sure what had happened on the asteroid.

When the end came, it was beautiful.

In orbit around Venus, Eros came apart like a puzzle box. The giant asteroid split into a dozen chunks, stringing out around the equator of the planet in a long necklace. Then those dozen pieces split into a dozen more, and then a dozen after that, a glittering fractal seed cloud spreading out across the entire surface of the planet, disappearing into the thick cloud layer that usually hid Venus from view.

"Wow," Amos said, his voice almost reverent.

"That was gorgeous," Naomi said. "Vaguely unsettling, but gorgeous."

"They won't stay there forever," Holden said.

Alex tossed off the last of the tequila in his glass, then refilled it from the bottle.

"What d'ya mean, Cap?" he asked.

"Well, I'm just guessing. But I doubt the things that built the protomolecule just wanted to store it here. This was part of a bigger plan. We saved the Earth, Mars, the Belt. Question is, what happens now?"

Naomi and Alex exchanged glances. Amos pursed his lips. On-screen, Venus glittered as arcs of lightning danced all across the planet.

"Cap," Amos said. "You are seriously harshing my buzz."

Epilogue: Fred

Frederick Lucius Johnson. Former colonel in Earth's armed forces, Butcher of Anderson Station. Thoth Station now too. Unelected prime minister of the OPA. He had faced his own mortality a dozen times, lost friends to violence and politics and betrayal. He'd lived through four assassination attempts, only two of which were on any record. He'd killed a pistol-wielding attacker using only a table knife. He'd given the orders that had ended hundreds of lives, and stood by his decisions.

And yet public speaking still made him nervous as hell. It didn't make sense, but there it was.

Ladies and gentlemen, we stand at a crossroads—

"General Sebastian will be at the reception," his personal secretary said. "Remember not to ask after her husband."

"Why? I didn't kill him, did I?"

"No, sir. He's having a very public affair, and the general's a bit touchy about it."

"So she might *want* me to kill him."

"You can make the offer, sir."

The "greenroom" was actually done in red and ochre, with a black leather couch, a mirrored wall, and a table laid out with hydroponic strawberries and carefully mineralized drinking water. The head of Ceres security, a dour-faced woman named Shaddid, had escorted him from the dock to the conference facilities three hours earlier. Since then, he'd been pacing—three steps in one direction, turn, three steps back—like the captain of an ancient ship of the line on his quarterdeck.

Elsewhere in the station, the representatives of the formerly warring factions were in rooms of their own, with secretaries of their own. Most of them hated Fred, which wasn't particularly a problem. Most of them feared him too. Not because of his standing in the OPA, of course. Because of the protomolecule.

The political rift between Earth and Mars was probably irreparable; the Earth forces loyal to Protogen had engineered a betrayal too deep for apologies, and too many lives had been lost on both sides for the coming peace to look anything like it had been before. The naive among the OPA thought this was a good thing: an opportunity to play one planet against the other. Fred knew better. Unless all three forces—Earth, Mars, and the Belt—could reach a real peace, they would inevitably fall back into a real war.

Now if only Earth or Mars thought of the Belt as something more than an annoyance to be squashed after their true enemy was humiliated...But in truth, anti-Mars sentiment on Earth was higher now than it had been during the shooting war, and Martian elections were only four months away. A significant shift in the Martian polity could ease the tensions or make things immeasurably worse. Both sides had to see the big picture.

Fred stopped before a mirror, adjusted his tunic for the hundredth time, and grimaced.

"When did I turn into a damned marriage counselor?" he said.

"We aren't still talking about General Sebastian, are we, sir?"

"No. Forget I said anything. What else do I need to know?"

"There's a possibility that Blue Mars will try to disrupt your presentation. Hecklers and signs, not guns. Captain Shaddid has several Blues in custody, but some may have slipped past her."

"All right."

"You have interviews scheduled with two political narrowcasts and a news source based on Europa. The Europa interviewer is likely to ask about Anderson Station."

"All right. Anything new from Venus?"

"Something's happening down there," his secretary said.

"It's not dead, then."

"Apparently not, sir."

"Great," he said bitterly.

Ladies and gentlemen, we stand at a crossroads. On one hand there is the very real threat of mutual annihilation, and on the other—

And on the other, there's the bogeyman of Venus, getting ready to crawl up out of its well and slaughter you all in your sleep. I have the live sample, which is your best, if not only, hope of divining what its intentions and capabilities are, and which I have hidden so that you can't just march over and take it from me. It's the only reason any of you are listening to me in the first place. So how about a little respect here?

His secretary's terminal chirped, and she consulted it briefly.

"It's Captain Holden, sir."

"Do I have to?"

"It would be best if he felt he was part of the effort, sir. He has a track record of amateur press releases."

"Fine. Bring him in."

The weeks that had passed since Eros Station had come apart in the thick skies of Venus had been good to Holden, but prolonged high-g dives like the one the *Rocinante* had sustained chasing Eros had long-lasting effects. The burst blood vessels in the man's sclera had healed; the pressure bruising was gone from around his eyes and the back of his neck. Only a little hesitation in the way he walked spoke of the deep joint pain, cartilage still on its way back to its natural form. Acceleration swagger, they'd called it, back when Fred had been a different man.

"Hey," Holden said. "You're looking pretty. Did you see the latest feed from Venus? Two-kilometer-high crystal towers. What do you think that is?"

"Your fault?" Fred suggested, keeping the tone friendly. "You could have told Miller to drive it into the sun."

"Yes, because two-kilometer-high crystal towers coming out of the sun wouldn't be creepy at all," Holden said. "Are those strawberries?"

"Have some," Fred said. He hadn't been able to eat anything since that morning.

"So," Holden said around a mouthful of fruit, "are they really going to sue me over this?"

"Unilaterally giving away all mineral and development rights to an entire planet on an open radio channel?"

"Yeah," Holden said.

"I would guess the people who actually owned those rights are probably going to sue you," Fred said. "If they ever figure out who they are."

"Could you give me a hand with that?" Holden asked.

"I'll be a character witness," Fred said. "I don't actually make the law."

"Then what exactly *are* you all doing here? Couldn't there be some kind of amnesty? We retrieved the protomolecule, tracked down Julie Mao on Eros, broke Protogen, and saved Earth."

"*You* saved Earth?"

"We helped," Holden said, but his voice had a more somber tone. Miller's death still bothered the captain. Fred knew how that felt. "It was a joint effort."

Fred's personal secretary cleared her throat and glanced toward the door. They'd need to go soon.

"I'll do what I can," Fred said. "I've got a lot of other things on the plate, but I'll do what I can."

"And Mars can't have the *Roci* back," Holden said. "Right of salvage says that's my ship now."

"They aren't going to see it that way, but I will do what I can."

"You keep saying that."

"It keeps being all I can do."

"And you'll tell them about him, right?" Holden said. "Miller. He deserves the credit."

"The Belter who went back into Eros of his own free will in order to save Earth? You're damn right I'm going to tell them about him."

"Not 'the Belter.' Him. Josephus Aloisus Miller."

Holden had stopped eating the free strawberries. Fred crossed his arms.

"You've been reading up," Fred said.

"Yeah. Well. I didn't know him all that well."

"Neither did anybody else," Fred said, and then softened a little. "I know it's hard, but we don't need a real man with a complex life. We need a symbol of the Belt. An icon."

"Sir," the secretary said. "We really do need to go now."

"That's what got us here," Holden said. "Icons. Symbols. People without names. All of those Protogen scientists were thinking about biomass and populations. Not Mary who worked in supply and raised flowers in her spare time. None of them killed *her*."

"You think they wouldn't have?"

"I think if they were going to, they owed it to her to know her name. All their names. And you owe it to Miller not to make him into something he wasn't."

Fred laughed. He couldn't help it.

"Captain," he said, "if you're saying that I should amend my address to the peace conference so that it wasn't a noble Belter sacrificing himself to save the Earth—if you're suggesting that I say something like 'We happened to have a suicidal ex-cop on-site' instead — you understand this process less than I thought you did. Miller's sacrifice is a tool, and I'm going to use it."

"Even if it makes him faceless," Holden said. "Even if it makes him something he never was?"

"Especially if it makes him something he never was," Fred said. "Do you remember what he was like?"

Holden frowned and then something flickered in his eyes. Amusement. Memory.

"He was kind of a pain in the ass, wasn't he?" Holden said.

"That man could take a visitation from God with thirty under-dressed angels announcing that sex was okay after all and make it seem vaguely depressing."

"He was a good man," Holden said.

"He wasn't," Fred said. "But he did his job. And now I've got to go do mine."

"Give 'em hell," Holden said. "And amnesty. Keep talking up the amnesty."

Fred walked down the curving hallway, his secretary close behind him. The conference halls had been designed for smaller things. Petty ones. Hydroponics scientists getting away from their husbands and wives and children to get drunk and talk about raising bean sprouts. Miners coming together to lecture each other about waste minimization and tailings disposal. High school band competitions. And instead, these work carpets and brushed-stone walls were going to have to bear the fulcrum of history. It was Holden's fault that the shabby, small surroundings reminded him of the dead detective. They hadn't before.

The delegations were seated across the aisle from each other. The generals and political appointees and general secretaries of Earth and Mars, the two great powers together at his invitation to Ceres, to the Belt. Territory made neutral because neither side took it seriously enough to be concerned about their demands.

All of history had brought them here, to this moment, and now, in the next few minutes, Fred's job was to change that trajectory.

The fear was gone. Smiling, he stepped up to the speaker's dais, the podium.

The pulpit.

There was a scattering of polite applause. A few smiles, and a few frowns. Fred grinned. He wasn't a man anymore. He was a symbol, an icon. A narrative about himself and about the forces at play in the solar system.

And for a moment, he was tempted. In that hesitation between drawing breath and speaking, part of him wondered what would happen if he shed the patterns of history and spoke about himself as a man, about the Joe Miller who he'd known briefly, about the responsibility they all shared to tear down the images they held of one another and find the genuine, flawed, conflicted people they actually were.

It would have been a noble way to fail.

"Ladies and gentlemen," he said. "We stand at a crossroads. On one hand, there is the very real threat of mutual annihilation. On the other..."

He paused for effect.

"On the other, the stars."

Acknowledgments

Like most children, this book took a village. I would like to express my deep gratitude to my agents, Shawna and Danny, and to my editors DongWon and Darren. Also instrumental in the early formation of the book were Melinda, Emily, Terry, Ian, George, Steve, Walter, and Victor, of the New Mexico Critical Mass writers group, and also Carrie, who read an early draft. An additional thanks goes to Ian, who helped with some of the math, and who is responsible for none of the mistakes I made understanding it. I also owe an enormous debt to Tom, Sake Mike, Non-Sake Mike, Porter, Scott, Raja, Jeff, Mark, Dan, and Joe. Thanks, guys, for doing the beta testing. And finally, a special thanks to the *Futurama* writers and Bender Bending Rodriguez for babysitting the kid while I wrote.

extras

orbit

meet the author

JAMES S. A. COREY is the pen name of fantasy author Daniel Abraham and Ty Franck, George R. R. Martin's assistant. They both live in Albuquerque, New Mexico. Find out more about this series at www.the-expanse.com.

interview

Leviathan Wakes *is the first book in a series called The* ***Expanse.*** *What kind of story are you telling in this series?*

There's a lot of science fiction that talks about the near future. There's a lot about great galaxy-spanning empires of the distant future. But there's not much that talks about the part in between. The Expanse is playing on that bridge. Whatever drives us off Earth to the rest of the solar system or from there to the stars, the problems we have are the ones we bring with us. What I want to do is write good old-fashioned space opera centered around human stories, but with an increasingly large backdrop.

It seems like **Leviathan Wakes** *is a science fiction book, but it borrows from a lot of other genres as well, including horror and noir. Did you intend to blend those genres? What kind of book do you feel this is?*

It's definitely science fiction of the old-school space opera variety. That's the story I wanted to tell. But half of the story was a detective story, and as soon as Detective Miller hit the page, he told me in a loud voice that he was a classic noir character. It was in his voice and the way he talked about things, you know? As for the horror feel, that's just the way I roll. I've never written anything in my life that didn't at least blur the line into horror. If I wrote greeting cards, they'd probably have a squick factor.

Leviathan Wakes *has two protagonists with very different worldviews, which are often in conflict. Can you describe those views and why you chose that particular conflict?*

You know how they say science fiction is about the future you're writing about, but it's also about the time you're writing in? Holden and Miller have got two different views on the ethical use of information. That's very much a current argument. Holden's my holy fool. He's an idealist, a man who faces things with this very optimistic view of humanity. He believes that if you give people all of the information, they'll do the right thing with it, because people are naturally good. Miller is a cynic and a nihilist. He looks at the dissemination of information as a game you play. He doesn't have faith in anyone else's moral judgment. Control of information is how you get people to do what you want, and he doesn't trust anyone else to make that call. I picked those two characters because they're both right, and they're both wrong. By having them in the same story, I can have them talk to each other. And that central disagreement is sort of underneath everything else that happens.

Leviathan Wakes *has a gritty and realistic feel. How much research did you do on the technology side of things, and how important was it to you that they be realistic and accurate?*

Okay, so what you're really asking me there is if this is hard science fiction. The answer is an emphatic no. I have nothing but respect for well-written hard science fiction, and I wanted everything in the book to be plausible enough that it doesn't get in the way. But the rigorous how-to with the math shown? It's not that story. This is working man's science fiction. It's like in *Alien,* we meet the crew of the *Nostromo* doing their jobs in this very blue-collar environment. They're truckers, right? Why is there a room in the *Nostromo* where water leaks down off of chains suspended from the ceiling? Because it looks cool and makes the world feel a little messy. It gives you the feel of the world. Ridley Scott doesn't explain why that room exists, and when most people watch the film, it never even occurs to them to ask. What kind of drive does the *Nostromo* use? I bet no one walked out of the film asking that question. I wanted to tell a story about humans living and working in a well-populated solar system. I wanted to convey a feeling of what that would be like, and then tell a story about the people who live there.

So how does the Epstein drive work?
Very well. Efficiently.

In your acknowledgments you thank the New Mexico Critical Mass writers group. What effect did having that workshop environment have on your work?
Well, Critical Mass is a lot more than a workshop or critical group. It's more like a writer's mafia. Just about anything you might need, someone in the group can get it for you. Walter Jon Williams, who wrote the brilliant Dread Empire's Fall space opera series, was there to give important tips about writing in that genre. S. M. Stirling and Victor Milan write some of the best action in the business, and there was a lot of action for them to critique. Ian Tregillis is an actual astrophysicist and made himself available for technical questions. Melinda Snodgrass is pretty much the Yoda of letting you know when you've wandered too far away from your plot. And the entire group, including Emily Mah, Terry England, and George R. R. Martin, was there to read and critique the early drafts of the book, and a lot of changes were made based on their advice.

You've worked with George R. R. Martin a lot in the past. What kind of advice did he have for this project?
Yes, I've done a number of projects with him in one incarnation or another. In this case, he was mostly just encouraging. He likes old-fashioned space opera, and he followed my progress on the book with great interest. He was also the first to read the final version. He was very complimentary. He said at one point that it

was the best book about vomit zombies he'd ever read. That was nice.

Where do you see the Expanse series going from here?

Well, I'm contracted with Orbit for at least two more books. They are titled *Caliban's War* and *Dandelion Sky*. I hope to keep exploring the idea of human expansion into the solar system and beyond, and balancing the very real threats that the galaxy poses for the fledgling human diaspora against the threats that those same humans will bring with them. For up-to-date information on what I'm up to and where the project is headed, people can visit www.the-expanse.com and get the latest.

introducing

If you enjoyed
LEVIATHAN WAKES,
look out for

CALIBAN'S WAR

Book Two of The Expanse

by James S. A. Corey

"Snoopy's out again," Private Hillman said. "I think his CO must be pissed at him."

Gunnery Sergeant Roberta Draper of the Martian Marine Corps upped the magnification on her armor's head-up display and looked in the direction Hillman was pointing. Twenty-five hundred meters away, a squad of four United Nations marines were tromping around their outpost, backlit by the giant greenhouse dome they were guarding. A greenhouse dome identical in nearly all respects to the dome that was behind her.

One of the four UN marines had black smudges on the sides of his helmet that looked like beagle ears.

"Yep, that's Snoopy," Bobbie said. "Been on every patrol detail so far today. Wonder what he did."

Guard duty around the greenhouses on Ganymede meant doing what you could to keep your mind occupied. Including speculating on the lives of the marines on the other side.

The other side. Eighteen months before, there hadn't been sides. The inner planets had all been one big, happy, slightly dysfunctional

573

family. Then the Eros incident, and now the two superpowers were dividing up the solar system between them, and the one moon neither side was willing to give up was Ganymede, breadbasket of the Jovian system.

As the only moon with any magnetosphere, it was the only place where dome-grown crops stood a chance in Jupiter's harsh radiation belt, and even there, the domes and habitats had to be shielded to protect civilians from the eight rems a day burning off Jupiter and onto the moon's surface.

Bobbie's armor had been designed to let a soldier walk through a nuclear bomb crater an hour after the blast. It also worked well at keeping Jupiter from frying Martian marines.

Behind the Earth soldiers on patrol, their dome glowed in a shaft of weak sunlight captured by enormous orbital mirrors. Even with the mirrors, most terrestrial plants would have died, starved of sunlight. Only the heavily modified versions the Ganymede scientists cranked out could hope to survive in the trickle of light the mirrors fed them.

"Be sunset soon," Bobbie said, still watching the Earth marines outside their little guard hut, knowing they were watching her too. In addition to Snoopy, she spotted the one they called Stumpy because he or she couldn't be much more than a meter and a half tall. She wondered what their nickname for her was. Maybe Big Red. Her armor still had the Martian surface camouflage on it. She hadn't been on Ganymede long enough to get it resurfaced with mottled gray and white.

One by one, over the course of five minutes, the orbital mirrors winked out as Ganymede passed behind Jupiter for a few hours. The glow from the greenhouse behind her changed to actinic blue as the artificial lights came on. While the overall light level didn't go down much, the shadows shifted in strange and subtle ways. Above, the sun—not even a disk from here as much as the brightest star—flashed as it passed behind Jupiter's limb, and for a moment the planet's faint ring system was visible.

"They're going back in," Corporal Travis said. "Snoop's bringing up the rear. Poor guy. Can we bail too?"

Bobbie looked around at the featureless dirty ice of Ganymede. Even in her high-tech armor she could feel the moon's chill.

"Nope."

Her squad grumbled but fell in line as she led them on a slow low-gravity shuffle around the dome. In addition to Hillman and Travis, she had a green private named Gourab on this patrol. And even though he'd been in the marines all of about a minute and a half, he grumbled just as loud as the other two in his Mariner Valley drawl.

She couldn't blame them. It was make-work. Something for the Martian soldiers on Ganymede to do to keep them busy. If Earth decided it needed Ganymede all to itself, four grunts walking around the greenhouse dome wouldn't stop them. With dozens of Earth and Mars warships in a tense standoff in orbit, if hostilities broke out, the ground pounders would probably find out only when the surface bombardment began.

To her left, the dome rose to almost half a kilometer: triangular glass panels separated by gleaming copper-colored struts that turned the entire structure into a massive Faraday cage. Bobbie had never been inside one of the greenhouse domes. She'd been sent out from Mars as part of a huge surge in troops to the outer planets and had been walking patrols on the surface almost since day one. Ganymede to her was a spaceport, a small marine base, and the even smaller guard outpost she currently called home.

As they shuffled around the dome, Bobbie watched the unremarkable landscape. Ganymede didn't change much without a catastrophic event. The surface was mostly silicate rock and water ice a few degrees warmer than space. The atmosphere was oxygen so thin it could pass as an industrial vacuum. Ganymede didn't weather. It changed when rocks fell on it from space, or when warm water from the liquid core forced itself onto the surface and created short-lived lakes. Neither thing happened all that often. At home on Mars, wind and dust changed the landscape hourly. Here, she was walking through the footsteps of the day before and the day before and the day before. And if she never came back, those footprints would outlive her. Privately, she thought it was sort of creepy.

A rhythmic squeaking started to cut through the normally smooth hiss and thump sounds her powered armor made. She usually kept the suit's HUD minimized. It got so crowded with information that a marine knew everything except what was actually in front of her. Now she pulled it up, using blinks and eye movements to page over to the suit's diagnostic screen. A yellow telltale warned her that the suit's left knee actuator was low on hydraulic fluid. Must be a leak somewhere, but a slow one, because the suit couldn't find it.

"Hey, guys, hold up a minute," Bobbie said. "Hilly, you have any extra hydraulic fluid in your pack?"

"Yep," said Hillman, already pulling it out.

"Give my left knee a squirt, would you?"

While Hillman crouched in front of her, working on her suit, Gourab and Travis began an argument that seemed to be about sports. Bobbie tuned it out.

"This suit is ancient," Hillman said. "You really oughta upgrade. This sort of thing is just going to happen more and more often, you know."

"Yeah, I should," Bobbie said. But the truth was that was easier said than done. Bobbie was not the right shape to fit into one of the standard suits, and the marines made her jump through a series of flaming hoops every time she requisitioned a new custom one. At two meters tall, she was only a bit above average height for a Martian male, but thanks in part to her Polynesian ancestry, she weighed in at more than 140 kilos at one g. It wasn't fat, but her muscles seemed to get bigger every time she even walked through a weight room, and as a marine, she trained all the time.

The suit she had now was the first one in twelve years of active duty that actually seemed to fit well. And even though it was beginning to show its age, it was just easier to try to keep it running than beg and plead for a new one.

Hillman was just starting to put his tools away when Bobbie's radio crackled to life.

"Outpost four to stickman. Come in, stickman."

"Roger four," Bobbie replied. "This is stickman one. Go ahead."

"Stickman one, where are you guys? You're half an hour late and some shit is going down over here."

"Sorry four, some equipment trouble here," Bobbie said, wondering what sort of shit might be going down, but not enough to ask about it over an open frequency.

"Return to the outpost immediately. We have shots fired at the UN outpost. We're going into lockdown."

It took Bobbie a moment to parse that. She could see her men staring at her, their faces a mix of puzzlement and fear.

"Uh, the Earth guys are shooting at you?" she finally asked.

"Not yet, but they're shooting. Get your asses back here."

Hillman jumped to his feet. Bobbie flexed her knee once and got greens on her diagnostic. She gave Hilly a nod of thanks, then said, "Double-time it back to the outpost. Go."

Bobbie and her squad were still half a kilometer from the outpost when the general alert went out. Her suit's HUD came up on its own, switching to combat mode. The sensor package went to work looking for hostiles and linked up to one of the satellites for a top-down view. She felt the click as the gun built into the suit's right arm switched to free-fire mode.

A thousand alarms would be sounding if an orbital bombardment had begun, but she couldn't help looking up at the sky anyway. No flashes or missile trails. Nothing but Jupiter's bulk.

Bobbie took off for the outpost at a dead run. Her squad followed without a word. A person trained in the use of a strength-augmenting suit running in low gravity could cover a lot of ground quickly. The outpost came into view around the curve of the dome in just a few seconds, and a few seconds after that, the cause of the alarm.

UN marines were charging at the Martian outpost. The year-long cold war was going hot. Somewhere deep behind the cool mental habits of training and discipline, she was surprised. She hadn't really thought this day would come.

The rest of her platoon were out of the outpost and arranged in a firing line facing the UN position. Someone had driven *Yojimbo* out onto the line, and the four-meter-tall combat mech towered over the other marines, looking like a headless giant in power armor, his massive cannon moving slowly as it tracked the incoming Earth troops. The UN soldiers were covering the 2,500 meters between the two outposts at full speed.

Why isn't anyone talking? she wondered. The silence coming from her platoon was eerie.

And then, just as her squad got to the firing line, her suit squealed a jamming warning at her. The top-down vanished as she lost contact with the satellite. Her team's life signs and equipment status reports went dead as her link to their suits was cut off. The faint static of the open comm channel disappeared, leaving an even more unsettling silence.

She used hand motions to place her team at the right flank, then moved up the line to find Lieutenant Givens, her CO. She spotted his suit right at the center of the line, almost directly under *Yojimbo*. She ran up and placed her helmet against his.

"What the fuck is going on, El Tee?" she shouted.

He gave her an irritated look and yelled, "Your guess is as good as mine. We can't tell them to back off because of the jamming, and visual warnings are being ignored. Before the radio cut out, I got authorization to fire if they come within half a klick of our position."

Bobbie had a couple hundred more questions, but the UN troops would cross the five-hundred-meter mark in just a few more seconds, so she ran back to anchor the right flank with her squad. Along the way, she had her suit count the incoming forces and mark them all as hostiles. The suit reported seven targets. Less than a third of the UN troops at their outpost.

This makes no sense.

She had her suit draw a line on the HUD at the five-hundred-meter mark. She didn't tell her boys that was the free-fire zone. She didn't need to. They'd open fire when she did without needing to know why.

The UN soldiers had crossed the one-kilometer mark, still without firing a shot. They were coming in a scattered formation, with six out front in a ragged line, and a seventh bringing up the rear about seventy meters behind. Her suit HUD selected the figure on the far left of the enemy line as her target, picking the one closest to her by default. Something itched at the back of her brain and she overrode the suit and selected the target at the rear and told it to magnify.

The small figure suddenly enlarged in her targeting reticule. She felt a chill move down her back and magnified again.

The figure chasing the six UN marines wasn't wearing a suit. Nor was it, properly speaking, human. Its skin was covered in chitinous plates, like large black scales. Its head was a massive horror, easily twice as large as it should be and covered in strange protruding growths.

But most disturbing of all were its hands. Far too large for its body, and too long for their width, they were a childhood-nightmare version of hands. The hands of the troll under the bed or the witch sneaking in through the window. They flexed and grasped at nothing with a constant manic energy.

The Earth forces weren't attacking. They were retreating.

"Shoot the thing chasing them," Bobbie yelled to no one.

Before the UN soldiers could cross the half kilometer that would cause the Martians to open fire, the thing caught them.

"Oh, holy shit," Bobbie whispered. "Holy *shit.*"

It grabbed one UN marine in its huge hands and tore the man in half like paper. Titanium and ceramic armor tore as easily as the flesh inside, spilling broken bits of technology and wet human viscera indiscriminately onto the ice. The remaining five soldiers ran even harder, but the monster chasing them barely slowed as it killed.

"Shoot it shoot it shoot it," Bobbie screamed and opened fire. Bobbie's training and the technology of her combat suit combined to make her an extremely efficient killing machine. As soon as her finger pulled the trigger on her suit's gun, a stream of two-millimeter armor-piercing rounds streaked out at the creature at a thousand meters per second. In just under one second, she fired nearly fifty rounds at it. It was a relatively slow-moving human-sized target, running in a straight line. Her targeting computer could do ballistic corrections that would let her hit a softball-sized object moving at supersonic speeds. Every bullet she fired at the monster hit.

It didn't matter.

The rounds went through it, probably not slowing appreciably before they exited. Each exit wound sprouted a spray of black filaments that fell onto the snow instead of blood. It was like shooting water. The wounds closed almost faster than they were created; the only sign the thing had even been hit was the trail of black fibers in its wake.

And then it caught a second UN marine. Instead of tearing him to pieces like it had the last one, it spun and hurled the fully armored Earther — probably massing more than five hundred kilos total — toward Bobbie. Her HUD tracked the UN soldier on his upward arc and helpfully informed her that the monster had thrown him not *toward* her, but *at* her. In a very flat trajectory. Which meant fast.

She dove to the side as quickly as her suit would let her. The hapless UN marine swiped Hillman, who'd been standing next to her, and then both of them were gone, bouncing down the ice at lethal speeds.

By the time she turned back to the monster, it had killed two more UN soldiers.

The entire Martian line opened fire on it, including *Yojimbo*'s big cannon. The two remaining Earth soldiers diverged and ran at angles away from the thing, trying to give their Martian counterparts an open firing lane. The creature was hit hundreds, thousands of times. It stitched itself back together while remaining at a full run, never more than slowing when one of *Yojimbo*'s cannon shots detonated nearby.

Bobbie, back on her feet, joined in the barrage but it didn't make any difference. The creature slammed into the Martian line, killing two marines faster than the eye could follow. *Yojimbo* slid to one side, far more nimble than a machine of its size should be. Bobbie though Sa'id must be driving it. He swore he could make the big mech dance the tango when he wanted to. It didn't matter. Even before Sa'id could bring the mech's cannon around for a point-blank shot, the creature ran right up its side, gripped the pilot hatch, and tore the door off its hinges. Sa'id was snatched from his cockpit harness and hurled sixty meters straight up.

The other marines had begun to fall back, firing as they went. Without radio, there was no way to coordinate the retreat. Bobbie found herself running toward the dome with the rest. The small and distant part of her mind that wasn't panicking knew that the dome's glass and metal would offer no protection against something that could tear an armored man in half and rip a nine-ton mech to pieces. That part of her mind recognized the futility in attempting to override her terror.

By the time she found the external door to the dome, there was only one other marine left with her. Gourab. Up close, she could see his face through the armored glass of his helmet. He was screaming something at her she couldn't hear. She started to lean forward to touch helmets with him when he shoved her backward onto the ice. He was hammering on the door controls with one metal fist, trying to smash his way in in his mindless panic, when the creature caught him and peeled the helmet off his suit. Gourab stood for one moment, face in vacuum, eyes blinking and mouth open in a soundless scream; then the creature tore off his head as easily as it had his helmet.

It turned and looked at Bobbie, still flat on her back.

Up close, she could see that it had bright blue eyes. A glowing, electric blue. They were beautiful. She raised her gun and held down the trigger for half a second before she realized she'd run out of ammo long before. The creature looked at her gun with what she would have sworn was curiosity, then looked into her eyes and cocked its head to one side.

This is it, she thought. *This is how I go out, and I'm not going to know what did it, or why.* Dying she could handle. Dying without any answers seemed terribly cruel.

The creature took one step toward her, then stopped and shuddered. A new pair of limbs burst out of its midsection and writhed in the air like tentacles. Its head, already grotesque, seemed to swell up. The blue eyes flashed as bright as the lights in the domes.

And then it exploded in a ball of fire that hurled her away across the ice and slammed her into a low ridge hard enough for the impact-absorbing gel in her suit to go rigid, freezing her in place.

She lay on her back, fading toward unconsciousness. The night sky above her began to flash with light. The ships in orbit, shooting.

Cease fire, she thought, pressing the thought out into the blackness. *They were retreating. Cease fire.* Her radio was still out. She couldn't tell anyone that the UN marines hadn't been attacking.

Or that something else had.